Praise for
Dianne Duvall

"Book after book, Duvall brings her readers complex, fascinating tales of romance, danger and loyalty."

—RT Book Reviews

"Duvall's storytelling is simply spellbinding."

—Tome Tender

"Dianne Duvall does an amazing job of blending paranormal with humor, romance, action, and violence to give you a story you won't want to put down."

—The SubClub Books

Praise for
A SORCERESS OF HIS OWN
The Gifted Ones Book 1

"Ms. Duvall excels in creating a community feel to her stories and this is no different... A Sorceress of His Own has a wonderful dynamic, an amazing promise of future adventures and a well-told romance that is sure to please."

—Long and Short Reviews

"Dianne Duvall has delivered a gripping story-line with characters that stuck with me throughout the day and continue to do so long after I turned that last page. A must read!"

—Reading Between the Wines Book Club

"A wonderful story and a great beginning to a new and different series."

—eBookObsessed

"Full of danger, intrigue and passion. Dianne Duvall brought the characters to life and delivered an addicting and exciting new series. I'm hooked!"

—Reading in Pajamas

"I enjoyed this world and can't wait to see more crossover as the series continues."

—Books and Things

"I think I loved Dillon and Alyssa's story as much as I loved Roland and Sarah in Darkness Dawns... The passion between the two was intense and lovely to watch."

—From the TBR Pile

Praise for Dianne's
Immortal Guardians Books

"These dark, kick-ass guardians can protect me any day!"

—Alexandra Ivy, *New York Times* Bestselling Author

"Crackles with energy, originality, and a memorable take-no-prisoners heroine."

—*Publishers Weekly*

"This series boasts numerous characters, a deep back story, and extensive worldbuilding... Ethan will seem familiar to sci-fi and fantasy fans, as he boasts the glowing charms of Twilight's Edward Cullen and the vicious durability of the X-Men's Wolverine."

—Kirkus Reviews

"Full of fascinating characters, a unique and wonderfully imaginative premise, and scorching hot relationships."

—The Romance Reviews

"Fans of paranormal romance who haven't discovered this series yet are really missing out on something extraordinary."

—Long and Short Reviews

"Paranormal romance fans who enjoy series like J.R. Ward's Black Dagger Brotherhood will definitely want to invest time in the Immortal Guardians series."

—All Things Urban Fantasy

"Ms. Duvall brings together a rich world and a wonderful group of characters... This is a great series."

—Night Owl Reviews

"It was non-stop get-up-and-go from the very first page, and instantly you just adore these characters... This was paranormal at its finest."

—Book Reader Chronicles

"Full of awesome characters, snappy dialogue, exciting action, steamy sex, sneaky shudder-worthy villains and delightful humor."

—I'm a Voracious Reader

Dianne Duvall

Rendezvous With Yesterday

The Gifted Ones

Titles By Dianne Duvall

The Gifted Ones
A SORCERESS OF HIS OWN
RENDEZVOUS WITH YESTERDAY

Immortal Guardians
DARKNESS DAWNS
NIGHT REIGNS
PHANTOM SHADOWS
IN STILL DARKNESS
DARKNESS RISES
NIGHT UNBOUND
PHANTOM EMBRACE
SHADOWS STRIKE

Anthologies
PREDATORY
(includes *In Still Darkness*)
ON THE HUNT
(includes *Phantom Embrace*)

Author's Note For Immortal Guardians Fans

Dear Reader,

Robert and Bethany's tale has been referenced several times in my Immortal Guardians books, so I wanted to mention that—although I've labeled Beth's time as "Present Day"—***Rendezvous with Yesterday*** actually takes place before ***Darkness Dawns***, Immortal Guardians Book 1. I chose to use "Present Day" instead of assigning her time a specific year simply to avoid dating the book since some ***Rendezvous with Yesterday*** readers have not read my Immortal Guardians series.

I hope you'll enjoy seeing the full story unfold.

—Dianne Duvall

Acknowledgements

I'd like to thank the many readers who have supported my leap from traditional publishing to indie publishing, as well as my launching of The Gifted Ones series. Every time one of you contacted me, asking me when *Rendezvous with Yesterday* would become available, it fueled my excitement and determination to bring you Robert and Bethany's story. Many more thanks go to Crystal and my fabulous street team, as well as the bloggers, reviewers, and wonderful readers who have picked up copies of my books and helped spread the word about them.

I would also like to thank Syneca for the awesome cover so many readers have deemed badass. I'd also like to thank my editor, copyeditor, formatter, and the other behind-the-scenes individuals who helped me bring you *Rendezvous with Yesterday*.

And, of course, I'd like to thank my Facebook friends who make me laugh and smile even when I'm stressing over deadlines. You rock!

Chapter One

BETHANY BENNETT FLIPPED THROUGH THE CDs piled at her feet. "Seriously, Josh, we need to scrape together enough money to put a new stereo in this piece of crap."

Without taking his gaze from the highway, her brother laughed. "What's wrong? Can't find anything you want to listen to?"

"No." Most of the CDs had belonged to their parents and featured music from the seventies and eighties. Beth was in more of a Disturbed kind of mood, but couldn't play her MP3s on the car's outdated system.

Josh reached down and retrieved another stack of CDs from beneath the driver's seat. "How about some Hendrix?"

Her mood lightened. "Okay." As she slipped a CD into the player, the air conditioner began to screech again.

She grimaced. Even with the AC on full blast, dragging wisps of hair from her long brown braid and tickling her bangs, the heat stifled Beth, raising beads of moisture on her skin and making breathing difficult.

Of course, the bulletproof vest she wore didn't help. Though the Type II wasn't as bulky as the higher classification vests Josh had tried to talk her into getting, she still found it uncomfortable. The white tank top beneath it clung damply to full breasts mashed flat. Her snug blue jeans made her wish she could have worn breezy shorts. And her feet, encased in heavy boots, felt as though they roasted in a barbecue pit.

She shifted uncomfortably. The shoulder holster encasing the Glock 9mm beneath her left arm pinched a bit as she adjusted the holster on her left hip that carried the Ruger 9mm.

She glanced at Josh to see if he was equally uncomfortable and smiled.

His short, wavy brown hair gleamed in the sunlight as he bobbed his head to the music. Pretty much every female friend Beth had had since middle school had deemed him *hot* and driven her crazy, drooling over him. Today his strong jaw bore dark stubble that lent him a rugged look. And his trim, athletic body was clad in blue jeans, a black T-shirt and his own Type II bulletproof vest.

Once they left the city behind them, Josh orchestrated a series of turns that landed them on a barely discernible dirt road.

When that road abruptly ended in a dense forest, he slowed the car to a stop and cut the engine. "Are you ready?"

Heart pounding, she nodded. "I'm ready."

He studied her carefully as he removed his sunglasses. "You look nervous."

"Maybe a little," she admitted.

He swore. "I wish Grant could've come instead."

"Grant is in San Antonio, so you're stuck with me," Beth countered. "Besides, you said this was a long, long shot."

"Long, long shot or not, I don't want you here if there's even the slightest chance we may run into Kingsley or Vergoma."

Both Kingsley and Vergoma faced murder charges and had jumped bail. Rumors of violence against women swirled around the duo as well, but such charges had yet to be brought against them.

Josh had done his damnedest to limit Beth's role in the family bounty hunting business to skip tracing—ferreting out information on the Internet and over the phone that could lead to the criminals' capture. Beth was particularly skilled at such. But with their partner Grant gone, Josh had had no choice but to extend her participation in his search for Kingsley and Vergoma and let her back him up on this jaunt.

After much digging, Beth had uncovered the name of a little-known ex-girlfriend of Kingsley's. A very bitter and vindictive ex, she had learned when she had tracked down the woman's phone number and contacted her. It had taken surprisingly little effort to weasel out the location of an old hunting shack Kingsley had used when they were together. That woman *really* wanted Kingsley to go down.

Though authorities believed the two men had either headed to San Antonio to seek shelter with known associates or fled to Mexico, Josh had thought the tip worth pursuing. Bail jumpers almost always returned to their comfort zones. And—according to Kingsley's ex—this hunting shack was his hidden comfort zone.

Beth raised one eyebrow. "Are we going to do this or what?"

Muttering beneath his breath, Josh exited the car and stuffed the keys into his back pocket.

She opted not to grumble over him not wanting her to accompany him. She knew he didn't mean it in a *you're-a-puny-girl-and-shouldn't-be-running-with-the-big-boys* kind of way. He just loved her and wanted to protect her. They had lost both of their parents by the time Beth turned eighteen and Josh twenty-four, so the two of them were all each other had.

As she opened the passenger door and got out, Beth's triumphant smile transmogrified into a grimace. No longer held at bay by the struggling air conditioner, heat and humidity assaulted her, sparking instant misery.

She opened the back door as Josh circled to the trunk. Kingsley and Vergoma's case files lay on the back seat, along with a stun gun, pepper spray, two pairs of handcuffs, leg irons, and a couple of navy blue jackets with BAIL ENFORCEMENT emblazoned on the back in bright yellow letters.

Beth reluctantly donned the smaller jacket, more to thwart West Nile-carrying mosquitoes than to identify herself as a bounty hunter and prevent any confusion if law enforcement should arrive on the scene.

Law enforcement wouldn't arrive on *this* scene. They didn't even know this place existed.

She pulled out the backpack.

Josh halted when he saw it. "What's that?"

"Marc made me promise to bring it."

"What the hell for? What's in it?"

"Water, first aid stuff, my cell phone, extra ammo..." She tucked her arms through the loops and hoisted it onto her back. "Marc packed most of it. He said it's best to be prepared for anything." Marc was their next-door neighbor and closest friend.

"You are *not* bringing that," Josh informed her. "Take it off."

"No. I told him I'd wear it."

"You only agreed to bring it because you're attracted to him."

Guilty heat stole into her cheeks. "I am not."

"Yes, you are. You know damn well if he weren't seeing someone else, you would have jumped him by now."

3

She sure as hell would have. Marc was hot. "What woman wouldn't? He's freaking gorgeous." Over six feet tall with a tight, muscled body. Black hair that fell several inches below broad shoulders. A neatly trimmed mustache and beard she had fantasized about abrading her skin. A chiseled jaw. Soulful eyes so dark brown they almost matched his hair.

Yeah. She would've totally jumped him if he weren't taken.

"Besides, Marc isn't a bounty hunter," Josh pointed out.

"No, but we've both suspected for some time now that he works for the CIA or FBI or one of those other agencies that has something to do with national security." Marc claimed he worked in the private security business, but... "All those weird hours he keeps. The monochromatic wardrobe."

"Dude always wears black," Josh muttered.

"The cloak-and-dagger secrecy crap, and the wounds we've seen him come home with late at night. It's like living next door to a freaking agent of S.H.I.E.L.D."

Josh shook his head as he pulled his jacket on over the shoulder holster that encased his Glock 9mm. "The pack stays, Beth." He thrust the handcuffs in one pocket, the pepper spray in the other, and clipped the stun gun to his belt. "It'll only slow you down. Especially in this heat."

The heat index was supposed to reach a hundred and ten today. Typical Houston summer.

Beth raised her chin as she looped the strap of their pistol-grip shotgun over one shoulder. "The pack goes."

Almost against his will it seemed, Josh smiled. "You think you have enough weapons there, sport?"

She glanced down. With two 9mms, the shotgun, and the tiny .22 Josh didn't even know she had tucked in one boot, she supposed she did.

Beth sent him a teasing grin. "I don't know. I think I could use a few more."

Shaking his head, he popped the trunk and reached inside. "You know how rarely bounty hunters have to draw weapons."

"When they aren't butching it up on TV," she added.

"Exactly. In all this time, I've only drawn mine once. And I've only had to use the stun gun twice."

She shrugged. "Marc said there was something about these guys that made him nervous. I trust his instincts." And her own. Despite the bravado

4

she attempted to convey, she kept feeling like something was going to go very, very wrong.

"Just keep in mind that legally we're only allowed to use lethal force if our own lives are threatened." He held out a sheathed hunting knife. "Here. Take this."

Beth took it and stared down at it, uncomprehending. "What do you want me to do with it?" Hadn't he just razzed her about having too many weapons?

He closed the trunk. "Strap it to your other thigh."

"Ooookay." She did, wondering what possible purpose the knife would serve.

"There's a compass in the handle," Josh reminded her.

"Oh. Right."

"Keep an eye on it. If we become separated or if something foul goes down, I want you to use it to find your way back to the car and get the hell out of Dodge."

Beth nodded, knowing she would never leave Josh behind but seeing no point in arguing.

"Okay, let's get going. Keep your steps quiet. And the moment you feel that pack slowing you down, drop the damned thing."

Keeping her steps quiet proved to be impossible. Texas still suffered from a severe drought, so the ground beneath their feet bore no grass. Dried and cracked, the heavy clay soil felt as hard as concrete beneath her boots. A thick layer of crisp brown leaves coated it, having fled the parched and dying trees above them. Weeds and saplings struggled to survive, their limbs snapping at the slightest touch.

Beth kept her face impassive, though inwardly she grimaced.

Oppressive heat pressed down on her like a pair of hands on her shoulders, weighting every step. Within minutes, sweat saturated her clothing and dampened her hair. Josh's, too. The plethora of leaves that crunched beneath their boots left gaping holes in the canopy above, allowing the sun to bombard them at will. And not even the hint of a breeze stirred the few leaves that still clung to brittle branches.

Though Beth worked hard to stay in shape, exercising and lifting weights six days a week just couldn't combat the effects of the weather. With every step, her backpack felt heavier. Her mouth grew drier. Several times she had to reach back and adjust the shotgun strap to keep it from sliding off when her shoulders slumped with weariness. No complaint crossed her lips, however, as she used the compass to monitor their location.

It felt as though they trekked through the trees for half an hour or more before Josh stopped and held up one hand. Beth halted, then moved forward as quietly as possible until they stood shoulder to shoulder.

Josh dipped his head and whispered in her ear, "The hunting shack should be just through those trees over there, maybe a quarter of a mile ahead. I want you to stay here while I go check it out."

"No way," she hissed back. "I'm going with you."

He shook his head. "I'm not going to try to apprehend them by myself, Beth. I just want to see whether or not Kingsley and Vergoma are there. If they are and it's just the two of them, I'll do a little recon, determine the best approach to make, then come back here and we'll go in and apprehend them together."

"And if they're not alone?"

"We'll have to see if Marc would be willing to come out and back us up since Grant isn't in town."

Beth wanted to protest further. But Josh crept forward before she could, amazingly light on his feet considering his height and heavy muscles.

Swearing silently as he disappeared through the brush, she eased the backpack off her shoulders and set it on the ground at her feet.

Minutes crawled by as her heart tapped out a nervous rhythm in her chest. Beth curled her right hand around the grip of her Glock, drawing it from the shoulder holster. She strained to hear any sounds beyond the buzzing of mosquitoes, twittering of birds and chatter of squirrels.

Swatting a mosquito, she mentally castigated Josh for leaving her behind like this to worry instead of—

Gunshots split the air.

Starting violently, she froze, eyes widening, heart racing. *Josh!*

Several interminable seconds passed before Beth could force her leaden feet to move. Adrenaline surging through her veins, she raced forward in the direction Josh had taken, terrified of what she might find.

Josh. Josh. Josh.

A gnarled tree root reached up and tripped her. But she managed to stay on her feet as she stumbled unexpectedly into a small clearing.

Josh stood several yards away, up and to her right, his back to a tree, Glock in hand.

Beyond him stood a ramshackle cabin barely bigger than a garden shed.

Josh's eyes widened when he caught sight of her.

More gunshots sounded. Bark splintered from the tree just above his head.

"Beth!"

A bullet slammed into her left shoulder.

Staggering backward, she glanced down as burning pain invaded her arm.

Josh fired into the brush on one side of the cabin.

Raising her own 9mm, Beth followed suit and fired half a dozen times as she backed toward the trees.

Branches snapped as a large body fell forward out of the brush.

Kingsley.

Her ears ringing from the shots, Beth ducked behind a tree. The stale smell of gunpowder filled the air. Her rapid heartbeat pounded in her ears. She tightened her hold on the 9mm, gritting her teeth as the throbbing in her shoulder and arm increased. *Damn*, it hurt.

Licking dry lips, she tasted the salt of her own sweat as she peered around the rough tree trunk.

Another gunshot sounded.

Bark exploded from the tree shielding Josh, no more than an inch from his face.

Her fear doubled. Where the hell was the second shooter?

She studied every tree and bedraggled shrub she could see without sticking her head out far enough to draw fire.

Nothing.

She swore. Josh was trapped. He would be totally exposed if he made a run for it. And, judging by the shots she'd heard and seen him fire, he was probably low on ammo.

Beth slid the shotgun off her shoulder, caught his eye, then tossed it to him.

He grimaced as he caught it. Leaning forward, he pressed the hand still holding his Glock to his side, drawing her gaze to the hole in his vest.

More bullets nicked the tree as he ducked back behind it. So close!

Panic invaded her. A terrible trembling began somewhere deep inside. Her breath shortened as she struggled to pull the Ruger 9mm from the holster on her hip and flip off the safety. She almost couldn't do it. Her left arm didn't want to cooperate.

"Run!" Josh ordered.

She shook her head helplessly. No way would she leave him here like this.

He peered around the tree, then squatted down.

Bark burst from the trunk just above his head.

Josh swore viciously. "Then cover me. He's at your nine o'clock."

Heart in her throat, she nodded, then leaned to one side and fired into the foliage up and to the left.

Josh took off running toward her.

Beth continued to fire, searching the brush for any hint of movement that would let her know exactly where the shooter hid.

Blood suddenly spurted from Josh's right thigh. His leg buckled, sending him to the ground out in the open with no cover.

Beth's breath stopped.

Before the dust had even settled, another bullet pierced his left arm.

"No!" Tears blurring her vision, Beth burst from the cover of the tree, firing blindly in the direction Josh had told her to with both the Ruger and the Glock. Before she could reach Josh, a bullet struck her in the back.

Pain careened through her. All strength seemed to leave her legs as she tumbled forward and landed facedown in the dirt. The hard-packed earth scraped her forearms like cement when she threw them up to keep her head from hitting the ground. Dust flew up and invaded her eyes as her body went limp. Her breath vanished, sucked away in an instant, filling her with terror.

Beth fought to draw air into her lungs, but couldn't. All she could do was listen to her abnormally loud heartbeat and futilely fight her body's attempt to suffocate her.

From what felt like a long distance, she heard Josh emit a roar of either grief or fury.

Even the blasts from the shotgun that followed seemed strangely muffled.

Terrified that Josh was on the receiving end rather than the firing end of those booms, Beth dug deep down into an unknown reserve of strength and struggled to draw her legs up under her. Bracing her hands on the ground, she managed to rise as far as her knees. Her Glock was empty, so she dropped it and rubbed her gritty eyes with quaking fingers in an attempt to clear her vision.

Josh struggled to his feet, his horrified gaze pinned to her.

Still gripping the Ruger, she twisted slightly and saw the second shooter lying dead, half-in half-out of the brush.

Vergoma. He must have circled around behind her. Unless...

Had others joined them? Were there more of them out there somewhere, watching with weapons drawn?

A clatter drew her attention back to Josh.

The shotgun now lay on the ground.

Beth shook her head sluggishly. She needed to warn him that there might be others. But she still struggled for breath and couldn't find her voice.

Dizziness assailed her, made worse by the wagging of her head—the only warning she could conjure.

"They're alone," Josh gritted, managing to gain his feet. Wavering, he stood hunched over with one arm pressed against his side. "B-Beth." He staggered toward her. Pain and apprehension tightened his features. He stared down at her chest, then met her gaze before his eyes rolled back in his head and his body sank bonelessly to the ground.

Beth tried to call his name, but could produce no sound. Nor would her legs support her when she tried to stand.

Feeling weaker by the second, she glanced down. Blood, warm and wet, stained the sleeve of her jacket. More warmth blossomed beneath her vest.

Dropping the Ruger, she parted the front of her jacket with uncooperative fingers and stared in astonishment at the substantial holes in her vest. Ruby liquid seeped from beneath the lower edge and began to stain her jeans.

Nausea rose. Blackness floated on the periphery of her vision.

Beth sank back on her heels, but even then could no longer remain upright.

Tumbling backward, she barely felt it when her head struck the hard soil. Dappled sunlight winked down at her between the green and brown leaves above her.

Turning her head, she focused on Josh with cloudy vision.

He lay, unmoving, only a couple feet away to her left.

Forcing her burning left arm to do her bidding, she reached out and just managed to brush his hair with her fingertips.

Tears filled her eyes and spilled down her temples. Was he dead?

She managed to draw in a short, jagged breath. Warm, salty liquid pooled in her mouth, threatening to choke her. When Beth coughed, flecks of blood flew from her lips and agony shot through her chest and back. Down her arm. So intense she almost lost consciousness.

But she didn't. She couldn't pass out. She had to get help.

Josh needed her. She had to find help.

Curling her fingers in her brother's hair, she clutched a dusty, silky fistful. She had to get help.

A shadow fell across her. Blinking, Beth stared up in confusion as a tall figure swathed in black robes and a cowl entered the clearing.

Fear rising, knowing she had to protect her brother, she dragged her left hand back to her side and curled it around the grip of the Ruger she had discarded. She groaned as she raised her arm. Tears of pain streamed down her temples. Her aim wavered wildly as her muscles trembled.

The new menace loomed over her, his dark robes fluttering and fanning a slight breeze across her that carried with it the scent of exotic spices.

"Wh-Who are you?" she whispered.

He sank onto his haunches beside her. "I have come for you, Bethany." His deep voice held the hint of a foreign accent.

His large hand closed around her wrist, his touch gentle.

Nevertheless, the Ruger fell harmlessly to the ground with a clatter.

The pain in her chest increased, clawing at her and tempting her to seek solace in oblivion.

A strange wind rose, tugging at his cowl and allowing her a brief glimpse of his face.

It was the last thing Beth saw before darkness claimed her.

England, 1203

Dense forest surrounded the four knights as they made their way home. Birds twittered and sang as the branches that supported them swayed in the cool breeze. Squirrels barked their displeasure at the figures that rode past, nearly drowning out the soft thumps the horses' hooves made each time they touched the ground.

Lord Robert, Earl of Fosterly, drew in a deep breath as they left Terrington's land and crossed onto his own. 'Twas foolish to think the air smelled sweeter here, but to a fourth son who had never thought to acquire either land or a title, Fosterly was the most beautiful place in all of England.

"I still think the air of Fosterly smells sweeter than any other," Sir Michael said, echoing his thoughts.

Robert smiled. "You will hear no arguments from me."

The youngest of the powerful Earl of Westcott's six children, Robert had been destined for the church until his two eldest brothers had been killed, the first whilst defending his king during the revolt of 1174 and the second in an accident whilst competing in a tournament. Both of his sisters, like their mother, had died in childbirth. When Dillon, the only sibling Robert had left, had accompanied King Richard to the Holy Land, their father had begun to worry he might lose all of his children and had advised Lord Edmund—the man to whom Robert had been sent to foster—to keep a careful eye on him and ensure he came to no harm.

Of course, Robert *had* come to harm.

Harm Lord Edmund had been unable to guard him against and one his father could not have anticipated. At the age of ten and eight, Robert had fallen deeply in love with Eleanor, a tiny bit of a girl with light brown hair and amber eyes so pale they were nigh golden. How he had adored her and the son she had borne him.

Then all had been taken from him.

Pain, like the ache of an old war wound, filtered through him as he remembered her brother finding him on the practice field that day. And, once more, he found himself wondering why the worst memories always seemed to be the most vivid and easily recalled.

There had been no recent rains. The river had not raged. There had been no reason at all for the bank to give way beneath her feet as Eleanor had walked alongside her brother with baby Gabriel snug in her arms. But give way it had.

Though her brother had lived, Eleanor and Gabe had both drowned. His son's precious little body had never been found. Robert had searched for days—in the water, along the banks, in the surrounding forest—beset by fears that animals might find Gabe first. Then Lord Edmund had forced him back to the castle and poured wine and ale down his throat until darkness had stolen the pain.

When Robert had awoken, it was to find a messenger from Westcott leaning over him, bringing news of his father's death.

It had been a dark time in Robert's life.

It had been a dark time in his brother Dillon's life as well. As soon as the news had reached him, Dillon had returned from the Holy Land. But it had been a different Dillon, greatly changed by whatever horrors he had witnessed in Outremer. Quiet. Grim. Haunted by Robert knew not what.

Until Alyssa had taught Dillon how to laugh again.

Robert's spirit lightened once more.

"And what has inspired that smile?" Michael asked.

He shook his head. "I was thinking of the many unexpected twists and turns the path of life takes."

"Any turn in particular?" he asked curiously.

"Alyssa."

Michael nodded. He and the two men who rode behind them were amongst the few who did not fear Robert's sister-in-law.

Poor Dillon. People had been wary of him and feared him for his ferocity on the battlefield long before he had married Alyssa. But, now that he had chosen for his wife a woman reputed to be a sorceress, England's populace was utterly terrified of him.

Of them both, actually.

"By marrying your brother," Michael commented, "and swiftly producing a son, Lady Alyssa has denied you the title of Earl of Westcott."

Robert nodded. Dillon had been grooming him for the title since their father's death. "And yet, had she not married my brother, I would not love her like a sister and would not have taken such offense when Lord Hurley heaped insults upon her head. So I would not have begged the king's leave to settle our dispute on the field of combat."

"Weasely little bastard," Sir Stephen spat. "'Tis no wonder he always hid behind those hulking guards of his, letting others fight his battles instead of facing one like a man. He had no talent with a sword."

Sir Adam grunted his agreement.

It had taken Robert mere minutes to defeat Hurley. But, after conceding the battle, the blackguard had attacked Robert's back as he had turned to leave the field. Had Michael not bellowed a warning, Robert would have been felled. Instead, he had deflected the blow meant to sever his head, then had driven his sword through Hurley's heart.

"And now you and your brother are *both* earls," Michael said with a grin.

"Aye, we are."

Since Lord Hurley had had no living heirs, King John had bestowed the former Earl of Fosterly's title upon Robert, granting him the lands and remaining wealth that accompanied it as well.

Robert did not delude himself regarding the reasons for this, however. King John had engendered many enemies and wished to curry the favor and acquire the loyalty of Robert and, through him, his brother Dillon, who commanded the largest garrison in the kingdom. Countless noblemen sent their sons to foster at Westcott, where both brothers were renowned for training the country's finest knights. King John was no imbecile. He knew that, should Robert and Dillon decide to join his adversaries, they could swiftly raise a formidable army against him.

"I believe King John is afraid of Lady Alyssa," Adam inserted softly.

Robert glanced at him over his shoulder.

"'Tis why he has never summoned your brother and his wife to court," Adam continued. "He fears she will see his secrets and expose them. Expose *him*."

Stephen whistled low. "'Tis something I would like to see. Would you not? Particularly since I can guess what some of those secrets are."

A distant discordant sound met Robert's ears, distracting him. Holding up a hand to halt his men, he listened carefully.

Seconds later it came again.

"Do you hear that?" he asked.

Michael frowned. "Aye. 'Tis a woman."

"Does she call for help?" Robert asked.

"I know not," Michael responded. "I can barely hear her."

All quieted.

The call came again, a fraction louder this time.

Stephen grunted. "I hear her now. But I cannot understand her words."

"Nor can I," Robert murmured. Mayhap distance muddled them. "But I hear the fear in her voice."

The others nodded.

Adam studied the trees in front of them. "It she to the north?"

"Josh!" the woman shouted.

"Nay." Robert pointed east. "There."

As one, the men turned their horses east and swiftly urged them forward.

Chapter Two

S OMETHING TICKLED HER FACE. REACHING up to brush it away, Beth encountered a strand of her own hair. It danced on a surprisingly cool breeze that wafted over her. Yawning, she tucked it behind her ear, then drew her hands above her head in a stretch, twisting first one way, then the other.

Dull pain traveled from her back to her shoulder, inspiring a wince.

Memory returned in a flash.

Beth bolted upright.

Looking down, she stared in dread at the red stains that covered her shirt sleeve and darkened her jeans almost down to the knees.

She had been shot. Twice.

She frowned. But, other than a slight stiffness in her back and shoulder, she felt fine.

She examined her vest. A substantial hole showed her where the bullet had exited her chest. A smaller one marked the place the other bullet had entered her shoulder. Reaching around behind her, she felt a second set of entry and exit holes.

Yet she felt fine.

Unfastening the Velcro tabs on the vest, she opened it and dragged up the sticky tank top she wore beneath it.

Aside from the blood, the only sign that a wound had ever marred her skin was a pale, barely visible... scar?

Confused, she pulled the top down and sat unseeing for several seconds.

Frown deepening, she yanked the tank top back up to double-check, then let it fall again.

For the first time, Beth noticed her surroundings.

The forest in which she had been shot appeared to have vanished, as had the St. Louis encephalitis and West Nile Virus carrying mosquitoes.

Dense, dark pockets of trees surrounded her instead, all beneath them a lush, beautiful green.

"What the hell?"

It was wrong. It was *all* wrong.

Texas was in the middle of a drought. The only place one could find lush green *anything* was at the heart of an urban sprinkler system. And that was only if the water restrictions had been lifted. The healthy grass before her should be brown and brittle, a major fire hazard.

No. Wait. Come to think of it, there had *been* no grass in the forest where she had died.

Well, *almost* died.

She bit her lip.

Had she died?

Because none of this looked familiar to her. The trees were different, healthy and thriving rather than parched and dying. And the sky...

The sky where she had fallen had been dominated by the harsh, blinding light of a summer sun, not hidden behind a blanket of soft gray clouds. The temperature should be over a hundred degrees, not pleasantly cool and lacking the usual cloying humidity.

Where the hell *was* she? How had she gotten there?

She gasped suddenly. And where was Josh?

Fear struck, hard and fast, as she remembered how still he had lain after being shot.

Beth swiftly refastened her vest and rose.

Dizziness assailed her.

Staggering, she threw out her arms for balance until the world stopped tilting and rolling.

Okay, so she was a little weak. That didn't explain how her bullet wounds had disappeared or healed or changed into scars or whatever. It just confirmed that she hadn't dreamed it all.

Bending, she picked up the Ruger 9mm that lay at her feet.

Her backpack and other belongings lay there, too, but she would tackle that puzzle later.

Beth ejected the empty magazine and replaced it with a full one from her pocket, advancing the first bullet into the chamber.

"Josh?" she called hesitantly, looking all around her. If Kingsley and

Vergoma's men lurked nearby, calling out was a very bad idea, but she didn't have much choice if she wanted to find her brother.

A moment passed. No answer came.

Backing away, she turned toward a stand of trees several yards distant.

Somewhere a bird stopped twittering.

"Josh, where are you?" she shouted, fear rising. "Josh!"

The forest beckoned. Turning this way and that, she started toward it, walking forward, then backward, then forward again, searching for some sign—*any* sign—of her brother.

Why was everything so unfamiliar to her? Had she gotten lost in the forest? *That* forest? The one in front of her?

"Josh!"

Maybe before she had passed out she had stumbled away from her brother in search of help, had ended up wherever she was now, and just couldn't remember it.

Grasping that small shred of hope, she took off into the trees, racing through them as fast as she could, praying she would zip past a tree trunk any minute and run smack into Josh's chest.

"Josh, where are you?"

He has to be nearby, she thought. *I mean, how far could I have gone with a gaping hole in my chest?*

"Josh!"

Her initial burst of energy dwindled at an alarming rate, confirming just how weak she had become. Her voice grew hoarse and fearful.

"Josh!"

She didn't know how long or how far she ran, tripping over fallen branches, crashing through shrubs and ferns and vines, always calling his name, before she saw light up ahead.

Another clearing? *The* clearing?

Hope reviving, breathing hard, she stumbled out of the trees and skidded to an astonished halt.

Four men on horseback stared down at her with equally stunned expressions as they pulled back on the reins to keep their mounts from plowing into her.

Falling back a step, Beth raised her 9mm and gripped it with both hands, aiming first at one man, then the next, not knowing upon whom to settle. "Where is he?" she gasped, so out of breath she could barely speak.

Three of the men looked to the one in the center.

Assuming him their leader, she transferred her aim to him. "Where's..." Her voice trailed away as she got a good look at them. "...Josh?" she finished weakly.

Lowering the gun, Beth gaped.

They created quite an image, lined up before her—side by side—on impressively large, horses with gleaming coats. Every single one of the men was handsome (especially the leader), with broad shoulders and muscled bodies that must surely be a challenge for the horses to carry.

But that wasn't what made her stare until her eyes began to burn.

All four men wore chain mail, sported long broadswords strapped to their trim waists, and looked as if they had just ridden off the pages of a medieval history book.

Or maybe a movie set.

Hope rose.

Shoving her gun into her shoulder holster, Beth eagerly moved forward. "Hey, are you guys actors? Is there a set nearby? Does it have security? Maybe HPD or sheriff's deputies? Because—"

The one on the far left barked something in a language she didn't recognize. He appeared to be the oldest of the four, boasting rich brown hair that grayed at the temples.

"English," Beth said. "In English, please. Are you guys actors?"

The leader said something she again could not understand. What was that—Gaelic?

"Do you speak English?" she asked. "Parlez-vous anglais? Sprechen sie Englisch? Habla used Inglés?" She had always had a knack for foreign languages, both for learning them and speaking them proficiently. She had learned Spanish in high school, then French in college. Marc, who was fluent in at least five or six different languages, had taught her enough German to carry on basic conversations. And her geography professor in college had claimed that knowing English, Spanish, French, and German had enabled him to communicate in every country he had visited throughout Europe.

So, if these guys were European, chances were good that they knew at least one of those.

"Well?" she prompted.

All looked to the leader, who spoke again. He almost sounded like a Scandinavian person speaking English for the first time.

Beth frowned. "Wait. Speak slower, please." For a minute there, it had sounded vaguely familiar.

When the leader merely looked confused, she said again, lengthening the words dramatically, "Speeeeeeeak slooooooooower, pleeeeeeese."

While he still didn't seem to understand her words, he did seem to catch her meaning and obligingly spoke much slower.

Beth stared. Middle English? *That's* what they were speaking? *Sheesh.* No wonder it sounded so weird. She had had a heck of a time learning it when her English professor mother had encouraged her to read rural English literature of the Middle Ages in its original form. And she doubted she would have learned to speak it at all without her talent for learning languages. Josh had had a heck of a time getting it down.

Why the hell would these guys be speaking Middle English?

"Oh, wait," she said suddenly. "I get it. You're one of those reenactment groups, right?" If they had learned to speak Middle English, they must be *really* dedicated to their roles.

When they all just sat there, looking puzzled, she did her best to translate, trotting out her rusty Middle English. But she couldn't always find a medieval equivalent for the modern words she wished to use. "Are you members of a reenactment group?"

The redhead frowned. "Can you not see we are knights?"

Right. Knights in an apparently fanatical reenactment group if they wouldn't deign to speak modern English. "Where are the rest of you?" she asked, still struggling to translate on the fly and get the archaic pronunciation right.

"There are only the four of us," the leader responded, eyebrows colliding as his gaze traveled over her. He had shoulder-length, wavy black hair and bright blue eyes that seemed almost to glow in comparison to his tanned skin.

"No," Beth said, then mentally cursed. "Nay, I mean where is the rest of your reenactment group? Do you have a club around here? Is there a paramedic there, or someone who—?"

"I know not what a reenactment group is, nor a paramedic for that matter. I am Lord Robert, Earl of Fosterly. And these are—"

"Look," she gritted, raw nerves and fear for Josh's safety rapidly eroding her patience as she regained her breath, "now is not the time to be stubborn, okay? I realize you guys are supposed to stay in character, and that sometimes you can be really anal about that kind of thing, but this is an emergency. How far are we from wherever it is you meet with everyone?"

"If you mean Fosterly," he said in his remarkably authentic accent, "'tis almost a day's ride from here."

Yeah, right. So was Florida.

Her fists clenched. "Damn it, this is serious! Quit screwing around!"

The fourth man—blondish-brown hair and chiseled jaw—bristled. "'Tis the Earl of Fosterly you address, girl. 'Twould be wise to—"

"Michael," the leader interrupted softly. "She is injured and likely out of her head with fever."

"I am *not* out of my head," she snapped. "I'm just trying to get some answers from you!"

"And we have given you them."

Beth paused and drew in a deep breath to calm herself. "Okay. I don't know what game you are playing, but let us put that on hold for a minute and just take a step back. I am standing here, covered in blood, asking for your help." Plucking at her sticky jacket, she fanned it a few times. "This is not fake, okay? This isn't studio blood. It isn't Karo syrup mixed with food coloring, or whatever else it is you use in your fake tournaments and reenactment wars. It is human blood. It's *my* blood. And Josh is still out there somewhere"—she motioned wildly to the forest around them—"either bleeding to death or killing himself trying to find me. And that is *if* the damned criminals we were hunting didn't have any friends. I passed out right after the second one went down."

As one, the men drew their swords, startling her into stumbling back a few steps.

"You were attacked by criminals in this forest?" the leader demanded.

She swallowed. Holy crap, they looked fierce. "Yes. No. Nay, I…" She shook her head. "Josh and I are bounty hunters. We were down here looking for two bail jumpers—Kingsley and Vergoma. But something went wrong and, to make a long story short, they shot me, then shot Josh and—"

"Shot?" the redhead interrupted.

"With arrows?" the man with the graying temples interrupted.

"What?" Beth asked.

"You said they shot you," the older man said. "Do you mean with arrows?"

"With *bullets*, Einstein."

"I am Sir Stephen, not—"

"I don't care *what* your freaking name is!" she shouted. Knowing that every minute these guys insisted on furthering their medieval knight roles, Josh could be slipping closer to death, Beth just lost it.

Robert stared at the woman in silence whilst she paced and bellowed her frustration in her peculiar tongue. When she spoke slowly, he could glean her meaning. But the angrier she grew, the more she slipped into that foreign language he could not understand, so he could only grasp a few words here or there.

"Josh could be dying! And you're sitting up there, pretending we're in freaking Medieval England or something! What the hell are you *thinking*? I…"

She seemed to believe they toyed with her in some way. But they had done naught but try to understand and help her.

He studied her carefully.

She was obviously gravely wounded. Delirious. Possibly nigh death.

Despite her assurances otherwise, the woman must truly be out of her head. Many of the words and phrases she used were unfamiliar to him. All but a few that he thought might be mispronunciations of epithets. And those increased in frequency as her agitation grew.

'Twas not just her speech that was odd, though. Her appearance confounded him as well. She was garbed in pale blue breeches, which hugged her slender legs down to her ankles, and a strange dark blue tunic that parted down the middle, revealing a shorter black tunic beneath it. Brown boots encased her small feet. A large knife was strapped to her right thigh. An empty leather pouch of some sort clung to the belt on her left hip. A similar pouch hung beneath her left arm. That one was filled with the weapon (at least, he assumed 'twas a weapon) that she had initially pointed at them, believing them a threat.

Her long, brown, disheveled braid dangled down her back almost to her waist. Dirt smudged her face. Blood coated her chin and cheeks, either coughed up or vomited he guessed from his experience on the battlefield. And most of her clothing was completely saturated with the crimson liquid.

What injuries had she sustained? Who had done this to her?

His fists clenched. And on *his* land?

Dismounting, he motioned for the others to join him.

Her words halted. Her expression lit with inspiration. "Hey, do any of you have a sellfone?"

He frowned. A *sellfone*? What was a *sellfone*?

"A what?" Michael asked beside him.

"A sellfone. I promise I will reimburse you if you'll let me use it."

All four regarded her blankly.

"Oh, come on! Everyone has one."

Silence.

"Seriously? *None* of you have a sellfone?" she asked incredulously. Then she clapped a palm to her forehead. "Wait! I have one in my backpack. I totally forgot about it." Spinning around, she took off running back the way she had come.

Actually, 'twas more of a stumbling jog.

Robert feared she was weak from blood loss. "Michael," he murmured.

Michael strode forward. Easily catching up with her, he took the woman by the arm and drew her to a halt.

Robert applied himself to removing his mailed mitts, then retrieved the bag of healing herbs tied to his saddle. Alyssa had prepared it for him, insisting he carry it with him at all times. He only hoped the herbs and whatever help he could yield would be enough to save the woman.

The sounds of a scuffle broke out behind him.

Frowning, Robert turned in time to see Michael knock that strange weapon from the woman's hand. Undeterred, she brought her heel down on his boot, then slammed the base of her palm up into his nose.

His friend grunted.

"Hold her still, Michael," Stephen barked as Adam started forward. "If she continues to struggle, she will be dead ere Robert even touches her."

The woman stilled, her face blanching.

Pouch in hand, Robert slowly approached them.

"She trembles," Michael murmured, wiping a smear of blood from beneath his nose.

Her features were now as pale as winter snow. Her eyes, glazed with fear, flitted from one to the other, then locked on him.

Robert's stomach clenched at the desolation he saw there.

"I just want to find Josh," she said in a small, choked voice, her unusual accent thicker.

"You will," Robert assured her, taking another step forward. "*We* will. But we must see to your wounds first." So saying, he held up his pouch.

She studied it. "What is that?"

"Herbs," he said simply.

"You mean like medicinal herbs? Or"—she seemed to search for the right words—"healing herbs?"

"Aye. 'Twill stop the bleeding and speed the healing of your wounds, whatever they may be."

"I'm not injured."

"You said you had been…" What had she told them? "…shot."

She said nothing, only watched him uneasily.

"If you vow you will not flee, Michael will release you and I shall tend your wounds," he told her.

"There *are* no wounds."

"Do I have your word you will not flee?" he pressed.

She bit her lip, looking so lost and vulnerable that, for a moment, he had an odd urge to sweep her into his arms and hold her until she felt safe again.

"All right," she grudgingly agreed. "I promise I will not run."

"Release her, Michael."

Michael did as ordered.

As soon as the women was free, she sidled away from his friend and rubbed her arm.

Michael's brow furrowed. "Forgive me if I held you too tightly. 'Twas not my intention to harm you."

She made no response, merely surveyed them all distrustfully.

Robert took another hesitant step toward her. "If you will show me your wounds, I shall do what I can to—"

"I'm not injured," she interrupted with a quick, nervous glance at the others.

"There is no point in lying. All here can see—"

"I'm not lying."

Robert sighed. She had no color to speak of and swayed where she stood. "You are covered in blood."

She lowered her head. Frowning, she dragged one hand across the stains that marred her clothing as though just recalling them. "It's not mine."

"You have already admitted otherwise."

She eyed him uncertainly.

Did she not remember? Considering the excessive amount of blood that streaked her face and saturated most of her clothing, he wondered if whatever she had suffered had damaged her mind.

If so, he could afford to waste no more time. "Enough foolishness," he said, his tone brusque enough, he hoped, to ensure that she would speak the truth this time. "Answer me truly. Where did the blood originate?"

Again she bit her lower lip. "My wounds."

Opening his drawstring bag, Robert closed the distance between them. It pleased him mightily that she did not flinch away from him. "Show them to me."

"I can't," she murmured. "They're gone."

He paused. "What?"

Eyes firmly focused on his face, she nervously licked her lips. "They're gone. My wounds are gone. They disappeared."

Robert dropped his gaze to her clothing. "You lie."

"I know how it sounds," she said miserably. "But it's true."

If proof of the contrary did not saturate her clothing and skin, he might believe her. "Remove your tunic."

"But—"

"Please. I know 'tis not proper for you to disrobe before me, but I assure you I have no wicked intentions. I only wish to help you."

A little crinkle formed in her brow, making her appear even more vulnerable. She was so small. The top of her head did not even reach his chin.

"Y-You guys are really on the up and up, right?"

He had no idea what that meant, but could tell by the inflection in her voice that she was hoping for confirmation. "Aye... Forgive me. You have not given us your name."

"Bethany."

"Aye, Mistress Bethany. We wish only to help you."

A long moment passed, after which she nodded warily. "Okay."

Her outer tunic clung to her in sticky patches as she peeled it off with trembling fingers and dropped it to the ground. Beneath it, her slender arms were bare.

High up on her left arm was a patch of pale skin. Skin that looked incredibly soft from where he stood. The rest, however, was varying shades of red and sticky with congealing blood.

Shrugging out of the strange leather pouch under her arm, she let it fall to the ground atop her tunic.

Another peculiar, smaller tunic covered her torso. All black, it boasted no brooches or clasps. In sooth, he could not see how she had donned it, for it fit her too snugly to have been pulled over her head.

Two ragged holes, he noticed, marred its surface: one in the left shoulder and one in the chest, just beneath the place where her breasts would be if her chest were not as flat as a boy's.

He motioned briefly to Michael with his hand.

When Michael started to walk around behind her, the woman hastily took a step away, tripping over her discarded tunic and the straps of her leather pouch.

Michael stopped and glanced at Robert.

The woman's leery gaze darted back and forth between them.

"I wished him to see if there were holes similar to those in the back," Robert explained, not bothering to hide his concern. Three years ago his brother had almost died from injuries similar to these. He *would* have died, in fact, had Alyssa not healed him in time.

"There are," she confirmed. "If he'll stay back with the others, I'll show you."

Robert did not know why he felt so satisfied that—of the four of them—she had chosen to place her trust in *him*, but he did.

At Robert's nod, Michael obligingly retreated.

Keeping one eye on the others, the woman turned partially away so Robert could see her back.

Adam, Stephen, and Michael moved to stand behind him at a distance, where they would have a better view.

Mistress Bethany swiveled back to face them.

"Where are the arrows?" Robert asked whilst she perused them anxiously. "Did you remove them yourself?"

"Arrows?" The spark of anger that had illuminated her eyes earlier returned. "You mean *bullets*? I didn't *have* to remove them." She motioned impatiently to the holes. "I think it's fairly obvious that they removed themselves." Fingering the hole beneath her small breasts, she scowled. "They must have used armor-piercing rounds, because they went straight through my vest."

"What are bullets?" Michael murmured.

Robert shook his head. He had only understood about half of what she had said and could only assume, due to her strange speech, that such was her word for arrows or quarrels. But it would have taken great force for them to pass straight through her body, and the damage they would have wrought whilst doing so would have been immense. How could she possibly have survived it?

"They entered you there?" he questioned, nodding to her front.

"The shoulder one did. The other one hit me in the back."

His jaw clenched reflexively as outrage flooded him.

His men spat a slew of curses that did not come close to expressing the fury that heated his skin.

"Remove your vest," he said, using her word for the strange tunic.

Offering no further objections, she tucked her fingers under the edge of a rectangular cloth patch on one side and ripped it away. She did the same with another above it and two more on the opposite side.

The vest was sewn together?

It remained fairly stiff as she peeled it away from her body.

Robert's breath left him in a rush as she dropped it to the ground.

One of his men gasped. Another swallowed audibly.

Beneath, a white tunic was molded to her flesh by the blood she had lost. Instead of sleeves, it boasted only two narrow bands of material that disappeared over her shoulders. The neckline dipped enticingly low and clung to full breasts like a second skin. Breasts that had previously been undetectable beneath the tight vest and now drew his fascinated gaze.

The tunic then shaped itself to a small ribcage and narrow waist before disappearing into her breeches.

Her form was too tempting by far. The only thing that kept him from

26

losing his train of thought entirely was the hole that had been shredded into the material just beneath those distracting breasts.

His gaze went to her shoulder, where a smaller hole appeared in the garment.

"It's gone," she spoke into the silence.

His eyes met hers. "Gone?"

"The wound," she clarified. "It's gone."

What did she mean it was gone? "And the other one?"

Without further ado, she peeled her bloodstained white tunic away from her skin and dragged it up to just beneath her breasts.

More crimson coated the skin on her flat stomach, but no wound marred it. She slid her hand across the place he had expected to find one, as though she could not quite believe it herself. "It's gone, too."

Robert stared. She seemed even more confused than they were.

"But there *were* wounds," Michael persisted.

"Aye." Her brow furrowed. "I know it sounds crazy, but it's true." Tugging her tunic down, she took a hesitant step toward Robert. "I *was* hit, okay? I felt the bullets go in. I went down. And I remember lying there, choking on my own blood and having trouble breathing, but..." Forgetting her fear, she finished closing the distance between them and spoke in a voice that grew faster and more agitated with every word. "I think something happened to me after I passed out, because when I woke up everything was different. I wasn't in the same clearing. My wounds were gone. Josh was gone. And the men who shot us..." She shook her head. "I don't know. I can't remember."

She stood close to him now, her head tilted back as she stared up at him.

"Let me see your back," he implored softly.

"Why?"

"Ere we decide what did or did not happen, I wish to make certain no wounds linger where you cannot see them."

She took a moment to consider, then nodded. Turning away, Mistress Bethany reached for the hem of her tunic and pulled it all the way up to her neck in back, her arms crossed over her breasts in front.

Robert swallowed. The skin of her narrow back was as ruby-coated as the rest of her. It was also crossed by three tiny black strips of material that puzzled him as much as the rest of her garb. One was the width of his forefinger and traversed her back from side to side, widening beneath her arms. Two others, narrower than his smallest finger, came down from her shoulders to join it. He could not guess their purpose. But at least one of them was in the way.

Reaching up, he carefully slipped one finger beneath the smaller strap on the left.

The woman jumped and hastily looked over her shoulder.

"I am only searching for injuries," he assured her.

Surprisingly, the strap came away from her skin with little urging. It actually stretched as he pulled it away. Curious, he drew the strap even farther away from her, marveling at its resilience… until it slipped off the end of his finger and hit her skin with a sharp *snap*.

She jumped.

He frowned. "Did that hurt?"

"*Aye*, thank you very much," she growled testily.

For some reason, Robert felt heat creep up his cheeks. "Forgive me. I did not intend to harm you."

"Whatever," she grumbled. "Just don't do it again."

Reclaiming the strap, he gingerly moved it aside, careful not to let it escape him this time, and peered beneath. There was so much blood that he found it hard to discern what it did or did not conceal.

Stepping closer to her, he ducked his head to get a better view.

She stiffened.

"Easy," he whispered in the same voice he used to calm Berserker. "There is so much blood I cannot see beneath it."

"Will it wipe off?" she asked, her voice conveying her anxiety.

"I do not wish to harm you further by putting pressure on the wound."

"There *is* no wound. Just do it."

When Robert hesitated, she reached back with her right hand and started scrubbing at her skin.

Robert grabbed her hand, stilling it before she could inflict further damage. "Cease!"

"It doesn't hurt!" she insisted.

Michael took a step toward them, intending to restrain her if necessary.

Bethany half-turned and backed into Robert, her fingers curling around his in a grip that bordered on painful.

"Michael," Robert instructed, "remain where you are."

He halted.

"Easy," Robert crooned to the trembling woman. "He will come no closer."

She nodded, her throat working in a swallow.

"Now, let me finish examining your wounds."

After a moment, she released his hand and turned her back to him once more.

When Robert returned his attention to her shoulder, he noticed that she had removed enough blood to show him that there was indeed no wound.

Frowning, he rubbed his thumb over the area the hole in her shirt had covered. "There is no wound here."

"That's what I've been trying to tell you."

"But there *was* one." 'Twas a statement more than a question.

"Yes. Is there a scar?"

He felt a raised irregular circle beneath the grit that covered it. "Aye."

"There's one in front, too."

Leaning into her, his chest pressing against her back, he peered down at the front of her shoulder and brushed her clothing aside. "Aye. There is a smaller scar right here." He touched it with his finger.

He noticed she was holding her breath about the same time he realized their bodies were pressed together.

Pulse leaping, he cleared his throat, stepped back, and dropped to one knee behind her so he could search for her other wound. "Tell me if I cause you pain," he uttered, staring at her slender waist and gently rounded hips.

She nodded, her breath soughing out.

With great care, he wiped at the red that coated her back where her injury should be and revealed a scar similar to the one in her shoulder.

An idea began to form. Ere he pursued it, he gently ran his hands over her back and sides in search of cuts or abrasions or *anything* else that could have produced this amount of blood.

There was nothing.

Taking her by the hips, he swiveled her around to face him. His position, kneeling before her, placed his face on a level with her breasts. But he steadfastly kept his gaze trained beneath them.

The scar he found in front was larger, suggesting a violent exit by whatever projectile had pierced her. And Robert again found himself wondering how she could have survived.

Chapter Three

BETH WATCHED THE HANDSOME KNIGHT rest warm, rough hands on her waist. When he smoothed his thumbs across her flat stomach, a shock zipped through her.

Her breath caught. It was almost as strong as the shock she received when she forgot to use dryer sheets in the winter and went pawing through the laundry as soon as she removed it.

She found *this* shock far from irritating, however.

Shaken, she stared down at him. "Did you feel that?" she whispered.

He made no answer, but the surprise that lit his sapphire gaze told her he had.

"Is there a wound?" the one he called Michael asked, breaking the leaden silence.

"Nay. Only blood and scars."

Beth tugged her shirt down and stepped away from the leader's hold. "I told you there were no wounds."

A look passed between him and Michael.

"Lady Alyssa?" the latter asked.

The leader slowly shook his head as he rose, graceful as a panther. "She is at Westcott. And Dillon would not let her risk her life, healing such severe wounds again." He returned his attention to Beth. "Did an old woman come to you whilst you lay dying?" he asked.

She frowned. "What? No. Look, I need to get to my cell phone, call for help, and keep searching for Josh. I'll answer any questions you have later if you'll just help me do that. Okay?"

An eternity seemed to pass before he agreed. "As you wish."

"Could we start with your telling me where we are?" She motioned to the trees around them. "None of this looks familiar. Everything in the clearing I was injured in was dying from the drought. And all of this looks healthy." She frowned, a notion occurring. "Are we near the Woodlands?" If so, she was far from where she should have been. "I seem to recall people on the news complaining about residents and businesses in the Woodlands ignoring the water restrictions." And she was pretty sure there was a state forest somewhere on the outskirts of it.

The knights stared back at her blankly.

Right. Too many modern words. "Are we near the Woodlands?"

"Woodlands?" The leader glanced around him, then nodded slowly. "Aye."

It wasn't much to go on. But it was something. "Can I have my gun back?" she asked, eager to get her things, get moving, and find Josh.

He followed her gaze to the discarded Ruger. "Nay. Your weapon will remain in my keeping for now."

Frustration coursed through her. "What if Kingsley and Vergoma weren't alone ? What if there are others out there who were helping them?" *Someone* had to have moved her here.

"We will dispatch any who choose to attack us."

Beth gave him a skeptical once-over. "With what—your sword?"

He frowned. "Aye. We are more than capable warriors, all of us."

Yeah, right. "I'll take my chances with the gun."

His scowl deepened. And damned if he didn't look insulted.

Seriously? Beth threw up her hands, unwilling to waste any more time. "Fine. But if you don't return it when help arrives, I'll report it stolen and tell the police you took it."

She wouldn't have given up so easily if she didn't still have a .22 strapped to her ankle. While it didn't pack much of a punch, it would do in a pinch.

Well, against a single attacker it would, if she hit him in the right places. Thank goodness these men hadn't turned out to be rapists or murderers. A 6-shot .22 wouldn't have stopped all four of them unless she managed to hit them all in the head.

The leader bent to retrieve the Ruger.

"You might want to make sure the safety is on before you put that away," she advised.

He gave the weapon an enigmatic glance.

"The little switch on the side," she elaborated. "Make sure it's— *Not that one! That's the trigger!*"

At her near-shout, he hastily jerked his finger away from the trigger.

Beth splayed a hand across her chest, covering the heart that threatened to burst from its confines. Stalking toward him, she reached for the 9mm.

He promptly raised it above his head, out of her reach.

"I'm not going to take it," she snapped. "I just want to make sure you don't accidentally shoot one of us."

Muttering something beneath his breath, he let her flick on the safety.

"You act like you've never seen a gun before," she grumbled.

"I have not."

"Not even in the movies?" When Beth turned away to retrieve her discarded clothes, the world spun crazily. "Whoa." Throwing out one arm, she fell sideways into the leader.

"Careful," he murmured as he wrapped strong arms around her and held her upright.

"Sorry. I just..." Beth blinked hard until everything swam into focus and stopped moving. "I got a little dizzy there for a minute." Straightening, she clutched a handful of the soft tunic that covered his chain mail, took a deep breath and released it slowly. "Much better. Thank you." She gave his chest a pat, then retrieved her clothes.

It only took her a minute to don her vest and refasten the Velcro tape on each side. She added the shoulder holster next, then her dirty jacket. While she no longer seemed to need protection from mosquitoes, she found she could use the added warmth. A freak cold front must have swept through or something, because the temperature had definitely dropped.

"What is that?" Michael asked, motioning to the words on the back of her jacket.

Blood must have obscured the words, making them difficult to read. "It says Bail Enforcement Agent. Josh and I are bounty hunters." She pointed in the direction from which she had come. "I think my backpack is that way." When she looked around, everyone was staring at her shirt. She glanced down and saw nothing amiss. "What?"

"Your clothing is passing strange," Michael commented, his tone bewildered.

"What's so strange about it? It's jeans, a bulletproof vest, and a jacket."

"Why do you wear breeches?" one of the others—Stephen?—asked with something akin to disapproval. "You are a woman."

"Last time I checked I was," she drawled. "What does that have to do with anything?"

"And the fastenings," the fourth one added. "How did you refasten your vest without needle and thread?"

"Ever heard of Velcro?"

"Nay," Stephen and Michael answered with every appearance of honesty.

These guys just didn't give up, did they? "Whatever. Let's just get going."

The leader motioned to his men, who moved to mount their horses. "You shall ride with me," he informed her.

Beth took one look at the mammoth-sized, stomping, snorting stallion he led toward her and abruptly turned coward. "Um, you know what? I think I'm going to walk."

He frowned. He did that quite often, she noted, and wasn't sure if it was because he disagreed with her words or simply couldn't understand some of them. "'Twill be faster if you ride."

"Nevertheless, I'll walk." She scuttled backward as the horse drew near.

The others all mounted their horses and sat, looking down at her as if she were certifiable.

Or perhaps just being difficult.

But she *wasn't* being difficult. She was being a wuss.

"Why?" the leader asked.

"Because I, um…." *Ah, hell.* How was she supposed to come up with a good excuse when that huge thing was peeling its lips back from its teeth and stretching its neck out as if it wanted to take a nice big bite out of her?

"You shall ride with me," he commanded again.

"No. I mean, nay."

Great. If the tightening of his lips and the muscle jumping in his cheek were any indication, she had offended him.

Beth sighed. "All right. Here's the thing," she confessed in a low voice the others leaned forward and strained to overhear.

The leader obligingly ducked his head to better catch her words.

"I have never been this close to a horse before," she told him softly. "And, as embarrassing as this is for me to admit, I just realized that I'm apparently afraid of them."

He blinked. "You have never been nigh a horse?"

Resentment bubbled up inside her, heightened by her embarrassment. "Look, not everyone in Texas owns a ranch, you know," she blurted defensively. "We aren't all cowboys. We don't all own horses and wear boots and fringed shirts and big belt buckles and cowboy hats and listen to country western music. That's such a stereotype! I grew up in the suburbs of one of the largest cities in the country, for crying out loud! The only time I ever even *saw* a horse was when my parents took me to the rodeo when I was a kid. And the horses there didn't look *nearly* as huge from my seat way up high in the nosebleed section as yours does now."

"Cowboys?" he queried, seemingly confused.

"Nosebleed section?" This from Stephen.

"Suburbs?" Michael parroted.

"Yes!" Her temper erupted in a growl of frustration. "I mean, aye!"

The leader held his hand out to her. "Berserker will not harm you."

"Berserker is your horse's name?"

"Aye."

"And that's supposed to reassure me?"

He didn't seem to know what to say to that. Not that *anything* he said would erase her qualms.

"I will not let you fall, Mistress Bethany. You have my word that you will come to no harm if you ride with me."

She stared up at him, taking in his handsome, earnest features.

Something about this man was starting to grow on her. Something that made her want to throw caution to the wind and give him her trust.

He must have sensed she was weakening, for he moved in then with a killing blow. "If you ride with me, we will cover ground more quickly and will have a greater chance of finding this Josh you seek before nightfall."

Great. He had found her biggest weakness. She would do *anything* to find Josh and see to his safety, even ride an oversized horse with an attitude.

Her wary gaze on Berserker, Beth placed her hand in the leader's much larger one.

It was warm and tanned and callused but capable of gentleness, she learned as he folded his fingers around her own.

"Your hand is as cold as well water," he exclaimed, frowning down at it. Curling his other hand around it, he brought it to his lips to blow warm breath on it.

Butterfly wings fluttered in her belly. "What was your name again?" she asked.

"Lord Robert, Earl of Fosterly."

She nodded slowly, his touch doing strange things to her insides. "Well, Robert, I'm going to hold you to that promise. So, I guess you'd better go ahead and give me a boost."

Something about the way she said his name surprised him. She saw it in his eyes and felt it in the tightening of his grip on her fingers before he frowned over the rest of her words.

Shaking his head, he dropped his hands to her waist, lifted her effortlessly and deposited her sideways on the saddle. It was an odd one, not like those she had seen in movies, but Beth barely registered it as she clutched the high pommel with a death grip.

Her heart raced madly. Her palms grew moist. The ground seemed miles away from her precarious perch. And every horror story she had ever heard about people being thrown from their horses and winding up either dead or paralyzed chose that moment to flood her mind.

She gasped as Robert launched himself into the saddle behind her, lifted her and settled her firmly across his lap. One heavily muscled arm locked around her waist while the other took the reins.

"Fear not, Mistress Bethany," he murmured soothingly in her ear. "I shall let no harm befall you." Then the horse beneath them moved, carrying them forward to retrace her path through the forest.

Beth had just enough time to convince herself that—under other circumstances—she might actually enjoy learning to ride horseback... eventually... on a nice, slow, elderly nag, before they broke through the trees.

The meadow in which she had awoken opened up in front of them.

Relief rushed through her when she saw her possessions. "My backpack!"

Berserker stopped at Robert's unspoken bidding. The others followed suit.

"I shall dismount first," Robert spoke gruffly in her ear. "Then I will assist you down."

"Okay."

35

Beth didn't realize how tightly she was holding his arm until he carefully peeled her fingers away and settled them on the pommel. "Just hold on here and you shall be fine."

She nodded jerkily.

Covering her hands with one of his, he gave them a comforting pat, then dismounted. Seconds later, he gripped her waist, lifted her and settled her gently upon the grass.

"Thank you." Beth hurried over to her backpack and dropped to her knees. As she began to paw through it, she heard the others dismount. "Where is it?" she muttered. "Where is it? Where is it? Come on, you son of a— *Aha!*" She cried out in triumph when she finally located her cell phone. Turning it on, she prepared to dial 911.

No bars.

"Shoot!"

Scrambling to her feet, she bumped into Robert and Michael. The two had apparently come to stand beside her and now leaned down to peer curiously at her phone.

"Sorry," she mumbled as she took several steps away to try again.

No bars. Not even a flicker.

"*Shoot!*"

She crisscrossed the clearing at least a dozen times, holding the phone high and low, this way and that, trying to get a signal with no luck, her worry increasing with every step.

"*Work, damn you!*" she shouted, and tried yet again with no luck.

No phone. No Internet. No nothing.

Sighing, she bowed her head. Her shoulders slumped. She lowered the hand holding the phone and let it dangle uselessly by her hip.

How was she supposed to summon help when her freaking phone wouldn't work?

"What precisely is it supposed to do?" Stephen asked.

Eyes narrowing, Beth turned to look at him.

Stephen and the one she now knew was called Adam had joined Robert and Michael. All stood a few yards away.

"I'm trying to call 911," she told him, thinking it pretty obvious.

She may as well have spoken in ancient Aramaic. All four regarded her blankly.

"You were not successful?" Michael asked.

"Nay. I can't get any service." Frowning, she tucked the phone into one of her jeans pockets. "Do you think it's the trees? Do trees block the signal? I don't think I've ever seen any this tall before."

Michael and Adam both looked up and around at the trees.

Robert stood with his hands on his hips, his tunic stained with her blood, a scowl marring his otherwise handsome features.

"Whom do you wish to call?" Stephen asked.

Clearly, he wasn't the brightest bulb.

"911," she repeated, returning to her backpack. "Josh, two dead men—at least I *hope* they're both dead—and who knows how many others are still out there." For the first time, she noticed the cylindrical nylon bag that was lying on the ground beside her backpack. She frowned. "That's weird."

"Is aught amiss?" Robert asked.

"I don't know." She opened the drawstring end and confirmed her suspicions. "It's our camping tent. Josh left it in the trunk after we got back from our trip last month. I don't know why it's here. Josh wasn't carrying it when we left the car. I *know* he wasn't. He didn't even want me to bring my backpack." Which *also* hadn't been with her in the clearing when she had fallen, come to think of it. So why was it here? What did it mean?

Kneeling down, she set the tent aside and began to rifle through her pack again in search of the bottles of water Marcus had included. Her mouth was so dry it felt as though no liquid had crossed her lips in days. She couldn't blame the heat since the air had cooled quite a bit. So it must be a result of the blood loss. She was light-headed, too, and hoped some water might help clear her head. "We need the police to organize a search. And Josh will need medical attention when we find him. The last time I saw him…" Her throat closed off. Tears blurred her vision.

After he had collapsed, he had lain so still.

Robert knelt beside her and placed a hand on her shoulder. "We shall find him for you."

Nodding, she dipped her chin and continued to rummage through her things. At last, her fingers brushed the familiar cold plastic.

When Beth stood with the water bottle and began to unscrew its top, she suddenly found herself encircled by four enormous men who gazed at the bottle as though it were a perfect, baseball-sized diamond. "Do you, uh, want some water?" she asked no one in particular, assuming thirst inspired their interest.

"'Tis water inside there?" Stephen asked.

Nodding, she held it up so they could read the label.

"What manner of container is that?" Michael queried.

"Is that parchment wrapped about it?" Adam followed. "Such colors!"

Beth looked down at the object in her hand, wondering what was so unusual about it. "It's a plastic bottle full of spring water. What's the big deal?"

When they continued to *ooh* and *ahh* over it, she raised puzzled eyes to Robert's.

"We have never before seen the like," he explained.

"You mean you've never seen this *brand*?" Improbable, considering one could purchase it in just about any grocery or convenience store in Texas. "Or you've never seen a bottle this size?"

Stephen reached out and gave the bottle a squeeze before she could stop him. It emitted a squishing noise as bubbles and large droplets of water oozed out from the base of the partially unscrewed lid. "It gives!" he cried, as excited as a child.

Then they *all* wanted to squeeze it.

"Hey—hey—*hey*!" Beth called out, backing away from them and swiveling to place her body between them and the water. When Stephen reached around to take it from her, she slapped his large, gloved hand away. "Stop that!"

"Stephen, leave her be," Robert ordered, even though he had squeezed the bottle himself a time or two.

Only when she was sure they would all obey him did she turn back around, both hands locked protectively around the bottle. "I don't mean to be rude or anything. I just didn't bring that much with me. It would've made the pack too heavy."

Their gazes remained fixed on the bottle.

Were they even listening to her?

"You're more than welcome to drink some," she offered. "But I can't afford to let you waste any of it on the ground while you pretend you've never seen plastic before. I want to save some for Josh."

"The flask is formed from plastic?" Robert asked.

Bewildered, Beth looked down at the bottle, then up at him. "Well, yeah. Aye."

"We have none of us ever beheld plastic."

Beth looked from one to the next, taking in their befuddled expressions and melding them with their strange garments. "Ohhh. Is this part of the whole reenactment thing?"

Robert frowned.

"It is, isn't it?" she persisted, removing the lid from the bottle they still sought to fondle and raising it to her lips. Cool, sweet water slid across her tongue and down her throat, quenching her fierce thirst. Feeling a little better, she offered the bottle to Robert. "Would you like some?"

His hand brushed hers as he took it, sending a little tingle through her. The plastic crackled and popped as he gave the bottle several more experimental squeezes, then downed a few swallows.

The anticipation on his friends' faces as they awaited his judgment was almost enough to convince her that this wasn't, in reality, all a game to them. She'd had no idea these reenactment groups carried things so far. It was... pretty weird, wasn't it?

Of course, she had heard that a few groups were quite fanatical about it, forbidding participants from carrying anything evenly remotely modern on or about their person, attempting to keep things as true to the time period as possible, allowing no modern language or inappropriate accents, even strictly abiding by the hierarchical stratum.

But she was not a part of their troupe or whatever they called it, so weren't they taking things a bit too far? Particularly considering the circumstances?

"'Tis water," Robert pronounced after taking another swig, "as she said."

If she weren't so worried, she would be amused. What had he thought it was—her secret liquor stash?

Beth returned her attention to her pack. When she tugged it up to rest it on its base, she was surprised to find her other 9mm resting beneath it, along with the pistol-grip shotgun she had last seen lying beside Josh. A large hand grabbed hers as she reached for them. Startled, she looked up into Robert's vivid blue eyes.

"I shall keep those with the other," he informed her as he picked them up.

Damn it!

He nodded at the smaller weapon and raised one eyebrow. "Is it safe?"

"Safe?" she asked, unsure of his meaning.

"Aye. Do you need to make it safe as you did the other?"

"Oh. No. Nay, this one doesn't have a safety. Just don't touch the trigger." She really wished they would give up the Middle English already. Translating on the fly when she was rattled and distracted and worrying about Josh was not easy.

Satisfied, he tucked the weapon in his sword belt. "And this?" He indicated the shotgun, holding it out for her inspection.

Beth pushed the small round button on the side, near the trigger. "It's safe."

Robert looked it over briefly, then slipped the strap over his shoulder.

Reaching for the zipper on her backpack, she started to close it and again found herself surrounded by four fascinated men. All wanted to know how she had done it and demanded she zip it and unzip it again. With very realistic exclamations and awed expressions, they crowded and buffeted her and reached for the bag.

Beth threw herself bodily across it to keep them from taking it from her. "I am *not* going to do this again!" she shouted, swatting at their grasping hands. "Come on! Cut the crap! We don't have time for this! We need to find Josh!"

"Cease!" Robert bellowed, shoving the men back as if he weren't just as guilty as the others.

Air whooshed out of her lungs as Beth cautiously sat up and clutched the heavy backpack to her chest. "Thank you."

"Forgive us," he entreated, his expression chagrined. "We did not mean to overset you, but we have never—"

"Seen a zipper before?" she finished for him.

"The marvelous fastening is called a zipper?"

"Aye," she said, her patience beginning to fray.

"Aye. We have none of us seen a zipper."

"Well, this whole medieval thing is all very entertaining. But right now I just want to look for Josh, okay? You can pretend to marvel over all of my twenty-first century gadgets later, after we've found him."

The men exchanged a look.

Beth stood with the backpack in her arms, a new need making itself known. She hadn't thought she had been unconscious for that long, but her full bladder suggested many hours had passed. And she had no idea how long it would be before she could find a restroom.

A quick survey told her there were plenty of thick bushes and trees behind which she could relieve herself, but having four men for an audience did not appeal to her in the least.

"So," she broached tentatively. "If I go out there to, ah, you know," she motioned to the surrounding forest, "you won't follow me and peek or anything, will you?"

She must have phrased it funny or something because they again gazed at her as if she had three heads.

"Did you say twenty-first century?" Michael asked, his face clouded with doubt.

"Oh, for crap's sake!" she exclaimed. "I am too tired and too worried to deal with this! Will you stay here or not?"

Robert held up a hand to silence Michael when he would have replied. "We will allow you your privacy."

"Thank you!" Spinning around, she marched off into the woods, muttering under her breath about stubborn men who never knew when to quit.

As Mistress Bethany disappeared into the foliage, Michael asked in a hushed voice, "Did I mistake her?"

"Nay," Stephen answered somberly. "She did say twenty-first century."

"Poor girl," Adam murmured. "Even with her peculiar speech I did not think her mad, but—"

"She is not mad," Robert denied, a sick feeling nevertheless lodging itself in his gut.

"Robert," Michael protested softly.

"She is overwrought, Michael. I know not what has befallen her, but it has left her covered in blood and consumed with worry for her husband or lover or whomever this Josh fellow is, and he is probably dead. Think you she does not realize that?" Hands on his hips, he took a few steps in the direction she had taken. "We bombard her with questions and try to pry the last of her belongings from her blood-encrusted fingers merely to satisfy our curiosity and you think her mad for offering a misplaced word or two?"

Adam pursed his lips. "'Tis true the lass has some difficulty with the language."

"I understand not half the words that emerge from her lips," Robert agreed. Lips that he suspected would be quite lovely if they and the rest of her face were clean.

"You are certain Lady Alyssa is not in the area?" Michael posed.

"Nay. She is at Westcott, struggling to keep Dillon from placing a wooden sword in their son's eager hands. And if she *were* here, she would not have healed the girl, then left her to wander the forest alone in such an addled state."

"*No peeking!*" Bethany shouted suddenly, startling them.

Stephen raised both bushy eyebrows. "Overwrought or nay, I think her mad as the miller's mother." Catching Robert's frown, he grinned. "I did not say I dislike her, only that she is mad. I cannot recall another woman who has entertained me so."

Robert's scowl deepened as something resembling jealousy sifted through him.

"If not Lady Alyssa, then who?" Michael went on. "Her grandmother?"

Robert shook his head. "I think not. Her grandmother has not the strength. Healing such wounds would kill her."

"What of the other *gifted ones*?"

"As far as I know, none of them possess the ability to heal and cannot do so without Alyssa or her grandmother present to channel their gifts."

"What of the giant?"

"The one who calls himself Seth?" Dillon had often described the man as a giant because of his impressive height, which was a head or more taller than Robert's six feet. "I know not his gifts. But Dillon said Seth did not heal Alyssa himself. He showed the others how to combine their strength and their gifts to heal her instead."

Stephen grunted.

"The scars could be from old wounds," Adam murmured.

Michael tilted his head to one side. "What of the holes in her clothing?"

Adam shrugged. "Are all of your tunics new and undamaged? Mayhap she has not the coin to replace hers."

Stephen nodded. "The blood could belong to this Josh fellow. Mayhap whatever she witnessed has made her retreat to a previous attack she suffered and she is confusing the two. Sir William once told me that when he saw a fellow crusader cut down a woman in the Holy Land, he flew into a rage and killed the man. When his thoughts finally cleared, William found himself weeping over the woman's corpse and calling her by his wife's name."

Robert frowned. "Was his wife not slain here in England?"

"Aye, and 'tis what Sir William saw whilst he defended the woman in the Holy Land and struck down her attacker."

"I *said* no *peeking!*" Bethany yelled. "Where *are* you guys?"

Robert called back, "We stand where you left us!"

"*All* of you?"

"Aye!" the men chorused loudly.

"Just making sure!"

"What do you intend to do with her?" Stephen asked, voice soft.

"If we do not find this Josh she seeks, I will offer her shelter at Fosterly until we learn more."

"And if you never learn more?"

"I know not."

Twigs snapped and foliage rustled as Bethany moved into view and headed toward them. The pouch with the fascinating zipper was now looped over one shoulder and rested against her back. "Sorry to keep checking," she said, "but I had a sudden vision of my bare bottom being plastered all over Facebook."

Michael's eyebrows flew up. "What?"

Robert gazed down at her dirt-smudged, blood-speckled face and found himself fervently hoping she was *not* touched in the head.

"So what's the plan?" she asked. "Are we going to split up so we can cover more ground? Or should we go wherever it is you guys came from and get help there?"

Beginning to see a pattern in her speech, which was an odd combination of familiar and foreign words, Robert considered the question. "'Twould take us mayhap half a day to reach Fosterly."

"What's Fosterly?"

"My castle."

"I assume by castle, you mean reenactment group meeting place."

43

Robert did not know how to respond to that, so he opted not to. "There is little light left, however."

Beth glanced at the sky and frowned. "I hadn't even noticed."

"If your Josh's condition is as dire as you say it is, I believe 'twould be wisest to continue searching for him."

Relief entered her greenish-brown eyes. "That would be my choice as well. The thought of leaving the area, of leaving him even for a few hours when he might be bleeding to death is…"

"I understand. Do you know where we may find him?"

"No." Her brow furrowed as she glanced around. "None of this looks familiar to me. But if we're near the Woodlands, we should probably head north. Or maybe west. Or northwest. I'm just not sure."

"Since you are uncertain, we shall each travel in a different direction. Will Josh recognize your possessions?"

"Aye."

"Then Michael will take your pack. Stephen will take that." He nodded at the long narrow bag on the ground.

"My tent?" she asked as Stephen bent to retrieve it.

"Aye," Robert said, though he failed to understand how the makings of a tent could fit into such a small bag. "And Adam will take this." He handed Adam Beth's largest weapon. "If any of you find Josh and he doubts Bethany has sent you looking for him, show him her belongings."

Beth nodded. "And please speak slowly when you see him so he can understand you."

The men all agreed.

Robert motioned to his destrier. "You may once more ride with me on Berserker."

The hazel eyes that met his carried both fear and dread. "We *will* find him, won't we?"

Robert tucked a stray curl behind her ear. "I hope so, Bethany."

"You can call me Beth."

He smiled. "As you wish, Beth."

Taking her backpack from her, he handed it to Michael. "Shall we?"

Chapter Four

MICHAEL RODE TO THE SOUTH, Adam to the west, and Stephen to the east.

Robert rode to the north with Bethany perched on his lap.

She had insisted on riding astride this time, her shapely bottom snug against his groin, her thighs molded to his, generating a heat that drove him to distraction. Because of her fear of horses, he had expected her to remain tense. But she had surprised him, relaxing and leaning back against him most of the time.

He held Berserker's reins in one hand. The other arm he wrapped around her narrow waist, smiling when she folded her hands comfortably atop it.

It would have been a pleasant journey had her concern not permeated the air around them. Every few minutes she would pull the odd *sellfone* from her pocket, stroke it with her thumb, then mutter and tuck it away again. Then she would draw a large hunting knife from its sheath on her thigh, hold it up in front of her like a cross, then put it away. A few minutes later she would shout Josh's name three times, pausing in between to listen for a response. When none came, she would rest a moment, then reach again for her *sellfone,* and the cycle would begin anew.

"Joooosh!" The shadows of the forest swallowed any echo her call may have otherwise generated. "Joooosh! Can you hear meeee?"

She had a powerful voice for such a small woman. His eyebrows had nigh met his hairline the first time she had bellowed the other man's name. Unlike most of the females of his acquaintance, her voice did not rise in pitch when she shouted and was not the least bit shrill. Rather 'twas deep and strong and almost loud enough to make his ears ring, growing only the slightest bit hoarse as the sun continued its descent.

"Joooosh!"

Berserker snorted, as if he knew she desperately wanted some kind of answer and thought it might help to give her one himself.

Sighing, Bethany slumped back against Robert. "Why is it so cool?" she asked wearily. "Earlier today I was worried about suffering heatstroke, and now the breeze is giving me chills. The cold fronts we get this time of year don't usually lower the temperature this much."

Robert thought the temperature quite mild for late spring and wondered if mayhap she grew feverish. Frowning, he worked his arm out from under hers and pressed his palm to her forehead.

"I'm not running a fever." She pulled his hand down. "Aren't you cold?"

"Nay, but the padded gambeson I wear beneath my mail is much warmer than your tunics."

She peeled the mailed sleeve of his hauberk back and tested the gambeson with her fingers. When one of those slender little fingers slipped beneath the thick material and glided across the inside of his wrist, a shock of desire zigzagged through him, catching him off guard.

"Wow. That *is* warm." Wriggling her hand, she managed to stuff the rest of her chilled fingers up his sleeve. "*Ahhhh.*"

Robert's heart thudded against his ribs when she slid her other hand along his and linked their fingers around the reins. How fortunate that he had not donned his mailed mitts again after checking her wounds.

"Mmm. Your hand is warm, too," she praised. "You don't mind, do you?"

"Nay," he answered, silently cursing when his voice emerged a bit hoarse. Her touch affected him far more than it should have.

When she tilted her head back to look up at him, he stared straight ahead and schooled his features into a bland mask.

"You sure?" she asked.

"Aye."

"Thank you." Facing forward, she seemed content for a while.

Her skin had not quite lost all of its chill when she abandoned his hand and wrist, retrieved her *sellfone* from the pocket on her breeches and stared down at it.

Curious, Robert peered over her shoulder and tried to understand just what this small, dark object did. There were what appeared to be several tiny, colorful paintings on it, all lined up in neat rows.

Bethany moved the phone to one side, then the other, up and down, all the while keeping a sharp eye on the object.

Robert failed to see it do anything, but thought the little drawings or paintings unusually bright. They seemed, in fact, to glow. "Is all as it should be?" he queried.

"Nay," she answered, frustration darkening her words. "I still can't get any bars. I don't understand it."

She shoved the *sellfone* back into her pocket, then leaned to one side, unknowingly grinding her hip into his arousal, and pulled her knife from its sheath.

A groan escaped him ere he could suppress it.

"Did you say something?" she asked.

"Nay."

She held the blade in front of her, handle up, and went still.

'Twas a most unusual weapon. The handle appeared to be somewhat tarnished silver that smoothed into a ball at its base. Between the handle and the blade lay a flat strip of metal that served as the guard. From this, two rounded spikes—each almost the width of Bethany's smallest finger—extended outward on either side of her small fists, offering protection from an opponent's strikes.

The blade itself was as long as her forearm. Mayhap as wide as her narrow wrist at its base, it thickened along its length and curved wickedly until it narrowed to a sharp point.

When she would have put it away, Robert spoke. "What do you do when you hold your weapon thusly? Do you pray?"

"Pray? Nay, I'm looking at this." Twisting so that one shoulder brushed his chest, she drew the knife in closer and tilted the handle toward him. "See?" She tapped the rounded ball at the base. "It's a compass."

Robert leaned down a bit to give it a closer look.

The rounded base was not metal as he had believed, but clear like glass. Inside lay a small ball marked with letters that represented the directions. His eyes widened as the little ball stayed in place while she turned the handle this way and that.

"Since I can't really get a good look at the sun because of all these trees, I've been using this to keep track of what direction we're traveling in." Leaning over to tuck her head beneath his chin, she looked at the miraculous little ball. "Right now we're heading north-northwest. We *were* heading due north."

Robert could only stare. What a wondrous weapon.

Straightening, she glanced up at him. "Pretty cool, huh? And that's not all." Holding the handle with one hand, she wrapped the other around the spherical compass and began to turn it. "This unscrews." Removing the compass, she showed him a hidden compartment within the handle. "And inside are waterproof matches, a fishing hook with fishing line, a safety pin, a needle and some thread."

Robert had no idea what *matches* were. They looked like large wooden splinters with blue tips. And the fishing line could not hold much strength. He could practically see through it. But the secret compartment, the compass and the fishing hook concealed in the blade's handle he found very intriguing.

"A most unusual weapon."

A sad smile briefly lit her face as she tucked her secrets back inside the handle. "Josh lent it to me."

Facing forward again, she secured the knife in its sheath.

Robert scowled at the back of her head. Affection laced her voice when she spoke the other man's name.

"Joooosh!"

"Who *is* this Josh to you?"

"*Joooosh!*" Sighing heavily, Bethany leaned back against him, her head resting against his chest. "My brother. I told you that, didn't I?"

"Nay, you did not." Had she done so, he would not have been jealous. Nay, not jealous. He would not have been... concerned?

His scowl deepened. Not if he were honest with himself. If it had been aught other than jealousy, he would not feel so relieved now.

"Have you other siblings?" he asked.

"Nay. It's just the two of us." Reaching up, she scratched her left shoulder. "My mother died of cancer when I was fifteen. My father was killed in a car accident just before I turned eighteen. Josh is all I have now. I don't know what I'm going to do if we don't find him."

"If our search bears no fruit, I shall send out a large search party the moment we reach Fosterly."

"Thank you. I'm not sure how long it will take the police to get here once we call them."

Once more, her words baffled him. But Robert opted not to question her. He was too busy trying not to notice when she scratched her chest just above her left breast.

"You know what else confuses me?" she asked.

"What?" he murmured.

"We haven't found our car."

Car? Did she mean cart?

It occurred to Robert then that he had never asked her how she and her brother had been traveling. He did not think she had come by foot. 'Twas plain she had not been traveling on horseback either. But if she had been riding in a cart as she stated, why had she seemed ignorant of horses?

"You journeyed here in a cart?"

"Car," she corrected. "A silver Toyota Corolla that has seen better days. If I'm not as far from where I fell as I thought and the forest just looks greener here because we're close to a river or a lake, then we should have found our car by now."

Her words failed to clarify the difference between a car and a cart for him, but he chose not to press her further. "Mayhap one of the others will discover it."

"I hope so." Sitting up straight, she arched her back and pushed one arm up behind her to scratch between her shoulder blades.

Robert suspected that her scars were itching. Either that or the dirt that had coated her and mingled with the drying blood was beginning to slip down into the folds of her tunic and the odd vest she wore, tickling her as it went.

Stopping, Bethany sat very still for a moment, then suddenly threw her hands up and shouted, *"How big is this freaking forest?"*

Berserker snorted and bobbed his head up and down.

Her frustrated outburst over, Bethany gave the horse's neck a tentative pat, then glanced at Robert over her shoulder. "Would you please scratch my back? This itching is driving me crazy."

Removing his arm from around her waist, Robert dutifully curled his fingers into claws and began to scratch her shoulder.

"Harder, please."

He applied more pressure.

"Harder."

And more pressure.

She curled her shoulders forward and leaned back into his touch, twisting this way and that, guiding his hand along the edge of her vest. "Mmmm, yes. Right there," she purred.

Sweat began to bead on his forehead. The heat already present in his groin increased.

"Now the other side."

Robert drew in a deep breath and proceeded to scratch her other shoulder. Bethany moaned in pleasure. "Mmm. A little lower," she murmured.

He obeyed.

"Lower."

He swallowed.

"Right there. That feels *sooo* good."

His whole body tightened.

She is directing you in scratching her back, you arse, not lovemaking, he reminded himself.

The voice of reason did naught to bring his body under control, however. Every purr and moan slid down his spine like fingers, leaving goose flesh in their wake as his breath shortened.

"Thanks," she said, the sensual hum leaving her words. "I really appreciate it."

Yanking his hand back, he offered a nod of acknowledgment she could not see.

If he spoke, he feared she would have little difficulty hearing the desire that would surely thicken his voice.

They rode in silence for some time, Bethany no doubt wrapped up in thoughts of her brother and Robert almost succeeding in bringing his body back under control... until she resumed her squirming and scratching.

"Jooosh!"

He would have to find water soon. Nice frigid water to cool his ardor and soothe Bethany's skin so she would stop wiggling around and rubbing her lovely bottom against his...

"Would you please scratch my back again?"

...groin.

50

Steeling himself to ignore her moans, Robert reached up and diligently began to scratch.

Beth estimated that when she and Robert began their search for Josh, they only had a couple of hours of daylight left.

Those hours proceeded to frustrate, confuse, and ultimately scare the hell out of her.

She had expected the lush, cool forest around them to gradually give way to drought-stricken trees that would at last begin to look familiar. Though she had caught no sounds of a river or stream, she had reasoned that they had perhaps begun their search near a lake or other waterway she simply couldn't see. This part of Texas was riddled with them, which was why Houston was commonly known as the Bayou City. Trees were always greener near water sources. But if that were the case, the farther they moved away from the water, the drier the trees and foliage should have become.

That just didn't happen. And she was pretty sure the forest on the outskirts of the Woodlands wasn't this large, so her belief that she had ended up there faltered.

Perhaps, she speculated in desperation, she had wandered onto private land after being shot. Private land that thrived because the owner had opted to ignore the water restrictions and regularly quenched the land's thirst with an excellent irrigation system.

But who would own *this* much land and spend *that* much money irrigating it when it wasn't farmland?

She wasn't sure how far a horse could travel in a couple of hours, but they should have encountered *something* by now. A house. A farm. A road. A rest stop. A barbed wire fence. A sign letting them know they were trespassing on private property or had wandered into some kind of wildlife preserve. *Anything.*

She frowned.

As far as she knew, there weren't any wildlife preserves outside of Houston that were this large. But there *was* a huge national forest north of Conroe that was bracketed by two large lakes and peppered with waterways. That might explain the lusher forest. There had been many times when the Houston area had suffered a drought while areas to the north or west flooded. And it was pretty common for cold fronts to stall north of Houston and cool things down there while providing no relief from the heat in Houston.

But this cool? She didn't think so. Besides, Sam Houston National Forest wasn't within walking distance of the one that boasted Kingsley's hunting cabin. She would've had to get in the car and drive to where she had woken up. But they had not found her car. And Beth knew she would never have left Josh behind.

It just didn't make any sense.

Nevertheless, Beth opened her mouth to suggest they turn around, convinced that they were too far north, but the words froze in her throat as the trees parted before them and Berserker carried them out of the forest.

Her stomach twisted into a nauseated knot as she took in their surroundings. Fear—entirely different from that which she felt for Josh's safety—sprouted within her and grew in tandem to her racing thoughts.

She and Robert had passed in and out of several clearings and meadows, but none had been large enough for her to see any farther than the trees on the opposite side. This...

This was different.

Robert guided Berserker onto a dirt road that stretched far into the distance. Beth stared straight ahead, then leaned over and looked behind them, fighting back panic as cries of protest filled her head.

Having been born and raised in Texas, she was pretty familiar with the Lone Star State's landscape. She and Josh and their dad had driven to Galveston, Dallas, San Antonio, Austin, El Paso and all the way down to Mexico through one small town after another. And there was one thing you could safely say about Houston: It—and the land around it—was flat for miles and miles in every direction.

Yet that wasn't what she saw and experienced as they continued along the road Robert had chosen to follow. The land sloped up behind them and down in front of them as they pressed on to the bottom of what could only be described as a substantial hill. Only one of many, she learned much to her dismay, when they topped the next even larger one.

"Jooosh?" She couldn't quite produce a shout this time, so stunned she could barely find her voice.

All the way to the distant horizon, the trees were as green and healthy as the forest she and Robert had just abandoned. Verdant grass and flowering weeds rolled like ocean waves in a breeze chilly enough to make her shiver. Now that the forest no longer kept the wind from buffeting them and hitting them head-on, she guessed the temperature must have dropped a good forty degrees while she had lain unconscious, something that should have spawned violent thunderstorms and left the ground saturated. Yet not a drop of rain had fallen.

"Jooosh!"

And the dirt road…

Though narrow, it gave all appearances of being well-traveled. Yet it lacked the assorted litter that usually made Beth grouse. No tissues. No soda cans. No fast-food napkins. No dirty diapers. No discarded potato chip bags, gum wrappers, or cigarette butts.

And no tire tracks.

Though she searched and searched, Beth could locate not one tread mark. Instead, deep grooves that looked as though they had been carved by large wooden wagon wheels marred the dirt's surface.

Her heart began to slam against her ribs.

The only people she could think of who used wagons like that—aside from those who offered downtown and midtown carriage rides—were the Amish. But the only Amish communities she could think of in Texas were up near Fort Worth and down by Corpus Christi, both of which were about a four-hour drive from Houston.

It wasn't right. *None* of it was right.

"*Jooooosh!*"

Fear must have crept into her voice, because Robert tightened his arm around her.

But this time she took no comfort in it.

In the blink of an eye, everything had changed.

Beth didn't know where she was, only that she was far from where she should have been. Much farther than she had guessed.

And until she discovered exactly how she had come to be there, she could give no one—not even Robert—her trust.

The rest of the ride passed in silence, broken only by Beth's frantic calls for her brother.

Concern for Bethany suffused Robert as he guided Berserker off the road and into the forest toward the clearing in which he intended to make camp.

She no longer leaned back against him as she had earlier. Instead she held herself stiffly erect.

All of his recent attempts to speak with her had begotten curt, one-word responses.

'Twas more than her missing brother that concerned her now. He was sure of it. But she would not confide in him.

"Why are we stopping?" she asked.

"We have lost the light. 'Tis time we make camp for the night."

A moment passed. "What about the others?"

"They shall find us anon."

Dismounting, he turned, grasped her by the waist and lifted her down.

As soon as her feet touched the ground, she stepped away from him, breaking contact. "Thank you."

Robert frowned as she sidled away, carefully avoiding his gaze.

She no longer trusted him.

Had he said or done something to frighten her or lead her to believe he lacked honor?

His mind raced as he removed his bundle, then the saddle from Berserker's back. "What think you, friend?" he whispered into the mighty destrier's ear. "My questions might have proven vexing to some, but she seemed happy enough to answer them at the time."

Berserker gave his shoulder an affectionate nudge, encouraging him to continue as Bethany wandered off into the brush.

"I know not why they would inspire fear. Do you? I vow 'twas not my intent to make her uneasy."

Troubled, he began to rub his patient listener down and sought some reason for her withdrawal. He had said naught untoward. His hand had not strayed whilst his arm had been securely locked around her.

Of course, his mind had. And where his thoughts had gone, his body had longed to follow.

Robert stilled. Bethany had not been aware of his body's physical reaction to her, had she? Though his mail and gambeson had not prevented his nether regions from responding to the lustful thoughts inspired by her moans of satisfaction as he had scratched her back or the ever-changing pressure of her shapely bottom wedged up against him, he had thought he was shielded well enough that she would be none the wiser.

If he were mistaken, however, such would explain her new wariness of him. A young woman, unescorted, alone with a knight whose body had betrayed his desire for her...

"Do you think she knew?"

Berserker snorted and nodded his head, as though confirming Robert's thoughts.

"Well, I am certainly not going to ask her. 'Twould only make things worse if you were mistaken."

"Do you always talk to your horse?"

Jumping guiltily, Robert spun around.

Bethany stood behind him, her arms full of branches.

He cleared his throat. "I see you have been busy."

She shrugged and nodded toward Berserker. "So who was consulting whom?"

Relief flooded him. She had not heard.

"Actually, er, Berserker was just seeking my advice on how he might woo a certain mare in my brother's stables."

"Ahhh." The faint shadow of a smile touched her lips. "I'll leave you to your manly discussion then and see if I can't put together a fire while we wait for the others to join us."

He shook his head. "I shall see to that. You should rest."

She stared up at him for a long moment, eyes haunted. "I need something to do, something to occupy my mind and hands while I wait for your friends to bring me news of Josh."

Again Robert felt tenderness rise within him. "Then we shall build the fire together."

Nodding, she turned and led the way to the center of the small clearing. A couple of additional trips into the forest were required to produce enough wood and kindling for a fire that would burn most of the night. When all had been arranged to their mutual satisfaction, Robert retrieved the flint he would use to strike a spark.

"You're going to light it with that?" she asked, kneeling beside him.

"Aye."

"Really? I've never seen someone do that before."

He looked down at the fine-grained quartz in his hand, then met her curious gaze. "How do *you* start a fire?"

"With matches."

He frowned. "Those wooden splinters secreted away within the handle of your blade?"

"Aye."

That seemed unlikely. Without flint, how would she spark a flame to burn the wood?

Tilting his head to one side, he cocked a brow. "I shall demonstrate the use of flint if you will do the same with your matches."

She smiled. "Deal."

Beth had a much more difficult time sparking a fire with the flint than Robert did with the matches. The expression on his face when the *little splinter* he held ignited after a single strike was classic.

"Had I not produced the flame myself, I would suspect sorcery," he breathed, eyes wide. "May I strike another?"

She couldn't resist his boyish smile, so full of delight and eagerness. Nodding her permission, she watched him remove another match from her knife handle and explained the purpose of the colored tip.

He did not seem at all like a man bent on treachery. She felt no bad vibes and read no deceit in his gaze, no subterfuge. Neither when he questioned her about the match, nor when he taught her how to use the flint with such patience, encouraging her and praising her when she succeeded.

For the past hour or so, Beth had fought an inner battle with herself. Her instincts, which had always guided her so well in the past, kept urging her to give Robert her trust while her brain forbade it. She simply could not understand what had happened to her, what—if any—role Robert and his friends might have played in it or what possible purpose it would serve.

Everything inside her told her she was no longer near Houston. And with the temperature dropping as the sun set, she had to doubt she was even in Texas. *No* place in Texas was this chilly at night during the summer, even after a cold front.

So where the hell was she?

She thought again of those wooden wagon wheel ruts.

Pennsylvania?

How in the world would she have come to be there? Someone would've had to move her. But who?

Logic would indicate that Robert and his friends must have played a role in it since they were the only people she had encountered since waking. But they could have harmed her in a hundred different ways by now and hadn't. They had all been kind to her instead.

Yes, they were weird. Their determination to adhere to their medieval role-play seemed insane under the circumstances. But, again, they hadn't harmed her.

Those instincts of hers kept telling her to trust Robert, while her brain advised her to run and seek help. But where would she run? She and Robert had encountered not *one* other person in the two hours they had searched for Josh. And she had seen no structures whatsoever on the road. So where could she go?

Even if she made it back to the road she and Robert had traveled, she doubted she would make it very far on foot. No streetlights had lined the thoroughfare. And the road's surface had been so rough and pitted that if she used her phone's flashlight to look for Josh instead of keeping it trained on her feet, she would probably step in one of the deep gouges and twist her ankle.

She glanced at the dense foliage around her.

Since she didn't know where she was, Beth had no idea what wild animals might lurk in these forests. And if she lucked out and actually ran into other people...

Based on what she had observed in the bounty hunting business, strangers would be just as likely to take advantage of the situation and harm her as they would be to help her.

With the sun setting and her lack of knowledge regarding the landscape, sticking with Robert—at least for the time being—seemed like the safest option.

Unless her intuition, for once, was wrong and he and his friends weren't members of a reenactment group at all, but instead were escapees from a mental institution who actually *believed* they were medieval knights.

Not all crazy people were violent, after all.

Her stomach twisted into a tighter knot.

Or perhaps *she* was the crazy one. What were the chances that she had gotten shot, passed out, and been transported to a place that boasted both a thriving Amish community *and* a medieval reenactment group?

She sighed.

If Robert and his friends were neither crazy nor acting, and she was of sound mind herself, what was she supposed to conclude? That they really *were* medieval knights and she had somehow traveled back in time?

Not. Time travel wasn't possible, not outside of fiction. Every member of the scientific community she had seen speak on the subject had agreed that time travel was a technological feat that had not yet been accomplished and thus remained purely theoretical.

Besides, she had seen no time machine. And if getting fatally shot made one travel through time, then thirteen thousand people in the United States would be hurled back in time every year. She was pretty sure that would've made the news.

Robert raised his head suddenly.

Beth followed his gaze to Berserker.

The horse stared into the forest, ears pricking as if it detected some sound she couldn't.

Robert rose abruptly. Gripping her arm, he pulled Beth up, dragged her behind him, then drew his sword.

Gaping, Beth offered no protest as he pressed her close to his back with his left hand and held his sword out in front of him with his right.

Someone or something approached.

Her eyes fell to his weapon.

He actually thought he could protect her with a sword?

Her heart began to beat a little faster, with nerves and with something else, too.

Relief, perhaps?

Robert didn't want to harm her. He wanted to *protect* her.

And she wasn't about to let him get hurt doing it. A sword, no matter how impressive its length, weight and sharpness, could not compete with firearms.

Turning slightly to one side, Bethany eased her knee up until she could reach her ankle and removed her .22. Robert's broad, mailed back blocked her view as she flipped the safety off and lowered her foot to the ground. Rising onto her toes, she clutched his tunic to steady herself and peeked over his shoulder.

"Beth," he warned in a low voice, his left hand clenching in her shirt, "remain behind me."

"I am." Even as she spoke, she extended her right arm beneath his and aimed her .22 at the forest Berserker studied so intently.

Robert's chin dipped as he glanced down at her weapon.

Berserker nickered a greeting to whomever or whatever approached.

The muscles beneath the tunic Beth clutched relaxed.

Robert spoke over his shoulder, amusement lightening his voice. "You may lower your weapon. 'Tis one of my men."

As soon as she did, he let go of her and turned around, lowering his sword tip until it nearly touched the ground.

Beth couldn't quite decipher his expression as she took a step back to place a little distance between them. "What?"

"You sought to protect me," he stated.

"So?" When his teeth flashed in a grin, she realized she should have denied it. "How do you know I wasn't just protecting myself?" she bluffed.

"Your flushed cheeks tell me otherwise."

Damn her fair skin for betraying her! "Okay," she admitted. "I was protecting you. So what? You were protecting me."

Robert shook his head. "Were I not so relieved to discover that you have not taken me into dislike, I would feel insulted."

Beth rolled her eyes. "Why? Because the tiny, helpless woman was trying to defend the big, bad— Wait a minute. What? What was that about being glad I don't dislike you?"

His smile contorting into a grimace, he motioned to her handgun. "Mayhap you should sheath your weapon now."

"Oh, no you don't. Answer the question."

He released a beleaguered sigh. "'Tis only that I thought mayhap I said or"—he looked away, a slight flush darkening his tanned, masculine cheeks—"did something to offend you. If I *did*," he hurried to say, "'twas not my intention and I do ask your forgiveness."

Beth stared up at him, another chunk of the ice her mind had struggled to fill her heart with melting. "You didn't offend me, Robert," she assured him softly. "I'm just worried. And scared. And confused. I don't understand what has happened to me. Or *why* it has happened. Or"—she shrugged—"whom I should trust."

"Trust *me*," he said, his gaze sharpening. "You can trust *me*, Beth. I vow it."

"I want to. I really do." And she did, though she probably shouldn't.

The heart that had just melted turned over in her breast when he offered her a gentle smile. "Then I hope that my men will bring you good tidings."

The foliage across the clearing parted as Adam's horse nosed its way into view. When his eyes lit upon them—standing a couple of feet apart, each with weapons in hand—the quiet man halted. "Is aught amiss?" he queried carefully.

"Nay," Robert answered.

Beth returned the .22 to her ankle sheath, then approached the warrior. "Did you find Josh? Is he okay?"

Adam dismounted, face sober. "I regret that I did not find him. Nor did I find any sign of the marauders who attacked you."

Her throat began to close up. "What about the car? Did you find our car? A silver four door in desperate need of a wash?"

His gaze went briefly to Robert. "Nay. I encountered no such thing."

Robert settled a large warm hand on her shoulder and gave it a light squeeze. "Michael and Stephen have not yet returned," he murmured, compassion in his gaze. "Mayhap they have had more success."

She swallowed hard. "And if they haven't?"

"Then I shall send two score men to search the forest as soon as we reach Fosterly."

Numb, Beth allowed him to guide her over to the fire, where Robert sat close without touching her, offering his support while they waited.

"Maybe we should have kept looking," she murmured. "Maybe we shouldn't have stopped." Images of Josh, lying out there, bleeding from his wounds, assaulted her.

What if he bled out overnight?

"Searches are best carried out in daylight," Robert said. "At night, even with torches, we could easily pass by him without seeing him. And if he is unable to call for help..."

She closed her eyes. *Please, let him be well enough to call for help.*

A short time later, the soft sounds of horse hooves accompanied by off-key whistling caught her ear.

She stood.

When Stephen entered the small clearing alone, her heart sank.

"What news?" Robert questioned him, rising beside her.

Stephen dismounted and somberly delivered his report. "My search bore no success. I regret that I could not bring you better tidings, Mistress Bethany."

Hope vanished. "Thank you anyway," she said through numb lips.

Beth retook her seat by the fire and stared blankly into the dancing flames. But its warmth could not penetrate the cold that encased her.

The men cast her sympathetic glances and tiptoed around the clearing as though they thought the slightest sound or disturbance might set her to weeping and wailing at the top of her lungs.

She swallowed hard. Perhaps they were right. As she awaited Michael's arrival, she felt as brittle and fragile as an eggshell. Easily shattered. As she feared she would be if Michael did not return with Josh riding behind him.

"Beth?"

Blinking eyes that burned, she looked over at Robert as he hunkered down beside her. "Yes?"

"I have a boon to ask of you." He spoke in soft, carefully modulated tones, as if he, too, feared she would break down at the slightest provocation. But unlike the others, his kindness made her want to give in to the fear pressing down upon her, lean into him, and seek catharsis through tears.

"What do you need?" she asked.

"Might I borrow your blade for a moment?"

"My hunting knife?"

"Aye."

"Sure." Her mind still on her missing brother and the mystery of how she had come to be wherever the hell she was, Beth removed the large knife from its sheath and handed it over.

"My thanks, Beth."

Nodding, she returned her gaze to the hypnotic flames and listened intently for sounds that would herald Michael's approach.

They did not come for another hour.

When they did, Beth rose, stomach churning.

Robert joined her, standing shoulder to shoulder with her as though they were criminals in a courtroom, awaiting a judge's sentence.

Beth slipped her hand into his much larger one, needing the warm contact in that moment.

His fingers curled around hers, and he drew her closer to his side.

When Michael rode into the clearing, his only company her bulky backpack alone, tears filled her eyes.

"Forgive me, mistress," he said, his handsome features full of regret. "I did not find him."

Beth nodded, afraid that if she tried to speak just then, she would fall apart.

When Robert tried to put his arm around her, she withdrew her hand and backed away.

If he did anything to console her, showed her *any* kindness at all, it would be her undoing. The sobs trapped inside her would find their release. And once started, she feared they would never end.

"Beth."

Shaking her head, she turned on her heel and strode into the forest, not really knowing where she was going, just needing to get away, to find time and privacy to compose herself.

Chapter Five

FOLIAGE CLOSED ABOVE AND BEHIND Beth, erasing most of the moonlight. Darkness surrounded her, plucking at her shirt with wooden fingers and tripping her every other step. She probably should have stopped long enough to retrieve the flashlight from her backpack, but hadn't wanted to wait. If she had, she might have succumbed to temptation and burrowed into Robert's waiting arms, weeping loudly and using his already abused tunic for a tissue.

She considered using the flashlight on her cell phone, but knew the battery was running low. And she wouldn't be able to use her solar charger until tomorrow.

A narrow branch, thick with leaves, slapped her in the face.

Beth swore softly. Just one more scratch to add to a host of others.

Freaking thing stung, though.

Pausing, she touched her cheek. Her fingers came away dry. Good. No blood.

The sounds of the forest swelled around her. Owls. Frogs. Things she couldn't identify.

Screeching things.

Scuttling things.

Reaching back to touch the pocket that cradled her cell phone, Beth peered into the night as disquiet crept in. Where the hell was she anyway? She hadn't meant to go so far, but could no longer see the light of the fire.

A twig snapped behind her.

Beth spun around and gasped as a large figure loomed over her.

Bringing up her fists, she prepared to fight.

"Rest easy, Beth. 'Tis me."

"Robert!" Wilting with relief, she dropped her fists. "You were so quiet I didn't hear you come up behind me."

His teeth flashed in a smile, though his eyes—what she could see of them in the darkness—remained watchful. "'Tis a skill my brother taught me."

"Well, you're very good at it," she praised with a faint smile. "Don't do it again."

He chuckled. "As you wish." He motioned to a large hump on his back. "I thought you might need your things if you wished to bathe and refresh yourself."

He had brought her backpack? That was thoughtful of him.

Wait. "Did you say *bathe?*" she asked. "Where?"

Robert glanced at something over her shoulder.

"The river," a low voice said behind her.

Beth jerked in surprise and spun around.

Adam now stood behind her, holding her knife and a string of what appeared to be enough fish to feed them all for a week.

Her mouth fell open. "How did you do that?"

"Do what?"

Sneak up behind her so silently and… "Catch so many fish."

"With the hook and line tucked away in your blade."

"'Twas why I asked if I might borrow it earlier," Robert explained.

"Oh." Her gaze went back and forth between the two warriors. And she truly *was* beginning to think of them in those terms now. "You're not assuming I'm going to cook and clean those fish, are you?"

"Nay," Robert answered. "My men will prepare them whilst we are away."

"Good, because I have no idea how to cook over an open flame, and cleaning and gutting a fish would just be too gross after the long day I've had."

Another of those strange pauses followed her words.

Robert nodded to Adam. "Return to camp. We shall join you shortly."

"Aye, my lord."

Adam passed them and disappeared into the foliage.

Robert settled a hand on Beth's lower back and guided her in the opposite direction.

"You don't expect *me* to address you that way, do you?" she asked, thinking of the way his men frequently addressed him.

Robert tilted his head to one side. "Others will think it odd if you do not." A slow smile stole across his face. "However, I find that I enjoy the sound of my name upon your lips."

Butterflies flitted about in Beth's stomach. Struggling to appear unaffected, she mustered a smile and nudged him with her shoulder. "Flirt."

"I am not familiar with that word."

"Yes, but you can probably guess its meaning, right?"

He laughed. "Aye."

As they walked, he solicitously held branch after branch out of the way so she could pass unscathed. Were she a gambling woman, Beth would bet he was also the kind of man who stood whenever a woman entered the room.

Not too many of those existed anymore.

The trees and undergrowth parted in front of them, revealing a lovely river that sparkled like diamonds in the moonlight. It looked fairly deep at its center, the current swift and strong, but shallow and fairly calm along its banks.

So they *had* been near a waterway.

"Yes!" Racing forward, Beth dropped to her knees and plunged her hands into the water. She was already in the process of splashing it up onto her face when she became aware of its frigid temperature. "It's freezing!" she gasped.

Behind her Robert chuckled. "I suspected you would think so."

Beth stared down at the water in dismay. She would really love to wash off the itchy, grisly remainders of her violent confrontation with Kingsley and Vergoma. But if she bathed in that, she would be blue from the cold by the time she finished. "I don't care. I'm going to wash this crap off of me anyway."

Robert lowered her backpack to the ground, along with another pouch she had not noticed. "You will be chilled afterward. Have you fresh clothing to don?"

"Yes." Marc had recommended that she add a change of clothes while he had loaded it up for her.

As Robert knelt beside her, Beth dug through the backpack and removed the flashlight. "Here. Would you hold this for me so I can see what I'm doing?" Flicking the *ON* switch, she handed the light to Robert.

Gasping, he turned it toward himself.

Beth held up a hand. "Don't—"

Too late. Blinking quickly, he rubbed his eyes with his free hand.

She sent him a wry smile. "Never mind. Just hold it like this." Clasping his wrist, she adjusted the flashlight's angle until the bright beam fell onto her backpack, then released him.

While Robert blinked to clear his vision, Beth rummaged through the pack, looking for all of the items she would need to get clean: a pair of rolled-up blue jeans, a black tank top, black bikini panties, white ankle socks, a bar of soap and a tiny bottle of shampoo. Unfortunately she had neither a towel to dry off with nor a clean bra to don underneath the tank top.

The latter bothered her more than the first. She didn't relish the idea of sitting before a campfire with Robert and three men she still considered virtual strangers all staring at her nipples, which the cold breeze would no doubt make prominent.

"Is aught amiss?" Robert asked, noting her frown.

"Nay. Well, aye. I don't have another bra, and the one I'm wearing is filthy." Though Beth wasn't as fanatical about cleanliness as the fictional character Adrian Monk, she disliked grime enough that her current state really nettled her.

She watched his face, clearly visible now thanks to the flashlight.

He had that cute, slightly befuddled expression again. And she wondered if he was going to pretend he didn't know what a bra was.

"'Tis necessary, this bra?" he asked cautiously.

"Nay." Irritated by the blush she could feel climbing her cheeks, she spoke more sharply than she intended. "Look, while I'm technically not shy, I'm not an exhibitionist either. My tank top isn't that thick and I don't want your men to spend the rest of the night staring at my breasts."

His blue-eyed gaze dropped to her chest, then swiftly returned to meet hers. A teasing grin stretched his lips. "I trust, however, you would not be averse to *my* staring at them."

A burst of laughter escaped her, catching her by surprise. She wouldn't have thought anything could amuse her under the circumstances. "Oh, shut up," she said, giving him a shove that landed him on his backside.

Deep masculine laughter washed over her, warming her and easing some of her tension.

"Forgive me, Beth. I did but jest. My men are all honorable and will not behave disrespectfully toward you. If you lack sufficient clothing to make you comfortable, however, you are more than welcome to don my spare tunic. Or you may wrap yourself in any of our cloaks and blankets. They are all at your disposal."

"Thank you, Robert."

A smile lingering on his handsome face, he shone the light down on her pile of belongings. "Have you any soap in there? Or do you wish to use mine?" His pack lay untouched where he had dropped it a couple of feet away.

"I have soap," she said, holding up the small bar of deodorant soap, "and shampoo." Beth frowned down at the little bottle. "I hope this is enough to get all of the crud out of my hair." Her tangled brown locks were matted with dirt and dried blood and reached her waist when not braided. She might have to use the soap, too, to get it clean.

"May I?" Robert asked, holding out his hand.

Beth handed him the bottle and watched him study it under the light.

"You use this to clean your hair?"

"Yes."

Turning slightly, he played the flashlight's beam across the riverbank until it landed upon a large semi-flat rock that jutted out above the water a few yards away. "That should do nicely."

"For what?"

Rising, his movements ever graceful and fluid, he tucked the shampoo into his fist beside the flashlight's handle and extended his hand to help her up. "For washing your hair. If you lie on your back with your head resting on the edge, I can—"

"Robert, I am perfectly capable of washing my own hair."

He smiled down at her. "You have been chilled for hours, Beth. If you remain in the water long enough to wash both your body and your hair, you will be half-frozen ere you emerge. I do not wish you to become ill."

He *would* have to echo her own thoughts. But she still couldn't let him wash her hair. The two of them were all alone out there. Surrounded by darkness. And the city girl in her kept reminding her that, though he seemed like a very nice guy, she didn't know him from Adam. "I'll just hang my head over the water and wash it myself."

He shook his head and pulled her along after him. "Do not be stubborn. 'Twill be easier if I do it for you."

"*You* are the one who is being stubborn."

Stopping beside the rock, he stared down at her for a long moment. "You have great difficulty trusting men, do you not?"

She shrugged. "I have met very few men who were trust*worthy*. Don't forget, I spend most of my time hunting down criminals, many of whom are men. Between dealing with *them* and knowing the statistics on sexual assault and infidelity in our society, I can't help but be cynical regarding your gender."

Raising their linked hands, he used them to tip her chin up, forcing her to meet his earnest gaze. "You can trust me, Beth." He spoke the words softly, his grave eyes almost hypnotizing.

Her treacherous heart began to pound again.

"I would never intentionally harm you," he continued. "Nor would I allow anyone else to do so. Were it necessary, I would give my life to protect you."

Beth stared up at him, astounded. "You *mean* that," she whispered, seeing it in his eyes.

She and Josh dealt with liars all the time. Not just the bail skippers, but their family members, too. As well as friends and associates who lied to buy the criminals time and divert the search. After a while, truth became easy to identify. Which was why confusion inundated Beth every time she worried and wondered if Robert and his friends had been involved in whatever twist had taken her away from Josh and brought her to this place, wherever they were.

All of her instincts told her that Robert was exactly what he appeared to be—a really nice guy who only wanted to help her.

"I do mean it," he confirmed. "Will you allow me to wash your hair now?"

Too tired to continue fighting her intuition, she nodded.

Robert removed his tunic and draped it over the rock.

"It's going to get wet," she warned.

He shrugged, his chainmail glinting in the moonlight. "It matters not."

Taking her hand, he helped her recline on the rock. "I will not ask if 'tis comfortable. But is it at least tolerable?"

Beth shifted around a bit until her spine no longer rested upon a ridge in the hard stone. "It's fine." Turning her head, she felt a jolt when she saw him removing his mailed shirt. "What are you doing?"

"I do not wish my armor to become wet and rust. Although 'twould give my squire something more to do upon my return." His mailed pants and his thick padded gambeson followed, leaving him in a soft shirt, trouser-like braies and hose.

Apparently medieval reenactors even wore authentic underwear.

Beth watched him wade into the water. Much to her astonishment, he didn't even flinch. "The water is freezing. Won't you be too cold?" she asked, tilting her head back as he moved around and knelt behind her.

The rock she lay upon only extended about a yard beyond the grassy bank, so the water did not quite reach his groin.

"I am accustomed to such." Motioning for her to relax and stare up at the sky, he picked up her crusty braid and bent to examine it. "Unlike most of my men, I prefer to bathe daily whenever water is available. When not at one of my own keeps or my brother's, I sometimes must resort to washing in whatever lake or stream is at hand, which is oft as cool or cooler than this one. And too, I am reluctant to trouble the servants with carrying bucket after bucket of hot water up to my solar every night."

Evidently he had a brother who was into the whole dungeons and damsels thing, too.

"Beth?"

"Aye?"

"I cannot fathom how to remove the fastening at the end of your braid. There are no ribbons to untie or—"

"It's elastic. Just pinch the hair above it and pull. It'll come right off."

"Will it not pain you, pulling your hair in such a fashion?"

"Nay. I do it all the time." When he hesitated, she smiled. "Go ahead, Robert. It won't hurt. I promise."

He must have been careful even so, because she did not feel even the faintest tug on her braid before his hand appeared above her, holding the dark brown elastic band.

"Thank you." That was probably the only tie she had with her. Afraid of losing it, Beth wound it around the middle finger of her right hand like a ring and rested both hands on her stomach.

Robert went to work on her hair, dunking the braid in the icy water, letting some of the dirt soften and rinse away before he gingerly began to untangle the long strands. When he cupped his hands and dribbled the first of many chilly drops on the hair at her temples and around her face, a shiver shook her, raising the hair on her arms.

"Wow. That is *really* cold." She rubbed her arms. "I don't know how you can stand it."

One large hand smoothed the hair back from her face, gliding over the crown of her head. "Mayhap you should postpone your bath until we reach Fosterly and you can do so in warmth and comfort."

"I can't." Her stomach soured. "I don't want to wait that long. I need to wash the blood off."

"I understand." Leaning away, he reached for the shampoo.

Did he? she wondered. Did he know the fear and revulsion that filled her every time she glanced down at her stained clothing? Did he understand the terror that claimed her whenever she acknowledged that most, if not all, of the blood had drained from wounds on her own body? Wounds that should have killed her? Wounds that—defying all comprehension—no longer existed?

And did he sense the disgust that pummeled her when she admitted that some of the blood that coated her back could have sprayed from Vergoma when Josh had shot him with the Remington?

Robert could see unrest growing in Bethany.

A crease formed between her brows. Her hands began to fidget and pluck at her clothing in restless movements.

Twisting the top off the container of *shampoo*, he wondered what he could say that might ease her.

He tipped the bottle sideways. A white, pearlescent liquid flowed into his cupped palm as a sweet aroma rose up to envelope him. "A most pleasant fragrance," he commented, bringing it closer to his nose for another sniff. "What is it?"

"I don't know. I've never used that one before. It was a free sample."

Setting the bottle aside, he began to work the strange liquid into her hair. Almost immediately, a thick white foam grew and spread throughout her long locks.

"You are troubled," he observed.

Her frown deepened.

"You may confide in me, Beth. Whatever words pass between us will go no further." At least, he hoped they would not. If she told Alyssa that he had teased her about her breasts, Robert feared he would find himself spending a night in his brother's dungeon.

He still could not say what had come over him and made him speak so familiarly to her.

Her throat worked with a swallow. "I'm just so worried about Josh." Her eyes shimmered as tears rose in them. "I keep seeing him, the way he looked when he staggered toward me. The blood on his clothes and the pain in his face. The fear for me in his eyes. How still he lay after he fell." Issuing a sound of impatience, she brought a hand up and rubbed the tears away. "And the sound he made when he saw me fall… I don't know how to describe it. He let out this… roar of grief and fury, as if he knew I would die from my wounds." She shook her head. "Not knowing what happened to him is eating me up inside."

Robert nodded. He had emitted such a roar himself the day he had watched his brother take three quarrels from a crossbow. Not knowing whether Dillon had survived or died from his wounds would have been unbearable. "You said you slew your attackers, did you not?"

She nodded.

Then there was still hope they would find Josh alive on the morrow.

"I've never killed anyone before," she confessed, her voice low and strained.

Another burden for her to bear. "You were protecting yourself and your brother. You had no choice."

"I know. And I would do it again if I had to. I guess it's just now hitting me."

He nodded, his eyes on his hands as they sifted through the tangles. "Killing is never easy."

While he had participated in numerous skirmishes, Robert had not engaged in his first major battle until his last year under Lord Edmund's tutelage. He had fought as he had been trained to fight, coolly and without emotion, spilling the blood of one opponent after another until no more had been left standing. The knights around him had heaped praise upon him as he had withdrawn his sword from the last man he had felled. Praise to which he had paid no heed. The scent of blood and death saturating the air around him, Robert had slipped away from the others and—out of sight and out of hearing—promptly lost the contents of his stomach in the brush.

It had been the first time he had taken another man's life. And it had disturbed him far more than he had expected it to, considering he would have lost his own life had he not done so.

That night, instead of celebrating the victory with the other warriors and boasting of his kills to any and all who would listen, Robert had sought solace in Eleanor's arms. Only she had seemed to understand.

Leaning closer to Bethany, he massaged the fragrant soap into her scalp and tried in vain to remember what magical words Eleanor had imparted so long ago to banish his turmoil.

Beth's chin rose skyward as she looked up at him. "Are you just trying to make me feel better? Or are you speaking from experience?"

"Experience." He moved around to her side so she would not have to strain to see him while he continued to work the lather through the hair at her temples.

"You've killed someone then?" she asked, her tone cautious.

"More men than I care to admit." He could see his words shook her and forced a casual shrug. "War cannot always be avoided." He shook his head. "At times it seems constant, so often is it waged, warranted or nay. I choose my battles as I can, fulfilling my duty to my country and ensuring the safety of my family. Yet even in the most minor of skirmishes, there are casualties. I have been one myself a time or two."

When she didn't cringe away from him, he relaxed. He had thought for a moment that she might turn away from him or again begin to fear him. "If you will slide a bit more toward the edge, I shall rinse your hair for you now."

Rising up on her elbows, she inched backward until her head hung completely off the edge.

Robert slid one hand beneath her mass of soapy hair and cupped her head for support. The other he combed through her dark locks, letting the current sweep the soap away.

When the last pale bubble had abandoned them, he gathered the gleaming strands together and gently twisted as he had seen Eleanor do to wring out the excess water.

"Thank you." Reaching back, Bethany liberated the thick bunch from him and sat up.

Rising, he left the cool water and stepped up onto the bank, where he proceeded to remove his shirt.

"Hey. What are you doing?" Bethany blurted. "Just because I let you wash my hair doesn't mean I want to play *I'll show you mine if you'll show me yours.*"

A burst of laughter escaped him, startling *him* more than it did her.

Her eyes narrowed.

"Forgive me, Beth." It took tremendous effort to choke back his amusement and reduce his smile to a mere twitch of the lips. "While I admit such a game sounds intriguing…" He raised his eyebrows and gave her his most charming grin, sparking a small smile of her own. "'Twas not my intention to engage in it now. I merely thought to have a quick wash since my garments are already wet and soap and water are both available."

"Oh." She twisted her hair to squeeze more water out of it. "So, where should *I* bathe then?"

"Here. I shall turn my back."

"I can't bathe with you here," she protested.

"I will not watch you, Beth," he informed her patiently. Though the temptation would be great, he felt confident he could resist it.

"Then go wait for me at the campsite. I can find my way back."

"I cannot leave you unprotected."

"Have you forgotten this?" Reaching down to her ankle, she removed the smallest of her weapons from her boot. "I have my twenty-two. I'll be perfectly safe."

He eyed the silvery object doubtfully, unsure exactly what such a weapon did. "You are not familiar with these woods and know neither the dangers they possess nor how swiftly they can come upon you. I will not leave you alone."

Her expression darkened with a mixture of frustration and dismay.

He loosed a heavy sigh. "I am here to *protect* you, Beth, not ravish you. Had the latter been my intention, I would have already done so. I vow I have never taken a woman by force in my life."

A flush mounted her cheeks.

"I have already told you I will turn my back. If 'twill make you feel better, then leave your undergarments on, though I assure you such is not necessary."

A moment passed. "Fine," she grumbled, scooting off the rock and stepping onto the grassy bank. "I guess it's nothing you haven't seen before anyway. Just don't take this as an invitation."

"As you wish."

Robert learned something new about her then. When Bethany decided to place her trust in someone, she gave her *full* trust.

After placing her *twenty-two* on the ground a few feet from the water's edge, she proceeded to disrobe without even asking him to give her his back. She discarded her boots and odd, thick, ankle-high white hose first. Then she parted her long-sleeved tunic down the middle and shrugged out of it.

He stepped forward and extended one hand.

A question in her gaze, Bethany handed him the *jacket*, he thought she called it.

"I thought to wash it for you whilst you bathe."

Her eyes narrowed. "Are you sure you're real?"

"I do not understand."

Shaking her head, she lowered her hands to the sides of her odd vest. "You're too good to be true, Robert. First you say you would give your life to protect me." *Rrrrip.* "Then you kneel in icy water and wash my hair." *Rrrrip.* "And now you're offering to wash my filthy clothes for me." *Rrrrip. Rrrrip.* She lifted the vest over her head. "*No* man is that nice." Tossing it aside, she reached for her belt. A few nimble pulls and it joined her vest at her feet.

Robert stood rooted to the spot, his mouth dry, breath quickening, as she tucked her fingers beneath the hem of her tiny sleeveless tunic, then dragged it up and over her head.

Heat seared him, racing through his veins and pooling in his groin.

Was that a *bra*? Those two tiny scraps of sleek black fabric that cupped her full breasts the way his hands itched to, barely covering the pale pink crests and held in place by the thin black straps whose purpose had eluded him earlier? More plump, pale flesh than he had anticipated rose above the edges, the shadowed valley between them drawing his hungry gaze.

Despite the fact that almost every inch of her skin was coated with dried blood, Robert found himself consumed with lust the likes of which he had not experienced in years.

"Mayhap I am not as honorable as you think I am," he admitted hoarsely.

Unconcerned, she handed him the sleeveless tunic, then started unfastening the front of her breeches.

"Mayhap I only offered to wash your garments in hopes of distracting myself from"—his gaze returned to her breasts—"other things."

Her eyes met his, then slid away. "Oh." He thought her cheeks darkened a bit. "Well, just pretend we're at the beach and this is a bathing suit," she mumbled, tucking her thumbs in the waistband of her breeches.

"You make a habit of walking along the shore garbed so— *By the saints!*" he practically bellowed.

Bethany jumped. "*What?*" Eyes wide with alarm, she scanned their surroundings.

Try though he might, Robert could not look away. He knew he should, but he could not. Nor could he pick his jaw up from where it had landed on the ground. All he could do was stand and stare and go up in flames.

Bethany's breeches now lay bunched around her ankles, leaving her long, slender legs and almost everything else bare. The only thing that shielded her… modesty… was a V-shaped piece of shiny black material that formed a triangle at the juncture of her thighs and narrowed to two thin strips that disappeared over her hips.

"Robert?"

For a moment, he thought he would not succeed in dragging his gaze away.

How those black scraps tempted him, beckoning him to abandon all honor and let his hands and mouth go exploring.

"Robert? You're starting to make me a little nervous."

He imagined so, slavering over her the way he was, like a wolf wishing to dine on a ewe.

"Not to mention self-conscious," she added.

At last, he managed to close his mouth. Clearing his throat, he tried to remember what he had been saying. "You wander along the shores garbed so sparsely?"

She glanced down and stepped out of the breeches. "Actually, no. I sunburn too easily. But I've seen women at the beach who wore less."

"Less than *that*?" he asked incredulously.

Her brow crinkled slightly. "Aye. Lots of times. Especially during spring break."

He didn't know what spring break was, but surely she jested.

"Are you all right?" she asked, eyeing him dubiously.

All right? Nay, he was not all right. He trembled with need. He was on fire. He was a breath away from losing both his control and his sanity. And she seemed completely oblivious to the effect her near nudity had on him.

Robert bent to scoop up her breeches and froze. "Your feet!"

"What about them?"

"Why did you not tell me they were injured?" Dropping the bundle of clothes he held, he knelt and reached for her left foot.

"They aren't. What are you—?"

She rested one of her hands on his shoulder as he carefully placed her cool foot on his bent knee and stared at her toes in dismay. She had shown no sign of injury, no limp or other evidence, so he had not thought to ask.

Swearing silently, Robert berated himself for letting her walk from the campsite when he obviously should have carried her.

"Oh," she said, understanding lightening her voice. "Robert, that's not blood. That's nail polish."

Robert squinted down at the red that coated her toes and realized that it only covered the short, perfectly shaped nails at their tips. "Nail polish?"

"Yes. I don't paint my fingernails very often. I have to keep them short because I spend so much time at the computer. And with all of the criminals and quote-unquote good ole boys I have to deal with, I've found that it's best not to add too many feminine frills to my appearance. So I paint my toenails instead."

This time Robert failed to decipher most of her words, apart from her admission that she painted her toenails. What a peculiar practice. He drew one finger across the nail of her big toe. Smooth, shiny, and oh-so-red. Peculiar indeed.

Yet he could not deny that it looked quite appealing next to her alabaster skin.

Again he frowned. That alabaster skin was as icy as the river water. Sliding his hand across the top of her foot and around her narrow ankle in an attempt to infuse some warmth into her, Robert made a second, even more astonishing discovery.

"Beth, you have no hair on your leg."

"I know. I just shaved."

"You shaved the hair off your leg? For what purpose?" Had she been ill? Was she recovering from some fever as well as the attack she had suffered?

"Legs plural. And I did it for the usual reasons."

If suppressing the need to touch her had been difficult before, it now proved impossible. He had to know what those smooth, sensuously curved limbs felt like.

Still holding her foot pressed against his thigh, Robert ran one hand up her calf, caressing his way to the back of her knee, around and down the front. So soft and tempting.

His heart thudded against his ribs. "What reasons might those be?" he asked hoarsely, repeating his slow foray up and down her leg, wishing he dared venture higher.

Goose flesh appeared in the wake of his touch. And he felt a shiver rock her.

Was it spawned by cold or by desire?

"B-because, like most women in our society," she began, voice quieter, "I've been conditioned by men and the media to believe that—on a woman—hairy legs are ugly."

The faint huskiness that entered her voice made his blood sing. But ere he could inch his hand up farther, eager to reach that shiny black triangle and *really* make her breath catch, his damnable honor resurfaced.

Was he not the one who had elicited her trust by assuring her he would not look and had no intentions of touching?

Swearing silently, he dropped her foot, collected her wadded-up garments and rose. He would have turned and, without another word, walked straight into the icy water to cool his raging ardor had she not stopped him.

"Wait!"

His pulse skipped, thrumming through his veins as he halted.

Would she call him back? Invite more caresses? Tell him it had been his touch, rather than the cold air or her wet hair that had made her shiver? "Aye?"

"On second thought," she said, "you better not wash my clothes. The police might need them for DNA evidence."

He sighed.

It must have been the cold.

Dropping the shirts without asking what *police* or *DNA* meant, he strode into the frigid water without removing his braies and hose.

"You forgot the soap," she called after him.

"You may toss it to me when you are finished with it." Under his breath, he muttered, "I have a feeling I will be here awhile."

Thankfully Bethany finished her bath in short order.

Keeping his back turned, Robert pushed aside thoughts of her enticing body and what every splash and gasp that sounded behind him signified. He forced himself, instead, to think of other things. Like whether or not the men who had attacked Bethany and her brother were part of the marauders who had been wreaking havoc upon his lands.

For months now he had traveled from one estate to another, attempting to capture them, always arriving a day or a sennight too late. There had been no deaths thus far. But crops and huts had been burned. Cattle had been stolen or slain.

Who were the bastards responsible? Why did they target him and his people?

Robert and his men had just returned from parleying with his nearest neighbors. None had suffered the slaughtered cattle, burned huts or terrorized serfs that he had. All were on good terms with him and had offered to aid him by sending out patrols to ensure the malefactors did not access his lands by crossing their own.

'Twas not enough, though. He wanted to capture the blackguards and have done with it.

Robert's anger and the glacial temperature of the water that buffeted his body at last succeeded in dampening his ardor.

Until Bethany spoke behind him.

"Here's the soap."

Staring at the opposite bank as though it held the answers to all of life's mysteries, he reached behind him and felt the block of soap drop into his hand.

Hard like a stone with streaks of varying hues of green crisscrossing it like veins in marble, it too puzzled him.

Vigorous splashing heralded her exit.

"Would you mind if I used your tunic to dry off?" she asked.

He looked without thinking and nearly lost his hold on the soap. All of his heedful concentration had been for naught. His overly chilled body defied the laws of nature and instantly turned hot and hard.

If he had thought Bethany pretty before, she was no less than stunningly beautiful now. Moonlight bathed her pale clean skin, so much more exposed now that the blood and dirt had been washed away, bestowing silvery highlights upon it and accentuating shadows and hollows that begged to be explored. Standing there, shivering, her knees clenched together to preserve warmth, her arms crossed tightly beneath her breasts, plumping them up for his ravenous inspection, her hair straggling down over one shoulder...

She looked utterly irresistible.

"The tunic?" she prodded, her teeth chattering audibly.

He blinked. "Of course. You are welcome to it. There is another in my pouch that you may don for warmth."

"Thank you. Now turn back around and don't look until I tell you to. I don't want you to see me naked."

Doing as she bid him, he bit back a groan.

Mayhap he should send her back to camp alone after all. That might be the only way he could walk out of the water without embarrassing them both.

Chapter Six

ROBERT TOOK SO LONG TO bathe that Beth began to wonder if he weren't part seal. Seated on a cold stone, she didn't know how he could stand the icy temperatures. Even covered in his dark tunic—which fell to the knees on him but reached her feet—she still shook like a leaf in high winds.

"You're going to get hypothermia if you don't come out of there soon," she cautioned, squeezing water out of the braies and hose he had tossed onto the bank.

Like him, she had failed in her resolve not to peek. And, *wow,* he had a magnificent body. Granted, she could only see him from the waist up. But his face and torso alone were enough to heat the blood in her veins. Broad shoulders that looked strong enough to carry any burden. Well-developed pecs. Rippling, washboard abs. Biceps that bulged with muscle.

Put those together with his handsome face, which now glistened with moisture in the flashlight's beam, and he was absolutely beautiful.

"You're turning blue," she called, striving to sound normal.

"I shall come out now," he announced.

More reluctant than she cared to admit, Beth turned her back.

Water splashed and clothing rustled as he emerged from the river and rubbed himself dry.

Well, at least I'm feeling warmer, she thought, then cursed her vivid imagination as her mind conjured tantalizing images to match every sound that reached her ears.

His hand abruptly appeared before her. "Shall we go?"

Startled, she glanced up.

He had hidden all of that lovely muscle beneath the fresh shirt and braies she had seen in his pouch, along with his boots. Both his pack and hers hung from one shoulder. His armor and their damp clothes dangled over his arm.

"Beth?" he prodded.

"Yeah?"

"Shall we go?" he repeated.

"Oh. Aye." Placing her hand in his chilly one, she stood, took two steps and tripped on the hem of his tunic.

Fortunately, Robert caught her before she hit the ground.

Beth shook her head at her own clumsiness and braced one hand against his chest. "Thanks, I—" Her eyes widened with alarm. "*Holy crap, you're cold!*" She pressed her other hand to his chest, felt the arctic temperature of his skin, the tremors that shook him, and panicked. "Robert, you're freezing!"

He was the one thing enabling her to keep her sanity. She sure as hell didn't want him to die of hypothermia.

Throwing her arms around him, she lowered her face to his chest, pressed her body against his, and began to vigorously rub his back, hoping to lend him a little warmth.

He stiffened. "I am well, Beth," he objected.

"Nay, you're not. You're an icicle! Here, let me warm your arms." She latched onto one of his arms and began to chafe it with both hands. *Sheesh*, his muscles were huge. "Here. Take your tunic back. I don't need it anymore. I'm warm now," she lied.

He grabbed her hands before she could remove the long garment and offered a frozen chuckle. "You are barely warmer than I, Beth. Let us hie ourselves back to the clearing, where a blazing fire awaits us. 'Tis not far."

A fire sounded wonderful. "Okay. But let's hurry." Linking the fingers of one hand through his, she chafed his arm with the other as he led her back to camp.

When the two of them stepped from the trees, relief filled her. A sizable flame roared and crackled in the center of the campsite.

Michael, Stephen and Adam glanced up from their positions around it, looked back down, then all did double takes.

Beth frowned. "What?" She looked behind her and saw nothing but trees.

Were they looking at *her*? Had she missed some of the blood on her face or something?

Reaching up, she ran her free hand over her features but found only clean skin.

So what had captured their attention?

After gaping at her like the fish they presently roasted over the fire, the men directed their gazes to her hand clasped in Robert's, then looked up at their leader.

Robert's fingers tightened around hers.

Almost as one, the men looked away.

Beth glanced up and caught the tail end of a glare Robert sent them.

Was he angry? Why?

Offering no explanation, he guided her over to the side of the fire opposite the others and invited her to sit upon a folded blanket Michael produced for her comfort.

Very thoughtful.

The temperature felt like it hovered somewhere around sixty degrees and was steadily dropping. This time of year in Houston, temperatures usually didn't even fall out of the eighties at night. Yet now it was cool enough for her butt to go numb if she sat on the bare ground.

She frowned as Robert handed her another blanket. She wasn't *really* in Pennsylvania, was she?

The others seemed neither surprised nor affected by the chill. Maybe that thick padded gambeson thing Robert had worn under his mail kept them cozy warm.

Since Robert no longer wore his own, Beth unfolded the blanket so they could share it. Crossing her legs beneath the somewhat coarse material, she patted the makeshift cushion at her side.

Robert draped two more blankets around her shoulders, then obliged her by seating himself close enough that their shoulders brushed.

"There's plenty of blanket," she said. "Why don't we share?"

"'Tis not necessary," he protested.

"Aye, it is. Look at us." Opening her arms, she drew half of the blankets around him. "We're both shivering." As added incentive, she stopped clenching her teeth and let them chatter at will.

Across from them, Stephen muttered something about it not being the cool air that made Robert shiver, earning another dark look. Robert nevertheless cocooned himself within the blankets with her and lent her his warmth as his own chill deserted him.

"Mayhap your brother will see our fire and be drawn to it," he suggested softly.

Thankful for that bit of hope, she nodded. "I hope so."

The rest of the evening passed as pleasantly as it could with dozens of unanswered questions swirling through Beth's brain and concern for Josh constantly prodding her. The fish ended up being rather tasty. In true warrior fashion, her four male companions wolfed down their share in less than five minutes, then set about attempting to assemble her tent while she slowly ate her fill.

"Why don't you just read the instructions?" she asked at one point, motioning to the single sheet of paper they had set aside.

"We need no instructions," Stephen muttered now, frowning over the way the slim metal rod in his hands bent. "This metal is of very poor quality."

Beth rolled her eyes. "It's *supposed* to bend. The tent is dome-shaped."

"The cloth is flimsy, as well," Michael added. "'Tis thinner than parchment."

"It's waterproof. It's windproof. It's fine," she countered.

The only one who didn't grumble was Adam, whom she had already identified as the quiet one of the group. He merely nodded his agreement with the others' complaints and scowled his frustration when nothing they tried seemed to work.

Beth glanced over at Robert, who also neglected to consult the instructions, and caught him staring at her across the fire. Rising, he abandoned the tent and the others and came to sit beside her once more.

"Giving up?" she asked.

He shook his head. "I find your company more pleasing than theirs."

"I heard that," Stephen groused, tossing the metal rod down and picking up another.

She smiled. "What is it with men and their refusal to read instructions? It's almost as bad as their insistence on not stopping to ask for directions when they get lost."

"I cannot speak to the latter. But, with regards to the first, I am the only one here who can read with any proficiency."

She raised her eyebrows. "Seriously?"

He nodded. "Michael can read a little. Lord Edmund, the man Michael and I fostered with, insisted that our training include learning to scribe. Alas Michael was often ill and was not made to suffer through as many of the tiresome lessons as I was."

He sounded, for all the world, as if he had really *had* such a medieval upbringing. As if he had been a page, then become a squire, and then the knight he was now.

"And the other two?" she asked.

He shrugged. "The knights who trained them had little use for such abilities."

She couldn't hide her shock.

"'Tis not uncommon, Beth."

"I know, but didn't they go to school?"

"Unless a boy either plans to enter the church or possesses estates he must oversee, he has little need for numbers or letters."

She studied him, trying to convince herself that this was simply his medieval-reenactment-group way of saying they had slipped through the cracks, that both the educational system and their parents had failed them.

But he really didn't seem to be acting. Her instincts kept telling her he was sincere.

You have great instincts, Beth, Josh had told her many times. *Trust them. They've never failed you.*

She glanced at the men across the campfire, then returned her gaze to Robert.

Had she inadvertently guessed correctly in her mental ramblings earlier? Were these guys mentally off? Did they actually believe they were medieval knights, guided by a code of honor?

There were worse delusions someone could have, she supposed. "Haven't you ever heard the saying *knowledge is power*?" she queried.

"Nay." He studied her thoughtfully. "However, I have often found such to be true."

"Me, too." Was that admiration in his gaze? "So, if you're the only one who can read, why aren't you over there reading the instructions to them?"

He hesitated. "They displeased me earlier."

"What did they do? Take the fish you wanted?"

He looked away. "'Twould not interest you."

"I wouldn't have asked if I wasn't interested."

A twinge of what looked to be chagrin rippled across his handsome features. "I did not care for the way they looked at you," he admitted.

"What do you mean? When we came back from our bath?"

Bad choice of words. Beth flushed as soon as they left her mouth.

His blue eyes twinkled with amusement as he gazed down at her. "Aye. When we returned from *our* bath."

Beth elbowed him lightly in the ribs for teasing her. "I looked like a drowned rat. You can't blame them for thinking it when they saw me."

A different spark entered his eyes then. "Verily, if that is what you believe, I wish I had a looking glass so that I might show you what I see."

She laughed ruefully. "I don't need a mirror, thank you, and would only grimace if I had one. I'm not wearing any makeup. I have scratches all over my face from racing pell-mell through the forest. And even though I found a comb in my backpack, I know my hair. If I don't use tons of mousse and spend half an hour blow-drying it straight, it kinks up as if it's been freshly permed."

To demonstrate, she reached up, tugged on a ringlet until it straightened, then let it bounce back into place.

He frowned. "You have beautiful hair. Why would you wish to straighten it?"

"Because straight is *in*. Straight is sleek. Straight is sexy. Straight is sophisticated." She wrinkled her nose. "Curly is cute."

He fingered one of the thick curls that rested upon her shoulder. "You truly dislike your hair?" He sounded as if he couldn't believe it.

Her pulse picked up. "Yes."

"'Tis soft," he murmured, his voice deep and hushed. "And radiant. See how it captures the light of the fire?"

Her throat closed up, silencing any self-derisive protest she might have made. As she watched, mesmerized, the brown lock twined itself around his long, tanned finger like the limbs of a lover.

"It coils itself around me, caressing me and making me your willing prisoner." Seizing a larger section of hair, enough to fill his callused palm, he brought it to his face, closed his eyes and inhaled deeply. "And so fragrant. The perfume of some flower I cannot name. Mayhap one of those that defies winter itself and blooms ere spring is even full upon us."

85

Sighing, he returned the curls to her shoulder as if he had not just enthralled her with his words.

Beth stared at him.

Who are *you?* she wanted to ask, her heart thudding loudly in her breast. *And are you really the man you appear to be?* Her gaze fell to his lips. *The kind I would just about beg to have wrap his arms around me and kiss me?*

"Beth?"

She blinked. Where had *that* thought come from? "What? Oh." Had he asked her a question while she had been mentally drooling over him? "I, uh, think I'd better go show the guys how to put my tent together. I'm about ready to call it a night."

Shrugging out of the blankets, she stood, lifted the hem of his tunic so she wouldn't trip again, and practically ran to the other side of the fire.

One day. She had known Robert for *one* tumultuous day. *Half* a day really, if that much.

All things considered, she couldn't possibly be falling for him.

Could she?

Hours later, Beth curled up beneath the pile of blankets the men had all volunteered and tried to sleep within the dubious safety of her tent. Once she had retrieved the instructions and begun barking out orders, the men had swiftly erected the small structure. Then they had once more behaved as though they had never seen such a thing and had all insisted upon crawling around inside it, inspecting it.

The tent was small, about six feet by five feet with a domed ceiling and two arched windows. Each window was comprised of mosquito netting on the outside and nylon (or at least if felt like nylon) on the inside that could be unzipped to let a breeze through.

Of course, all four men had been eager to zip and unzip them. It was a wonder she had been able to make them pause long enough to remove their boots so they wouldn't track in too much dirt before they clambered around inside.

Beth just couldn't get over their childlike fascination with zippers and Velcro and the rest of her belongings. It was annoying, amusing and confusing all at once because, again, the more time she spent with them, the more she began to believe they weren't faking it.

A breeze rattled the tent. Shivering despite the protection of its walls, she burrowed deeper under the blankets.

It just didn't make any sense. Not where she was, whom she was with, or even the fact that she had lived through that violent confrontation with Kingsley and Vergoma.

Had Josh survived, too?

She could only pray that he had. And that tomorrow would bring her the answers she so desperately needed.

Her limbs trembling from the unseasonable cold, Beth sighed and gradually let the world around her fade away.

"Bethany?"

"Hmm?"

"Beth," someone whispered.

"Answer the door, Josh," she grumbled, snuggling deeper into the blankets. Hadn't he heard the doorbell?

"Beth," the deep voice called again, this time laced with amusement.

Sleep receded. Her eyes flew open. "What?" Shoving disordered curls out of her face, Beth rolled onto her stomach, propped herself up on her elbows, and reached out to unzip the window in front of her.

The nylon fell away, revealing Robert, propped on his elbows just on the other side. Golden light from the fire lit half of his handsome face and left the other half in darkness.

She glanced over his shoulder.

The other three warriors appeared to be sleeping soundly.

"What is it?" she whispered. "Did you hear something?"

He nodded. "You were talking in your sleep. I feared you might be—"

"I talk in my sleep?" she interrupted, surprised.

"Aye."

"Really?"

"Aye."

She'd had no idea. But then, how would she? She had never had a lover who would tell her that she did, or that she hogged the covers, or... "I don't snore, too, do I?"

His lips twitched. "Like a warrior."

"I do?" she squeaked.

He laughed. "Nay, Beth. I jest. But you do talk in your sleep."

Scowling, she thumped the netting in front of his nose, barely missing it. "What did I say?" Hopefully nothing embarrassing.

"Much that I could not comprehend. At the last, when I called your name, you thought me Josh and bid me answer the door."

"Hmm."

"I feared you might be trapped in a nightmare, and sought to wake you ere it became too violent," he told her.

"Oh." A moment's thought failed to reveal whatever she had been dreaming.

A brisk wind wound its way through the window, inspiring a shiver.

"You tremble," he murmured.

"Yeah. It's cold, isn't it?"

"Secure your window against the breeze and I shall leave you to your rest."

"Okay." She reached for the zipper. "And, Robert?"

He stopped in the process of lying down again. "Aye?"

"Thank you."

He offered her a tender smile. "Sleep well, Beth."

She tried to. Sleep well, that was.

But she couldn't. Not because of nightmares. The temperature kept her awake. It was even colder now than it had been when she had turned in. The ground beneath the tent radiated an almost wintery chill that seeped through the thin material and settled in her bones.

She wished she had a nice warm sleeping bag.

Beth tucked one of the blankets beneath her, using it as a bed of sorts. But it didn't make much difference other than to leave the rest of her colder.

Tossing and turning, chafing her arms and legs, Beth's frustration mounted. This was ridiculous! It was August! She should be sweating! Where the hell was she?

She blew on her fingers.

And what the hell did she have to do to get warm already?

Sitting up, muttering several curses, she folded each of the three blankets that covered her in half, then stacked them one atop the other. She might have to sleep in a fetal position beneath them, but maybe six layers would finally insulate her well enough to sleep.

Beth flounced back down, curled up into a little ball and tucked the folded blankets around her, pulling them over her head.

So they were a little itchy and smelled like horse. Who cared? At least they were warm.

Or they would be.

Given time.

Yep. The warmth would kick in any minute now.

Damn it! It's not working!

How did those guys stand it out there? They all either slept on the ground or leaned against a tree, exposed to the wind with nothing but their cloaks for protection.

Movement sounded outside the tent, distracting her.

She jumped when the zipper at the tent's entrance began to unzip itself. Struggling to unbury her head, she peered over the edge of the bunched-up covers. "Robert?"

As the man himself ducked inside and resealed the tent's entrance behind him, she propped herself up on her elbows.

What had already been a small space now seemed positively Lilliputian.

"What's wrong?" she whispered as he turned to face her.

Crouched down on his haunches to avoid scraping his head on the top of the tent, he smiled. "Your muttering and chattering teeth are keeping me awake."

"I'm sorry. I didn't even realize I was doing it."

Robert waved away her apology, then motioned for her to scoot over. "Move over a bit. We will have to sleep with our heads in one corner and our feet in the other if we are going to do this. Otherwise I will not fit."

"I beg your pardon?"

He grinned at the challenge in her tone. "Do not question my honor again. I only wish to offer you the heat of my body, naught more."

"Oh." It seemed downright intimate as she scooted over to make room for him beside her. "So, we're just going to sleep, right?" Best to put it right out there and make doubly sure.

"Aye."

Robert was a big man and took up a lot of room as he stretched out as much as the tent would allow him. His arm pressed against hers. Their hips and thighs touched. Taking the blankets from her, he unfolded and shook them out to settle over their bodies.

Oooh. And he was warm, too. So wonderfully, deliciously warm. She didn't even wait for him to finish getting comfortable before she eagerly turned toward him and tucked her frosty toes between his calves.

He hissed in a sharp breath as the cold penetrated the thin material that covered his legs.

Beth felt a shudder ripple through him and laughed. "That's nothing. Wait until you feel my hands."

He groaned. "You had best give them to me now and get it over with."

She gratefully thrust her icy digits at him, sighing with pleasure as his warm fingers closed around them and carried them to his mouth to be bathed in warm breath.

"Saints, woman! Your dip in the river did not leave you ill, did it?" Freeing one hand, he pressed his palm to her forehead in search of aberrant heat.

"I might ask the same of you. You're so warm! You aren't running a fever, are you?"

"Nay." The backs of his fingers touched her cheek, then her neck, before leaving. "You do not feel overly warm," he murmured doubtfully.

"I'm fine. I'm just not used to this kind of weather."

He grunted. "In truth, I do not find it unseasonably cool."

"Well, you must have been born in Alaska or something."

"Nay. I was born at Westcott."

"Oh. Where is that?" Maybe that would give her a clue as to where she was.

A lengthy pause ensued, during which he stopped blowing on her hands. "You have never heard of Westcott?" His tone suggested she should have.

"Nay."

"Lord Dillon, Earl of Westcott?"

Was he another medieval reenactment friend of Robert's? "Nay."

"Feared throughout the land for his ferocity?"

"Not by me."

"Wed to a sorceress?"

"Good for him. But nay."

"Lionheart's fiercest champion?" he prodded almost desperately.

"Who is Lionheart?"

He sucked in his breath. "Do you jest with me, Beth?" He sounded very serious all of a sudden.

Frowning, she tried to see him—a shadow among shadows—more clearly. "Nay. Why?"

He offered no answer, as though he were too appalled to think of one.

"*Should* I know him?" she asked tentatively. "Or is it an it? Is Lionheart the name of a charity or a rock group or something?"

His thumbs began to stroke her hands in tandem. "Nay, Beth."

"Then, who—?" She lost her train of thought when she felt his lips touch her knuckles.

"We shall discuss this on the morrow."

She wished he would discuss it now. He sounded shaken. Indeed, there was an odd texture to his voice. Indicating sadness? Concern? Something weighty she soon forgot entirely when he released her hands and urged her to roll away from him and onto her side.

Before she had a chance to feel disappointed, he curled his large body around hers, his chest warming her back, his hips cupping her bottom, the fronts of his thighs cushioning the backs of her own. He slipped one of his thick biceps beneath her head to form a surprisingly comfortable pillow. The other arm he looped around her, capturing both of her hands in his and nestling them against her chest just above her breasts.

His gentle touch and presence both warmed and soothed her.

Well, *part* of her was soothed. The other part had trouble catching her breath and was, in fact, trying unsuccessfully to calm her racing pulse as a different kind of heat pooled low in her belly.

Especially when she became aware of the obvious evidence of his arousal trapped between them.

"Um... Robert?"

"Ignore it." Despite the increased beat of his heart against her back, he sounded completely unaffected.

"But—"

"You are a beautiful woman, Beth. I cannot help my body's natural response to your nearness. But I will not betray your trust by acting upon it."

"Oh." Beth winced, silently cursing herself for sounding disappointed. "Do you want me to move away?"

His arm tightened around her. "Nay, you are perfect where you are."

Relaxing into his embrace, she waited for sleep to come.

Instead of dreams, however, doubts returned to plague her.

"Robert?" she whispered after some time had passed.

"Hmm?"

"Would you think less of me if I told you I was afraid?"

He stiffened. "Of me?"

"Nay." Though the city girl in her still thought she *should* be.

His muscles relaxing, he settled against her once more. "Then what? What frightens you?"

She bit her lip. "I think something is wrong. I think something is very, very wrong. I think I'm far away from where I should be. And I don't know how I came to be here."

A sigh wafted across her shoulder as he nuzzled his face into her hair, inspiring a sensual shiver. "All will be well, Beth. I will help you find your brother and the answers you seek."

Just hearing those words helped her. "Thank you."

He gave her a little squeeze. "Try to sleep."

Too weary to argue, she closed her eyes.

Wide awake, Robert lay motionless.

His heat gradually suffused Bethany, stilling her shivers and drawing a sigh from her lips as she slipped into slumber.

'Twould be a long night, he thought, closing his eyes and willing his body not to respond when she snuggled her shapely bottom into his groin.

Unfortunately, his body had a will of its own. He had been so long without a woman that even a gentle breeze could make his manhood stand at attention. His brother Dillon would be shocked, convinced that Robert very cheerfully spent each night in a different woman's bed.

In truth, Robert had been celibate for months. And this would be the first night he had actually *slept* beside a woman since Eleanor.

He could not decide how he felt about that.

He experienced some guilt, of course. Not *because* he was sleeping with a woman. Aside from his body's involuntary response, there was nothing sexual about their embrace. He simply wished to warm her and comfort her.

But it felt so damned good to just lie there with Bethany's fragile body nestled trustingly against his own, her breath a soothing whisper.

He had almost forgotten what moments like this could be like.

One of the horses nickered softly. The fire beyond the tent continued to crackle and snap whilst insects and occasionally larger beasts voiced their accompaniment.

Robert sighed, his breath ruffling Beth's hair. His thoughts and his body's rampaging response would no doubt keep him far from sleep this night. Concern would as well.

How could Beth have failed to hear tales of Dillon and Alyssa? Plentiful stories of the couple circulated the country and were carried as far away as the Holy Land. Even the damned minstrels sang of them, feeding the fear the two inspired.

And how could she not know of King Richard? He had only been dead for four years, succeeded by his treacherous brother John. Was she simply unaware that some had begun to refer to King Richard as Lionheart, giving testament to his bravery and ferocity in battle?

Aye, mayhap that was it.

He frowned and closed his eyes.

At least he *hoped* that was it.

His friends' suggestion that she was mad followed him into troubled dreams.

Chapter Seven

Waking up with Robert's large, warm hand kneading her breast should have warned Beth that the day would not go as planned.

Of course, none of the surprises that followed were as pleasant as that one.

Whew! What a way to wake up. All warm and tingly and snuggled up against a man's strong, muscular, very aroused body. It was a first for her. And one she hated to see end, which it did as soon as Robert woke up and realized he had been fondling her in his sleep. Swiftly apologizing in a voice gravelly with slumber and no little desire, he rolled away from her, rose, and left the tent.

The other men didn't tease her or make any sly remarks about Robert's having spent the night with her, though she had expected them to. For whatever reason, some men tended to be juvenile about such things.

Instead they seemed to be on their best behavior. They didn't jump on her as soon as she opened her backpack. They didn't pester her about her possessions. They didn't fight over who got to dismantle and put away her tent. And they developed the most peculiar habit of addressing her as *my lady*.

Are you warm enough, my lady?

Will you take my cloak, my lady?

Shall we stop for a rest, my lady?

It was all very odd.

And the surprises kept coming, each more disturbing than the last.

They returned to the road she and Robert had traveled the previous day.

The narrow hard-packed dirt, deeply rutted with those strange wagon-wheel impressions, never changed. It didn't widen and smooth over to indicate they approached civilization. No rubber tire tread marks appeared. No gravel covered the dirt. Nor did blacktop or pavement. No candy wrappers appeared in the grass alongside the road. No soda cans. No plastic bottles. No cigarette butts. No billboard advertisements. No street signs or markers of any kind.

It just continued on as it was, seemingly endless.

And the people…

Twice they encountered other people on the road. Both times Beth remained silent, so shocked the words she wanted to spill froze inside her.

First came the merchant. (Traveling salesman just did not seem an appropriate title for him.) He rode atop a rickety wooden wagon full of who-knows-what pulled by an ancient, swaybacked nag that plodded along at the speed of a snail and boasted matted fur interspersed with bare patches irritated by flies.

Absolute astonishment temporarily supplanted her fears for Josh when the man spoke Middle English.

Beth could not help but gape while Robert told the merchant he wasn't interested in any of his wares and questioned him to determine whether to not he had encountered Josh or anyone who might have met Josh's description.

She couldn't even *guess* the man's age. His leathery skin and blond hair could've used a scrubbing. One of his teeth was missing. The others were discolored. She was pretty sure one was rotting.

And he wasn't Amish. He bore no beard and wore no hat. Nor did he wear the black suit she had seen Amish men wear so often in pictures and movies. Instead his clothing looked to be that of a down-on-his-luck tradesman or merchant raised in the era Robert and his friends were mimicking, as if he were part of their reenactment troupe.

Except he acted as though he had never met Robert or the others before.

She glanced around to assess their responses, expecting to see recognition, and found none. Stephen and Adam weren't even paying attention. They just evinced boredom and a desire to continue their journey. Michael seemed more interested in her own horrified reaction than in the newcomer's identity.

When Robert said something sharply, Beth looked back at the merchant in time to see him hastily avert his gaze from her. She had noticed him looking at her strangely throughout the exchange—her jeans in particular—but didn't know why. Nor did she have time to ask as Robert dismissed the man and nudged Berserker forward.

"Does aught trouble you, my lady?" Michael asked, riding abreast of them.

She hesitated. "Don't you know that man?"

"I have never met him, nay."

She sensed no lie. "Robert, do *you* know him?" she asked over her shoulder.

"Nay." The arm wrapped around her waist tightened. "Is he one of the men who attacked you, Beth?"

"No," she denied. "Nay, it's naught. Never mind."

But it wasn't nothing. The next travelers they came across confirmed that.

A man and a boy headed in the same direction as she and the others. The duo resembled each other so closely they must be father and son. Both were garbed in shabbier, more threadbare clothing than the merchant had worn but seemed clean and could easily have walked off the production set of a medieval movie. The man looked to be in his late thirties, with stooped shoulders and lines bracketing his eyes and mouth. Lean and hungry. Barely more than skin and bones. She suspected that every spare crumb he came across he fed to the scrawny six – or seven-year-old boy at his side.

Both bowed deferentially to Robert, offering several *milords*. Neither appeared to have previously met him.

And the father spoke and understood Middle English.

The whole time the man answered Robert's questions, the boy stared up at Beth with rapt fascination, as though she were Lady Godiva. The boy's father seemed uncomfortable, his eyes darting to and from her in the manner of one who did not dare look too long.

She didn't know why. She wore Robert's freshly washed, big linen shirt over her jeans and tank top. And she wore her bra beneath the tank top. So it wasn't as if her breasts were hanging out or anything.

"Follow this road to Fosterly," Robert told them. "Find my steward, and he will see that you and your son have a warm meal."

The man bowed several times. "Thank you, milord. 'Tis most generous of you, milord. And I'll work for it, I will. I am a hard worker."

"*I* am a hard worker," the boy piped, dragging his attention away from Beth long enough to offer an energetic nod.

A chill skittered down her spine. The boy spoke Middle English, too.

"I have many talents you might find useful," his father promised. "And I am always willing to put in a hard day's work."

"I am good with horses," the boy boasted.

Robert nodded. "We shall speak more of this at Fosterly. I am certain my steward will have need of some of your talents."

"And mine?" the boy pressed eagerly, ignoring the swift shake of his father's head.

Robert's chuckle vibrated Beth's back. "Aye, and yours as well."

The bowing and scraping began anew.

Robert kneed Berserker forward once more, leaving the two to follow on foot.

Beth glanced back and felt her throat tighten at the hope that shone on their thin faces as they smiled at each other. The boy took his father's hand and skipped along at his side, grinning in anticipation of the warm meal the two would soon share, the new home they might find ahead of them.

Those could *not* have been actors. They just couldn't have been. Beth had encountered enough homeless men and women in Houston to tell the difference between those who were truly hungry and in need of shelter and those who merely panhandled in their free time to make an easy buck.

That man and his son weren't out to make an easy buck. They had suffered some very lean times.

"Does aught trouble you, my lady?" Adam asked.

She faced forward, feeling sick. "Aye."

Though an expectant pause ensued, she offered nothing more.

Robert leaned to one side and ducked his head, trying to read her expression. "What is it, Beth?" he asked, his voice gentle and coaxing.

She shook her head, swallowing hard.

How could she tell him that a thought so unbelievable as to be labeled lunatic had entered her mind, making her question her own sanity?

Robert. Michael. Adam. Stephen. The merchant. The poverty-stricken father and son. Strangers to each other, yet all garbed and behaving the same. All speaking and understanding Middle English. As though they truly *were* medieval and not merely playacting or performing a role.

It was inconceivable, right? That they were medieval?

"Beth?"

Of *course* it was inconceivable. The notion that she had gone back in time was absolutely ludicrous. It just wasn't possible. On *any* scale. The entire scientific community agreed that time travel remained purely theoretical.

So, she *couldn't* have gone back in time.

Yet, realistically speaking, what other explanation was there?

If this were all part of some sick, twisted, incredibly extravagant joke that was being perpetrated at her expense, who was doing it? Who in his or her right mind would take it so far? And why had they chosen *her,* of all people, as their victim? She was a bail enforcement agent. A bounty hunter. A woman who had no knowledge of *anyone* who might possess the kind of wealth and connections that would be necessary to pull off something this big.

Robert abandoned his attempts to draw her out and began a whispered conference with Michael and the others. Beth paid them little heed, too busy trying to rationalize her situation.

So, as far as explanations go, the two choices appear to be—she closed her eyes—*time travel, or a bizarre conspiracy with what*—revenge—*as the motive?*

Both sounded equally deranged.

Which led her to a third option: that whatever wounds she had suffered had left her either brain damaged or mentally unbalanced, and all of this was just some massive delusion.

The fact that she was tempted to laugh maniacally did not ease her worries.

Time travel didn't exist yet, so that one was pretty much out.

Insanity left a bad taste in her mouth, so Beth decided to nix that one, too.

That only left her with the implausible scheme or joke.

Okay. So someone with a lot of money (never mind that everyone she knew lived from paycheck to paycheck) *must have arranged for me to be abducted from that clearing after I was shot. They... drugged me?*

Yes. That was it. They drugged me, patched up my wounds and—while I was still sedated—transported me to someplace else. Maybe Pennsylvania? Ohio? Indiana?

Someplace cooler than Texas, that was for sure.

Then, after my injuries healed, they stopped drugging me. Or maybe I was in a coma. That would've worked, too. So, when I came out of the coma, they left me in this forest and hired actors to pretend they are medieval knights. And peasants. And a merchant.

So I would...

So they could...

Beth sighed. Even if all of the other stuff were true, which it only would be in a really bad B movie shown very late at night, what was the point? What was the end game? To make her think she was in Medieval England?

Yeah, right.

To make her think she was crazy?

They're succeeding.

Why? If someone had wanted her to lose her mind, there were far easier ways to go about it. And except for the bail skippers she and her brother hunted down, who she was fairly certain did not possess such grand connections, she couldn't think of a single person who might wish her harm.

Nor could she believe that Robert would participate in such a deception.

Feeling utterly confused and defeated, she let her head drop back against Robert's chest and closed her eyes.

Maybe this was just another in a long line of crappy television reality shows: Thrust a modern woman into a medieval setting without telling her and watch her crack up.

Yeah, right. And get sued six ways from Sunday when she realizes what's happened. Besides, how stupid would it be to do that to an armed bounty hunter? After shooting her! Because all of this had begun with her getting shot and nearly dying.

No television studio would be that stupid. And anyone crazy enough to pitch such an idea would be shut down by the studio's legal team.

And, again, she couldn't bring herself to believe that Robert would be a part of something that devious. Or Michael. Or Adam. Or even Stephen, as aggravating as he could be.

They could have harmed her in so many ways since they found her, yet they had all been perfect gentlemen.

Perfect gentlemen with no apparent knowledge of objects commonly used in the twenty-first century.

Again she sighed.

Maybe this was an *Occurrence-at-Owl-Creek-Bridge* thing and everything around her was a very elaborate fantasy crafted by her mind in the moments before she died. It would make sense, in a weird kind of way, since the last thing she had seen before losing consciousness was Josh. And, when they were younger, she and Josh had used Middle English as their *secret language*, confusing friends who—upon asking what language they were speaking— wouldn't believe them when they had said they were speaking English.

But, damn, that was an unsettling notion. She wasn't ready to die.

Lifting her head, she opened her eyes.

Terror engulfed her, as great as that which had pummeled her when she had watched blood spray from Josh's wounds.

Gripping the arm Robert kept around her waist with one hand, she dropped the other to his thigh and clutched it so tightly the chain mail dug into her fingers.

"Stop," she whispered through stiff lips.

Robert dipped his head. "What?"

"Stop," she repeated louder.

"You wish me to—"

"Stop. Stop! *Stop!*"

Berserker did an edgy little dance when Robert halted him. Either the fearsome creature wanted to keep going or he sensed her fear.

Twisting to the left, Beth wrapped both hands around Robert's big arm. "Help me down. I need to get down." Too impatient to wait, she threw a leg over the saddle, slid off the huge horse, and landed on the ground with a stagger.

"Beth, what is amiss? Are you ill?"

She barely heard Robert over the sudden pounding in her ears as she turned away. Her heart felt as though it might explode at any moment. Her breath came faster and faster until she feared she might hyperventilate.

Stumbling a few yards to the crest of the hill that Berserker's height had allowed her to peer over prematurely, Beth absorbed the fresh scenery before her with something akin to horror.

Below them spread a valley dotted with cattle and plump white sheep, grazing idly on the lush green carpet that overlaid the land. Small huts with thatched roofs appeared and grew in greater frequency as her gaze moved on, ultimately clustering together and forming a sizable village. Farmland, rich and bountiful, wove a gargantuan quilt. People, whom she didn't need to see clearly to know were dressed much the same way the merchant and peasants had been, bustled to and fro as they performed the day's labor.

Beyond them a moat slithered in the shadow of a stone wall whose height and width she could not begin to estimate from this distance. And beyond that, atop the opposite rise, standing proud and majestic in the brilliant sunlight, rose an enormous medieval castle.

Her whole body began to shake.

Not a few stones piled here and there amidst tangles of overgrowth.

Not the *remains* of a medieval castle. Or the *shell* of a medieval castle. Or a *refurbished* medieval castle preceded by a paved drive, carefully planned flower beds and a parking lot arranged for tourists' convenience.

But a medieval castle that stood in pristine condition.

A castle that looked as though it could have been built yesterday.

A castle with absolutely nothing modern surrounding it.

No city. No suburbs. No small town.

No sidewalks. No paved streets. No old-time brick-and-mortar streets.

No cars. No trucks. No SUVs. No buses. No motorcycles. No bicycles.

No telephone poles. No cell towers.

No grocery stores—neither large chain nor mom and pop.

No post office. No police station.

No motels or bed-and-breakfasts welcoming tourists with colorful signs.

"It can't be," Beth whispered as full-blown panic paralyzed her. "It can't be."

Robert paced back and forth from one side of the road to the other, his gaze fastened on Bethany's back.

For almost an hour, she had stood motionless at the top of the hill, limbs stiff, fists clenched, eyes wide, face bloodless. Occasionally her lips would move, but damned if he could hear one word of whatever she spoke.

Every once in a while she would squeeze her eyes shut and shake her head as though in denial.

Glancing to one side, he gauged the response of his men. The three of them lounged in the grass at the edge of the forest, having grown weary of waiting. Though they talked in low voices that eluded him, he did not doubt they speculated about whatever madness afflicted her.

His gaze swerved back to Bethany, unsurprised to find she had not moved.

She just stood there, staring at his castle, his domain, his grandest possession, with what appeared to be revulsion.

A sour feeling invaded his stomach.

Fosterly was the largest of his estates. Today he had found himself anticipating their arrival home with joy and pride, eager to show it to her, hoping she would be impressed by it.

It was everything he had dreamed of and thought he would never have.

And she abhorred it.

Why?

Losing patience, he marched toward her. "Beth," he issued curtly as he reached for her shoulder, "I insist that you tell me what is amiss."

He had not truly expected her to cooperate since she had ignored all of his previous attempts to communicate. So she caught him off guard when, at the first touch of his hand, she turned on him.

"What have you done?" she demanded.

Robert frowned. Was she angry or frightened? He couldn't tell.

"*What have you done?*" she shouted, backing away from him.

His own ire rising, he strove for patience. "Beth, I fail to comprehend why you are behaving so strangely. If you dislike Fosterly…"

In the next instant, she reversed direction and advanced on him with large, angry strides, quickly eating up the distance that separated them. "Where are my guns? I want them back."

His frown deepened. "You are safe here. I have told you many times that you have naught to fear from us." In truth, he was growing tired of having to repeat himself.

"I want my weapons back."

"Beth—"

"Now!"

He stiffened. "'Twould be wise to—"

"I need them back!" she bellowed, eyes wild, breath short. "You have no right to keep them! You never should have taken them in the first place! Now give them to me!"

Had he not seen the absolute terror that glowed in her hazel eyes, he would have been furious that she dared speak to him thusly. Particularly in front of his men.

Not privy to her fear, they no doubt wondered why he did not deal out retribution.

It mattered not. Bethany's entire body was quaking with fear.

"If you would but calm down," he coaxed.

She took another step closer, so close she had to crane her neck to look up at him. "Give them to me, Robert." Her voice softened to a whisper imbued with desperation. "You said I could trust you. If that's true, then give them to me. *Please. I need them.*"

He had seen men dying on the battlefield who had held this same look of fear in their eyes. Dreading the inevitable, they had only been comforted by those things that were most familiar to them, things that lent them a false sense of security they could cling to until death claimed them. Naught else would appease them.

Nor, it seemed, would aught else appease Beth.

Swiveling, Robert crossed to Berserker and retrieved the two dark weapons that filled his palms, as well as the one that was the length of his arm.

His men watched in silence, faces alert, bodies tensing.

Beth waited for him in the road, shifting from foot to foot, chewing her lower lip, her gaze darting all around.

Returning to her, Robert held them out.

As he had expected, she reached for them as though they were strips of roasted venison and she were perishing of hunger. She confiscated one of the smaller weapons first. Giving it a swift inspection, she removed a thin object from the part of it that fit into her palm and replaced it with another she had tucked in a pocket of her breeches. Once satisfied, she put it in the leather sheath she had strapped to her hip over his tunic. The second weapon she inspected as well, then slid it into her belt.

The third and largest weapon she took in both hands. It appeared to have a handle similar to the others. Holding that with her right hand, she slid another part of it back with her left, revealing within a green object with a gold base.

Robert would have leaned forward for a closer look, but she closed it and looped the weapon's strap over her shoulder in a way that left the weapon dangling beneath her arm, able to be raised at a moment's notice.

That done, she looked up at him with wrinkled brow and chewed her lower lip.

"Beth." How could he ease her fears if she would not speak them?

Swallowing hard, she glanced at the men behind him, then turned her gaze to the castle.

Why did the gray stone edifice disturb her so? He had seen many more imposing structures in his travels, beginning with his brother's.

She wagged her head from side to side in silent despair. Her eyes met his once more, filling with moisture she didn't bother to blink back.

"Tell me," he urged. His movements slow and careful, he brushed a tear from her cheek, then cupped her face in his palm.

A muscle worked in her jaw as she closed her eyes. "Thank you."

'Twas only a shadow of a sound.

When next she opened her eyes, she backed away from him, forsaking his touch. And kept backing away, trekking steadily downhill, away from Fosterly.

Confused, he cautiously started after her. "Beth?"

Shaking her head, she turned and bolted.

His men leapt to their feet.

"Nay!" Robert threw out a hand to stay them, then gave chase.

Beth was fast. A lot faster than she looked. One would think he would have little difficulty catching someone with legs so much shorter than his own. But with her astonishing speed and head start, he didn't reach her until they were at the base of the hill.

"Beth, cease!" Grabbing her by one arm, he dragged her to a halt, careful not to harm her or hold her too tightly.

She put up a brief struggle, then collapsed against him in tears.

"Why did you run from me?" he asked, baffled, as he folded his arms around her. Her own arms encircled his waist as she burrowed deeper into him. "I told you I would never harm you."

Her sobs increased, almost violent in their intensity. Her small hands clutched his back, fisting in his surcoat.

"Why does Fosterly frighten you so? You were well until you saw it. Have you been here before? Mayhap when Lord Hurley was earl?" A sick feeling invaded his stomach. "Did he harm you in some way?" Fury flooded him at the notion.

"You don't understand," she sobbed into his chest.

"Then tell me. Help me to understand. What inspired such fear?"

"I c-can't tell you," she wailed miserably.

"You *can*. I would no more use your words against you than I did your weapons. You must trust me in this." Cupping her face in both palms, he forced her to look up at him. "I vow I only wish to help you, Beth."

Her hazel eyes shimmered with liquid. Her cheeks were blotchy and shiny with tears, her nose rosy. She inhaled with short choppy gasps.

Nevertheless, Robert thought her beautiful.

Speaking softly, he drew his thumbs across her cheeks. "Calm yourself now and tell me what has overset you."

"W-When I saw the castle, I th-thought I was in England," she choked out.

He frowned. "You *are* in England."

His words only seemed to upset her more.

"Don't you see?" she cried. "I c-can't make it work!"

"Make what work?"

"N-no one is going to drug me and s-send me to England!"

"Someone drugged you?" he demanded, outraged.

"N-No! Nay! That's just it!"

He paused. "You think someone *intends* to drug you?"

"N-Nay."

"Beth, I do not understand. Why are you so distressed?"

"B-because it means I'm c-crazy after all!" Her sobs grew louder, her breath hiccuping in between them. "I'm m-mad! I'm looney! I'm w-wacky in the wicky woo! I'm c-completely nuts!"

Rendered helpless by her tears, Robert let her duck her head and bury her face in his surcoat once more. "You think you are mad? That is why you ran?"

"Yes. Th-This can't be real. It's just n-not possible. It's all some c-crazy hallucination."

"Nay, Beth, 'tis not. You are not mad. You are merely weary."

"Of c-course you'd say that. Y-You're a hallucination, too."

He smiled. "I assure you I am quite real."

"N-no you're not. I m-made you up in my head. I *knew* you were t-too good to be true! I kn-knew it!"

Chuckling, he tipped her chin up with one finger. "You think me a mere apparition conjured by a broken mind?"

She nodded miserably and bit her lip again, drawing his gaze to it.

His pulse leapt. "Then I suppose I shall have to prove otherwise."

She was mid-hiccup when he dipped his head and touched his lips to hers. He meant it to be a brief kiss, as light as a breeze. But lightning struck.

At least, that was how it felt.

One tiny taste and sizzling heat arced through his veins, robbing him of his will and coaxing him to deepen the contact.

Beth froze in his arms, her only movement the erratic lifting of her breasts against his chest by residual sobs, and the softening of her full, pink lips.

Then she tentatively returned the gentle pressure.

And he was lost.

Combing his fingers through her soft, fragrant hair, Robert cupped the back of her head, tilting it to allow him greater access. He splayed his other hand across her back, urging her closer until her body was flush against his own. She tasted so good. As good as she had in his dreams last night. Heated, erotic fantasies that had led him to fondle her sweet curves in his sleep and awaken hard and longing to fulfill every one.

Her hands crept up his chest, slid over his shoulders, and dove into his hair.

Heart racing, Robert drew his tongue across the seam of her lips.

They parted on another gasp.

Groaning, he took swift advantage and delved within, exploring, caressing, stroking, and inflaming.

She moaned in response and rose onto her toes, sinking fully into him as her tongue dueled with his own.

Robert felt his control begin to slip and fought the need to slide his hands down those formfitting breeches, cup the bottom that had been rubbing against him, and grind her hard against his arousal.

A sensual shudder shook him.

Or, better yet, lift her up so she could wrap her legs around him and cradle him in between.

Dragging his lips from hers, he clutched her tightly for several heart-pounding seconds, then forced himself to relax his hold.

Both were breathless.

He leaned back just enough to look down at her. Tears no longer fell, he was pleased to see. Instead, desire lit the eyes she raised to meet his own.

"Would an apparition do that?" he inquired, voice husky, already regretting the moment he would have to release her.

Her lips tilted up in a ghost of a smile. "Probably. But n-not half so well. My imagination isn't that sharp."

He laughed.

She sobered. "I'm serious, Robert. I really do think I'm crazy."

"And I am just as certain you are not." Tenderly, he smoothed the hair back from her face. "Either way I will not abandon you."

"You say that now, but..."

"You may tell me all once we reach Fosterly," he assured her. "You *will* accompany me the rest of the way to my home, will you not?"

She sighed. "Aye."

He had a feeling she agreed simply because she believed she had nowhere else to go. "I must ask a boon of you first."

Her gaze turned wary. "What kind of boon?"

"That you do not use your weapons to harm any of my people."

Her eyebrows rose. "You'd take a crazy person's word for it?"

"I would take *your* word for it."

She nodded. "Okay. I promise not to shoot anyone."

"You have my gratitude."

"*Unless* they try to hurt me. Or you. Then all bets are off."

He smiled, understanding her meaning, if not all of her words. She still wished to protect him. "As you wish. Now, what say you? Shall we continue our journey?"

"Wait." She grabbed his arm as he started to turn away.

"Aye?" She had not changed her mind already, had she?

A small, curious smile lit her tear-ravaged features. "Give me another kiss first. Just to settle my nerves."

Grinning, Robert was more than happy to oblige.

Chapter Eight

ETH'S LIPS STILL TINGLED AS the group approached the village that preceded the castle. She could not believe she had asked Robert to kiss her when she was on the brink of a mental breakdown. But for a moment, after that first tentative contact, her worries had deserted her.

Pure, sizzling heat had supplanted them, stealing her breath and robbing her of all reason. She had had no idea desire could consume her so swiftly.

It certainly never had in the past.

Granted, she wasn't very experienced in that area. She hadn't really dated much in high school.

Okay, she hadn't dated *at all* in high school. She had been a late bloomer, something her blushing father had awkwardly assured her ran in the family when Beth had bemoaned the fact that she still hadn't gotten her period by the time she had turned fourteen, even though her friends had all long since *become women.*

Her diminutive height combined with her flat chest and slim hips had made her appear several years younger than the other girls her age. Far too young, it seemed, to interest hormone-driven teenage boys who were too busy chasing girls with big boobs to even notice her.

By the time Beth had finally acquired some curves, she had been studying her ass off in college and forcing her way into the family business, which had left little time to socialize.

She *had* managed to go out with a few guys, though. Some more than once. She'd shared kisses. Touches. But nothing more. Not after what had happened with Josh.

When he was nineteen, Josh had received a phone call from a former girlfriend who had informed him she was HIV positive and advised him to get tested. Beth had found out quite by accident and had almost wept with relief when the test had come back negative. But the incident had scared them both so badly that neither Beth nor Josh even *considered* engaging in casual sex. Condoms didn't offer one hundred percent protection, and neither one of them believed a moment's pleasure with someone they didn't love was worth the risk. So in the years since, Josh had only had two lovers.

And Beth had had none. Which hadn't been that big a deal. None of the guys she had dated had knocked her socks off or fueled her desire. Not the way Robert had.

Whew! That man could kiss! She had been so stimulated that just having his arm looped around her waist now kept her heart pounding and left her breathless.

Until they reached the village.

Every once in a while, foul aromas would assail her. Beth didn't know if the odors originated from the animals or poor sewer drainage or what. She didn't think it came from the people, but more than one didn't exactly appear to make good personal hygiene a high priority.

None of the men and women—or children for that matter—appeared slothful, though. Each seemed to have his or her own purpose and duty to perform. Each went about performing that duty diligently, pausing to greet Robert with friendly smiles full of respect and what appeared to be an almost overabundance of relief.

And to stare at Beth, of course.

What was it about her that made so many gape? Sure, her hair wasn't braided and curled uncontrollably. Thanks to Robert's plunging fingers, it was probably more messy than usual, too. But she didn't exactly resemble Medusa.

Was it Robert's shirt? It did hang on her like a flour sack, constantly slipping off one shoulder to reveal the dark tank top beneath.

She didn't really mind the slippage, though, because Robert always dragged it back up with his big hand, leaving a wicked warmth behind that provided a welcome distraction.

"These are your people?" she inquired softly.

"Aye."

Her knowledge of world history was fairly limited, so she wasn't sure how the whole peasant/nobleman infrastructure worked. As she looked around her, though, she decided that here it appeared to work pretty well.

These people seemed to bear true fondness for Robert. And, though she didn't see many elderly men and women, the people she did see all seemed in good physical condition. Some were in need of a bath or missing a tooth here or there, but their bodies seemed healthy and strong and lacked the gauntness of the man and his son they had encountered earlier.

"You must be a good leader," she commented.

Robert waved to the children who ran alongside their horses, teasing smiles and giggles from them. "What makes you say so?"

"Look at them. They all love you."

"Nonsense," he grumbled, dropping his hand and shifting slightly.

Beside them, Michael grinned. "He will swear he is a harsh taskmaster, severe and lacking leniency, beating subservience into them all. But in truth, he knows every one of these people by name and has earned their fierce loyalty through his kindness and generosity."

Robert retorted with a spate of blistering French Beth failed to understand. Apparently the French language had undergone a lot of changes, too, since the Middle Ages.

Michael laughed. "The previous earl was all that Lord Robert is not. All you see around you suffered greatly under his brutal rule. Many villeins died. A majority of the rest sickened and starved. Yet during the four years we have been here, even the most bitter inhabitants of Fosterly have come to admire Robert for his fairness and benevolence. There is not a man amongst them who would not give his life to protect Robert. And not just out of duty."

More grumbly French followed.

Beth turned to look at Robert.

He scowled down at her, his face red.

"You're blushing!" she exclaimed, reaching up to touch one hot, bristly cheek. "That is sooo cute!"

"Cute?" Robert questioned.

She sought a medieval equivalent. "Fetching. Delightful."

Michael exploded with laughter, urging his mount forward before Robert could reach out and knock him from the saddle. The curses Robert uttered then were in English and quite impressive.

"Oh, stop that," Beth chided. "Do you know how many people in your position would abuse their power? Michael was just bragging about what a good man you are. There is no reason to get upset over it. He's obviously very proud of you."

His blue eyes began to twinkle with a smile as his embarrassment faded. Turning his head, he nuzzled the hand she still held against his cheek, pressing his lips to her palm.

Her own face heating, she hastily withdrew her hand and faced forward.

Robert picked up their pace a bit as they approached the castle. The moat in front of it was a lot wider than she expected and *beyond* disgusting.

Eyes watering, she covered her mouth and nose and wondered how the others could cross the heavy drawbridge lowered over it without gagging and losing their breakfast.

Dark. Muddy. With green slime floating on the surface. Clogged with she-didn't-want-to-know-what. The stench overpowered all else.

If the moat was meant to prevent intruders from approaching the castle walls, she declared it a grand success. She couldn't imagine *anyone* being willing to dive into that muck. And it was so thick she doubted a boat could get across it. *Blech!*

The horses' hooves thudded on the sturdy wooden drawbridge.

Beth stared up at a huge iron gate with pointed spikes on the end as they crossed beneath it.

Shadows engulfed them. Cold air embraced her, making her shiver as she studied their surroundings with wide eyes. The walls were huge! Ten, maybe twenty feet thick. A man called a greeting to Robert from a doorway on their right. More greetings rained down upon their heads from above as sunlight washed over them, restoring a modicum of warmth. Beth looked up and back over Robert's shoulder.

She wasn't very good when it came to estimating height and distance. But, were she to guess, she would say the walls were at least three stories high.

"Who are you looking at?" Robert asked curiously, following her gaze.

"Not who. What."

He considered her thoughtfully. "The curtain wall?"

"That's what you call it?"

"Aye. Do you not?"

She shook her head, unwilling to go into all of that just yet. "Do you think it's big enough?" she joked weakly, still awed.

Robert seemed to take her question seriously. "Aye. 'Twas the first modification I made when I acquired Fosterly, to strengthen its defenses. The original wall was neither deep enough nor high enough to suit me. Mayhap you noticed as we approached the village that I have begun construction of a second, outer curtain wall."

No, she hadn't. All of her attention had been on the villagers. And his kiss. And his big, warm body behind her. "Why do you need a second one?"

"To protect the village and provide Fosterly with an outer bailey. Having been raised at Westcott, I find that one is not enough."

"You mentioned Westcott last night." And had been appalled that she had not been familiar with it.

"Aye. My dream is to eventually make Fosterly its match in both grandeur and indestructibility."

"Well, you are definitely on the right path." With some reluctance, Beth abandoned her study of the wall and faced forward.

More people bustled about in the bailey, soon to be the inner bailey if Robert had his way. A number of structures and buildings also occupied it, though she couldn't guess their purpose. Except for the stables. The only reason she recognized that one was because a horse's butt disappeared inside it just as she glanced over at it.

Berserker stopped at Robert's invisible instruction. Beth had learned fairly quickly that he had a number of them.

Robert dismounted, then placed his hands on her waist and lifted her down.

Michael joined them.

"My lord!"

A teenager, perhaps seventeen or eighteen years of age, loped toward them, a wide smile splitting his handsome face. "You have returned!" He skidded to a halt before them. Even though he was taller than Beth, he, too, had to look up at Robert. And he did so with a fair amount of hero worship in his deep brown eyes.

Was this...? Did Robert have a son?

Robert didn't seem old enough to have fathered a boy this age. Yet the boy had the same black hair (cut short), was obviously from the same class, and wore the same colors Robert wore.

Robert reached out and ruffled the boy's hair. "Aye. I trust you have been lazing the days away, toasting your feet before my fire, consuming every morsel Cook fails to keep under guard, and wooing every maid in the castle during my absence."

"Of course," he admitted cheekily, engaging in a brief, mock-wrestle with his lord.

His eyes fell upon Beth. Filled with inquisitiveness, they roamed her from head to toe with far more knowledge of women sparkling in them than she thought he should possess at his age. "And what have *you* been doing in your absence, my lord?" he asked, never removing his gaze from her. His meaning could not have been more clear.

Robert cuffed him on the side of his head. "Insolent pup. Hold your tongue. I have brought an honored guest home with me and expect you to trot out all of those courtly manners I have gone to such lengths to drum into you these past years. Lady Bethany, I present to you my faithful squire, Marcus, heir of Dunnenford."

Straightening his shoulders, Marcus took her hand, offered her a gallant bow, and pressed a light kiss to her knuckles. "'Tis both a pleasure and an honor to meet you, my lady," he pronounced gravely. "I pray you will forgive my earlier impertinence. I meant no disrespect and would in no way wish to injure the tender feelings of one so comely as yourself."

Beth looked up at Robert and fought back a smile. "I see you've imbued him with some of your charm as well."

"Mayhap too much of it," he commented dryly, removing her hand from Marcus's. "See to Berserker, whelp. I've a mind to thrash you in the lists later ere I set you to polishing my armor."

Marcus groaned, though his grin indicated that he had no true objections. Taking Berserker's reins from Robert, he spoke softly into the mighty stallion's ear as he guided him toward the stables.

Another boy raced up to liberate Michael's horse.

When Beth looked around, she realized that Stephen and Adam had continued on and now stood conversing with another group of soldiers some distance away.

If seeing four men in mailed armor had been strange, being surrounded by a castle full of others similarly garbed was downright bizarre.

Someone called out to Robert.

Beth turned. Her mouth fell open when she saw the figure briskly approaching them, "What is *he* doing here?" she blurted.

Robert glanced at her in surprise. "He is my steward. Do you know him?"

She stared up at Robert in astonishment as the man halted before them. "Captain Kirk is your steward?"

That confirmed it. She really *had* lost her mind.

"I believe you have mistaken me for someone else, my lady," the man offered with a puzzled smile. "Since my skill lies with numbers, not with swordplay, I am no soldier. Though I admit to being flattered you might believe otherwise."

"His name is Edward, not Kirk," Robert informed her. "And a better steward you will not find. Edward, this is Lady Bethany. She was traveling with her brother when their party was set upon by ruffians."

Edward's brow furrowed with concern as he studied her, his gaze lingering on her face. "I do hope you were not badly injured, my lady."

Beth had forgotten the marks on her face that had been left by low-hanging branches whipping her during her flight through the woods. "Nay, I'm fine." She hated to lie to the man, but what could she do—admit that she was either mad or a modern marvel, accomplishing something twenty-first century scientists, physicists, and whoever else it was that studied time travel had yet to achieve?

She just could not get over the amazing resemblance this man bore to William Shatner.

"Almost all of her belongings were lost, Edward. Might Lady Alyssa have left some things behind that would suit her?"

"Aye, my lord. She has taken to keeping a trunkful in her chamber so that she might travel more lightly when she visits."

"Good. See to it that the chamber is prepared for Lady Bethany. I want every comfort afforded her."

"Aye, my lord." He hesitated. "And her brother, my lord?"

"Taken." He turned to the man standing silently beside him. "Michael, organize the search party. Two score men with hounds. Have them comb the forest until they find Sir Josh. You have his description."

Edward's eyes widened. "They were attacked on your land, my lord?"

"Aye."

"Think you it was—?"

Robert shook his head quickly, cutting him off.

Beth frowned up at Robert. "What? Who does he think it was?"

"'Tis naught," he said. "Naught to concern yourself with."

Folding her arms over her chest, she raised her eyebrows. If Robert knew something that might help, he'd better tell her.

He sighed. "Very well. We shall discuss it later. I have been away from Fosterly longer than I proposed and have business I must attend to. Edward will escort you to your chamber and see that you are made comfortable until I return."

What?

When Robert started to leave, Beth latched onto his hand. "Wait! Where are you going? You aren't leaving me, are you?" On the slim chance that she wasn't hallucinating all of this and had actually traveled back through time, she did *not* want to let Robert, the one man she trusted, out of her sight.

Weren't medieval times and people supposed to have been rather barbaric? Peering around her, she took in the strange stares directed her way.

Weren't the people also supposed to have been extremely superstitious? What if she said or did something wrong and they all decided she was a witch? Would they try to burn her at the stake or drown her or stone her to death before Robert returned?

Robert raised his free hand and drew his fingers down her cheek in a brief caress. "You are safe here, Beth. No one at Fosterly will harm you on penalty of death. You have my word."

"Yes, but—"

He touched a finger to her lips, silencing her. "You have my word."

Reluctantly, she nodded. "Are you sure you don't want company? I could come along for the ride." She *really* did not want to let him out of her sight.

Smiling, he shook his head. "You have suffered much. I will not drag you hither and yon and exhaust you further. You need rest."

Beth didn't think rest was going to help her. "All right. But hurry back."

Though the command seemed to astound Edward, Robert chuckled.

Bowing, he brought her hand to his lips for a kiss, then released it. "Take good care of her, Edward."

"I will, my lord."

Somewhat forlorn, Beth watched him leave, then met Edward's curious stare. "Are you sure you're not William Shatner?"

His friendly face puckered with a perplexed frown. "I thought you mistook me for a soldier named Kirk."

"I did."

"Do I also bear a resemblance to this Shatner?"

"Actually they're one and the same. Captain Kirk is William Shatner's, ah, title. And it isn't a minor resemblance. The two of you could be twins. Except I've never heard Shatner speak English with a British accent. It's a bit disconcerting."

Edward motioned for her to walk with him. "I noticed you bear an unusual accent yourself, my lady."

She nodded. "I apologize if my words are difficult to understand." She tried hard not to stare with gaping mouth at the towering castle that loomed before them. Large, rectangular, with rounded towers at each corner, it was like something out of a fairy tale. "I'm not from around here."

"You are from the continent then?"

"Aye." It wasn't a lie. She *was* from another continent, just not the one he meant.

They climbed a long set of stone steps that led to a pair of massive double doors. Edward opened one, then motioned for her to precede him inside. "My lady?"

Taking a deep breath, Beth crossed the portal.

Exhaustion weighting his steps, Robert climbed the stairs to the donjon. He had meant to return earlier so he would have plenty of time to bathe and change into fresh clothing before escorting Bethany down to supper. Instead, a goodly amount of dirt and soot coated him and he smelled no better than his horse.

The marauders had struck again. They had watched him leave, then attacked in his absence, damn them. Two dozen sheep had been slaughtered, which Robert thought even worse than their having been stolen for profit. Greed was a familiar malady. Such malicious destruction as this, however, was something entirely different.

This was personal. This was meant to anger. To frustrate. To send a message Robert could not discern since none of his attempts to discover his enemy's identity had met with any success.

And his people were suffering the consequences.

A crofter and his two eldest sons had been slain when they had challenged their assailants and protested the burning of their cottage. The crofter's youngest son, a lanky lad of twelve, had been badly beaten when he had leapt into the fray and fought by their side.

By the boy's account, the marauders had outnumbered them three to one. And though the will to defeat them might have been there, the crofters had lacked the weapons and skills needed to do so.

Thankfully the wife and daughter remained unscathed, both having left before the attack to attend the childbed of a relative. Had they been present, Robert feared they also would have been slain.

He stepped into the donjon.

Robert did not doubt that the marauders acted under the directions of one man. He must find some way to identify and defeat his enemy before the man claimed more victims.

Again bemoaning the fact that he came to her so filthy, Robert entered the great hall, then stopped short.

The chair Beth should have occupied beside his own at the high table sat empty.

A quick survey of the room failed to locate her. Frowning, he turned and climbed the stairs in search of an answer. At the top, he passed the closed door of the solar and continued on to Bethany's chamber—the same one his brother and Alyssa occupied during their visits.

Michael, Stephen, and Adam lounged in the hallway outside it.

Noting his approach, they straightened.

Robert could not decide what their expressions indicated but feared it did not bode well. "Where is Lady Bethany?"

"In her chamber," Michael answered, face somber.

"Why is she not supping below? Is she ill?"

"Nay."

"Not in body," Stephen muttered.

Robert stiffened. "What say you?"

"She is mad," Stephen declared, then grunted when Adam's elbow promptly lodged itself in his ribs. "*Oomph.* That is to say, we think... ah, the three of us... fear she may be a bit"—he glanced uncertainly at his friends—"daft. Just a bit. Mayhap."

Bethany's flight from him earlier leapt to Robert's mind. Her heartrending sobs.

I'm m-mad! I'm looney! I'm w-wacky in the wicky woo! I'm c-completely nuts!

All but one of those expressions were foreign to him. However, her meaning had been clear. And his most trusted men seemed to agree with her.

"What happened?" he asked grimly.

"After you left," Michael informed him, "she insisted that I show her the kitchen."

Robert frowned. "Did Edward not ensure she was served a light repast in her chamber?" The customarily reliable Edward would feel his wrath for neglecting his guest's needs after Robert had specifically instructed him to see to her comfort.

"He had not the chance. He had no sooner shown her to yon chamber and left her with a change of clothing than she threw open the door and, upon finding me outside, made her demand. Or request. 'Twas more of a request. For all of her bold speech and bravado, Lady Bethany is a sweet lass."

Robert had long since discovered that fact on his own. "Why were you lingering outside her door?"

Michael shrugged. "I merely thought to watch over her in your absence, to ensure that all was well with her."

"As did we," Stephen inserted.

Adam nodded.

Robert eyed them suspiciously. "Are you certain you were not simply seeking an opportunity to coax her into showing you more of her intriguing possessions?"

"Nay!"

"Of course not!"

Robert bit back a smile as the knights flushed and stammered and drowned each other out in their rush to deny it. Even Adam joined in.

'Twas obvious Robert had guessed their true motive, though he suspected that, in addition to curiosity, something more had driven them to seek her out.

They liked her and enjoyed her company.

Hopefully not as much as he did. But he wasn't quite ready to explore that yet.

"All right. All right," he interrupted. "Michael, you escorted her to the kitchen. Did she find aught pleasing enough to satisfy her hunger?"

Michael shared an uneasy glance with the others. "Nnnay. I believe she was rather disturbed by the state of the kitchen."

Stephen snorted. "I would say disgusted."

Robert winced. "As is Alyssa whenever she and Dillon visit. But I have not the time to see to all of the little details Edward has no time for, which makes keeping an immaculate hall difficult." In truth, he had been so consumed with making Fosterly a prosperous holding that he had had little energy left to dedicate to the more mundane household tasks. "Desiring cleaner kitchens does not indicate Lady Bethany is mad. Did she return to her chamber?"

Michael shook his head. "After gawking at the goings-on in the kitchen for nigh onto an hour, Lady Bethany began her search."

Her search?

"Stephen and Adam had accompanied us," Michael continued, "and we all watched in dismay whilst she lowered herself to her hands and knees and began to crawl about the floor like a babe. Under tables. Under benches. Underfoot of many of the shocked servants. She even pulled things away from the walls and ran her hands across them."

"The walls, not the goods," Stephen clarified.

Confusion sifted through Robert. "She was feeling the walls?"

"Aye," Michael confirmed. "Every crack, crevice, and corner."

"Why? For what did she search?" A doorway to a secret passage mayhap? Had she discovered so quickly the one in her chamber and thought to look for more?

How *could* she have when no one else had guessed its presence in the four years he had resided at Fosterly?

"She sought a number of things apparently," Michael said. "First and foremost was something called an eklectical..." He frowned. "Nay, an *electrical* outlet."

An *electrical outlet*? What was that?

"From what I understand, 'tis something small that is commonly found on walls in her homeland," his friend said with furrowed brow.

Well, if 'twas something from her homeland, mayhap her desire to find it was not so odd. Although the way she went about looking for it was. She could have simply asked. "What purpose does it serve?"

"I know not."

Robert would have to ask her later. "Very well. What else did she seek?"

"A light switch."

Robert's eyebrows flew up. "She wished to beat someone?" Who? And why?

He scowled. Had someone insulted her? Threatened her? Harmed her in some way?

Stephen must have seen the thunderclouds gathering in Robert's expression because he quickly tried to head off the storm. "'Tis what we thought as well until she told us that the light switch she sought was not a rod used for whipping, but rather an object similar to the electrical outlet."

Michael nodded. "She would not take our word that Fosterly boasted none of those."

Stephen frowned. "'Twas insulting, really, her refusal to believe us."

Indeed it *was* an insult, but Robert had no interest in pacifying his friends at the moment. "Continue, Michael."

"So intent was she upon finding these outlets and switches that she ordered a ladder to be brought in, climbed to the top of it, and felt those parts of the wall that were out of reach. By the time she gave up, she was almost as disheveled as when we found her."

The unknown objects must be of great important to her. "A light switch and an e-lec-trical outlet," Robert murmured, struggling to pronounce the last. In all of his travels, he had heard no mention of such things.

"And something called a micro *wave* oven. She seemed to think every kitchen should have one, and was very disappointed that Fosterly's does not."

Robert knew not what that was either, but vowed to acquire one if 'twould please Beth. Alyssa could help him. She knew about kitchens. He had been remiss in not requesting her assistance earlier.

Michael propped his hands on his hips and frowned. "What was the other thing she sought, Stephen? The one that sounded like plumage?"

"Plumming," Adam supplied.

"Aye!" Michael agreed. "Indoor plumming. Something else she thought no castle should be without."

Hmmm. He would have to ask Alyssa about that one, too. No sense in questioning Dillon. His brother was as oblivious to the inner workings of a household as Robert.

Wondering what to make of Beth's strange behavior, why she had felt the desperate need to run her hands across the walls when she could plainly see that what she sought was not there, Robert finally noticed his friends' unkempt appearance. All three bore dusty, mussed hair, smudges on their faces and hands, and stains on their surcoats.

"I know why Lady Bethany may be disheveled, but what is your excuse?" Again the three shared a look.

Much to his surprise, Adam broke the silence. "I saw her cross herself," he uttered in his gravelly voice, a scowl darkening his features.

"Lady Bethany?" If she had not crossed herself whilst covered in blood and faced with four armed warriors on horseback, he found it difficult to believe that aught she found in the kitchen would make her do so.

Then again...

"Nay, a kitchen maid," Michael corrected. "Lady Bethany's unusual garb and peculiar behavior began to make some of the servants uneasy as she moved from room to room."

"I thought her search was restricted to the kitchen," Robert said.

Stephen shook his head. "I vow she searched every room in the castle. Except for the solar, that is. We would not allow her to search in there."

Michael grimaced. "She even searched the garderobes. She mentioned the plumage—"

"Plumming."

"—again there. And I thought she would weep upon discovering the castle had it not."

Robert frowned. "You have not yet said how you all came to be so soiled."

Michael nodded to Adam. "'Twas his idea."

Adam flushed a deep red under Robert's scrutiny. "I could not let them all think her mad or bewitched, could I?" he demanded belligerently. "Leave her to face the same condemnation and fearful glances Lady Alyssa was subjected to on those first few visits?"

And continued to face on occasion.

What exactly had Adam done?

Stephen grinned, enjoying the quiet man's discomfort. "When Adam saw the servant girl cross herself, he got down on his hands and knees and pretended to join Lady Bethany in her search, dragging us down with him."

Michael laughed. "He even said—loudly enough for everyone in the great hall to hear, mind you, for that is where we were by then—how kind it was of Lady Bethany to help him find what he had been so careless as to misplace, that many ladies of her station would have thought it beneath them and her concern was evidence of a kind heart."

Pleased by the big man's clever attempt to divert suspicion away from Beth, Robert clapped him on the shoulder.

Adam cursed and turned even redder.

Robert laughed. "What did Lady Bethany say?"

Stephen's grin widened. "Naught. She simply looked at Adam as if *he* were the daft one, then continued with her search."

"Soon enough the servants assumed Adam had indeed misplaced something," Michael went on. "A few even offered their services, which we graciously declined."

"You have my thanks," Robert said. "I do not wish Lady Bethany to feel unwelcome here."

"Nor do we," they chorused.

Stephen lost his grin. "We heard about Donald, Henry, and Douglas. How fares young Davie?"

"One arm is broken. Two teeth are missing. Both eyes are swollen shut. And I suspect a few of his ribs are cracked."

All three swore fiercely.

Robert turned toward Bethany's door. "Hie yourselves off now. I shall see to Lady Bethany's care. And tell Edward I want a bath prepared and a tray brought up to the solar. Mayhap I can convince her to sup with me here, away from prying eyes."

Nodding, the knights trudged down the hallway.

Pushing open the heavy oak door, Robert took two steps into Bethany's chamber, then halted. 'Twas empty.

His heart jumped. "Beth?"

This chamber was arranged much like the solar. An enormous bed allowed his brother, who was a bit taller than Robert, to stretch out without his feet hanging off the end. Beside it rested a small table upon which sat parchment and ink that Alyssa used to record her prophetic dreams. A trunk at the foot of the bed contained Alyssa's possessions. Another against the far wall by the window contained Dillon's. Two chairs and a larger table, at which Alyssa repeatedly bested Robert at Nine Men's Morris, rested before the hearth.

Hurrying inside, Robert thrust back the curtains that cloaked the bed. Empty.

A quick inspection confirmed that Beth was not down on her knees, hidden from his view as she conducted another of her odd searches.

Robert started toward the door, his mouth already opening to bellow for his men's return, then stopped abruptly. His eyes went to the large, elaborate tapestry that hung on one wall.

Behind it lay a secret door.

With his men standing guard, she would have had no other means of exiting.

Leaving the room, Robert closed the door behind him, strode down the hallway, and threw open the door to the solar.

It, too, appeared to be empty.

"Beth?" he called.

"Aye?" came her response, muffled, but welcome.

Relief trickled through him as he closed the door and crossed to the center of the large room. "Where are you?"

"Is that you, Robert?"

"Aye."

"Good. I'm under the bed."

He circled the foot of his large bed and found two slender, trouser-clad legs poking out from beneath the blankets, heels up, toes down. "What are you doing under there?"

"Waiting for you. Would you do me a favor?"

"You have but to ask."

"Good. Grab my ankles and give them a good yank, would you? I'm stuck."

Laughing, he knelt beside her, curled his fingers around her ankles just above her small mannish boots and pulled her out from underneath the bed.

The shirt he had lent her rucked up almost to her neck. Beneath it she wore her small black sleeveless tunic and blue breeches that hugged her like a second skin. As luck would have it, the *tank top*, he thought she called it, wanted to linger beneath the bed, too, sliding up and leaving her slender back bare.

Robert took eager advantage of the few moments he was granted to admire her curves before she rolled over onto her back and sighed.

Poking her lower lip out, she blew her hair out of her eyes and stared up at him. "Hi."

He smiled and returned her unusual greeting. "Hi."

Her pretty face and hands were even more smudged than his men's. Curls surrounded her face in enchanting disarray.

As she lay there, staring up at him with her arms stretched loosely above her head, Robert felt his body harden.

Her tiny tank top had caught on the base of her breasts and climbed no farther. Beneath the pale skin of her flat belly lay muscle, smooth and sleek, faintly defined. He had never seen such on a woman before. All of those he had been with had been soft and malleable, more than a few of them round.

Robert found Beth's form to be a fascinating combination of strength and vulnerability. Of hardness coupled with softness. The muscle he had marked on her arms and legs and now on her abdomen was by no means large and bulky like his own. Nay, 'twas more subtle, creating soft shadows and gentle ripples that warned one not to be fooled by her seeming delicacy. This woman was a warrior and could take care of herself.

Even as the thought formed in his mind, he noticed again the ragged scar just beneath her breasts.

Gently, he brushed two fingers across it.

Her breath caught.

His eyes met hers. "Does it hurt?"

"Nay."

Resisting a sudden urge to bend and press his lips to it, he slipped his thumbs under the edge of her black tank top and tugged it down until its hem met her breeches.

Beth said nothing. Just watched Robert as little sparks ignited all along her torso where his hands brushed her as he adjusted her tank top.

His hair was windblown. His clothes looked as though he had been rolling around in a barbecue pit. And the skin alongside his mouth bore a tightness it had lacked earlier.

"Did you find what you sought?" he asked when the silence stretched.

She sighed. "Nay. I didn't really expect to, but I had to look anyway."

He nodded.

"I guess they told you everything, huh?"

"Who?"

"The motley crew out in the hallway. Your overly curious knights in somewhat tarnished armor." All of whom had shadowed her throughout the day and seen her attempts to find proof that what stared her in the face was not true.

"Aye."

She didn't know what spin Stephen had put on her actions, but guessed it probably involved pointing an index finger at his temple and swirling it in circles in the universal *cuckoo* sign. "Do you believe me now?" she asked, not really wanting the answer.

"About what?"

"Being mad. Do you believe I'm crazy?" The servants certainly had before Adam had begun his ruse.

She wasn't sure *what* they thought now.

"Nay, I do not," he responded, then smiled. "I do not believe you are wacky in the wicky woo."

That almost made Beth laugh. "Do you have any idea how strange that sounds coming from the mouth of a medieval knight?"

"No less strange than it does coming from your own sweet lips."

Her amusement faded. "I screwed up, didn't I?" He said nothing, because he agreed or because he didn't understand her? "I made a mistake," she clarified. "I know I did. Your friends wouldn't have gotten down on their hands and knees and pretended they knew what the hell I was doing if I hadn't. I *knew* I was making a spectacle of myself, but I couldn't help it. I had to know. I had to be sure. I—"

Robert touched a finger to her lips to halt the sudden rapid flow of words. "You did naught wrong, Beth."

"Yes, I did. You're just trying to be nice."

"Mayhap your behavior was a trifle odd, but there was no harm done."

She shook her head, touched by his constant kindness. "Everyone here thinks I'm mad, Robert. Everyone but you."

"Nay, Beth."

"Your men do. Stephen and Michael and Adam. They think I'm nuts."

"They do not."

Damn, he was nice.

Beth lowered her arms and held her hands out to him. "You know what?"

Grasping her hands, he drew her up to sit beside him. "What?"

"You're a terrible liar." And she thought it one of his most endearing qualities. She had dealt with *so* many liars over the years. Closing her eyes, Beth leaned into him and rested her face against his dirty surcoat. It smelled of fresh air and soot. "What am I going to do?"

He wrapped his arms around her. "You are going to give me time enough to bathe the stench from my body, then join me for a light supper."

She rolled her head from side to side. "If you knew what I was thinking... how crazy this all seems..." She had traveled back in time to medieval England.

How the hell was that even possible?

He pressed a kiss to her hair.

Her heart fluttered in her breast.

"Tell me, Beth. I will not betray your confidence."

She couldn't. Not yet. Not while she was still trying to understand it herself. "One more day, Robert." Sliding her arms around his waist, she held him close. "Give me one more day, then I'll tell you everything. I just hope..."

"What?"

"I hope you'll still like me after I tell you." He had been raised in a time when superstition governed thought and action as much religion and politics did. She had no idea how he would react to her telling him she was from the future.

His hold tightened. "You need not fear, Beth. Naught you say will change the way I feel about you."

Chapter Nine

Beth turned Robert's words over and over in her mind that night as she huddled beneath the covers, trying to fend off the mental demons that plagued her long enough to fall sleep.

Naught you say will change the way I feel about you.

Robert had coaxed her back to her own chamber and had a bath prepared for her.

She could see what he had meant about not wanting to trouble the servants nightly. It had taken a *lot* of buckets to fill that tub. And Beth hadn't even let them fill it as full as they'd wanted to.

Robert had bathed in his chamber, or solar, then had invited her to join him there for a meal, presenting her with a trencher full of food she was too afraid to eat after her inspection of the kitchen.

Seated across from him at the table before the hearth, she had peppered him with questions about his life.

It was all real.

This was real.

This place. Fosterly. This time.

How had she come to be there? How had she accomplished something men and women who were far smarter than her believed was only possible theoretically?

How had she not died in that clearing after being shot twice?

Had traveling through time healed her wounds? She could have broken countless laws of physics, for all she knew. Somehow healing her wounds and bringing her back from the brink of death didn't seem as inconceivable as landing in the Middle Ages did.

Curling into a ball, she wiggled her toes.

The fire in the hearth seemed to do nothing to warm her feet. They were like ice. As was her nose. And pretty much everything in between.

She sighed.

Robert was a great storyteller. Beth was so glad her mother—a literature professor at the University of Houston—had made both Beth and Josh learn to read English literature of the Middle Ages in Middle English, even teaching them how to speak it aloud. Had she not, Beth would've had difficulty understanding Robert.

Even so, she had a little trouble. Every age had its slang and words unique to that era. Words that didn't always make it into books, particularly at a time when such were rare.

But Robert patiently explained anything she didn't comprehend and, at the same time, seemed to do his best to decipher and learn modern words she inadvertently used or for which she couldn't find a Middle English alternative.

He really was something.

As he had recounted the mischievous escapades he and Michael had embarked upon as pages and squires, his vivid blue eyes had sparkled and danced. Beth had been fascinated and amused and so grateful to him. He had tried so hard to distract her and lift her spirits.

Shivering, she drew the covers up over her head.

Where was Josh? Why had he not traveled back in time with her? Why had he not been by her side when she had awoken?

Those questions nagged her more than any others.

If he had traveled back in time with her and roused before her, he would have remained by her side. He wouldn't have left her alone in that clearing. Even if he had noticed how different the trees looked and decided to do some recon, he wouldn't have ventured out of earshot. And her shouts would have swiftly drawn him back to her side.

So he must not have come with her.

Had he died? Was that why he hadn't traveled through time?

Her eyes burned with tears she had no wish to shed.

If he hadn't died, had he woken up in their time, found her gone and believed *she* had died? Or worse, had he thought some of Kingsley's comrades had abducted her? Was he still in their time, searching for her and fearing the worst?

Another shiver rocked her.

Frustrated, angry, and drowning in despair, Beth threw back the blankets and rose.

Robert lay in his bed, staring up at the ceiling, and wondered if Beth slept on the other side of the wall that separated them.

One night. He had spent *one* night with her soft presence beside him. Her siren's curves relaxing back into his hard form. Her cold toes seeking the warmth of his calves. Her sweet-smelling hair tickling his nose.

And he found, much to his dismay, that tonight he had difficulty sleeping without it.

Curling one arm up so he could rest his head on his palm, he drummed the fingers of the other on his stomach.

Did she sleep? Had she drifted easily into slumber after he had left her presence? Or did she feel as restless as he?

Did nightmares plague her as they had last night? Did she talk in her sleep again? Would she rest better or worse without him there to wake her when she murmured anxiously?

A scraping sound met his ears just before the tapestry on the wall opposite his bed twitched. Lowering his lids, Robert watched through his lashes as it swelled outward.

Keeping his breath deep and even to simulate sleep, he prepared to reach for his sword.

The material rippled, then folded back as Bethany's pale face peeked out at him. Her eyes squinted in the light of the dying fire.

Wondering if his thoughts had conjured her, he watched her duck behind the tapestry once more. Ears straining, he heard the secret door close. A moment later she stepped out from behind the heavy cover and let it fall soundlessly back into place.

Robert's pulse quickened.

She wore naught but one of his thin linen shirts. Gone were her breeches, her boots, her vest, her little black tank top, her even smaller scraps of shiny black material. Now he saw only soft skin, as pale as moonlight, and material rendered almost transparent by the waning flames as she crossed in front of the fire and made her way toward him.

Tiny bare toes with red tips peeked at him below slender calves left bare by the shirt's hem. Her long hair—now clean—gleamed like waves of satin.

Robert did not move. He was afraid to. If he did, he feared his hands would betray him and drag her down atop his body, clasp her head in a firm grip, and force her lips to merge with his in an attempt to quench the heat igniting within him.

Why had she come to him? And so sparsely garbed?

"I can't sleep," she said softly as she stopped beside his bed and stood staring down at him. "It's too cold and—"

Frowning, Robert propped himself up on his elbows. "Forgive me, Beth. Let me build you a fire and—"

"Nay, I… There *is* a fire. It's just…" Releasing a frustrated sigh, she glanced around the room and pressed the fingers of one hand to her forehead.

Robert reached out and captured her other hand in his own. "What is it, Beth?"

"Look, I know this is a lot to ask"—she dropped her arm—"but could I sleep in here with you tonight?"

Even as his body hardened with desire, Robert's heart went out to her. She had not come to him for lovemaking. She merely sought comfort and reassurance.

Giving her hand a squeeze, he scooted over and folded back the blankets. "Come."

Some of the tension in her face eased. Placing one knee on the side of the bed, she hesitated. "We're *only* going to sleep, right?"

He doubted he would sleep at all with her sensuous body so nigh, but smiled nevertheless. "Aye, Beth."

Offering him a faint smile of her own, she climbed in and pulled the blankets up to her chin. "Mmm. I'm warmer already."

He grinned. "Let me have those fingers and toes."

Rolling onto her side to face him, Beth offered him her hands. Robert hissed when her icy toes made contact with his shins, but spoke not a word of complaint. Instead, he sandwiched her hands between his much larger ones and warmed her feet with his own.

His heart began to pound.

'Twas different tonight. More intimate.

Instead of being squeezed into a tent with his men sleeping just outside, they were alone in his chamber, in his big sumptuous bed, with a cozy fire burning in the fireplace. Where last night, both had been fully clothed, now Beth wore only Robert's thin shirt and Robert...

She cleared her throat. "Umm, Robert? Are you naked?"

"Aye."

"That's what I thought."

Robert waited for her to protest, to express shock or dismay.

When she didn't, he blew on her hands. "Is the rest of you this cold?"

"Aye."

"Come along then. Let me warm the rest of you."

Curling his arm around her, he lay on his back and encouraged her to snuggle up against his side.

She rested her head upon his shoulder, draped one cool, smooth thigh across his.

If his arousal surprised or alarmed her, she made no comment. What she did instead was steal his heart with two featherlight touches.

Reaching up, she brushed his hair back from his forehead, then oh-so-gently trailed her fingers down one bristly cheek in a brief caress.

"Thank you, Robert," she whispered.

She sealed his fate in that moment. An innocent caress before she wrapped an arm around him, burrowing closer as she abandoned herself to slumber, and his heart became hers.

"Damn you, Marcus! Pay attention!" Robert growled seconds after the tip of the blunted training sword he wielded struck his squire's shoulder with enough force to knock him to the ground.

A flush mounting his cheeks, Marcus scrambled to his feet and stuttered a hasty apology. "Forgive me, my lord."

"Had this blade not been blunted I would have taken your bloody arm off! The moment your concentration wanes, your life is forfeit!"

The boy nodded, shamefaced. "Aye, my lord."

Marcus had not erred so gravely in a long while. He had a true talent for the sword, rarely made the same mistake twice, and strove for perfection in all that he did.

Robert enjoyed training him. "'Tis the first time in months your diligence has faltered. What distracted you?"

Marcus swallowed miserably. "'Twas Lady Bethany."

Robert quickly looked around, but did not see her. "Lady Bethany?"

"Aye, my lord. There."

Robert looked in the direction Marcus pointed and found Bethany sitting on a bench that butted up against the keep on the far side of the practice field. Her long hair cloaked her shoulders and back in rich brown curls. A dark green kirtle borrowed from Alyssa fit her alluring curves snugly and fell a bit short, exposing her odd mannish boots.

Something that looked like her *sellfone* lay beside her on the bench.

"Hie yourself over and train with Michael and Ned for a time," Robert murmured absently as he sheathed his sword.

"Aye, my lord."

Robert approached Bethany slowly, noting her pensive expression. She had been his shadow for a fortnight now, following him everywhere he went, watching him train or work on the wall or perform any duty that did not take him far enough away that he must ride.

She had not yet confessed her troubles as she had promised she would that first night. Nay, she had told him naught in the days since, though she continued to ask him questions about himself and his past. Though he became more accustomed to her accent and learned more of her odd words every day, he was unable to coax her into speaking of her own past.

She seemed beset with melancholy whenever he wasn't luring laughter from her with wild tales of his youth. Dark circles bruised the skin beneath her hazel eyes, indicating how little she slept. She ate very little, as well. Already slender when he had met her, Beth had lost enough weight to leave her cheeks hollow and her arms thinner.

Robert had doubled the number of men who searched for her brother, but she had long since lost hope that they would find him. Robert knew not how else he might help her. He alone seemed able penetrate the fog of despair that enveloped her. And not just during the day.

Every evening, as the fire burned down and he lay sleepless, Beth would slip into his solar, climb into his bed, and seek warmth, safety and—he hoped—some sense of peace.

Though his body burned for her and he seemed to walk around in a constant state of arousal, Robert never pressed her for more. Nor did he implore her to fulfill her vow and tell him from whence she came, why her speech was so different, and all of the rest she was so reluctant to share. He feared if he did, she would cease coming to him.

So he waited. Waited until her breathing deepened into sleep (sometimes it took hours as she lay awake, agonizing over her troubles), then rolled toward her and embraced her fully, nestling her soft curves into his hard body, pressing kisses to her forehead and dozing until the sun peeked over the horizon and 'twas time to carry her slumbering form back to her own bed ere she awoke, so the servants would be none the wiser.

"My lord!" Sir Rolfe's voice stopped him just as Robert reached Bethany. "My lord! Come quickly!"

Robert swung around as the pale man-at-arms skidded to a halt. "Tell me."

"'Tis Sir Winston and Sir Miles," the man said breathlessly. "Both nigh dead. Whilst searching for Lady Bethany's brother, they came upon the marauders' camp. They were badly outnumbered, my lord."

Robert looked beyond him and saw a cluster of men carrying two bodies toward the stairs of the keep. He raced toward them.

"Robert!" Bethany called after him. She sounded frightened again, and he regretted that he had not the time to reassure her.

"Marcus!" he called over his shoulder. "Remain with Lady Bethany and guard her with your life!"

"Aye, my lord!" his squire vowed.

"Wait a minute!" Beth called. "Where are you going? What's happening?"

"We will speak later, Beth!" Both fallen knights appeared to be unconscious. "Until then, Marcus will keep you safe."

"But…"

Whatever else she said faded into the distance as he sprinted up the stairs and into the donjon.

He would learn where the bastards were hiding this time. Then he would slay them all and end this torment.

Dozens of men, along with boys Robert's squire's age, swarmed into the bailey, the latter leading warhorses that pranced and moved about restively.

The numbness that had permeated every element of Beth's being while she had adjusted to the knowledge that she had traveled back in time left her so quickly that her head swam.

Robert, her anchor in this frightening sea of medieval surrealism, was leaving. He was riding off to fight who knows how many men armed with swords that were practically as long as she was tall in hand-to-hand combat. And it was quite conceivable that he would not survive.

"*Robert!*"

When she would have hurried after him, Marcus gripped her arm with surprising strength. "You must not, my lady. The destriers are very dangerous and may trample you."

Beth watched the men struggle to keep the enormous horses in check.

"You must wait until they have departed," Marcus told her.

"But I can't just let him leave. I have to go with him!"

The boy looked appalled. "My lady, nay! 'Tis too perilous."

"Then he shouldn't be going," she snapped, scared to death that something might happen to him.

"He could not do otherwise, my lady. Lord Robert wishes to protect his people."

"But that guy said those two men were almost killed."

"'Twas Sir Rolfe, not Sir Guy. And Sir Winston and Sir Miles are not the first to fall. These blackguards have plagued my lord's holdings overlong, taunting him with their cruelty to those who cannot defend themselves sufficiently. Their attacks have weighed heavily on his heart. He is most eager to capture those responsible and put an end to their violence."

This had happened before? When? How many times? "Who is doing it?"

"We know not, or Lord Robert would have long since dispatched them."

Robert, Michael, and Stephen stormed from the castle and launched themselves into the saddle.

Seconds later, they and the rest of the mounted men thundered across the drawbridge.

"You need not fear for him, my lady," Marcus stated. "Lord Robert is one of the finest swordsmen in all of England. I vow only the Earl of Westcott can match him."

That did little to alleviate her anxiety. When two men hacked at each other with broadswords—their only protection a bunch of metal links, a padded shirt, and a helmet—how could they not get hurt? And without satisfactory medical care, even small wounds could turn septic and result in death.

Speaking of which…

Beth grabbed the solar charger she had placed on the bench in the sun, turned toward the castle, and headed for the steps leading up to the entrance.

Marcus remained at her side, even when she quickened her pace, his long legs having no difficulty matching her stride.

Shoving the heavy doors open, she marched into the great hall and elbowed her way through the throng of men gathered around a trestle table servants had hastily erected. "Excuse me. Excuse me. Pardon me. *Would you move?* Excuse me."

When, at last, she made it to the front of the pack, she actually felt the blood drain from her face. "Holy crap," she whispered, and swallowed hard.

"Lady Bethany, you should not be here," Adam said behind her. Strong hands clasped her shoulders and tried to turn her away.

She shrugged them off, her horrified gaze surveying the carnage.

Two men, laid out head to head, their faces indiscernible for the gore. Eyes closed. Enough blood gushing for four.

A young priest, who couldn't be much older than she was, muttered something in Latin above them.

"Who are they?" she asked when she could find her voice.

"Sir Miles and my cousin, Sir Winston," Adam answered, motioning to one, then the other.

Winston's eyelids twitched a little at the sound of his name.

"Are they married?"

"Sir Winston is."

Her eyes rose to meet those of the men standing across from her. "Fetch his wife," she ordered in a voice that brooked no argument.

One of the men looked to Adam, then departed.

"Does Fosterly have a healer?" Beth asked.

"Nay," Adam answered. "None will reside here because they know they will be carefully scrutinized by Lady Alyssa when she visits."

"What about a midwife? Do you have one of those?"

"Aye."

"Fetch her, too."

A second man took his leave.

Beth gripped her charger tighter and wiped the sweaty palm of her other hand on her dress. "Remove their clothes," she said, gesturing to the motionless victims. "I need to see what I'm going to be dealing with here."

A dozen rough, scarred hands flew into motion.

The priest's eyes widened as he was shouldered aside and layers of clothing and armor began to fall away.

Beth looked around at the men towering over her, unable to locate the face she sought. "Where's Kirk?"

"Who?"

"Captain Kirk." What was his name again? "The, uh… the, um…" She snapped her fingers impatiently. "The steward."

Adam turned his head. "Edward!"

"I am here, my lady." Edward's somber face appeared as the men to her right parted.

"You're the go-to guy, right?"

His forehead twisted into a confused pucker. "What?"

"The go-to guy. You're the one everyone goes to when they need something?"

"Aye, my lady."

"Good. I need boiling water and clean cloths for bandages." How could she prevent infection? The little tube of antibiotic ointment in her first aid kit wouldn't cover this. Since she had been drinking well water, she didn't know what kind of alcohol they drank or what proof it was, so she had no idea if it could be used as an antiseptic. And she could have sworn she had read somewhere that alcohol might not be the best choice to sterilize a wound because it killed good cells along with the bad. "Honey," she blurted. Hadn't she seen on the news that honey could be just as effective as antibiotic ointment when applied to wounds? "I need lots of honey."

Air whooshed out of her lungs in a rush as the men's shirts and braies were cut away. "Hhho boy," she said shakily, surveying the deep gashes on their limbs and torsos. "I'm going to need a needle and some thread. Soak both in boiling water for me, Edward. And I'll need a basin of hot water to wash my hands in, along with clean cloths to dry them."

"Aye, my lady." He turned and disappeared into the crowd.

Beth glanced at the men across from her. "Tear their shirts up and use them as padding. Apply pressure to the worst wounds and keep it there to staunch the bleeding until I get back."

"Where are you going?" Adam asked as she turned away.

"I need some things from my backpack. It will only take a minute."

The throng of concerned soldiers parted swiftly for her this time.

Beth hurried up to her chamber. Her backpack was on the chest by the window. Setting the charger down beside it, she took the backpack to the bed, unzipped it, held it upside down, and shook it violently until it vomited all of its contents onto the blankets.

Marcus appeared in the doorway. "My lady?"

"Here," she said. "Hold this."

Leaping to her side, he obediently held out his arms as she began thrusting items toward him.

The travel-sized first aid kit was first (as if anything it contained could seal the kind of lacerations she'd just seen). Then a bottle of ibuprofen. A small box of butterfly closures. What was left of her antibacterial hand wipes. Her bar of deodorant soap.

What else? What else? What else?

There *was* nothing else. Help was supposed to be a brief 911 phone call away.

"Okay," she announced. "That's it. Let's go."

The basin of water and cloth towels Beth had requested awaited her when she returned to the great hall. All eyes followed her as she approached the table.

No pressure, she thought hysterically.

A young woman, blond and pretty, about twenty-three or twenty-four years old, sobbed over Winston.

"Are you his wife?" Beth asked her.

She nodded, sniffling. "Aye, my lady."

"Can you sew?"

Her red-rimmed, blue eyes widened, then flew to the wounds three soldiers applied pressure to on Winston's shoulder, arm, and thigh. "Y-you do not wish *me* to...?"

"Can you sew?"

Reluctantly she nodded. "Aye, my lady."

"Then pull yourself together. I need your help."

Adam moved to Beth's side.

"Where's the midwife?" she asked him.

"Attending a birth. She will come as soon as she is able."

Crap. That meant this was all on *her* shoulders, because—even though she'd had no medical training—she still probably had more knowledge of wound care than the men in this room.

Beth motioned for Winston's wife to follow her to the basin of water. "What's your name?"

"Mary."

"Okay, Mary, I want you to watch me and do everything I do. All right?"

"Aye, my lady."

"First, we're going to wash our hands and forearms." Extending her arms before her, Beth glared at the long sleeves that trailed to the floor. "Adam, these sleeves have to go. Would you please remove them?"

A dagger appeared in his hand. "Where shall I cut them?"

"At the shoulder, please."

She suffered not even a scratch as he trimmed the material away.

"Much better. Thank you."

Taking her bar of deodorant soap from Marcus, Beth worked up a good lather and scoured her hands and arms up to her elbows. Mary did the same as soon as another man cut her sleeves away, too.

Beth frowned down at the basin of dirty, soapy water that resulted. "Edward, would you—?"

"Right here, my lady." Anticipating her request, he set a second basin of hot water down beside the first.

"Thank you. Mary, let's do it one more time just to be safe."

Several men continued to apply pressure to the more severe wounds while the two women finished.

"Now wipe your hands with one of these." Beth handed her one of the antibacterial hand wipes, then used another on her own hands.

Drawing in a deep, fortifying breath, she tried to ignore the metallic scent of blood combined with the pungent odor of sweat. "Mary, you work on Miles. I'll tend Winston."

Mary wrung her clean hands. "But, my lady—"

"Trust me. It's for the best." If Winston didn't pull through, Beth didn't want Mary to have any reason to blame herself. "Which wound is the worst?" Beth asked the men staunching the bleeding.

The man beside her removed wadded up linen from Winston's thigh and stepped back.

Beth's stomach lurched. *Holy crap, that's deep.* "I'll have to clean it, then stitch it. Mary, you do the same for Miles. More water, please, Edward."

Beth bent over the man's thigh. "Light. We need more light, too."

Torches appeared in several hands, bestowing ample illumination.

It was all too horrible. Thank goodness she hadn't eaten anything earlier. If she had, it would have come right back up as she pried apart the ragged edges and began removing bits of cloth and broken metal links from Winston's flesh. "Make sure you get it all, Mary. Every bit of it. Every little speck."

"Aye, my lady." She sounded as shaken and nervous as Beth felt.

Winston awoke with a moan and began to thrash about with amazing strength, considering.

"Hold him down," Beth ordered.

Rough hands gripped his limbs to still his movements.

Mary turned and reached toward her husband's face.

"Mary, don't touch him," Beth cautioned.

The blonde hastily jerked her hands back without making contact.

"Keep working on Miles. You can comfort Winston when you're finished."

Mary hesitated, clearly wanting to abandon her gory ministrations in favor of sitting and holding her husband's hand.

Someone moved to Beth's side.

When she looked up, she found stony, silent Adam glaring at the other woman.

Mary cast one last longing look at Winston, who seemed ignorant of all around him save the pain, then returned to her ministrations.

Unlike Winston, Miles neither moved nor made a sound while Mary tended the worst of his wounds.

Mary's gaze met Beth's.

That couldn't be a good sign.

"Stitch it," Beth told her, "then move on to the next." She glanced around. "Where's Marcus?"

"Here, my lady." He peered around Adam, her things still clutched in his arms.

"Set that stuff on the table."

He hurriedly obeyed.

"Now open the bottle of ibuprofen. That one there." She had to tell him how since plastic pill bottles with childproof caps were foreign to him. Ibuprofen was a pain reliever, a fever reducer, and an anti-inflammatory. With these wounds, Beth assumed the men would need all three.

"Shake out two caplets." She glanced around. "Would someone please bring me some water for him to drink?"

Winston looked up at her through glazed eyes. "You are Lord Robert's woman," he whispered hoarsely.

"Yes. I mean, aye. You have suffered some serious injuries, Winston. But I'm going to do everything I can to help you. All right?"

He nodded weakly.

"Good. Marcus is going to put some things in your mouth. I want you to swallow them with the water he gives you next. Don't chew them. Just swallow."

He did, then lost consciousness again.

Thank goodness. She didn't think she could poke a needle through his skin with him awake and watching.

"Okay. I'm ready for the honey, a needle and thread, Edward."

Edward diligently produced them.

"I can do this," Beth whispered to herself.

"Aye, my lady," Adam said with confidence. "You can."

Time blurred as she painstakingly stitched Winston's thigh, then moved on to the next wound.

Clean. Apply honey. Stitch. Then move on to the next.

Clean. Apply honey. Then stitch.

Once the more serious injuries were taken care of, she treated the rest of his abrasions the same way without sewing them.

She applied antibiotic ointment to every minor cut and scrape, rapidly depleting her small supply. She would've applied it to the harsher wounds, too, but the ointment's directions advised against applying it to open wounds.

Bandages followed. The larger wounds she bound with clean cloth torn into fairly neat strips. The smaller wounds she covered with either butterfly closures or adhesive bandages.

The odd tubes of ointment, plastic containers, and adhesive strips all sparked curiosity in her audience. Thankfully, the men were either too smart or too courteous to interrupt her work.

Adam's quiet, protective presence was no doubt responsible for that. Though she supposed concern for their friends could've kept them silent as well.

When at last she and Mary had done all they could, Beth stepped back.

Miles had not roused once. Considering all of the crud she had dug out of Winston's mangled flesh, she feared infection and fever were unavoidable and thought she should try to get some ibuprofen into the other man as well. Antibiotics would have been far better. Unfortunately, Fosterly lacked both a qualified physician and a twenty-four-hour pharmacy.

Beth used a mortar and pestle Maude produced to crush two caplets into a powder. After mixing it with water, she raised Miles's head a bit and dribbled several bitter drops between his lips.

No response.

Mary reached down and massaged his throat until—miracle of miracles—he swallowed.

Beth smiled. "It worked. Do it again."

Together they coaxed him into swallowing it all.

Stepping back, Beth stared down at the two fallen men.

"Now what, my lady?" Marcus voiced the question that hovered on the tips of all tongues.

She sighed. "Now, we wait."

Wait for fevers to rise? Wait for them to slip into comas? Wait for death to claim them?

No, she tried to deny. *Wait for them to heal. To recover.*

Was that really likely though? Beth wasn't a doctor. She wasn't a nurse. She didn't know how injuries this severe should be treated. Everything she had done had been wrought by instinct and desperation. What if she had done something wrong?

Idiot!

She had marched forward and barked orders as if she had actually known what the hell she was doing. What if she had skipped some crucial step? What if she had given them too much ibuprofen? Or not enough? Or maybe she shouldn't have given them any at all. What if the honey she had used contaminated the wounds instead of speeding their healing?

These men's lives were in her hands. Why hadn't she waited for the damned midwife? Or waited for Robert to return. Hadn't he mentioned something about knowing healing herbs?

What if these men died?

Beth would never know if it was because of something she had done wrong or something she was *supposed* to have done, but hadn't or if they had simply lost too much blood.

"My lady?"

She met Mary's anxious gaze. "Aye?"

"May I sit with Winston now?"

"Of course, Mary. Thank you for helping me. You did very well."

The woman nodded and bobbed a curtsy.

"Adam?" Beth said.

"Aye, my lady."

"You might want to clear the hall. Either that or stay and watch over Miles and Winston. All these men have been very nice." She motioned to her substantial masculine audience. "But I have a feeling they'll start picking at the Band-Aids and butterfly closures as soon as I turn my back."

And they would. All were fascinated by the bright white strips that held some of the cuts on their friends' faces closed and by the flesh-colored strips that covered the others. Clearly they wanted to test them and find out what kept them from falling off.

Adam must have known he would have a battle on his hands, for he instantly and none-too-gently began to herd the men out of the hall.

Beth gathered together what was left of her first aid supplies and carried them to her chamber. The contents of her backpack were strewn across the bed. It wouldn't do to have one of the servants see any of it. Even Marcus shouldn't have seen it, but she couldn't do anything about that. So she stuffed everything except the soap back into her pack and hid it in one of the two trunks the room boasted.

Restless, she paced to the window and looked out over the bailey. Or tried to. The glass wasn't crystal clear here, but thick and warped. She could see enough, though, to know the sun would set soon. Bright oranges and pinks painted the clouds rolling in from the north.

Beth hadn't realized how long it had taken her to patch up the injured men. Had Mary not assisted her, she would have been working on them long into the night.

If they hadn't died first.

Her stomach performed a queasy somersault. Her insides began to tremble, as did her hands now that she wasn't using them.

There had been so much blood.

She had never *seen* so much blood. Not even the day she had been shot.

Crossing to the basin of water on the table near the hearth, she grabbed the soap and began to viciously scour her hands.

She could still feel it. The blood. Could still see it, trapped beneath her fingernails. She scrubbed and rinsed and scrubbed and rinsed while the fear she had held at bay clawed at her in an attempt to gain purchase.

Her breath hitched. Tears blurred her vision. Furiously dashing them away, she grabbed the soft cloth some diligent servant had provided and dried her hands. No dirt. No specks or streaks of crimson. Just freckled pink skin rubbed raw by her efforts.

This was the second time in two weeks that her hands had grown slick with warm blood. She doubted any soap on the planet would make them feel clean again.

Clenching them into fists, she closed her eyes.

"Robert." His name emerged a ragged whisper.

Where was he? Would he return in even worse condition than the two men below? Would she have to toil over his mangled body, too?

She couldn't. *He* couldn't. He couldn't do that to her. She couldn't lose him, too. She had lost Josh. And her father. And her mother. She'd lost everyone really. And not just to death. Everyone she knew and loved was beyond reach of this foreign time and place. If she lost Robert, too…

A sob caught in her throat.

He had been so good to her, giving and giving, asking nothing in return. Nothing except the truth of who she was. And she had withheld that from him.

She had been afraid to tell him where she came from. Or rather when. Afraid and ashamed. Because, while she should have been wholly mourning

Josh, a part of her was falling for the handsome, unbelievably thoughtful man who let her seek solace in his arms each night and offered her comfort without making any demands regarding the desire she roused in him.

Who else would do that?

Spinning around, Beth left the room.

Chapter Ten

DOWN THE CORRIDOR, PAST ROBERT'S chamber Beth strode, descending the stairs and exiting through the donjon's heavy double doors. She stood at the top of the steps for many long minutes, breathing deeply of the cool, fresh air and looking out across the bailey.

That was one difference she hadn't noticed immediately upon awakening in the clearing. The air here was so fresh. So fragrant. So clean.

There was no air pollution. No daily ozone warnings. No health-threatening haze blanketing the land like milky fog each morning, leading meteorologists to warn people with asthma and other lung ailments to remain indoors or advise parents to keep children inside.

As long as one avoided close contact with the moat and didn't stand downwind of the stables, the air here smelled wonderful.

Stepping to one side, Beth seated herself on the top step. Resting her feet upon the third step, she propped her elbows on her knees, cupped her chin in her hands, and waited, cold stone chilling her bottom.

The sun sank behind the curtain wall. Pinks and oranges morphed into purples and blacks. The flickering light of torches appeared at intervals upon the battlements. Periodically men's faces, mostly hidden by helmets, faded in and out of view as the guards paced and kept watch, ensuring the safety of all within.

It was quiet here, too. There were no airplanes or jets roaring past above. No police helicopters circling as they searched for criminals from the safety of the sky. No cars creeping past, booming bass so loudly it rattled the house's windows. No car alarms screeching or honking. No horns blaring. No sirens screaming. No gunshots shattering the night. Or day. There wasn't even the familiar hum of the refrigerator, beep of the microwave, flush of the toilet or whoosh of the air conditioner turning on.

Just quiet.

Here and there a dog barked. Occasionally the low murmur of conversation drifted to her on the breeze.

It was so peaceful here.

How ironic, considering Robert might at that very moment be engaging in a violent, bloody battle for his life.

The door opened behind her.

Beth didn't turn around, hoping whoever it was would leave her alone.

"My lady?"

She looked up. "Oh. Hi, Marcus."

Closing the door, he frowned down at her. "Are you well?"

Nodding, she looked toward the gate. "Aye."

The teenager shifted his weight from one foot to the other. "A storm approaches."

Again she nodded. Here, she could actually smell the rain coming.

"'Tis cool. Would you not be more comfortable in the great hall?"

She shook her head. "I'm fine where I am. Thank you, though."

He lingered a few minutes longer, then went back inside.

Beth's gaze remained fastened on the gatehouse as she willed Robert's safe return.

In the distance, thunder rumbled, almost fooling her into believing the men were returning on the backs of galloping steeds. Patches of clouds flashed golden with lightning before blending again into the night sky.

Two men exited the castle and tromped down the stairs, casting her curious looks. She watched them cross the bailey to one of the towers. No doubt they worried for their friends.

Would they blame her if Miles and Winston died?

She would blame herself, either way.

The door behind her opened, then closed once more.

A cloak fell about her shoulders.

Surprised, she glanced up. "Thank you."

Marcus shrugged and seated himself beside her. He was a tall, thin, yet muscular boy who might very well attain Robert's height before he stopped growing. "I would not wish you to catch a chill, my lady."

146

Tugging the warm material more closely around her, she realized it was Robert's.

It must be. His scent clung to its folds.

Burying her nose in it, she breathed in deeply.

Please come home safely, Robert. Please.

"After the hours you spent toiling over Sir Miles and Sir Winston, I thought you might be hungry." Marcus held up a wineskin, a goblet, and a hollowed-out loaf of bread piled high with food. A trencher, they called it.

She would have refused, but her stomach chose that moment to growl.

The boy's lips twitched. "Please, my lady. Lord Robert has been sorely concerned over your meager appetite, and will be displeased should he return to find you have not supped."

Sighing, she chose a piece of what she hoped was overcooked chicken and forced herself to chew and swallow it. Marcus swiftly offered her additional morsels with his knife.

"Aren't you going to have any?" she asked. Maybe if he was distracted with satisfying his own substantial appetite, he wouldn't notice if she ate less. A *lot* less.

If she ended up trying to make a place for herself here, she would have to have a serious talk with Robert's cook.

Marcus declined at first. A few prods and encouraging words later, however, he dug in with amusing enthusiasm. For every five mouthfuls he devoured, she nibbled another piece of chicken.

Boy, she hoped it was chicken.

A somber though companionable silence sifted down around them. After a while, Beth gave up even pretending to eat. Her stomach was still unsettled by the wounds she had plunged her fingers into earlier. She didn't want to end up vomiting all over Robert's squire.

"You need not worry so, my lady," Marcus told her softly. Having demolished the food, he reclined beside her, unwilling to leave her alone despite her assurances that she would be all right if he would rather be somewhere else. "Lord Robert will return whole."

She bit her lip. "How do you know? How can you be so certain he won't return the way *they* did?" She nodded toward the keep behind them.

Marcus smiled, so handsome Beth thought he must make all of the girls his age swoon. "Had you paid attention when you watched him train, you would not ask that. There are none greater, my lady, in all of England. None fiercer. I have watched him take down two or three men at once. Even his brother, the much-feared Earl of Westcott, can no longer best him. Their sparring ever ends in a draw."

The boy's brown eyes glowed with pride as he spoke of his hero.

Beth felt a smile touch her lips. "Admire him a little, do you?"

"More than any other, my lady."

She nodded. "Me, too. He's a good man."

"That he is, my lady."

"You are, too, Marcus. I hope you know that."

He ducked his head shyly.

Her gaze inexorably returned to the barbican.

How much longer?

Lightning flashed, skeletal white fingers reaching across the sky above them and tunneling through the clouds. Thunder fleetly followed, a lion's harsh roar of warning. Around them, the temperature dropped as a brisk wind whipped through the bailey, climbed the steps and lifted her hair from the back of her neck.

Normally, Beth would close her eyes and let the storm vibrate through her, reveling in the wildness of it. Not tonight, though. Tonight she sat and watched and waited, her fear for Robert rendering her nearly oblivious to nature's turmoil.

"Marcus?"

"Aye, my lady?"

"You're not one of those Neanderthals who thinks that all men are strong and all women are weak and will pounce on any feminine exhibition of fear, are you?"

Marcus frowned and remained silent for a moment. He wasn't quite as adept at deciphering her odd accent and words as Robert. "I know not what a *Neanderthal* is, my lady, but know well the kind of man you describe. I am not such a man, nay."

"Good." Beth reached over and took his hand, lacing her fingers through his substantially larger ones. She thought she heard him suck in a breath as he looked down at her pale hand enclosed in his, shocked no doubt by her boldness. But she needed the contact. And the more time she spent with Marcus, the more familiar he seemed to her, odd as that might be.

Beth needed a little familiarity just then. Needed someone she could trust as much as Robert. And that intuition that had told her before her mind would accept it that she could trust Robert now told her that she could trust Marcus.

He gave her hand a gentle squeeze. "He is well, my lady. You shall see."

She nodded, acknowledging his words silently, and continued her vigil.

Jagged streaks of lighting illuminated the writhing clouds with increasing frequency. Thunder raced to catch up until, at last, the two spilt the night simultaneously.

Beth didn't move when the first big drops spattered her arm, her cheek, her hair and dappled the steps around them with damp spots.

When Marcus tried to entice her to wait inside, warm and dry, she politely refused.

Rain began to fall in earnest, the wind unrepentantly throwing it in their faces. Yet Marcus neither left her side nor forced her within.

Both were soon drenched. Though Robert's cloak didn't succeed in keeping Beth dry—nothing short of a roof over her head could accomplish that in this deluge—it did provide a modicum of warmth, as did Marcus when he cautiously eased closer until his shoulder brushed hers.

Her hair hung about her face in loose, sodden curls. Water beaded on her spiked eyelashes and dripped off the tip of her nose.

And still Beth did not move.

The storm seemed to rage for hours.

Robert studied the abandoned campsite. Blood painted the ground and foliage where Sir Winston and Sir Miles had fallen. Flies buzzed around the bodies of five men Miles and Winston had slain before sheer numbers had defeated them.

The marauders had left both their dead and a few belongings, fleeing into the forest.

"How many were there?" Robert asked young Alwin, Winston's squire.

"Mayhap a score."

Twenty armed men against two knights and two squires.

"Why did they not kill you all?"

The boy swallowed hard. "I knew Sir Winston could not win against such numbers."

Behind them, Stephen grunted. "He would have fought to the death rather than accept defeat."

Alwin nodded. "I knew as much, my lord. So, I told Hugo to ride for help."

Hugo, Sir Miles's squire nodded. "I did not wish to leave the battle, but hoped the others who searched for Lady Bethany's brother would be nigh enough to help us."

Both boys bore minor wounds, their clothing marred by rips and smudges of dirt and blood.

"When I saw Sir Winston sorely wounded," Alwin continued, "and saw Sir Miles stumble, I turned and called into the forest behind us, *Over here! Quickly, my lords! Ere they flee!*"

"And I," Hugo said, "upon hearing him, stopped and called back, altering my voice so it would appear more than one man answered."

"Swift thinking," Robert praised them. "They believed you were not alone."

"Aye, my lord," the boys responded.

"Osbert!" Robert called.

From the trees behind the knights, a man trotted forward, four hounds at his heels.

At Robert's nod, the man guided the hounds into the campsite.

Noses to the ground, tails wagging, the dogs swiftly caught the marauders' scent and took off into the trees.

Robert and the others launched themselves onto their destriers and raced after them.

The dogs led them to another body, then continued on to an unconscious man Robert knew would be dead by nightfall. Both had clearly been amongst the group that had wounded Sir Miles and Sir Winston. And Robert did not doubt that they were also the blackguards who had injured Davie and slain the boy's father and older brothers.

Were they also the same men who had attacked Beth and her brother?

Fury simmered beneath the surface as Robert gripped Berserker's reins.

Onward the hounds led them as the sky above them blossomed with the colors of sunset and daylight began to dim.

"There!" Michael shouted.

Robert followed his gaze.

Up ahead, men fleeing through the forest halted at Michael's cry.

Robert drew his sword.

Berserker lunged forward.

The marauders turned to fight.

Loosing mighty war cries, Robert and his knights descended upon the ragged band. Steel met steel, glanced off and slipped past into flesh. Cries of pain erupted all around him as Robert deflected a blow, then slid from the saddle and fought in earnest.

Curses flew and blood spewed as bodies began to fall.

Sellswords. Men who did not care who they slew as long as they were paid the proper coin for it. Each fought with surprising skill. And not one of them would allow himself to be captured. Nor would they reveal who directed their actions.

"Who hired you?" Robert roared, his powerful swings driving his latest opponent backward. He needed a name. Needed to know who the cursed whoreson was who kept plaguing his lands and people. Needed to know where he could find the bastard, because Robert did not think his enemy was amongst those who fought. Needed to know if the man held Beth's brother captive. "Is he here among you?"

The man merely growled, refusing to reveal the source of his coins.

Robert continued to hammer him with blows the man soon struggled to deflect. "Tell me!"

The man tripped on a body behind him. His sword arm lost strength as he fought for balance, offering little defense against Robert's next strike.

Robert swore when blood spurted from his opponent's throat. He hadn't meant to the kill the man. But years of training and battle had rendered dealing death blows instinctual.

Another swordsman leapt over his fallen colleague and attacked.

Robert deflected his blow, then delivered one of his own. And another. And another.

When the fierce battle ended, Robert and his men all remained on their feet, though some bore minor wounds.

All of the marauders lay dead.

He looked at his men. "Did any of you get a name?"

Heads wagged from side to side as most of the knights winced or grimaced over having failed to deliver what Robert had asked of them.

Breathing hard, Michael motioned to the last man he had felled. "Every one of them chose to fight to the death rather than reveal who hired them."

Which left Robert no closer to dispatching his enemy. "Search the bodies."

They did so, but found no hint of whence the sellswords came or who they followed.

Eyeing the carnage around him, Robert loosed a string of epithets.

Once more he had failed his people.

He had failed Beth as well, if these men were amongst those who had attacked her and her brother.

Grim silence accompanied Robert and his men as they rode home.

Dismounting, Robert handed Berserker into the care of one of the stable lads and waited for Michael and Stephen to join him.

"Mayhap your enemy *was* amongst those we slew," Stephen commented.

Michael nodded. "'Twould explain why the others would not name him. They feared he would retaliate if they defeated us."

Robert shook his head. "Or mayhap I am right, he was not amongst them, and 'twas simply their love of coin that kept them silent. That or the knowledge that they would die whether they spoke his name or not."

"'Tis possible the attacks will cease now that they are dead," Stephen commented.

Frustrated and weary to the bone, Robert removed his helm. "He will only hire others."

"Not if he lacks the funds additional mercenaries will require," Michael said.

Stephen nodded. "If he cannot raise enough, he will hire men of lesser experience who will be more likely to make mistakes."

"Not to mention less loyal," Michael added. "They will sing his name as quickly as a raven when our swords touch their throats."

"Aye. Next time we will unmask him," Stephen vowed.

Robert appreciated their efforts to lift his spirits from the bottom of the deep pit into which they had sunk. But naught could accomplish such a feat. His failure to find and defeat his enemy could result in more lives lost. Lives for which he was responsible.

Stephen whistled suddenly. "Now I *know* she is mad, the poor girl. And it looks as though her madness has infected your squire."

Robert followed his gaze to the steps leading up to the keep, and frowned at the soggy pair huddled atop them.

The two rose as one, hands linked.

His scowl deepened.

Marcus dared to touch Beth so familiarly?

"If your face gets any redder, your head will burst," Michael commented. "What ails you?"

Jealousy, Robert thought with more than a touch of self-disgust. He was jealous of his damned squire, but would never admit it.

His gaze fastening on the pair's linked hands, Robert marched across the muddy bailey.

"Go easy on her, Rob," Stephen said behind him. "I spoke hastily when I said she was mad. 'Twas obviously concern for you that drove her to brave the elements. There are worse things a man can come home to than a beautiful, though somewhat bedraggled, woman waiting upon the steps for his safe return."

Robert ground to a halt. Spinning around, he gaped at the big knight, unsure which stunned him more—the idea that Beth cared about him enough to sit in the rain and watch for his return or the words his rough-about-the-edges friend had just uttered, which contained what sounded distressingly like a longing for a wife.

Michael, too, stared at Stephen in fascination.

Stephen shifted his weight from one leg to the other and reached up to tug on his earlobe. "What?"

"Since when have *you* craved hearth and home?" Michael exclaimed. "I thought we had all agreed that no woman would have you."

Robert's lips stretched into a smile as he turned back toward the steps.

Cursing erupted behind him. Bickering followed, then the sounds of a scuffle.

Now his spirits lightened. And they climbed even higher when Beth abruptly grew tired of waiting for him.

Dropping Marcus's hand, she flew down the stairs and launched herself into Robert's arms. The force of it knocked him back a step. A sound—half-laugh, half-grunt—escaped him as he locked his arms around her waist and clutched her to him, breast to chest, hips to hips, her feet dangling a foot or so above the ground.

Her body trembled as she wrapped her arms around his neck and clung tightly.

Burying his face in her cold, damp hair, Robert enjoyed the moment, not knowing when or if he might ever experience another such homecoming.

She loosened her hold.

With much reluctance, he released her and let her slide down until her boots sank into the mud.

Retreating an arm's length, she stared up at him with red-rimmed eyes.

Did tears mingle with the moisture the storm had left glistening on her pale cheeks? Her nose did look a little pink, but that could simply be from the cold. If *he* felt a slight chill, he knew Beth must be half-frozen.

Her gaze dropped to his chest, his arms, and lower. "Are you hurt?" She began a hasty exploration of his limbs and torso with her small hands. "Is that *your* blood? Were you injured?"

"I am well, Beth. I incurred no injuries." And wished there weren't so much material and chain mail separating those hands of hers from his skin.

"Are you sure?" she prodded.

Her concern warmed him as much as her wondrous greeting had. "Aye."

Ceasing her frantic search for wounds, she took one of his hands in both of hers and looked beyond him to the others. "What about you, Michael? Were you hurt? Stephen, were you?"

Surprise and pleasure lit their eyes.

"I am well, my lady," Michael said.

"As am I," Stephen told her.

"Your chain mail is torn, Michael, there on your arm. *Were* you injured?"

He glanced down at the broken links in his hauberk, high on his left arm, near his shoulder. "'Tis but a scratch, my lady."

"Scratches can kill if they fester."

He smiled. "Lady Alyssa has been schooling me in the art of healing. I have the proper herbs and vow I will tend it anon."

She eyed him doubtfully.

His dark brows furrowed suddenly as he glanced at the donjon. "I should see to Miles and Winston first. I regret I was able to do so little for them earlier. Do either of them still live?"

Beth blanched. Her throat moved in a swallow. "I don't know. I think so. I hope so." She turned troubled eyes up to Robert's and squeezed his hand. "I need to talk to you."

No sooner had she spoken the words than she turned and began to drag him after her up the steps and into the keep.

Robert would have continued on into the great hall to check on his men, but Beth had other ideas.

Tightening her hold on him, she veered left to the narrow staircase and tugged him up behind her.

"Beth?"

"I want to make sure you really aren't hurt."

He struggled to keep his attention off the shapely bottom swaying in front of him. Her sodden clothing and cloak clung to every luscious curve. "I assure you I am well."

"I know. But when you thought I was injured, I showed you *my* wounds or lack thereof. It's only fair that you do the same for me."

A wicked grin curved his lips as he followed her down the corridor and into his solar. Closing the door behind him, he faced her. "Ahhh. So *that* is it," he teased. "You wish to play that fascinating game you mentioned down by the river: *I'll show you mine, if you'll show me yours.* Well, I am more than happy to oblige you."

She did not laugh as he had expected her to. Nor did she force a scowl and try unsuccessfully to keep her lips from twitching as she delivered one of her jesting punches.

Nay, she did none of those things.

Shocking Robert to his core, she dropped her cloak, closed the distance between them, and stretched up onto her toes to capture his lips in a kiss that stole his breath. Her small hands tunneled through his hair, her fingernails lightly raking his scalp and raising goose flesh on his arms.

Robert groaned.

Giving his hair a little tug, she drew his head down and deepened the contact. Her tongue stroked the seam of his lips, then delved within.

Lust pierced him like a knife, so quick and intense it was almost painful. Cupping her neck with one hand, he splayed his other across her back, collapsed back against the door and braced his long legs a shoulder's width apart. "Beth."

Beth's heart, already pounding fit to burst from her breast, leapt when Robert whispered her name with such longing. She might have initiated the kiss, but he swiftly took control, seducing her with every stroke of his tongue and every caress of his hand on her back, her waist, her hip. Eager to kindle the flames stirring to life inside her, she moved between his legs and leaned into his muscular frame.

A low groan rumbled from his chest. The hand at her hip slid down to clasp her bottom and draw her even closer. "Help me out of this damned armor," he growled. "I want to feel you against me."

Nodding, unable to produce a coherent word, Beth hastily divested him of his wet surcoat and began tugging on his mailed hauberk with fingers that shook.

She had never felt this way before. Had never needed someone so badly. Had never wanted a man so much that she thought she would shatter if he didn't touch her again.

Only their jagged breaths broke the quiet as they worked, soon accompanied by the *chink* of mailed links moving and the *plop* of sopping-wet fabric hitting the floor.

When at last Robert stood only in his shirt, braies and hose, Beth stared. Moisture rendered the pale garments nearly transparent, gifting her with a heart-stopping glimpse of his beautiful, very aroused body.

Her mouth went dry as she met his gaze. Desire burned brightly in his arresting blue eyes, darkening them until they appeared almost black.

But they held tenderness, too. And concern.

Unbidden, tears stung the backs of her eyes.

Robert gently cradled her face in his palms. "Tell me, Beth."

"I was so afraid you would be killed," she whispered brokenly. "I don't know what I would do if anything happened to you, Robert." She hadn't realized just how attached to him she had become until she had watched him ride through those gates to risk his life in battle.

He had been her rock, her anchor, since she had come to this place and time.

He had been her friend. And so much more.

Robert stilled at her words. Bending, he pressed a light kiss to her forehead, touched his lips to hers, then drew her into a tender embrace. "Your words warm my heart, Beth, for I feel the same way."

Sighing, she snuggled closer. "You're not upset, are you? Because I was worried?" He didn't believe she thought him weak, did he?

"Nay. I know you meant no insult. But you should trust me when I tell you that I am more than capable of defending myself. There are many who think me quite skilled in battle."

She did not doubt that. Sniffing back tears, she actually found a smile. "Marcus thinks you're the best. He thinks you're invincible."

"Ahhh. My faithful squire, who failed the test of chivalry and did not coax you in out of the rain."

"He tried to, but I wouldn't budge." Beth tightened her hold on him and looked up. "I know you're supposed to be this big, bad, unconquerable warrior. And I believe you when you say you're good, but I'm just not used to this sort of thing, Robert. Sword fights and mangled bodies and..." She shook her head. "It's all new to me."

His gaze sharpened. "Why *is* that, Beth? Whence came you?"

She closed her eyes. "I'm afraid to tell you."

"You need not be. You can trust me, Beth."

Sighing, she met his gaze. "I know." He had proven as much again and again.

He waited quietly. "Well?"

She pursed her lips. "You want me to tell you now?"

"Aye."

"But we're..." His large warm body, still pressed to hers, left no doubt that he was still very aroused. "I mean, I thought we were going to..." Heat crept up her neck into her cheeks.

Damn it, why did she feel so shy all of a sudden?

Robert grinned. "'Tis not that I do not wish to, Beth, as I know you are well aware."

Though her blush deepened, she returned his grin. "Soooo, what are we waiting for?"

He laughed. "You to tell me what has been preying upon my mind night and day since I found you."

Lowering her head, she plucked at the front of his shirt. "I think we should get out of these wet clothes first." And she would do just about anything to postpone telling him the truth.

"I agree."

"Okay. See ya later." Spinning around, she lunged for the door.

Robert caught her around the waist and pulled her back against him. "Ohhh, nay," he said, laughter in his voice. "I know you too well. If I allow you to leave this chamber without telling me what I wish to know, you will spend the next sennight avoiding me."

He was only half right on that one.

Melting back into him, she reached up and cupped the back of his neck, tilting his head down so she could look into his eyes. "Only during the day," she promised, a little bit surprised by the sultry quality of her voice.

It was the first time she had mentioned spending the night in his bed.

Only now she had little interest in sleeping.

Those eyes of his dropped to her breasts. His arms tightened. Groaning, he buried his face in the hollow of her shoulder. "What a temptress you are."

"Only for you," she admitted softly. "I've never been this way with a man before." She pressed a kiss to his temple, his wet hair cool against her flushed skin. "I've never *been* with a man before. Only *you* make me want more, Robert. Only you."

"Ah, Beth." Every muscle in the big body pressed to hers seemed to go taut as his arms tightened even more. He turned his head, pressed a heated kiss to the base of her neck.

Her pulse leapt madly.

His arms loosened as he shifted his hands to her ribcage and slid them up until his fingers almost touched her breasts.

Fire raced through her veins. Her breath shortened. Anticipation rose.

Then he took a deep breath and gently set her away from him. "Remove your gown, don my robe, and tell me what you seek to avoid telling me so we can move on to better things."

Barely able to hear him over the heartbeat pounding in her ears, she turned around and blinked up at him. "You... I... What did you want me to do again?"

His lips twitched, though desire blazed brightly in his eyes. He took a step toward her. Halted. And swore. Crossing to the bed, he picked up his robe and tossed it to her. "You'd best remove those wet clothes, sweetling. Your lips are turning blue."

As much as she hated to admit it, now that he no longer touched her, she was cold as hell. "Spoilsport," she muttered and began tugging at the laces of the gown she wore with fingers that trembled. She would much rather *he* keep her warm but understood his desire to know her story. She had promised she would tell him two weeks ago and had yet to deliver.

"I did not mention it earlier, Beth, but you look lovely in that kirtle," he murmured.

"Thank you," she said. Twisting this way and that, she tried to figure out the tangled laces. "I feel like an idiot. I'm not used to wearing dresses. Particularly dresses like this one. It's so cumbersome and restricting. You have no idea how relieved I was when Adam cut the sleeves off."

"Adam cut your sleeves off? Why would he do that?"

Damn it. The material clung to her like a second skin, heavy from the gallons and gallons of rainwater it had absorbed. "Because I asked him to." Why couldn't this dress have a nice convenient zipper? Or maybe some massive buttons. Or Velcro. *Anything* that would make it easier to take off.

Ceasing her contortions, she scowled up at him. "How the hell do I get out of this thing? I didn't really pay attention when that girl came in to help me dress this morning." She had still been too weirded out over a complete stranger pulling off the nightgown Beth had borrowed and helping her dress.

Emitting something between a laugh and a groan, he closed the distance between them. "You cannot resist tempting me, can you?" Turning her away from him, he went to work on the laces and deftly relieved her of the dress.

"Thank you," she breathed when the sodden material fell to the floor.

Robert said nothing.

She turned to face him.

His gaze had fallen to her black bra and bikini panties.

The fire crackled behind him.

His hands curled into fists.

He looked as though he wished to devour her.

"I just had a very naughty thought," she whispered, her heart again pounding in her chest.

Robert's eyes rose to meet hers, so full of desire.

"I was thinking," she continued softly, "that you were looking at me as if I were good enough to eat, and—"

"Beth?" he interrupted, his voice deep and hoarse.

"Aye?"

"I *beg* you not to finish that sentence."

She laughed. "It's *your* fault, you know. I'm not like this with anyone else. You're just so hot you make me want to—"

"*Beth!*" he barked.

She held up her hands, laughing again. "All right. All right. Where's your robe?"

For a moment, she thought he would suffocate her as he grabbed his robe and attempted to get her covered as quickly as possible.

Amusement taking the edge off her own desire, she turned away and slipped out of her bra and panties. The robe was too long, of course, the hem pooling on the floor and the sleeves ending well beyond her fingertips. But it was warm and carried Robert's amazing scent. Tugging it closed in front, she spun to face him and caught him staring down at her bra and panties.

"Do I get to help you take off *your* clothes?" she asked, only partially teasing.

"Nay," he insisted.

"Spoilsport," she muttered again and moved to warm her hands in front of the fire.

She could have sworn she heard a faint chuckle as material rustled behind her.

Beth told herself not to look, but ended up glancing over her shoulder anyway.

She frowned.

He had already divested himself of his wet clothes and donned dry braies and a shirt.

"How did you do that so fast? I didn't even get a chance to peek!"

Grinning, Robert joined her before the hearth. "There will be time for that later." He sank into one of the two chairs there. "Now I am ready to hear your story."

Beth bit her lip, any urge to tease him vanishing. "You're really going to make me do this, huh?"

His expression sobered. "Nay, Beth. If 'twill distress you overly, you need not tell me. I merely wish to know more of you."

She sighed. If she told him it was too painful or upsetting, she knew he would allow her to retreat and likely never say another word about it. But she had put it off long enough. He deserved to know. She had slept with him every night for two weeks now. She couldn't start sleeping with him in the nonliteral sense without telling him where or *when* she was from. And that she didn't know how she had come to be there. Or how long she would be able to stay. Or what in the world would take her back, if anything.

"Let me ask you something first," she began tentatively.

He gave her a nod of encouragement. "As you will."

Having witnessed firsthand some of the bizarre superstitions of this time, she thought it best to test the waters first and see how bad this might get. "How do you feel about witches? Do you think they should be burned at the stake or weighted down with stones and tossed into a lake?"

The change her words wrought in him both fascinated and frightened her.

His body went completely still. He didn't breathe. He didn't blink. He didn't make a sound. It was as though he had turned to stone.

Then his nostrils flared. A muscle in his jaw jumped as he ground his teeth. His eyebrows lowered. His eyes glinted dangerously. His hands tightened on the arms of the chair until she thought the wood might crumble into sawdust.

"To whom have you been speaking, Beth?"

She had never heard that particular tone of voice from Robert before. It actually sent a chill darting through her. "I don't know what you mean."

"Of course you do." He rose, the movement graceful, yet vaguely threatening. "Someone has been filling your ears with tales of Alyssa, have they not?"

As unobtrusively as possible, she took a step backward. "Tales of whom?"

"Dark tales, no doubt. Malicious lies spoken by loose tongues."

"Um..."

He stalked her with slow deliberate steps, like a panther on the prowl. "Did they tell you she sold her soul to the devil in exchange for her gifts?"

"Her what?"

"Did they tell you she is Lucifer's daughter? Or, better yet, Lucifer's lover?"

"I have no idea what you're—"

"I do not blame you, Beth, for listening. I merely want you to give me the liar's name so that I can *cut* his *tongue* from his *devious, filth-spewing mouth!*"

Okay, now she was worried.

Robert's face mottled with fury.

Her ears rang from his roar as he pursued her across the room.

"Tell me who it was." His tone softened, became well-modulated, even conversational, though she found it no less terrifying. "Who was it, Beth?"

"It was no one," she stammered, glancing behind her to ensure she didn't back herself into a corner. She didn't care for the murderous glint that had entered his eyes.

"You have no reason to fear."

"You'd think differently if you could see yourself right now," she retorted.

"It was lies. All lies. I promise you."

"I'll go along with that." Whatever would lessen his fury.

"Alyssa is all that is good in this world," he vowed fervently. "She is kind and thoughtful and beautiful. As beautiful on the inside as she is on the outside."

Beth frowned, her steps slowing. *Wait. What?*

"She has devoted her life to aiding others," he continued, "healing them and bringing them back from the brink of death time after time, with no care for the pain it causes her. Only *once* has she lifted a finger to harm another. And despite what you may have heard, it was in defense of her own life when the villain tried to plunge a dagger into her breast. Her soul is pure and innocent, free of any taint of evil. And I know of no other who would sacrifice so much for so little."

Beth stopped.

Robert no longer stalked her, too consumed now with listing this other woman's virtues, rambling on and on about how good she was and how beautiful and wonderful.

Beth's blood began to boil as he continued to praise his precious Alyssa, whom she hadn't even *mentioned*, damn it.

"I am certain Father Markham would be more than happy to correct any notions you may have to the contrary," Robert informed her. "She is sweet and generous and..."

He made this Alyssa sound like a bloody saint! A wholesome, generous, spiritually perfect, physically exquisite saint. The man was in love with her!

And it made Beth want to scream, which she did when Robert continued to gush over his goddess's virtues. *"Who the hell is Alyssa and what the hell does she have to do with anything?"* she bellowed, unable to take any more of the torture.

Robert stopped mid-sentence. Startled into silence, he took a step backward and lost his scowl. "What?"

"I said, *who*... the *hell*... is *Alyssa?*"

Though not as deep, his scowl returned as he propped his hands on his hips. "What game do you play, Beth? You asked me about her yourself."

"I did not! You just started gushing over her. Who is she?"

"You know who she—"

"Is she your wife?" she demanded furiously. "Why didn't you tell me you were married?" When she recalled how he had held her and kissed her and let her snuggle up to him in bed when he'd been married all along, it made her want to explode. What, was the woman away visiting family or something?

"I am not wed," he denied.

"But you *want* to be, don't you? Are you engaged? Is that it? You're engaged or betrothed or however the hell you want to put it?"

"Betrothed to whom?"

"To Alyssa!"

"Alyssa is my brother's wife."

Oh, this just got worse and worse. "You're *sleeping* with your brother's *wife*? How could you, Robert?"

"I am not! I *did* not!"

"But you *want* to! You love her, don't you?"

"Nay! Aye! That is, I—"

She took a combative step toward him. "You put me in your *mistress's* room and dressed me in your *mistress's* clothing?"

"Alyssa is not my mistress!"

"But you just said you want her to be!"

"I did not! Why are you shouting at me?"

"Because I'm *jeal-ous!*"

She roared the last word so loudly—lengthening and extending it in almost a growl—that the people down in the great hall probably heard her.

Beth drew in a deep breath and struggled to bring her fury under control.

"Robert," she said, making her voice low and even the way he had, "so help me if you don't wipe that grin off your face, I am going to wipe it off for you. And that is *not* a threat you should take lightly."

The grin fled, replaced by sparkling eyes and a look of innocence she found equally aggravating.

"I'm warning you…"

"I am *not* grinning," he protested. His lips twitched.

"That does it."

Robert caught her fist before it could connect with his nose and brought her white-knuckled fingers to his lips for a kiss. "Beth," he said tenderly, foiling her attempts to withdraw her hand, "Alyssa is my sister by marriage, but I love her as if she were my sister by blood. 'Tis all there is to it. I assure you there is *naught*"—he gave her fist a little shake—"in my relationship with her that should inspire jealousy, nor has there ever been. Verily, there was a time when I treated her most abominably because I thought her a wicked sorceress."

Beth did not doubt his sincerity.

The anger left her in a rush. "Oh." When Robert pulled her into his arms, she tucked her head beneath his chin. "That makes me feel both better and worse at the same time."

His lips touched her forehead. "I know why you feel *better*…"

"If you tell anyone I threw a jealous temper tantrum, I will deny it unequivocally."

He chuckled. "As you will. Now tell me why you feel worse."

"Because, when I asked if you thought witches should be burned at the stake…"

"Aye?"

"I wasn't talking about *Alyssa the Magnificent*." Okay, it might take a little longer for her jealousy to subside. "I was talking about myself."

His head came up. "You?"

"Yes. Aye." Thank goodness Robert seemed to have a knack for languages, too, because her Middle English tended to slip quite a bit when her emotions ran high. Or when she was tired. Or rattled.

In the short time she had known him, he had already learned quite a few of her modern words and was becoming pretty adept at deciphering her accent and occasional mispronunciations. Michael, Stephen, Adam and Marcus were, too.

"Are you telling me you are a witch, Beth?" Robert asked now.

"No, I'm not. I'm really not."

"If you are, you need not worry. I have a particular fondness for witches and wisewomen."

Ire rose once more.

"Nay, do not stiffen up on me," he said, giving her an affectionate shake. "I already assured you my feelings for Alyssa are merely those of a brother."

"I'm not a witch, Robert. I just asked you that because I'm afraid that once I tell you where I come from, you will *think* I'm a witch."

He pressed a kiss to her temple. "I will not turn from you, Beth. Whatever secrets your past may hold, I will always be here for you... to seek comfort from... or to scuffle with..."

She grinned.

"Or to ply with kisses."

"Is that a hint?"

"Just planting the notion for later." Turning her in his arms, he placed a hand on her lower back and guided her back toward the hearth. "Indulge me now ere I let you distract me again. I would have you fret over this no more."

Anxiety returning, Beth waited while he arranged the two chairs so they faced each other with only a few feet separating them. He seated her in one, then lowered himself into the other.

Robert leaned back casually, his face open and expectant. His knees were comfortably splayed, his big feet planted on the floor, his tanned, long-fingered hands laced upon his flat, muscled abdomen.

He looked good enough to eat.

"Oops. Sorry," she said without thinking, her eyes flying up to meet his.

"For what?"

"I just had another naughty thought."

"Beth."

"I know. I didn't mean to. I was just looking at you and it popped into my head."

He groaned, dropping his head back against the chair, which only fired Beth's imagination more.

Closing her eyes, she pressed her fingertips to her temples. "Okay. Give me a second to banish the image, then I'll get started."

It took longer than a second.

She opened her eyes.

Robert sent her a smile. "Ready?"

She nodded. "I guess I'll start by asking you another question."

"As you will."

"When were you born?"

"I was born in the year of our Lord eleven hundred and seventy-three."

Her jaw dropped. "Holy crap," she whispered. He had been born in the twelfth century. The twelfth freaking century!

Robert's smile faded. "You seem surprised."

"I am." The *twelfth century* for crying out loud!

His brow puckered. "You think me old?" He shifted slightly. "I have no gray hairs yet and—"

"No! No-no-no. I don't think you're old, Robert. It isn't that." Perhaps it would help if her eyes weren't wide and her mouth didn't hang open. It obviously made the poor guy self-conscious. But the *twelfth century*? Really? She hadn't realized just how far back she had traveled. "What is today's date?"

"'Tis the fifth of June."

Leaning forward, Beth tucked her hands between her knees. "The *whole* date, please."

His expression went blank. "'Tis the fifth day of June in the year of our Lord twelve hundred and three."

"Twelve hundred and three," she repeated softly. *1203.* The beginning of the thirteenth century.

Robert waited patiently as she mulled it all over. Beth had known him long enough to realize that the total lack of expression on his face was an indication of concern.

What was he thinking?

What *would* he think when she spelled it all out for him?

Her hands grew clammy. "The day you found me in the forest, after I woke up in that clearing…," she began.

"Aye?"

Please, let him believe me. "The day Josh and I were shot, and I collapsed and thought I was dying…"

He nodded, watching her closely.

"Robert, when I passed out in that clearing, I was in the twenty-first century."

Chapter Eleven

BETH HELD HER BREATH, AWAITING Robert's reaction.

He said nothing. He made no sound at all, offering not even a grunt of acknowledgment.

Did he not understand?

"What I'm trying to say is, I'm not only from another continent, I'm from another time. I'm from eight hundred years in the future."

Robert just stared at her, unmoving.

The silence stretched.

Her anxiety mushroomed.

Just when she thought she would scream from the tension of it, he leaned forward and rested his elbows on his knees.

Tugging her hands free, he clasped them in his own and locked gazes with her. "Beth, I wish to ask you a question."

Just one? Were she in his place, she would ask hundreds. "Okay."

"In the other clearing you spoke of, the one with your brother…"

"Aye?"

"When your wounds felled you, did you strike your head when you hit the ground?"

A laugh full of despair tumbled from her lips. "Oh, Robert, don't you think I wish it were that simple? Yes, I bumped my head on the ground, but not hard. Or rather not hard *enough*. It didn't give me amnesia. I know damned well who I am and where I'm from, even though I know how crazy it sounds."

Rising, she began to pace the large chamber. "It didn't give me a concussion either. And even if it had, a concussion couldn't explain *this*." She gestured to the room around them as well as the world outside the windows. "Concussions may cause confusion or make it difficult to think clearly, but I've never heard anyone mention massive hallucinations. And this is way too detailed, not to mention historically accurate, for a delusion or a hallucination anyway." She shook her head. "I *thought* it was a delusion when I saw your castle and the village for the first time. I mean, it felt real. But I just couldn't believe that it was, because it didn't make sense and shouldn't be possible. Then you brought me here and I couldn't deny it anymore, because people just don't live like this in my time, Robert. I know there is hunger and poverty every damned place you go, but let's face it. Anyone who could afford to buy or build a castle this size could also afford to install electricity and indoor plumbing. And their servants would all be paid by the hour."

"By the hour!" He looked astounded.

"Yes, by the hour."

"I have not the coin to pay all those who work for me so richly!"

"Look, I didn't say that to insult you. It's just… feudalism ended a long time ago. This way of life no longer exists in my time. Not in America, where I'm from. And not in England." She frowned. "Not that I know that much about England, in all honesty. But I guarantee you no one over there, or rather here, but in the future, would be willing to labor for nothing."

Robert stiffened. "My people do not toil for naught. Though recent events may have made it appear otherwise, I offer each and every one of them my protection."

Beth abruptly stopped pacing. She hadn't meant to upset him. "I know you do."

"And they may have starved under the rule of my predecessor. But since Fosterly came into my possession, not one of them has gone hungry. I—"

"Robert, I know." She gave him a smile full of the tenderness she felt for him, hoping to eradicate his belligerent expression. "I know. I've watched you with them. I know how much they love you and how well you care for them. You almost treat them as if they are part of your family." Again she frowned. "Which is really weird. You aren't at all what I expected a medieval nobleman to be like. I thought they were mostly narcissistic jackasses who treated peasants like dirt and ran around molesting and forcing themselves on all of the women and girls who weren't born with a title. And in some cases, I'm sure, the boys."

His eyes widened. Because he had never heard of noblemen behaving so vilely? Or because he was shocked that she knew of such things? Was Robert the exception to the rule? Or had Hollywood and some of the history programs she had watched gotten it wrong?

"Is your brother like you?" Beth didn't realize until the question popped out that she was curious about Robert's family.

"Hmm?"

"Your brother. Is he like you? Does he treat his people like family the way you do?"

"Nay, though I often think he would if given the chance."

She didn't bother to hide her distaste. "So, he impregnates all of his serving girls and—"

Robert released a short bark of laughter. "Nay. Not Dillon. His desire lies only with his winsome wife. And I can say with nigh absolute certainty that my squire has bedded more women than my brother had ere he wed."

Beth stared. "You mean Marcus? He's just a boy!"

Robert chuckled. "That *boy* has many admirers who fight every night over who will share his pallet. Whereas Dillon..." He tilted his head to one side. "I believe my brother had precious little knowledge of women and intimacy ere Alyssa stole his heart. Which is not to say he went to his marriage bed a virgin," he hastened to add. "He merely rarely indulged those needs as far as I could tell." His look turned thoughtful. "I never understood it, really. He is wealthy and powerful. Women think him handsome. They must have offered themselves to him fairly frequently."

"But he declined?"

"Aye. I know not why. And he refused to discuss it despite my prodding. I admit it troubled me."

"Why? I think it's admirable that he exercised a little self-restraint. Goodness knows other men don't."

Robert shook his head. "'Tis not *a little* self-restraint I speak of. My brother was nigh as chaste as a monk. Did I not know better, I would have thought he had sworn some vow of celibacy."

"Is that so bad?"

"I thought so at the time. He lived such a solitary existence and was always so solemn. Surely he could have benefitted from a little tenderness and love play. But whenever I would encourage him to tumble one comely wench or another, he would find an excuse not to."

Beth bit her lip. "Did you ever think that maybe he might have some trouble in that area?"

His lips curled up in that familiar, handsome smile. "Alyssa was already carrying their first child when they spoke their vows."

"Oh." She smiled back. "Well, I guess that answers that."

Robert nodded, his pleasure with the outcome plain to see. "He is happy now. Far happier than I ever dreamed he could be. It gladdens my heart to hear him laugh so often."

Yet, something didn't quite click for Beth. "If he's so happy, why does he treat his people badly?"

Robert looked surprised. "He does not."

"I thought you said—"

"His circumstances differ, Beth," he interrupted. "Dillon is one of the most feared warriors in all of England. On the continent, as well. Those who followed Lionheart and King Philip in the crusades were all witness to Dillon's ferocity on the battlefield."

"You're talking about Richard Lionheart, aren't you? As in King Richard?"

"Aye." He perked up a bit. "You recall him now? You knew him not when last I spoke of him."

"What can I say? History isn't my strongest subject. All those dates and names. I'm doing good to remember American history." She shrugged. "As far as England's history goes, unless it was in a movie, in a novel, on the news, in a History Channel program, or mentioned by my mom and her medieval literature cronies, chances are good that I don't know it."

His face went slack with patent disbelief. "We speak of King Richard! He perished only four years ago!"

"He's dead then?"

"Aye!"

"Well, how was I supposed to know that?" she asked defensively. "Honestly, Robert, how much do *you* know about events that took place on another continent eight hundred years ago?"

His lips tightened. "Then you maintain this fantasy that you have come to me from the future?"

"It isn't fantasy. It's fact."

His expression said, *I'm not buying it.*

She groaned. "I know, I know. It sounds insane. It can't be true. Well,

I have news for you. Time travel is no more possible in the twenty-first century than it is now, even with all of the technology we have. And, Robert, you would not *believe* the technological advances we have made."

"I know not what *technology* means, but if mankind will truly accomplish whatever future advances you have imagined they will by the twenty-first century, why think you that time travel will not be possible?"

"Because," she told him earnestly, "if time travel were possible in my century, the world would be even more screwed up than it already is. All it takes is one brief look at the past to know that the dumb-butts powerful enough to control the research and development it would take to make time travel possible would then abuse the *ability* to travel through time to change things for their own gain and say to hell with everyone else. And I am not *imagining* the technological advances of my time. I don't even know how to begin to explain all that the term technology comprises, but it's real. If I were a resident of your time, I would never even conceive of the things I see on a daily basis at home."

"Why is that?"

"Because compared to us—and by us, I mean inhabitants of the twenty-first century—the average person of your time doesn't know diddly squat about science and medicine."

Robert folded his arms across his chest and raised one eyebrow in what she took as a cold challenge. "Then by all means, enlighten me with an example or two and we shall see how difficult it is for my poor backward brain to conceive of it."

Groaning again, she resumed her pacing. "Robert, I didn't mean it like that. It's just… for Pete's sake! You guys probably still think the Earth is flat and that—"

"The Earth is not flat. It is round," he interrupted.

"Really? You knew that?"

"Scholars have known that for some time now, though the church continues to insist it is flat."

"Oh." She frowned. "Teachers should really stop teaching that *everyone-was-afraid-Columbus-would-sail-off-the-edge-of-the-Earth* crap in school then."

He blinked.

"Right. Too far off topic." She resumed her pacing. "Okay. So you know the Earth is round. But you probably think that the sun—and pretty much everything else in the universe—revolves around the Earth. And you probably know little to nothing about solar systems or galaxies or just how big this universe really is. *We* do. All of those stars up there," she said, motioning to the ceiling, "are suns just like our own with their own little groups of planets that revolve around them or circle them just like the Earth does our sun. And we're pretty damned sure that there's life on at least a few of them."

She paused to take a breath, then dove back in. "And Earth isn't the only planet that revolves around *our* sun. There are eight planets and three dwarf planets. Although, honestly, I still think of Pluto as a planet, not a dwarf planet. And with our technology, we've taken close-up pictures of some of these planets, and taken soil samples of at least one, and even studied their weather patterns. We've sent men to the moon, Robert. In the twentieth century, men actually walked on the moon. We've built a station up in space, where astronauts live for months at a time with great big rockets that take them to it. If I were born in your time, would *any* of that have occurred to me?"

He didn't answer.

"Well, would it?"

The silence stretched.

Had she tossed too many modern words in there for him to get the gist of it?

She studied him. No. Something she had said had gotten to him. Some fragment of her ramblings had actually reached him.

His face lost quite a bit of color. He gripped the arms of his chair so tightly that his knuckles whitened. He looked positively shell-shocked.

"Robert?"

Leaning forward, he braced his elbows on his knees again and clasped his hands between them.

"What is it?" she asked.

"'Tis naught," he answered, his face full of unease.

"I don't think so," she protested, watching him. "Something I said unsettled you."

He stared down at his hands for a moment and seemed to weigh his words very carefully. Either that or he debated the wisdom of speaking them aloud. "You do not believe the sun revolves around the Earth?" he asked finally.

That wasn't what she had expected. "No. Nay, the Earth, along with the other planets in our solar system, all revolve around the sun. But Europe didn't—or rather *won't*—figure that out until..." She frowned. When *had* they figured that out? "I'm not sure. Maybe the 16th century. I think Copernicus came up with a model somewhere around then." She had a vague recollection of writing an essay on it in middle school.

Robert looked none too pleased.

"Maybe I shouldn't have told you that," she murmured. Sure, he hadn't been thrown by the Earth being round thing. But the Earth revolving around the sun instead of vice versa must have come as a shock.

As she studied Robert, she frowned, then narrowed her eyes.

Or had it?

Shouldn't he be shouting denials or accusing her of madness or witchcraft or heresy or laughing it all off as a joke by now? Because he wasn't doing any of that. He was just sitting there, staring at her. Almost as if he were wondering how the hell she had known.

Her eyes widened. "You knew!" she exclaimed, pointing a finger at him with a combination of accusation and triumph. "You knew the Earth revolves around the sun and now you're trying to figure out how *I* knew it!"

"How *did* you know it?" he asked softly.

"We're taught that and a lot more, beginning at a very early age in school. If I didn't have such a hard time remembering numbers, I could probably tell you the Earth's dimensions, too."

"As could I."

She blinked. "What?"

He quirked one supercilious eyebrow.

"Seriously?"

The eyebrow's twin rose, as did the corners of his lips as he leaned back in his chair.

"No freaking way!" Beth hurried across the room and reclaimed her seat. "How is that possible? You're not supposed to know about that stuff yet."

"You must first vow you will not repeat what I tell you," he cautioned.

"Done. Now give it up."

He grinned. "You have the most peculiar way of issuing demands."

"I know. Just tell me."

"Very well. My brother's wife is a wisewoman, as were her mother and grandmother before her and so on. I know not how far back it goes, only that members of her family have more often than not been born with certain gifts that have driven some to travel the world in search of knowledge and to escape persecution as witches."

"What kind of gifts?"

"I shall disclose those later."

"Now I'm *really* curious."

He smiled. "I know."

"Wait a minute. Your brother's wife? You mean Alyssa?" If he started waxing poetic over the woman's beauty and many virtues again, Beth was going to hit him over the head with something.

"Aye." His teeth gleamed in a grin. "Your eyes are lovely when they sparkle with jealousy."

"Oh, shut up and keep explaining." *Damn it.* He was right. Even after his earlier assurances, she burned with jealousy whenever he mentioned the other woman's name.

"Alyssa has in her possession numerous tomes and scrolls so old that the language written upon some is no longer spoken."

"Can she read them?"

"Many of them, aye. Her grandmother taught her and she in turn has shared with me the knowledge she gleaned from them whenever I pestered her with questions."

The image of him bending over dusty old manuscripts with some gorgeous babe made her want to strangle him.

"And my brother," he added, clearly amused. "Did I mention that my brother is often present during our discussions? I am certain Dillon knows far more than I do."

"Good save." Forcing her jealousy aside, she pondered the probability of books or scrolls containing that kind of information actually existing at this point in time. "You said they're really old?"

"Ancient in some cases. Alyssa will not let me touch them for fear I will crumble the pages in my clumsiness."

"You aren't clumsy," she declared, a little offended on his behalf. Robert was the least clumsy man she had ever met.

"My thanks for your defense."

"You know, I saw a documentary once that said the great pyramids of Giza are *exactly* proportional to the radius and diameter of the Earth, which—contrary to popular belief—isn't perfectly round. *So* exactly proportional, in fact, that it couldn't have been a coincidence. Those pyramids were built at least as early as 2500 B.C., although some now argue they were built much earlier than that. And clearly astronomy played a huge role in the alignment of their structures, their calendar, and more. So it wouldn't surprise me at all if Egyptians were hip to the heliocentric model early on. Did any of Alyssa's scrolls, or whatever, by chance come from Africa? And, just in case you don't call it Africa yet, Africa is sometimes called the Dark Continent and is the one located south of the Mediterranean. You might refer to Africans as Moors."

All cockiness left him, along with the color that had managed to creep back into his features. His blue eyes widened. "Those scrolls and their origins have been very carefully guarded. How is it you know of them and of the place they originated?"

How did *she* know? She was as shocked by *his* knowledge as he was by hers. Though she couldn't help but be delighted.

No wonder he was more open-minded and seemed more progressive than his peers.

Beth leaned forward and gave his knee a gentle pat. "I told you. Everyone who goes to school or watches the History Channel knows that in my time."

Beth could almost see the thoughts racing through his mind as he scrambled for an explanation for her knowledge that would prove easier to digest than time travel.

What more could she say to convince him? What more could she do? She needed proof. Tangible proof.

She clapped a palm to her forehead. "I can't believe I didn't think of this. My things!" Grabbing his hand, she jumped up and drew him over to the tapestry that hid the secret door.

Robert remained silent, still reeling from Beth's revelations.

He held the tapestry aside for her as she passed through the doorway and into the narrow corridor that lay between his chamber and hers.

Dusty and ornamented with the wispy lace of countless cobwebs, the corridor was part of a maze of hidden passageways that afforded the lord's family several possible exits should an enemy take the keep by force.

"What's down there?" Beth pointed along the dark passageway.

Robert grimaced, thinking of the oubliette he had discovered down one of the lower passages. Wooden spikes—their points facing the ceiling—lined its floor in such numbers that anyone tossed inside from the trapdoor above would have no hopes of avoiding them. Skeletons of those who had been impaled upon them in the past now littered the floor like chalk. "You do not wish to know."

"Enough said."

Robert stared down at the top of Beth's head with disbelief. "You will issue no protests nor insist that I show you?"

She smiled up at him over her shoulder. "No. I trust you." Pushing the next tapestry aside, she entered her chamber.

The tapestry almost hit Robert in the face, so stunned was he. Catching it at the last moment, he stepped through, closed the door and let the heavy material settle back into place.

His heart began to thud heavily in his chest as he watched Beth hurry over to the trunk that contained Alyssa's clothing and various belongings. Her simple declaration of trust awoke feelings within him that had long lain dormant. He did not think he had experienced such an intense rush of affection since before he had lost Eleanor and Gabriel.

Emptiness had plagued him since their deaths. For years, he had done what was expected of him, performed his duties, and feigned good cheer around his brother, all with a heavy heart.

Until Beth had stumbled in front of his horse and aimed her peculiar weapon at him.

Her rare smiles and laughter had warmed him, forcing out the cold. Her boldness and lack of concern regarding propriety amused and entertained him. Her touch and her kisses enflamed him. Bringing her happiness made *him* happy. Her worry and anxiety became his own.

He was falling in love with her.

What a hell of a time to realize it.

Beth dropped to her knees and began pawing through Alyssa's clothing.

Eight hundred years. Beth thought she was from a time eight hundred years in the future.

'Twas mad. 'Twas unthinkable.

But she was Bethany. *His* Bethany. His *Beth*.

And she had known the Earth traveled around the sun.

Aside from himself, Dillon, Alyssa and the other *gifted ones*, he did not think anyone else in all of England knew that. Nor would they believe him if he told them.

He had been reluctant to believe it himself at first. Had anyone other than Alyssa suggested the sun did not travel around the Earth like the moon, he would have dismissed it outright. As would Dillon have. But Alyssa possessed extraordinary wisdom and abilities. How could one argue with her, having witnessed both firsthand?

Robert had not thought he would ever have reason or opportunity to discuss such with someone outside the family. Then Beth had blurted out the information as confidently as if she were stating that grass was green and the sky blue.

As if such were common knowledge.

Beth rose, lifting her strange pack out of the trunk. "I hid it here so the servants wouldn't see any stuff from my time and freak out." Her gaze made a quick foray about the room, then settled on the bed. "Over here."

Robert followed her to the bed, still shaken by both her revelation and his realization that he was falling in love with her.

Clambering up onto the mattress, she knelt, then sat on her feet and patted the covers in front of her. "Come on. Sit with me."

He settled himself cross-legged, facing her, as she upended her sack full of wonders between them and began to sort through it all. "Beth, there is something that puzzles me," he broached.

She glanced up. "Just one thing?"

He smiled. "One thing to begin with," he clarified.

Grinning, she went back to rummaging through the pile. "What's on your mind?"

"'Tis something you said earlier. You told me that traveling through time is no more possible in the twenty-first century than it is here in the thirteenth. Yet you seem to be trying very hard to convince me that you have indeed accomplished this feat."

She paused. Her forehead crinkled as her eyes met his. "That's right. I did say that. It doesn't really make sense, does it?" Releasing a frustrated sigh, she shook her head. "I don't know what to tell you, Robert. I'm as puzzled as you are. I honestly don't think a working method of time travel has been invented in my time. Scientists don't either. And, if mankind had accomplished time travel and the scholars just didn't know about it, everything would be totally screwed up."

Screwed up was one of the first of her odd terms that he had learned to translate. "How so?"

She pondered it for a moment. "Well, I'm guessing women wouldn't be as powerful as they are now, both in politics and society."

Robert stared. How powerful were they?

"In fact, the whole Women's Liberation Movement would probably have been quashed before it even began. With all of the bitching and moaning that's been going on in my time over women gaining power, running for president and getting elected in some countries... Yeah. That would've been nipped in the bud *really* fast. The Civil Rights Movement probably would have been stopped, too. And since greed seems to motivate everything, the richest men on the planet—the ones wealthy enough to fund the research and development needed to create time travel—would gain an even larger percentage of the planet's wealth than they have now. I mean, they'd have years of Wall Street numbers they could capitalize on and use to get richer. Not to mention lotto numbers. And I'm sure they'd manipulate things so they could have more power. I hate to even *think* what would happen war-wise. Preemptive strikes to head off World War I and World War II? Preemptive invasions that would just make things worse? Biological weapons and atom bombs implemented sooner than they were?" She shook her head. "Yeah. Time travel has definitely not been invented in my time." Her frown deepened. "And yet, here I am. I seem to have done the impossible, and I have absolutely no idea how I did it. I don't even know how to explain it."

Robert frowned. Could one travel through time without knowing it? Would not something momentous, if not frightening, take place during such an unnatural feat?

"I know it makes no sense," she said, "but don't give up on me yet. I may not be able to tell you *how* I came back in time, but I *can* prove to you that I did. I really can."

A small, colorful, cylindrical object the size of his smallest finger rolled toward him, coming to rest against his shin. Robert picked it up and examined it. "What is this?" It appeared to be made of the plastic material she possessed so much of.

"That's lip balm. You rub it on your lips to protect them from the sun and keep them from getting chapped. Keeps them nice and soft."

He could attest to the softness of her lips, having explored them thoroughly with his own.

Robert set the small tube down and contented himself with staring at the many fascinating objects arrayed before him. Amazingly, each appeared more interesting than the last. "For what do you search?"

"Something with a date on it," Beth murmured, wadding up the bloody tunic she refused to wash and dropping it over the side of the bed.

Robert leaned forward so he could better see the items she uncovered as she moved things around. "Are there, perchance, more small scraps of black material in there?"

Beth's hands stilled. Her head came up. A teasing smile bloomed on her pretty face as her eyes met his. "Like my bra and panties, do you?"

Unaccountably, Robert found himself blushing.

She winked. "I'll let you know if I find any."

As soon as she resumed her search, Robert directed a quick look down at his lap to ensure the loose shirt he had donned earlier concealed his arousal.

"Aha! Here it is!"

His pulse leapt as he looked up, expecting to see scraps of midnight dangling between her fingers.

Alas, she held a folded pouch of some sort.

"What is it?"

"My wallet." She unfolded it into a rectangle. "My birth date is on my driver's license. So is the expiration date. See?" She withdrew a small, shiny piece of what appeared to be thick parchment from the wallet. Glancing at it, she started to lean forward and hand it to him. Her face fell. "Damn. It only gives the last two numbers, not the whole year. And I bet my credit card does the same thing."

As she started to tuck it away again, he caught a glimpse of the front of it. "Wait."

Pausing, she looked up. "What?"

He motioned to it. "Is that a portrait, Beth? A miniature, mayhap?"

She considered the card. "In a manner of speaking. It's a picture ID. See?"

Robert took the card she offered him and stared at it with amazement. Beth's fair face smiled up at him beside a collection of numbers and words. "'Tis you! And 'tis so clear!"

She shrugged. "As far as driver's license pictures go, I guess it's a pretty good one. My last one was horrible. My eyes were half-closed and my mouth was open because I was answering a question the DMV lady asked just before she snapped the picture. I looked like a zombie."

Robert knew not what a *zombie* was, but could not imagine Beth looking less appealing than she did in the miniature he held. "'Tis beautiful. The artist captured you perfectly. Though he added a bit of color to your eyes and lips."

Beth laughed. "Actually, that was me. It's makeup. A little eye liner, a little shadow, and some lipstick. After that last picture, I was trying to look my best."

Robert frowned. "You stained your lips and eyes?"

"Aye."

"Why?"

"I told you. I was trying to look my best, enhance what nature gave me, work with what I got, however you want to put it. That's what women do in my time."

He let his disapproval show. "You have no need of enhancement. Your beauty transcends such senseless artifice."

Beth seemed taken aback.

Did she think he insulted her?

Leaning forward onto her hands and knees, she touched her lips to his. Once. Twice. Almost making him forget where they were and what they discussed.

"What was that for?" he asked hoarsely when she leaned back an inch or two.

She smiled. "For being you." A third kiss followed, heating his blood and robbing him of rational thought. Just as he decided to drop the portrait and drag her up against him, she broke away and sat back on her heels.

Robert's heart pounded as he watched her retrieve her wallet once more. "There must be something with a date on it in here," she muttered.

Only half-listening, Robert returned his attention to the miniature in his rough hands. He rubbed his thumb across the cold, smooth surface, trying to suppress thoughts of lunging across the pile in front of him and stripping Beth of the robe that now gaped in marvelous places. "What manner of portrait is this? I can feel neither the texture of the canvas nor the paint. And it shines like glass."

"It isn't a portrait. It's a photograph." She spelled the word for him. "Look. Here's my dental appointment reminder card. It has the full date written on it." She handed him a small piece of thick parchment. "Photos are more common than paintings in my time because they're pretty much instant. You point your camera or phone or tablet, press the button, and the image is recorded. Then you just hook your device up to a printer, pop in some photo quality paper, and *voila*, instant picture."

The card in Robert's hand boasted an unfamiliar coat of arms, along with printed and scrawled words he could not understand. "What language is this?"

"English."

"It cannot be. I cannot read it."

"I know. English has changed quite a bit since the thirteenth century. If my mom hadn't been a literature professor, she wouldn't have made me learn Middle English and I wouldn't have been able to understand a word you said." She wrinkled her nose. "Actually I still have trouble on occasion."

"I thought you understood me well."

"Then I must fake it better than I thought. Anyway, the words on that card aren't that important. It just lists my doctor's address, email address, phone number and fax number and gives the date. Can you read those numbers there?"

"Aye."

"Well that's the year."

Robert stared at the four digit number.

"See. Twenty-first century." Suddenly, her eyes widened. "I can't believe I didn't think of this! Coins!" She flipped her wallet over.

His head snapped up. "Coins?"

"Yes! Coins. Each one has the year it was minted imprinted on it." She unzipped a small pocket and dumped a number of very small coins into her palm. Some were copper colored. Some were a dull silver. Some had smooth edges, some slightly rough. "Look, here's a quarter from 2006." She pressed it into his palm.

With a face on one side and a mountain range on the other, it resembled no coin Robert had ever seen and was indeed stamped with the date 2006.

"There are two dates on this. 2006 and 1876."

"Oh. 1876 must've been the year Colorado achieved statehood. Look. Here's a penny from 2014. And a nickel from 1993. Another nickel from 2001. A quarter from 1998. A penny from 2001. 1994. 1976. 2004. 1990. Ooh, here's an old one. A dime from 1953."

One after another, she handed them over. All had faces and profiles on one side and a variety of images on the other. All boasted dates that ranged from the mid-twentieth century to the early twenty-first.

"Wait," she said suddenly. "My phone." She reached for the object she had repeatedly used to try to *call nine one one* the day he had met her. Snatching it up, she clambered over her pile of belongings and settled herself close beside him.

"What are you doing?" he asked.

"Taking our picture. Now look at the phone and smile."

She pressed her cheek to his and held up the cell phone. A flash of light blinded him.

Blinking, he raised one hand and rubbed his eyes.

Beth lowered the phone, looked down at it, and touched its smooth surface.

She laughed. "I said smile, not frown."

Robert followed her gaze and felt his jaw drop. A miniature image of himself stared back, his cheek pressed to Beth's. Beth was grinning and looked adorable. He was scowling and looked suspicious. The image was as crisp and clean as the one on her I. D. And Robert had no explanation for how she could have created it other than the one she had given him.

Beth had traveled back in time.

All of these miraculous things that baffled and amazed him had been created in the future.

Beth wasn't mad. She really *had* come to him from the twenty-first century. A handful of coins cupped in his palm, Robert slowly met her gaze.

Her breath caught. "You believe me," she whispered.

"I believe you."

She rewarded him with a tight hug. "Thank you."

Closing his arms around her, Robert feared for a moment she might weep, but her eyes bore no tears when she released him.

The gaps where the edges of her robe did not quite meet widened as she settled herself once more at his side, leaning into him. Her hip pressed intimately against his, as did the length of her thigh. Tucking her small bare feet to the side, she tugged the hem of the robe down to cover them.

She seemed disinclined to talk for the moment. Mayhap she knew not what to say now that she had convinced him of the truth.

Robert retrieved her wallet and returned the coins to the pocket from which they had come. The zipper on this, though shorter, intrigued him no less than the one on her backpack, compelling him to unzip and zip it several times before setting it atop her breeches.

He was loath to part with her ID, though.

Glancing up, he caught her smiling at him. His fascination with zippers and other things she considered commonplace must amuse her.

He held up her portrait. Or rather her *photograph*. "May I keep this, Beth?"

Her gaze shifted to the license. "Sure. If you want to. I don't really need it anymore, do I?"

He looked from her to the photograph. "'Tis strange."

"The driver's license?"

"Nay. That you are here beside me, touching me, when you have not yet been born. 'Tis difficult to reconcile in my mind." He shook his head. "You will not be conceived until nigh eight hundred years from now, long after I am dead."

Her face clouded. "Neither will Josh. Or Marc. Or Grant." Her eyes darkened with either grief or defeat when they met his. "Losing Mom and Dad was hard. I didn't think anything would ever be that hard again. But now I've lost *everyone*. Everyone who was important to me. Everyone I considered family. My friends. My home. Everything that was familiar to me. It's all gone." She gave a disconsolate shrug. "What am I going to do, Robert? Where do I go from here?"

Troubled by her distress, he cupped her cheek in his rough palm. "Nowhere, Beth. Remain here at Fosterly and begin a new life with me."

Chapter Twelve

ETH'S HEART TURNED OVER IN her chest.

Robert's intense gaze held hers as he awaited her response. So much emotion swam within that cerulean blue. Understanding. Strength. A determination to protect her.

And no little desire.

The passion they had shared earlier that had temporarily been dampened as she had poured out her story now returned, growing and sparking between them as he caressed her face.

Dare she hope it might be fortified by something deeper? A hint of love perhaps? A tiny ember she might fan into flame?

What else would explain the faint shadow of vulnerability lurking behind the rest?

"You really mean that?" she whispered.

"Aye."

"What if I don't fit in? What if I screw up all the time and can't do things the way you do them here?"

His lips twitched. "I believe your greatest obstacle will be overcoming the language differences."

She pursed her lips and adopted an exaggerated Southern drawl. "So, what are ya sayin', I have an accent?"

"'Tis barely noticeable," he lied merrily.

"Or barely understandable," she corrected dryly, daring him to deny it. She knew her tendency to slip and use modern colloquialisms made it sound as though she spoke a foreign language.

"Wellll..."

She gave him a playful shove.

He laughed. "I think we understand each other well enough."

He actually *had* learned quite a few modern words since they had met.

Beth nibbled her lower lip. "Seriously, Robert. I don't think you understand how different life in my time is. How independent women are, and how much more control we have over our lives in the future. I may not know a lot about the history of England, but I know that the women of this time in general were totally dominated by the men and were little more than chattel. *Are* little more than chattel."

"Not in my family," he asserted without hesitation.

She tilted her head to one side. "What do you mean?"

"The men of my line have always admired intelligence and strength in a woman."

"You're not talking about Alyssa again, are you?" she grumbled.

His lips twitched. "Aye. She is strong, and wiser than anyone I know. And though she is wed to my brother and expected to obey him in all things, she has more control over her life and decisions than you may think."

"Not as much as *I* am used to experiencing, I'll bet."

He sobered. "I did not say 'twould be easy, Beth. Or immediate. Or that there would not, of necessity, have to be concessions made by both of us if you choose to begin a new life with me." Setting her license aside, he braced one hand on the bed behind her and leaned in close. "But would the reward not be worth a few compromises on both our parts?"

Heat bled into her back from his large, muscled arm.

Beth licked lips that suddenly felt too dry.

His eyes followed the motion of her tongue.

"Yes," she decided.

"Aye," he corrected, with affection, not censure.

"Aye." It was hard to think straight when he was so close and tempting.

"Then you will stay?" he asked, still staring at her lips with growing hunger.

"What if I can't?" she posed softly. "I don't know how I came to be here, Robert. I don't know what brought me here. What if whatever did it takes me back one day?"

Something dark flickered briefly in the gaze he raised to meet hers. "Then we shall revel in whatever time has been allotted us and not waste another moment of it."

Beth nodded, her pulse picking up. "If that's the plan," she whispered, "then you'd better hurry up and kiss me."

He did not hesitate to obey.

Combing the fingers of his free hand through her hair, he cupped the back of her head in his palm and lowered his head. His lips touched hers. Clung. Seduced. Sparked heat. Then withdrew.

Beth found it difficult to catch her breath as she looked up at him.

One masculine eyebrow rose.

She managed a slight nod. "That was great." Even to her own ears, her voice sounded husky. "Now do it again."

Laugh lines appeared at the corners of his eyes. Shifting slightly, Robert smiled. "I believe I am going to enjoy this independent spirit of yours."

"Remember you said that later," she advised, "when it makes you want to scream."

He leaned forward, hesitating when only an inch separated their lips. Those mesmerizing eyes of his were dark and stormy with desire. His nose brushed hers as their gazes met and held. Anticipation rose. A half inch closer. Mouths still not meeting. Tempting without touching. Teasing with the knowledge of what would come, what she would feel, until she could bear it no longer and moved the last fraction of an inch closer, pressing her lips to his and surrendering with a moan.

Lightning sizzled through Beth's veins, heating her blood and speeding her pulse until she thought her heart might burst. The things he did...

Parting her lips, he slipped his tongue inside to stroke and scintillate with heart-rending tenderness and a growing urgency that soon had precious parts of her body tingling and longing for his touch. *Never* had she been so turned on by a kiss. Never had she wanted so much more.

Just as she decided to throw her arms around him and climb onto his lap, he broke the kiss.

Her heart slammed against her rib cage as he shifted.

He gave the nape of her neck a last caress, then slid his hand around and down ever so slowly, pausing fractionally so his thumb could trace circles over the pulse that beat wildly at the base of her throat. Then that callused heat slipped beneath the neckline of her robe and eased it across her shoulder.

Beth followed his avid gaze, watched his tanned hand mold itself to her pale, lightly freckled skin, massaging gently, enthralling her with the difference in the texture of his skin and hers.

The robe slipped over his knuckles and fell almost to the bend of her elbow. Midnight material dipped low in front, baring the upper curve of one breast.

He stilled.

Beth did, too.

Then he moved those rough-to-the-touch fingers again, creating a delicious friction as he abandoned her shoulder and trailed a path of fire across her chest. He followed the line of her collarbone, fondling the faint hollow above it, then eased the robe lower.

Her whole body flushed with desire as he cradled her bare breast in his palm. Her breath caught as he gave it a squeeze.

His eyes rose, met hers, as his thumb brushed across the taut, rosy peak.

Gasping, she arched her back, leaning into his touch as sensation rocked her.

His voice, when he spoke, dropped an octave. "Mayhap tonight I will make *you* scream."

Excitement skittered through her. "Holy crap."

A devilish smile curled his lips as he eased her back on the bed, stretching out beside her. Cool air made her shiver when he bared her to her waist. Then all was forgotten in a rush of heat as Robert bent his head to her breast and laved the sensitive bud with his tongue.

Robert groaned as Beth's nails scored his scalp. Her body arched against him as he took the taut tip of one breast between his teeth and teased the other with deft fingers. Urging her onto her back, he rolled half on top of her and inserted a thigh between hers.

His tenuous control begin to weaken.

He should not be doing this. *They* should not be doing this. 'Twas beyond improper. And he did not wish to dishonor her.

Had he not harshly criticized Dillon for taking Alyssa to his bed outside of wedlock? How could Robert do the same with Bethany?

But she made it damned hard for him to resist the temptation. She made *him* damned hard.

And she has slept in your bed for a fortnight with none the wiser, a wicked voice reminded him.

Beth moaned when he transferred his lips to her other breast. Writhing in pleasure, she ground her hips against his arousal.

Robert ignited. His whole body burned with the need to possess her. To be inside her. His hands shook. His caresses grew bolder, rougher as he nearly tore the robe off of her in his desire to see more, to see all.

When she lay bare before him, Robert stared, awed, hardly able to draw breath. "You are beautiful, Beth."

So perfect. Soft, milky white skin dotted with pale freckles atop gentle ripples of muscle that flexed as she reached for him. No black scraps of material hid what he had spent far too many hours imagining. His hungry gaze devoured pink-tipped breasts that were surprisingly full for one with such a small frame. Beneath them, the ridges of a narrow rib cage led to an even narrower waist. Full hips spread beneath, bracketing a thatch of dark curls that beckoned him as water would a man in the desert.

He rose above her, eased his other knee between her thighs, urging her to spread them wider so he could settle himself in between. He sought her mouth with his own, plundering and consuming as his pulse pounded in his head. He was frantic for her, his hands roaming at will, too rough surely for an innocent.

But rather than frightening her, his passion merely seemed to inflame her.

Beth fisted her hands in his shirt. "Take it off," she demanded hoarsely. "I want to feel your skin against mine."

No sooner had she asked than 'twas done.

The coarse dark hair on Robert's chest abraded her sensitized nipples. Gasping, Beth wrapped her arms around him and explored the heavy muscle of his back with her fingers. He was so warm. Both hard and soft at the same time.

The flesh beneath her hands bunched and flexed as he slipped an arm beneath her shoulders to elevate her breasts. He took one tight, aching bud into his mouth, teased it with his tongue and his teeth.

It felt sooooo good.

The other he pinched and rolled between thumb and fingers, kneading the mound and sending shards of pleasure slicing through her.

Beth moaned his name, undulated beneath him, felt the long, hard length of his erection pressing against her core. She moved her legs restlessly against his as the burning ache inside her intensified, begging to be assuaged. She wanted more. She wanted all of him. Burned for him.

Stroking her hands down his back, she molded them to his muscled ass and squeezed, urging him against the heart of her.

He groaned. The hand at her breast tightened. Dizzying currents of sensation swept through her.

She couldn't think. Could only feel. Want. Need. More.

Too breathless to ask him to remove his braies and hose, she instead delved beneath them, smoothing her palms across bare skin. His lips left her breast and scorched a burning path down her stomach. His tongue dipped into her navel.

Then he rose and sat back on his heels between her legs. His hands stroked her thighs as his heavy-lidded gaze roved over her, arrayed before him like a banquet, as though he could not decide which morsel he wanted to sample next.

Beth said nothing, merely watched, panting, while he slipped off the bed long enough to remove the rest of his clothing. His thighs were thick with muscle and dusted with dark hair as she had known they would be. But what she really had been waiting to see made her eyes widen and diluted her rampaging desire with a trickle of unease.

The few glimpses R-rated movies had given her of full-frontal male nudity had never featured an aroused male. And even if they had, she suspected Robert would've outshone most of them.

She met his heated gaze. "Okay. Now I'm a little nervous."

"Then mayhap I should distract you."

Before she could register his words, he climbed back onto the bed, slid his arms beneath her knees, then bent his head and took her with his mouth. Pure, unbridled ecstasy raced through her. Closing her eyes, Beth buried her fingers in his hair and clung as he laved and sucked and teased, rushing her toward a first climax more intense than anything she could have imagined.

Her chest rising and falling with rapid breaths, she lay sprawled beneath him as he crept up her body, trailing kisses along the way.

Robert braced himself above her on his elbows, gently settling his weight upon her.

As heavy as he was, it should have been uncomfortable. But it felt good. Incredibly good.

She stared up at him, feeling dazed and sated, yet hungering for more.

He quirked an eyebrow. "Still nervous?"

A disbelieving laugh crossed her lips. "Hell, no!"

Chuckling, he pressed his lips to hers. "Only you could make me laugh while I am clinging to control by my fingertips."

"You are?"

He pressed a soft kiss to her lips. "Can you not feel me trembling?"

He was, she realized, amazed that she could affect him so strongly. His whole body practically vibrated with restraint.

She cupped his face in her hands. "Then take me, Robert. Make me yours."

A shudder rippled through him. His hands fisted in the covers on either side of her face. "I do not wish to hurt you."

"It's my first time. That's unavoidable. Besides…" She trailed a series of kisses along his deliciously stubbled jaw, then nibbled his earlobe. "I want to feel you inside me."

He surrendered with a groan, plundering her lips, then stimulating her anew with his talented hands and mouth.

She did feel pain when he entered her despite the care he took, but it faded quickly, eclipsed by the wonder of being joined with him so intimately. He moved inside her with long, slow strokes, rekindling the flames that had engulfed her earlier, then quickening his pace and fanning them higher until—clinging together, muscles straining—they reached the precipice.

Sheer ecstasy.

I'm so glad I waited, she thought as breath returned to her body and her pulse began to slow. *No one else could've made me feel like this.*

No one.

And she had had to travel back in time to find him.

When Robert shifted as though to move away, she hugged him tighter. "Not yet." She loved the feel of him against her, inside her.

He pressed a kiss to her forehead. "I'm too heavy for you." Locking his arms around her, he rolled them to their sides, bodies still joined.

Neither spoke.

Was he as stunned by what they had just shared as she was?

He combed his fingers through her damp hair and pressed another kiss to her forehead.

Beth didn't think she had ever felt so relaxed in her life.

And Robert seemed content to lie quietly with her snuggled up against him, lightly stroking her back, her arm, her hip.

As their passion cooled, so did her skin.

When a light shiver rippled through her, Robert raised his head and glanced toward their feet.

Beth did the same and took stock of the bed. Almost all of her belongings had been knocked to the floor. Though the two of them lay atop the rumpled covers, a blanket adorned the foot of the bed.

Reaching down, Robert drew it up and cocooned them in its warmth.

Beth closed her eyes and snuggled closer.

How had he come to mean so much to her in such a short amount of time?

And how much time would they have together?

She frowned. No. She wouldn't think about that. Not tonight.

Tonight she would just live in the moment and forget about tomorrow.

Sighing, she embraced the peace Robert inspired and let sleep claim her.

Beth awoke to Robert's chuckle rumbling in her ear.

"I already did," he murmured, his voice laced with amusement.

She smiled, eyes closed, head pillowed on his chest. "You already did what?"

"Showed you my sword." Amusement warmed his voice.

She laughed. "Robert, what are you talking about?"

"You were speaking in your sleep again."

She opened her eyes to near darkness. "I was?"

"Aye."

Shifting, she folded her hands atop his chest, then rested her chin on them so she could see his handsome face and tousled hair. "What did I say?"

His lips twitched. "You were begging me to show you my sword."

His sword?

When she realized where his thoughts lay, she grinned. "I did not!"

He laughed with obvious delight and drew her up until she covered him like a blanket. "I vow 'tis true."

"I did not beg you to show me your *sword*."

"You did." He winked devilishly. "And I told you I already had."

"No kidding," she drawled.

He rolled, taking her with him, until she lay beneath him.

Beth looped her arms around his neck and offered him a teasing grin. "If I'd known how well you wielded it, I would've asked to see it sooner."

He laughed again and pressed a quick, hard kiss to her lips before settling beside her once more and holding her close.

Beth decided there was nowhere else in the world she would rather be at that moment.

"I wish we could remain thus forever," he said softly, mirroring her thoughts.

"That's what your lips say, but the rest of your body is telling me you're ready to make love again." His arousal and the effect it had on her proved impossible to ignore.

"I believe now would be an appropriate time to tell you, sweetling—in order to avoid any confusion in the future, you understand—that I am *always* ready to make love to you."

She grinned up at him. "All I have to do is ask you to show me your sword?"

He laughed. "That would do, aye." His boyish smile softened. "But you are no doubt tender." She wrinkled her nose in protest. "So I should not."

"Yes, you should. You *really* should." Her smile faded as a thought intruded. "But not yet."

His gaze sharpened at the change in her tone.

Dread soured her stomach. "I need you to hold my hand while I do something I don't want to do."

He brushed his knuckles down her cheek. "What is it, love?"

"While you were gone, I tried to help your friends. The ones who were wounded."

His brow furrowed. "Sir Miles and Sir Winston?"

She nodded.

"Then you have my gratitude."

"Don't thank me yet," she protested. "All I did was clean their wounds as well as I could, stitch those that needed to be stitched, apply some honey and antibiotic ointment and bandages, and give them both some ibuprofen. I'm worried I might have done more harm than good. I've never even *seen* injuries like that before, Robert, let alone sewed them shut. What if I didn't do it right? Or what if I forgot something or did something I shouldn't have and… I don't know… made things worse?" She shrugged miserably. "I'm afraid to go down and find out."

"You did what you could for them, Beth. And, coming from where you do, from such an enlightened time, I am confident you did the right thing." Sitting up, he grasped both of her hands and brought them to his lips. "Come. Let us see how they fare."

While he donned his tunic and hose, she tugged on his robe. Everyone else in the castle was probably asleep, so she didn't think what she wore mattered as long as she was covered and warm. A pair of socks helped, but didn't completely insulate her feet from the frigid floor. Unfortunately, her boots were still wet from sitting in the rain, so socks would have to do.

Robert took her hand and led her from the room, down the stairs, and into the great hall.

They found the large open room deserted for the most part. Winston and Miles still lay on the table where she had left them. Someone had covered both with blankets and placed pillows beneath their heads. Most likely Mary, who had fallen asleep in a chair beside her husband.

Adam must have taken her request to guard the injured men seriously, for he sat in a chair on the opposite side of the table with his arms crossed over his broad chest, keeping watch. Michael and Stephen had joined him. But those two now sprawled on nearby benches, snoring.

Adam rose as they approached and bowed. If he was shocked by their appearance or her improper attire, he didn't show it.

Beth tightened her hold on Robert's hand and tried to smile, but doubted she hid her concern with any success. "How are they?"

"Sleeping soundly, my lady."

She studied the large, still forms with trepidation.

Robert moved to stand behind her, placing his hands on her shoulders.

When she glanced up, she saw his jaw clench as anger darkened his features. She hadn't asked him what had happened while he was off looking for the men responsible. But assumed that, since frustration rather than relief had marked his features upon his return, things had not gone well.

Reaching up, she covered one of his hands with her own, then turned her attention to Adam. "Are they *sleeping*," she asked, "or unconscious?"

Adam slid a covert glance Robert's way, as if he wasn't sure how blunt he should be. "Winston sleeps. Miles has not yet roused."

Fear and regret filled her. "You see?" she said, looking at Robert over her shoulder. "I did something wrong."

"Nay, Beth. Both men would be dead now had you not tended them so carefully. They look far better than when I last saw them."

"Aye," Adam inserted. "Michael was impressed by your efforts. And his dealings with Lady Alyssa have given him more knowledge of healing than anyone else here at Fosterly."

His words failed to ease her worry. Nothing short of both men recovering swiftly would do that.

"Thank you for watching over them, Adam," she said, though, appreciating it.

He nodded.

She looked to Winston's wife. "Do you think we should wake Mary and send her to bed? She looks really uncomfortable."

Adam shook his head. "I already tried. She will not leave his side, my lady."

Nodding, she looked up at Robert. "I wouldn't either if I were her."

Robert offered her a tender smile and gave her shoulders a squeeze. "Come, Beth. 'Tis late. You can do no more for them this night."

Nodding reluctantly, she turned away, then paused and looked back at Adam. "If anything happens... if they should get worse or... anything, please come and get me." Glancing around furtively, she leaned forward and whispered, "I'll be with Robert." And damned if she didn't feel a blush climb her cheeks.

His face impassive, Adam responded, "As you wish, my lady."

"Thank you."

Robert seconded her thanks as he wrapped an arm around her shoulders and steered her back the way they had come.

Robert woke Beth before dawn with a kiss, then lifted her into his arms.

She smiled, practically purring with contentment. "What are you doing?" she mumbled sleepily, snuggling against his chest as he carried her through the secret passage to her own chamber. "Still trying to preserve my reputation?"

"Aye," he admitted, lowering her with great reluctance to her cold bed. "Though I doubt we can fool them for long. My people have sharp eyes and possess an overabundance of curiosity."

"Particularly when it comes to their hero," she murmured, then shivered. "Come here and give me another kiss."

Grinning, he obliged.

It began simply, but she was so damned tempting that he could not seem to prevent himself from ravaging her lips with a hunger reminiscent of the long night they had just passed.

Until duty reasserted itself and forced him to draw back.

Beth moaned her disappointment. "Why don't you take your clothes off and join me? These sheets will get a lot warmer a lot faster if you and I create a little friction."

He laughed. "No doubt they would. But if I join you now, I will pass the day here. And I must leave."

"Leave?" He couldn't tell if her eyes reflected surprise or alarm. "You're leaving? Where are you going? How long will you be gone?"

Sitting on the edge of the bed, he took one of her hands in his. "There remains a threat to my people, Beth. I cannot rest until I have eliminated it. The attacks grow more frequent, more violent. And the man who launches them was not amongst those we fought last night. I must continue my search for him and end this ere more lives are lost."

"Oh." Sitting up, she shoved tangled curls back from her face. "I'll go with you, then."

He stared at her, horrified by the notion. "Nay!"

She rolled her eyes. "Robert, this is what I do—or *did*—in my other life, in my time, in the future. I tracked down criminals."

"And were nigh killed doing so," he reminded her.

"That was a freak, onetime thing."

"I care not. You will *not* accompany me."

"I'll be careful," she promised. "I'll wear my vest. I'll carry my weapons. I'll—"

"You will remain here within Fosterly's gates, where I know you will be safe," he intoned, unmoving.

She considered him a moment.

Did she think she could change his mind?

"Last night you said you *liked* my independent spirit," she reminded him.

"I do." Mayhap more than he should. "But indulging it in this instance would mean risking your life. You are neither proficient in our methods of fighting nor confident on the back of a horse. Should you need to flee swiftly, you would not be able to do so."

She smiled wryly. "In other words, I would be a liability."

He frowned. "A what?"

"A hindrance."

Aye, but he did not wish to say it and injure her feelings. So he shook his head instead. "I will not risk your coming to harm."

"Fine," she conceded grudgingly. "I won't go. *This* time. Just promise me you'll be careful."

He smiled. "I will."

She frowned, acquiring a rather adorable petulant expression. "What should I do while you're gone? I'm not used to being idle. If I hadn't been so busy obsessing over the whole time-travel thing the past couple of weeks, the sitting around doing nothing would've killed me."

He shrugged. "Do as you wish. I meant it when I said I want you to make Fosterly your home. Mayhap you would like to take command of the servants and put the kitchen in order. I know its current state displeases you, as does the fare. You have eaten little since your arrival."

"You can blame that on a fear of botulism."

Robert did not know what that meant, but suspected it again revolved around the state of either the kitchen or the fare. "You are welcome to make whatever changes you desire."

She chewed her lip. "*Any* changes? Really?"

"Any changes that do not involve moving stone," he cautioned, only half in jest. "I would prefer that my walls remain where they are." He could almost see her mind working as she considered the possibilities.

"Will the servants listen to me?" she asked. "I'm a complete stranger, after all."

"Of course they will. I shall ensure that they do ere I depart."

"And by *ensure* you mean what exactly?"

He grinned. "I will not beat them or threaten them, if that is what you are imagining in that violent mind of yours. I will simply inform them that they are to follow your orders as though they were my own and that by pleasing *you* they will please *me*."

Doubt pursed her lips. "That's it? Just *I want you to do what she tells you to* and they'll jump to do my bidding?"

"Aye."

"They don't even know me, Robert."

"They *will*. And, until they do, they know you are important to me."

Color crept into her cheeks. "You mean they know we, ah…"

"Made love?"

"Yes."

"Nay, sweetling. They do not, although I fear 'twill not remain a secret for very long."

"Then why would they think I'm important to you, if they don't know?"

He tucked a lock of sleep-snarled hair behind her ear. "Word of the embrace we shared last night in the bailey will have spread to every ear ere you have broken your fast."

"It was just a hug."

He raised her hand to his lips for a tender kiss. "Men and women of my time do not express affection so freely in the presence of others."

She snorted. "I beg to differ. A couple of nights ago on my way to the garderobe, I heard moaning coming from the shadows and—"

"Let me rephrase that," he hastened to interrupt. "Men and women of the *nobility* do not express affection for each other so freely. Even husbands and wives share only the most innocent of touches when not alone."

"Oh." A moment passed. "Does that mean your brother and his wife don't touch in public?"

He laughed. "They are an exception. Dillon has great difficulty keeping his hands off his sweet wife and has raised many an eyebrow—as well as inspired a number of tart criticisms and jealous murmurs from the women—with his open pursuit of her. Their circumstances are a bit different, however." The two were wed. And both were feared by so many that none would dare to openly criticize them.

Beth's brow puckered. "Should I not have hugged you like that last night, Robert?"

"What?"

"You said everyone is going to be talking about it, and that things are different with Dillon and Alyssa. I thought maybe you were trying to tell me that you didn't like it, or that I shouldn't do it again because—"

"Do it again," he inserted.

"What?"

Leaning forward, he pressed a warm kiss to her lips. "Do it again," he repeated softly. "I care not who approves or disapproves. Were I to receive such a greeting each time I returned home, I would forever be a happy man." While he thought it best to keep the people of Fosterly from knowing he had bedded her, he found himself unwilling to forgo *all* of her gestures of affection. He craved them too much.

"In that case," she murmured with a smile, "'twill be my pleasure."

He rewarded her with a longer, deeper, heat-inducing kiss that left them both groaning in frustration when he forced himself to pull away. "I must go."

She nodded, clinging to his hand a moment longer before releasing him. "Be careful."

"And you as well." Rising, he adopted a stern expression and pointed an authoritative finger at her. "Do not slay any of my people whilst I am away, my fair warrioress."

She responded with an exaggerated sigh of disappointment. "All right. If you insist."

Chuckling, he pulled the tapestry aside and slipped back to his room.

Chapter Thirteen

A S IT TURNED OUT, ROBERT had exaggerated the ease with which
Beth would begin her new life at Fosterly. She didn't think he had
done it on purpose. His expectations regarding his servants just
didn't pan out the way he had said they would.

Not that it really surprised Beth.

Robert seemed to have sincerely believed the servants would accede to
Beth's wishes and carry out her *requests* without questioning them or giving
her a hard time.

Unfortunately, that ended up being quite a miscalculation.

After Robert's departure, she rested for a couple of hours to make up for
a sleepless night of lovemaking.

No complaints there.

Then, wanting to make a good impression on the people of Fosterly,
she carefully donned more of Alyssa's clothing.

There were two parts to the gown, if that's what it was called. The first
was a fairly shapeless, cream-colored dress that was shaped like a great big
T. Beth pulled that on over her head, glad it was shapeless or she wouldn't
have been able to tug it down over her shoulders and hips. (She had taken
the stretchy materials of the twenty-first century too much for granted.)

Next came a rust-colored kirtle decorated with elaborate hand-stitched,
cream-colored embroidery. The sleeves fit fairly tight until halfway down
her forearm, then widened dramatically, falling almost to the floor. The
kirtle laced up the back like the others she had worn, necessitating the help
of a maid she flagged down outside her door. The hem fell to the tops of
her boots. A gold belt looped around her waist and hung low on her hips.

Though the overall effect was pretty, it really just made her miss her
comfy jeans and tank tops.

Once dressed, Beth made her way down to the kitchen, unsure what to expect.

It took her very little time to realize that Robert's servants fell into two categories. The majority of the servants were just as Robert had predicted—eager to please *him* by pleasing *her*. Admittedly, they were a bit wary of her differences, probably because she had made such a spectacle of herself that first day, crawling around looking for electrical outlets, but offered no complaints when she explained what she wanted to accomplish and how she would like them to help.

Her strange speech didn't seem to concern them overly. She had learned since arriving at Fosterly that, although the peasants spoke English, the nobility often spoke French, which seemed weird to Beth, considering they were in England. Apparently some members of the nobility—those who lived up to the ugly reputations given them by several of the period piece movies she had seen—refused to speak English at all, even if they knew it, causing communication problems for which the servants were more often than not blamed.

So the servants of Fosterly appeared pleased that she spoke English, albeit an English that was different from the one to which they were accustomed. She tried extra hard not to insert too many modern words, but still had to repeat herself periodically.

Beth didn't mind, as it helped her gain an even better grasp of Middle English. It was pretty fascinating, seeing just how much the English language had changed in eight hundred years.

Michael helped. He remained nearby all day. Beth didn't know if Robert had ordered him to watch over her or if Michael had volunteered for the duty, but she appreciated his attempts to help her convert modern to medieval slang whenever she slipped, if he understood it. The children were particularly tickled when such happened.

Enlisting their aid in correcting her pronunciation astounded, amused, and eventually made Beth's helpers warm right up to her. They even shared a few laughs over it.

Most of them did, anyway.

The second group of servants quickly became a problem.

There were only a handful of them, all women around Beth's age. In appearance, they ranged from average to pretty, tall to short, slender to plump. Vocally they ranged from stonily silent to obnoxiously outspoken. One characteristic they all shared, however, was their resentment of Beth and Robert's obvious affection for her.

The one Beth quickly came to think of as the leader of the group boasted long, dark blond hair, pale blue eyes, and substantial—if a bit saggy, despite her youth—breasts. Her name was Alice.

According to Michael, the kitchen was a relatively new structure that had been attached to the great hall shortly after Robert took command of Fosterly. The kitchen had formerly been located across the bailey, which made Beth think the inhabitants of the keep must not have had many hot meals if the servants had been forced to lug the food that distance through snow and rain.

Beth considered the kitchen's being a new addition something of a blessing. She hated to think of the sooty, grimy buildup that would have covered its walls and surfaces if it were as old as the rest of the keep.

Not that it was filthy. It just really needed a good scouring with modern disinfectant cleaners.

Since those were not available, she ordered all supplies and foodstuffs removed to the great hall until the walls, floors, tables, stools, cauldrons, kettles, utensils and everything else the kitchen contained could be scrubbed thoroughly with the harshest soap available. Most of the men, women, and children were busily engaged in doing just that when a spate of harsh, angry whispers sounded behind her.

The room abruptly went silent.

Beth looked up from the sack she had been hesitantly peering into, hoping she wouldn't find any rodents or insects peering back, and found herself surrounded by an exhibition of statues and statuettes whose eyes regarded her with varying degrees of shock and horror.

"What?" As she glanced at the frozen faces around her, their gazes slid away from hers. "What did I miss?"

"'Tis naught to concern yourself with, my lady," Maude, a plump woman who looked to be in her fifties, offered briskly. Maude had behaved in a warm, almost motherly fashion toward Beth from the instant they had met, bustling around and directing the servants in carrying out her wishes.

Now displeasure pinched her round, time-worn features as she glared at Alice.

Beth looked at the troublesome blonde, whose stance screamed stubborn defiance, then back at Maude. "You want to tell me what's going on?"

"As I said, my lady, 'tis naught. Some here do not know their place is all."

Alice muttered something beneath her breath that made her comrades snicker. A little boy near her gasped and stared at Beth with wide eyes. Michael straightened away from the wall he had been propping up, his eyebrows lowering in a suspicious frown.

Her hackles rising, Beth crossed to stand a few feet in front of the much taller woman. "I didn't quite catch that. Would you care to repeat it?"

Lips clamped shut, Alice glared at her mutinously. Unbridled anger oozed from her sapphire gaze. That and a certain grating smugness.

"If you have something to say to me," Beth told her, "I suggest you say it to my face instead of behind my back like a coward."

"I am no coward!" the woman hissed, swallowing the bait. "I said I know my place and 'tis not serving Lord Robert's whore!"

Michael lunged forward with a furious growl.

Beth planted a hand on his chest before he could storm past her. "Let me handle this, Michael." She kept her tone neutral, her expression calm and her manner unruffled, though she snarled and growled a bit on the inside.

Keeping her gaze on Alice, she raised a brow. "Excuse me?"

An unattractive sneer twisted the woman's face. "All here know you share his bed."

"Really," Beth commented, letting her tone drop on the second syllable. "Well, since I'm pretty sure the earl doesn't invite you all to sleep in his chamber every night, I suppose that means you can see through wood and stone? Or do you forego sleep and keep your ear pressed to his door instead?"

"We need not be there to know 'tis true," Alice declared disparagingly. "We have all seen the way you throw yourself at him like a camp follower. 'Tis obvious he was bedding you long afore you arrived at Fosterly."

"You deceitful slut!" Maude shouted furiously. "'Tis not true and you know it! She was a virgin ere last night! You saw the sheets yourself!" As soon as the words left her lips, the older woman gasped and clamped a hand over her mouth. "Oh! Forgive me, my lady. I did not mean... I only thought to... Oh, dear!"

Michael groaned.

Lovely. Beth had never tried so hard in her life to suppress a blush. "Be that as it may, what business is it of yours, Alice?"

The blonde's face darkened as Beth continued.

"Lord Robert is the earl. Fosterly is his. And all who inhabit it are subject to his authority. Is that not correct?"

"You have it aright, my lady," Michael spoke behind her, barely restrained by the hand she still pressed to his chest.

"Lord Robert asked me to set his kitchen to rights," Beth said. "He also said that *my* will is *his* will and that to please *him*"—she took a step forward and stared Alice directly in the eye, uncaring that she had to look up to do so—"you will have to please *me.*"

"You will not last!" Alice screeched. "You will never please him the way I do. He will tire of you quickly. Then he will come back to me. He *always* comes back to me!"

A fist fastened itself around Beth's heart and slowly began to squeeze.

Alice and Robert had been lovers?

Michael took a step closer, ready to interfere. "You *dare* to—!"

"Shut up, Michael. I'm handling this," Beth snapped, then gritted her teeth. *Damn it. Don't show any reaction. Don't let her see that she's rattled you.*

And she had. Vivid images of Robert and Alice making love filled her mind as a primitive urge to do violence rose up within her.

Jealousy, rage, and insecurity all buffeted her as she stood there, outwardly impassive.

Wait a minute. What was she doing, taking this woman's word that Robert had slept with her? Josh had taught her better than that.

While all of the other occupants of the kitchen waited amidst a fascinated hush, Beth examined Alice and the situation as objectively as possible, then drew the only conclusion she could, knowing Robert as she did.

Her eyes on Alice, Beth shook her head, a slow, steady wagging from side to side. One corner of her lips she lifted in a patronizing smile as she released Michael and folded her arms across her chest. When next she spoke, she infused her words with condescending amusement. "You've never shared Robert's bed."

Alice's lips tightened. "I have. Lord Robert has sought me out many ti—"

"Not even once," Beth interrupted. "You're not his type."

Michael grunted. "Aye. Lying bitches in heat do not appeal to him."

Male laughter and female giggles and snickers filled the room.

Alice's face twisted with rage as she leapt forward.

Beth didn't know who the intended target was—herself or Michael. She simply reacted according to all of the self-defense drills Josh had put her through.

Dodging to one side, Beth grabbed Alice's wrist, knocked her off-balance, and—seconds later—pinned her to the floor, facedown, with one arm twisted up behind her back and Beth's foot planted firmly between her shoulder blades.

While their audience gaped, Alice struggled in vain for several seconds, most likely believing her size would give her the advantage, then subsided as Beth forced the woman's captive arm up a fraction higher.

Alice whimpered.

Not even out of breath, Beth frowned at their astonished audience. "Everybody out."

After an instant's pause, a stampede ensued, leaving her alone with her antagonist and Michael, whose mouth hung open.

"Michael, would you give us a minute, please? We need to have a little talk."

He closed his mouth, but made no move to leave.

"We'll be fine," she coaxed. "I promise."

He frowned. "I shall be right outside the door should you need me."

"Thank you. I appreciate that."

Beth contemplated Alice's messy hair for a long minute after he left. "I'm going to let you up now. But if you give me any trouble—I mean *any* trouble—I will take you right back down again. Do you understand me?"

No response.

With a mental shrug, Beth released her hold on Alice and backed away.

The other woman lurched to her feet, stumbled once, then spun around and glared at Beth while she rubbed her aching shoulder.

"I'm going to give you a little advice," Beth began, "that is frequently passed around where I come from. You would do well to keep it in mind." She would have to clean it up a bit, but the message should get across all the same. "You shouldn't provoke people. You never know who you might be dealing with."

The woman's scowl deepened.

Beth rolled her eyes. "Look, I have neither the need nor the desire for enemies, Alice. Your name *is* Alice, isn't it?"

Again, no response.

"I have enough problems as it is," Beth continued. "I don't need *you* causing more. Now, I don't blame you for wanting Robert. I really don't. I am well aware of his appeal and his many good qualities. But I want to make this perfectly clear to you." She took a step forward. "You *cannot* have him," she declared, voice stony. "He's mine."

Boy, it felt good to say that. So good that she decided to say it again. "Robert is mine. Whatever happens between us in the future is exactly that... *between us.* Just him and me. If you or any other woman who has her eye on him—don't think I haven't noticed that there are several of you—ever try to deceive us or come between us with schemes or bullshit lies like this again, I will have no other choice but to grind you into the dirt."

Her tone left no doubt that despite her diminutive size, she would have little difficulty doing so if challenged.

Alice's scowl shifted into a worried pucker of her brow. "How did you know?" she asked with a hesitance she hadn't displayed earlier.

"Know what? That you and Robert have never been lovers?"

"Aye. Even those who live here were uncertain."

Beth shrugged. "I just knew. Why did you lie and say you were?"

Alice cast the doorway an uneasy glance.

"It's all right. No one is listening." She had sparked Beth's curiosity now.

"The men mock me," Alice admitted uncomfortably. "As do some of the women. Because of my height. I thought they would cease if Lord Robert showed an interest in me or if I could at least make them *think* he did." Her gaze fell. "It worked for a time, but then you came and their taunts grew worse."

Beth sighed. She could see the men making Alice miserable for being taller than they were. And there were always petty, malicious people who enjoyed saying nasty things about others because of differences in their appearance. Beth had been ridiculed herself often enough to know the hurt such could generate. During her childhood and adolescence, she had been made fun of for being short, pale, freckled, and more. To this day, she did not understand people who had to jeer at and look down on others in order to feel good about themselves.

She never would.

"Okay, here's the deal," she announced. "If you intend to continue whispering behind my back, glaring, sulking, scheming and turning your friends against me, or if you *ever* try to seduce Robert, then I will kick your ass out of here, because I do *not* need the headache. And by *here* I mean Fosterly. I don't want to see you in the keep. I don't want to see you in the inner bailey. And I would rather not see you in the village. *If*, on the other hand, you cut the crap and start anew, just do your job and don't give me any grief, then you are welcome to stay."

"But what of my punishment? I shamed you in front of the others." Her nose and eyes reddened. "Will you have me whipped?"

"Whipped?" Beth repeated, appalled. "Hell, no!" *Sheesh.* She couldn't believe she was actually starting to feel sorry for the woman, but damned if Alice didn't look like she was struggling not to cry.

Beth frowned. Hadn't Michael mentioned something about the previous owner of Fosterly treating the servants harshly? And that a lot of them had died because of it?

Had the bastard actually whipped women for mouthing off?

"Why don't we just start with a public apology?" Beth proposed.

Alice lifted a hand to wipe her nose, and Beth realized that the obnoxious, contemptuous act she had put on earlier had been precisely that—an act. "As you wish."

Beth turned to the doorway. "Michael—"

"I shall send them in right now," he said, out of sight.

She closed her mouth and looked at Alice. "Do you think he heard it all?"

Alice nodded miserably.

Ignoring the stares of the servants who shuffled back into the room, Beth swiftly thought back over their conversation, recalled all of the things she had said about Robert, and wished she could go back to bed and start the whole day over again.

Since she couldn't, she simply avoided looking at Michael, who was the last to reenter.

When everyone had reclaimed their former positions, keeping their distance from Alice this time, Beth did not have to say a word.

Alice dropped to her knees and bowed her head. "My lady, I do beg your forgiveness." Beth opened her mouth to grant it, but the woman spoke again before she could. "I did shame you by calling you whore, not because I believed 'twas true—for I know otherwise—but because I was jealous of the affection Lord Robert holds for you, an affection that I admit he has never bestowed upon me, though I have led many to believe so. I was angry from the taunts I have suffered since your arrival and ashamed of the lies I have told. I should not have sullied your name when 'tis clear you make him happy. I vow I will never speak against you again and do humbly beg your forgiveness."

Speechless, Beth stared at the top of the woman's bent head.

Wow. She had expected a quick, grudging, *Sorry I called you a whore* and had gotten quite an impressive speech instead. Alice must feel thoroughly humiliated and know good and well that the taunts she had endured during the past few days were nothing compared to those she would be subjected to when all of this became common knowledge.

"Thank you, Alice." Beth smiled as the woman rose. "That is the nicest apology I have ever received."

Alice bobbed a curtsy.

A snide male voice spoke behind Beth. "I knew Lord Robert would not take up with a behemoth like her." Several snickers followed.

Alice's face flushed crimson.

Beth swung around furiously. "*Hey!*"

Everyone jumped and stared at her, wide-eyed.

"I do not want to hear *one* more word spoken about this, not to me and not to her," Beth ground out. "Anyone who does will have to scrub every garderobe in the castle from top to bottom. Is that understood?"

In the blink of an eye, the smirking audience turned into bobble-head figures, hastily nodding their agreement.

Beth gave them a curt nod of her own. "Good. Now let's get back to work."

It took a while, but eventually conversation began to flow once more as hands resumed lifting and scrubbing.

Few spoke to Alice.

Those who did were careful not to taunt her.

Strolling over to Michael, Beth decided to help him prop up the wall for a few minutes while she considered how she might extract a promise from him not to repeat what he had witnessed. It took her several minutes to gather the nerve to glance up at him.

When she did, she groaned.

He was grinning from ear to ear.

"So help me, if you say one word to Robert about all of this, I will—"

"Grind me into the dirt?" he suggested cheerfully.

"Aye," she growled.

He laughed. "Fear not, my lady. If 'tis your wish, I will not inform Lord Robert that *he is yours.*"

Groaning again, she covered her face with her hands.

Robert whistled a cheerful ditty as he entered the bailey, his spirit lighter than it had been in some time, despite his inability to locate his enemy. Another fortnight had passed, and no further attacks had ensued, leaving him with the hope that Michael and Stephen had been right and his enemy had moved on.

Work on the outer wall progressed rapidly.

Davey was up and walking about.

Sir Miles and Sir Winston had both survived their wounds and were slowly recovering as well.

And somewhere in the keep before him, he would find the woman who had brought joy and passion back into his life.

A roar of masculine laughter swelled on the air, echoing off the stone walls.

Pausing, Robert glanced around, seeking its source.

All was as it should be. No men loitered anywhere that he could see in groups large enough to have created such a ruckus.

Curious, he continued on toward the practice field.

Another roar of laughter buffeted him.

Cupping his hand above his eyes to shield them from the sun, Robert looked up at the men atop the curtain walls. Not only were they not laughing, they, too, seemed to search for the source of it.

A stern frown sent them hieing back to their posts.

When Robert reached the practice field, he found it deserted.

His captain slumped on a bench against the keep, glowering fiercely and muttering to himself.

"Why are the men not training?" Robert demanded, bearing down on him.

"Lady Bethany called them away," the burly warrior spat, obviously furious at having had his authority usurped by a woman.

"All of them?"

"Aye."

"For what purpose?"

"I told her the men would be at her disposal once their training was done for the day, that the threat remained and the men must be ready to defend the keep."

"For what purpose?" Robert repeated.

"'Twas women's work, I told her! Not fit for a man's attention, not when he has training to complete! But she would hear none of it."

"For. What. Purpose?" Sooner or later the words would penetrate.

"I thought she understood when she left, but here she came, dragging a blanket piled high with the men's gear, determined to toss it into the moat if they did not—"

"*Faudron!*"

His captain jumped. "Aye, my lord?"

"Where is Lady Bethany?"

"Entertaining the men in the north tower."

Fury struck like lightning. Grabbing Faudron by the throat, Robert hoisted him off the bench and shoved him back against the wall.

Face mottling, eyes bulging, the man struggled to get his next words out before he suffocated. "N-not *that* kind of entertaining."

Robert drew him forward, then slammed him against the wall again.

"C-cleaning!" Faudron sputtered. "Cleaning, my lord."

Irritated beyond belief, Robert opened his fists and let the man drop down onto the bench again. "Explain."

Coughing, Faudron complied. "She is forcing the men to clean the north tower, my lord. Called it a filthy pig sty and insisted that if they left it for *her* to do, she would toss aught she found lying on the floor into the moat. The men did not take her seriously until she began to do just that."

"The men ignored her request?" Robert found himself torn between anger that the men had disobeyed her and dismay that she had asked them to abandon their training for so trivial a task.

"I, ah, did not think you would wish them to cease their training and, ah…," the man stammered, searching for an answer that wouldn't increase Robert's ire.

Shaking his head, Robert turned and started toward the north tower. "Never show her disrespect again, Faudron, or you shall answer to me."

"Aye, my lord." The man did not sound thrilled by the notion.

As Robert approached the open doorway of the tower, another wave of laughter poured through it. A couple of men lingering outside grinned and nudged each other until they caught sight of the approaching earl. Then, smiles vanishing, they bowed and hurried away.

Frowning, Robert slowed his pace and actually found himself slinking closer to the wall outside the doorway so those inside would not see him.

"Give us another, my lady!" a boisterous male voice called out. 'Twas one of Robert's more spirited knights, young and having only recently earned his spurs.

Several others seconded his plea.

Give them another what?

"Where should I put this, my lady?" a quieter voice asked near the entrance. Hugh.

"What is it?" he heard Beth respond.

"'Tis my favorite tunic," Hugh answered as though 'twas obvious.

"That's a tunic?"

"Aye. My youngest sister made it for me."

"Awwwww. That's so sweet. Put it in the to-be-washed pile. We'll see about mending it once it's clean."

"My thanks."

"Sure." Beth raised her voice over the din. "I don't know, guys. I think maybe I should stop."

Vociferous complaints erupted.

"Seriously," she spoke above them. "I don't think spouting dirty limericks could exactly be considered proper behavior for a lady."

Dirty limericks? What were *dirty limericks?* And why would she think reciting them improper?

His men evidently saw naught amiss with it, because they all denied any impropriety and begged her to continue.

"Are you sure?" she asked next. "I know you're bored, but I don't want to do aught that might make Robert angry. And some of these are quite…" She emitted a little huff of frustration. "What's the word I'm looking for?"

Beth had confessed that she sometimes had difficulty finding the *medieval equivalent* of some of her *modern* words. Robert aided her whenever he could, committing her peculiar words and phrases to memory and using them himself on occasion. He wished to do aught he could, after all, to make her feel more comfortable in this place and time.

"Bawdy?" Marcus suggested.

Robert's eyes widened. She was telling his men bawdy tales?

"I was going to say crude," Beth murmured, "but bawdy might cover it." She spoke louder so the others could hear her. "Don't you think these limericks are too bawdy? I don't want to upset Robert."

A brief moment of silence ensued that led Robert to believe they were clearly misleading her and having second thoughts about it. Then they jumped in as one and insisted he would approve.

Robert's eyes narrowed as he crossed his arms over his chest.

Just how bawdy were these tales? Surely his men would do naught to incur his wrath.

"All right, all right," she laughingly agreed. "Let me see if I can remember another one."

A couple of quiet minutes passed, accompanied by assorted rustling sounds and occasional whispered comments.

"Okay, I've got one," she announced.

A loud cheer split the air.

"Tell us! Tell us!" the men chanted.

Beth laughed. "Okay. But before I do, you need to know that *Stormy Weather* is the name of a song."

"Will you sing it for us, my lady?" one man called.

"Maybe in a fortnight when you clean this place up again," she said not unkindly, eliciting many a groan. "Oh, and brass is a metal. I haven't seen any here, so I wasn't sure you knew that. Come here, Marcus. I need you to translate a word for me. What do you call…?"

A split second later, Robert heard his squire sputter and cough. "My lady!"

"Look how red the boy's face is!" someone belted out with glee.

"Aye! 'Twill be a good one, I vow!"

"My lady," Marcus whispered desperately, "I cannot."

"Sure you can. If I don't use the right term, they won't get it."

"Lord Robert would geld me if he knew I discussed such with you!"

Exactly what word did she seek?

Though curiosity begged him to wait and see, Robert opted to save his squire further embarrassment.

Assuming a foreboding expression, he stepped into the doorway.

Seated upon a tall stool just inside the doorway of the north tower, Beth felt a shadow fall across her. Turning, she smiled as her heart leapt. "Robert!"

Hopping off the stool, she took two steps toward him, then noticed his expression.

Uh-oh. He looked rather displeased. Had he heard one of the dirty limericks?

Behind her, the knights quieted and anxiously stood at attention.

Robert raised one eyebrow, daring one and all to offer an explanation.

"Um…" Without looking at Robert's men, Beth flung one arm out and pointed at them. "They made me do it."

Gasps ricocheted through the room.

Beth peeked over her shoulder to gauge the reactions of the accused. The looks of shock and abject horror that painted the men's rough faces were absolutely priceless.

She burst into laughter. "I'm just kidding, you guys."

"Jesting, my lady," Marcus corrected softly, his gaze darting back and forth between her and Robert.

"Jesting," Beth amended, waving her hand at the men, who seemed uncertain how to react. "I'm just jesting. You guys should see your faces. It's hilarious."

Still chuckling, she strolled forward, slid her arms around Robert's waist and leaned into him. There was nothing sexual in the gesture. Just another expression of affection that probably astounded all present. "It was me," she admitted freely, rocking slightly from side to side. The glint of amusement she saw enter Robert's eyes confirmed her guess that he wasn't truly angry. "I was desperate to get them to clean this place up and thought it might distract them. Although they *did*," she said, raising her voice, "assure me that all was good and proper."

Robert closed his arms around her and locked his hands at the base of her spine. "I suspect you knew otherwise."

She winked. "Guilty as charged. I missed you today." Rising onto her toes, she kissed his chin. "Did you miss me?"

A smile tugged at his lips. "Aye."

"Good." She lowered her voice so that only he would hear her. "I'm sorry, Robert. I know it wasn't proper. But this place was a real health hazard. When I walked past it earlier, I almost gagged at the stench. Something had to be done. And the men were whining so much about having to clean up their own mess and doing what they considered women's work that I had to hurry and distract them before I gave in to the desire to strangle them all."

"Why did you not simply assign some of the women from the castle to…" He trailed off when she narrowed her eyes.

She had fielded that question far too often today. "Because there is absolutely no reason these men can't pick up after themselves. They're not children, for crying out loud. Besides, I was afraid any women I sent in here would end up with their skirts tossed over their heads."

"*You* are a woman, are you not?" he asked, his expression unreadable.

"Aye, but we both know none of them would dare touch me. And as you can see, my skirts are still down around my ankles." Her voice sank to a whisper. "Plus, if anyone ever *did* try aught, I would totally kick his arse."

"*I* know that. *Others* do not."

She frowned. "What do you mean? Someone might actually think the men have been in here gangbanging me all afternoon?" She kept forgetting that appearances meant everything here. "Well, it doesn't matter anyway, because here everyone already thinks I'm a—" She broke off, remembering that he didn't know about the whole *whore* thing.

He frowned. "A what?"

"Nothing. I mean, naught." Alice had done a complete turnaround since the kitchen incident, going out of her way to help Beth despite the continued ribbing and belittlement of her peers. The two of them were actually becoming friends. Beth didn't want to get her into trouble, so she changed the subject. "Hey, while you're looking all fierce and murderous, would you order the men to finish their cleaning so we can sneak off and be alone together?"

"You would not perchance be attempting to distract me, would you?"

"I would," she conceded. "I have been indulging in some very imaginative fantasies about you today, and thought maybe we could try a few of them out."

Robert scowled over her head. "Finish the task she has set before you."

Beth whispered, "And repeat it every fortnight."

"And repeat it every fortnight," he ordered.

No one protested, though Beth suspected he would hear a few grumbles tomorrow.

"You're wonderful," she praised him with a smile.

"I know."

Beth laughed. Releasing him, she tucked one of her small hands into his and faced the men. "It's been fun, guys. I had a great time getting to know you all and shooting the breeze with you today. There isn't a single one of you that I don't like."

Uncertain of Robert's mood and whether or not there would be ramifications later for misleading her, the men all offered tentative smiles.

And, of course, she thought many of those smiles also held a good bit of confusion over her peculiar words. But they seemed to glean her meaning.

"See you later." Beth drew Robert out of the tower and led him across the bailey, swinging their linked hands between them. "I'm sorry."

"For what?"

Squinting against the descending sun, she sent him a wry smile. "I'm never going to fit in around here, am I? I keep forgetting the rules."

He shrugged. "You shall learn them all in time. And once you have, I shall be endlessly entertained, watching you choose which ones you will follow and which you will discard."

Shouldn't he be more concerned than that? "You won't be angry if I decide to buck the system every once in a while? You won't send me packing?"

The pause that followed, she felt, was due more to his need to decipher her meaning than think through his answer.

"Nay, Beth, my feelings for you are not contingent upon you obeying

216

the rules." He smiled and raised her hand to his lips for a kiss. "And I shall only become angry if you place yourself in danger."

She grinned up at him. "So, you like me a little, do you?"

"More than a little."

Good. Because she was crazy about him. "You know what?"

"What?"

"I'll bet Edward could scare up enough hot water for a bath if we asked him nicely."

His eyes sparkled with interest. "Could he now?"

She nodded. "Of course, there probably won't be enough to fill two tubs, so we would have to share."

"With the right incentive, I believe I could resign myself to such a fate," he murmured thoughtfully.

"The right incentive, huh? How about…" Beth stopped. Moving in close, she slid her hands up his chest, over his shoulders and into his hair. "This?"

Robert's heart stuttered as Beth rose onto her toes and fastened her lips to his in a kiss so rife with hunger that he forgot they were standing in the middle of the bailey. Locking his arms around her, he dragged her against him and lost himself in the feel of her. Her warm, slick tongue stroked his own. Her full breasts teased his chest. Her fingers clenched in his hair. And her hips…

Cupping the back of her head with one hand, Robert slid the other down to urge her hips closer and assuage the ache she inspired.

"Ahem." Something thumped Robert's shoulder. Hard.

Reluctantly abandoning Beth's sweet lips, he raised his head. Michael's back swam into focus. Apparently he had bumped into them on his way to…

Actually Michael did not seem to have any particular destination in mind. Why had he bumped them?

Blinking, Robert glanced around and gradually became aware of the gaping stares directed their way by virtually every man, woman, and child in the bailey. A quick look up confirmed the avid interest of the guards atop the walls. Even the hounds that had been romping with the children seemed to have paused in their play long enough to goggle.

Beth's face flushed a bright red.

"We seem to have attracted a bit of attention," he understated.

"Believe it or not, I only meant to give you a quick kiss."

Robert smiled. "If you think I am objecting, you are mistaken, love."

"Really?" She plucked at the front of his tunic. "You aren't angry?"

"Shall I repeat what I have already told you? I care not who approves or disapproves. Were I to receive such a greeting each time I returned home, I would forever be a happy man."

Pursing her lips, she cast him a flirtatious look. "But you would be happier if we were both naked in a bath, right?"

Robert groaned and laughed at the same time. "Unless you wish me to take you here before all of Fosterly, sweetling, I suggest you restrain that wicked tongue of yours."

"I will do aught with my wicked tongue that you request," she countered in a sultry voice, nigh making his knees buckle with the passionate images her words evoked.

Latching onto her hand, Robert practically ran up the stairs to the keep, her light laughter following and making him grin.

A resounding cheer followed them through the huge double doors.

"I could be wrong," Beth proclaimed breathlessly as they raced up the narrow stairs inside, "but I think they may know what we have in mind."

Robert laughed, feeling lighter and younger than he had in years. At the top of the steps, he swept Beth into his arms and claimed another kiss.

A kiss that didn't end as he staggered down the corridor, trying to carry her and fondle her at the same time, the lust she incited robbing him of his usual finesse.

Never had he been so frantic with need.

He groaned when she eagerly wrapped her legs around his waist and locked her ankles behind his back. His mouth never leaving hers, Robert pressed her up against the wall just outside the solar and supported her weight with one arm. The other hand he slipped up between them to knead one full, tempting breast.

Beth moaned, tightening her thighs around him and urging him to rock against her. "Off," she whispered raggedly, tugging on his tunic. "I want it off. All of it. Now."

Pushing away from the wall, Robert carried her inside his chamber and kicked the door closed behind them. Their laughter resurfaced, shaky with passion now, as he set her down and they began to fumble with each other's clothing, their hands clumsy in their haste. When both at last were naked, he urged her back onto the bed, then slipped his hands beneath her knees and dragged her back toward him until her bottom rested near the edge of the soft mattress. For many long seconds, he stood staring down at her, his hands kneading her spread thighs, his chest rising and falling swiftly.

Finally, Beth said hoarsely, "Robert, if you don't touch me soon, I'm going to scream."

She almost *did* scream when he gave her a heated smile, knelt on the soft rushes at his feet and buried his face in the soft curls at the juncture of her thighs. Moaning, she sank her fingers into his hair and clenched them into fists while he laved the tiny hidden nub with his tongue. She tasted so good. Was so passionate. So eager for him, crying out as a first climax overtook her.

Her breath still came in gasps as Robert rose above her.

Her beautiful breasts beckoned. Fastening his lips on her breast, he sucked hard, nipping her with his teeth.

She moaned.

He guided her legs around his waist once more, his body trembling with need. Every muscle was taut. And he clutched her so tightly he feared she would have bruises the next day.

When he reached between them and positioned himself at her entrance, she increased the pressure of her legs and drew him in.

He groaned, burying his face in her neck as he sank into her. "Do you know how good this feels?" he asked hoarsely.

She nodded, her hands roving his back.

Unable to remain still any longer, Robert began to move. Long, deep strokes he mimicked with his tongue as he claimed her lips and teased her breasts with rough hands, driving her swiftly toward a second climax.

"Robert!" she cried.

"More," he growled.

And the pleasure began anew.

Chapter Fourteen

A PERSISTENT POUNDING ON THE DOOR heralded the dawn and roused Robert from a sound sleep.

Beside him, Beth stretched, then settled back into slumber. Content to join her, he cuddled her close and sighed.

Boom! Boom! Boom! "My lord?"

Robert groaned.

"I don't think he's gonna to go away," Beth mumbled.

"My lord?" Marcus called.

Boom! Boom! Boom!

Growling epithets, Robert threw back the covers and lunged out of bed. Beth squealed when the icy morning air hit her sleep-warmed skin.

Laughing, he tossed the blankets over her head, then drew the bed curtains closed and called to his squire to enter.

"Forgive me, my lord," Marcus said upon entering. His gaze darted to the concealed bed and back again as he closed the door behind him. "A missive has arrived."

Robert crossed to his trunk and retrieved his braies. "From?" he asked as he donned them.

"Terrington. The messenger insisted it be brought to you at once."

As Robert reached for the rolled parchment, Beth poked her head through an opening in the curtains, clutching them closed beneath her chin. "Good morning, Marcus," she offered with a cheerful smile.

Marcus jumped and lowered the scroll, his head whipping in Beth's direction. Face flushing, he bowed. "Good morrow, my lady."

"Would you do me a huge favor and light a fire in the hearth? It is frrrreezing in here!"

"At once, my lady." Tossing the missive to Robert, Marcus hurried to the hearth and began to carefully construct what Robert guessed would be a great, roaring conflagration.

Robert glanced over at Beth and fought a smile.

Her hair was loose and adorably mussed from sleep, her eyelids a little heavy. The many kisses they had shared the previous night had left her lips puffy and rosy. The coarse stubble that coated his own jaw had abraded hers enough to leave it a bit pink.

Just the sight of her made his heart light.

Forcing a frown, he nodded his head toward Marcus, whose back was to them, and motioned for her to duck back behind the curtains. Even though her head was the only thing visible, he did not want any other male to see her so enchantingly disheveled.

A teasing glint entered her warm hazel eyes. Glancing at Marcus to confirm he couldn't see her, she suddenly flung the curtains wide, giving Robert a thrilling look at her beautiful bare body bathed in the morning sunlight that sifted into the room, then yanked the curtains closed again.

Robert laughed silently as she tucked the heavy material beneath her chin, her face alight with amusement and feigned innocence.

Setting the missive down on his trunk, Robert quietly crossed to the bed.

Beth grinned up at him, daring him to do he-knew-not-what.

Grinning back, he palmed her face and gave her a little push that sent her tumbling backward amidst blankets and giggles.

Ensuring no gap remained in the curtains, he returned to his trunk and grabbed a linen shirt. Marcus, he noticed as he tugged the material down over his head, concentrated overmuch on his task, adding to Robert's amusement.

"Robert?" Beth called sweetly.

He could not seem to stop smiling this morn. "Aye?"

"May I please borrow your robe?"

"For what reason?"

"I'm awake. I may as well get up."

"'Twould be best if you remain where you are until my squire has left the chamber."

Marcus rose. "Shall I leave now, my lord?"

"Nay. Stay until I have read the missive."

Beth cleared her throat pointedly. "The robe, Robert?"

Sighing with exasperation, Robert retrieved his robe and strode to the side of the bed that was hidden from Marcus's view.

One of Beth's pale hands extended through a gap in the curtains.

Instead of placing the soft material in it, Robert took her hand in his and pressed a kiss to her palm.

Beth drew the curtains back and smiled up at him. "Thank you."

Robert shook the robe out and draped it around her shoulders, helping her arms find the sleeves. "I was attempting to be discreet, love, and would not have alerted Marcus to your presence had you not spoken."

"Marcus is family. He won't gossip."

Her words pleased him. Had Beth learned of Marcus's painful past? If so, 'twas kind of her to claim him as kin since the boy wanted no part of his own.

"Besides," she continued, "I think discretion is sort of a moot point now, don't you? We weren't exactly subtle yesterday in the bailey."

Nay. They had left little doubt as to their intentions.

Robert helped her out of bed and took care to cover every inch of her pale skin from the neck down.

"Besides," she said, "I'm cold. And Marcus is building me a nice, big fire. I plan to take full advantage of it."

When he frowned down at her, seeking some other excuse to keep her in bed, she leaned up on her toes and kissed his neck just below his ear.

"Still like my independence?" she whispered.

"Aye," he grumbled.

Beth laughed and started around the foot of the bed. As soon as her back was turned, Robert smiled and shook his head.

"*Ooh.* That looks wonderful, Marcus. Thank you!"

Flushing anew, Marcus smiled as she skipped past him and held her hands out to the crackling flames.

"Ahhhhh. I love the gigantic fireplaces you have in this place. They let you warm everything at once."

As Beth turned around to warm her back, Robert picked up the missive and scanned its contents.

He stiffened, his fingers tightening on the parchment.

Beth's smile faltered. "Robert? What is it?" She crossed to his side.

"Lord Edward thinks he has captured my enemy."

"Who is Lord Edward?"

"His land abuts mine to the south."

"And he caught your enemy?"

Robert nodded. "He says he is holding him at Terrington and has requested my immediate presence."

"Where did he find him? Did he say who your enemy is?"

"He says naught other than that his men found a wounded man nigh Fosterly's border who claims I was the one who ran him through."

Beth groaned and threw up her hands. "Well, didn't he think you'd be curious? The suspense is going to kill me!" Suddenly, she perked up, her face brightening in a way that warned Robert he would not like the next words that emerged from her lips. "I'm going with you."

"Nay, Beth," he countered, hoping to head off the determination he could see raising her chin and straightening her shoulders. "You will remain here."

"No way." Turning, she started to hurry away.

"Beth—" He broke off when she spun around and returned to his side.

Leaning up onto her toes, she grasped his shoulders, tugged him down until her lips could reach his ear, and whispered, "Does Marcus know about the secret passage?"

"Aye." Dillon, Alyssa, Michael, Marcus, Adam and Stephen—all of those he trusted absolutely—knew.

Her heels hit the floor. "Good. Don't leave until I get back."

While Robert frowned and a bemused Marcus watched, she raced for the secret passage, opened it, and disappeared into the darkness.

Robert looked at Marcus. "Think you I can don my armor and leave ere Lady Bethany comes charging back in here, intent on accompanying me?"

"Nay."

"Nor do I. But let us try."

Beth catapulted herself back into the solar via the passage just as Robert was buckling on his sword belt. "Okay. I'm ready," she announced, breathless. She had managed to don another of Alyssa's gowns in record time. The kirtle was olive green and laced up the sides. The linen undertunic was bright white. Both were just short enough on her to leave the toes of her boots exposed.

"Beth," Robert began with a forbidding expression, "you will *not* accompany me."

"Aye, I will," she insisted, fastening the end of her long braid with her elastic tie. "I don't know how the justice system works here, but if you're heading over there to kick your enemy's arse, I'm damned well going to be there to cheer you on."

Marcus stifled a laugh.

Robert, however, looked less than amused. He crossed his arms over his chest and widened his stance. "I know you better than that, love. You say you want to watch me punish the blackguard who has been attacking my people, but, in truth, what you wish to do is guard my back."

Beth opened her mouth to protest, then closed it again. Bringing her own arms up and crossing them under her breasts, she mirrored his stance. "So? A man can't have too many friends at his back. Isn't that right, Marcus?"

Marcus eyed Robert warily before answering. "Though my lord's glare advises me to say otherwise, my lady, I must agree with you. Why do I not go in your stead? Then I can ensure Lord Robert's safety as well as your own."

Robert threw his arms up in apparent frustration. "*Saints!* Have you both forgotten that I am fully capable of fighting my own battles? Has my inability to apprehend my enemy myself so eroded your faith in me?"

"Nay!" Marcus hastened to deny.

"No!" Beth practically shouted at the same time. She did *not* want Robert to think they doubted him and proceeded to praise his skills as a warrior as effusively as she could.

Marcus did the same, each of them talking over the other.

"Enough!" Robert barked.

Silence settled upon them.

"Maybe," Beth suggested tentatively, "we could *all* go. Then I could meet your neighbor."

"Beth, you will remain here at Fosterly. With Marcus," he added, glaring at his squire. "Michael, Stephen, and Adam will accompany me. We will be in no danger."

"You don't know that," she persisted. *Damn it.* She *had* to go with him.

"I am not riding into battle, sweetling," he said with exaggerated patience. "The man has already been taken. Lord Edward has no doubt confined him to his dungeon."

"Well, how do you know this isn't a trap?" Beth countered, the anxiety that had crept up on her as she had dressed increasing, every instinct telling her she needed to remain by Robert's side. "Maybe there are two of them. Or more." When her hands began to shake, she drew her damp palms down the sides of her skirt. Her heart began to beat more quickly. Her body began to tremble.

She felt panicky all of a sudden as memories converged on her and fear for Robert's safety grew.

Unable to stand still, she began to pace. "Maybe there are others out there, lying in wait for you somewhere along the way. I mean, maybe the man Lord Edward found isn't even your enemy. Maybe he's just posing as your enemy while your real enemy actually waits to ambush you on the road. It's possible, Robert. You can't deny it's possible."

"Beth." His voice turned soft, coaxing. "You admitted yourself that you are unfamiliar with our methods of fighting, so you will have to trust me when I say that even were I ambushed and outnumbered four to one, I would emerge the victor." Snagging her hand, he halted her nervous movements. "I say this not as a boast, but to ease your mind. 'Tis a simple errand I am about. Verily, you need not worry."

She stared up at him, the backs of her eyes beginning to burn. "Josh and I were on a simple errand. Look what happened to *him*."

A simple errand. A long shot. So *long* a long shot that Josh had felt secure in bringing her for backup in place of Grant.

Beth had actually been excited, full of adrenaline.

Then the first shots had rung out and she had forgotten everything he had taught her.

But she knew better now. She could protect Robert. She *would* protect Robert. She wouldn't make the same mistake twice. She wouldn't lose him the way she had lost Josh.

"You never told me what happened to you and your brother that day," he broached. "Not really."

And she would rather not do so now, but... "It was my fault," she said, a kind of weary hopelessness suffusing her. "I should never have hung back when he told me to. I just stood there and let him go on alone. And then the shooting started and..." Beth shook her head, grief and guilt a constant, heavy weight in her chest. "I should have been with him. If I had been with Josh when he entered the clearing, it might have all ended differently. Kingsley and Vergoma might not have caught him off guard. Or maybe they wouldn't have fought being taken into custody if they knew he wasn't alone. Maybe they would have just cut their losses and surrendered themselves. Or slunk away. Then they wouldn't have shot him or shot me and we wouldn't have both fallen in that damned clearing and I never would have—" A sob checked her words.

Blinking back the moisture that blurred her vision, she saw Robert's jaw tighten.

"You never would have come here," he finished for her.

His words struck her like a punch to the chest. "What?" she whispered.

"Was that not what you were going to say?" he asked, his eyes reflecting the hurt he wouldn't allow his face to show. "You never would have come here. You never would have met me or—"

"Robert, no," she interrupted, forcing the words past her tight throat. "I was going to say I never would have failed Josh so miserably."

Robert's Adams apple bobbed up and down as he swallowed hard. Marcus quietly left the chamber, closing the door behind him.

"You believe me, don't you?" she pressed, holding Robert's gaze.

"Beth, after everything you have told me of your world—"

"You can't think I regret coming here. That I regret what we've shared. The time we've had together." Never had she intended to even *imply* such a thing. "You can't think that, Robert. Because I don't. Not one minute of it. Not one second. I promise." And did not want him to feel the pain that would crush her if he were to say *he* regretted it.

"Come here, love," Robert said, his stony face softening. Sliding his arms around her, he drew her into a loose embrace. "'Twas not my wish to distress you further."

Beth buried her face in his chest and squeezed him closer for a moment, then tilted her head back so she could meet his tender gaze. "I love you, Robert. You know that, right?" And how wonderful it felt to say it.

He pressed his lips to hers. "I do. And I love you, Beth. Forgive me for dismissing your concerns for my safety. I knew not that you were thinking of your brother."

Warmed by his words, she rested her face upon his chest. "I wasn't at first. Not consciously anyway. It just sort of crept up on me while I was rushing to get dressed."

Robert lifted her into his arms. How effortless he made it seem.

Crossing to the hearth, he seated himself in one of the chairs before it and settled her comfortably in his lap. "Tell me again what happened that day."

Smoothing her hand across his tunic, Beth leaned into him. "You don't have time for this, Robert. You need to go to Terrington."

"As I said, my enemy—if the man Lord Edward has captured is indeed the man for whom I have been searching—is being held at Terrington. He will keep."

"But—"

"You are more important to me, Beth. Please, tell me what happened that day."

Her stomach churned. "I screwed up," she told him, almost sick with shame as she admitted both to Robert and to herself what pained her most when she thought of it. That Josh was most likely dead because of her.

Tears clogged her throat, making it impossible to speak for a moment. Robert waited patiently, caressing her back in long soothing strokes.

"We were looking for two men accused of murder who had skipped bail. Or escaped," she added for clarification purposes.

She told him everything then, recounting as best she could the events that had transpired. Admittedly, some of it was fuzzy. And despite her resolve not to, she ended up breaking down and crying, her tears soaking the front of Robert's tunic. The guilt of failing Josh crushed her. The pain of not knowing if her brother had survived or died, of suspecting the latter and believing her actions had contributed, was like a virus that ate away at her and wore her down no matter how busy she kept herself or how hard she tried not to think about it.

"In truth, Beth, you did what any of us would have done," Robert said when she finished. "You knew your brother was in trouble, and you acted."

"But don't you see?" She swiped impatiently at her tears. "I didn't think. I just charged into the clearing, right into the line of fire."

"I have done the same myself on numerous occasions," he pointed out.

"But I was useless! I was just a distraction!"

"You were another weapon at Josh's disposal."

"I should've circled the clearing instead of just racing in there. I could have worked my way around and come up behind Kingsley and—"

"Did you not tell me that drought afflicted the forest that surrounded you?"

She frowned. "Yes, but—"

"Even the most cautious individual cannot avoid making a sound when stepping upon brittle leaves and grasses. Had you attempted to sneak up behind them, they would have heard you coming."

"Even if they had, it might've worked in our favor, because Josh could've gotten the drop on them when they turned their attention on *me*."

"Would he not have been more likely to do something rash to draw their attention back to himself and protect you?"

Yes, damn it. That was exactly what Josh would have done. "I could've called 911 before I ran to the clearing."

"Do you mean call for help? On your cell phone?"

She had tried to explain how her cell phone worked, but had received an *I-trust-you-so-I'll-take-your-word-for-it-but-it-seems-unbelievable* look. "Aye," she answered.

"Was your cell phone not in your backpack?"

"Aye," she said again, aware of how long it would have taken her to dig it out.

"Help would not have arrived in time, and your brother would have been left to face them alone, without the additional weapon you threw to him."

Beth stared at him helplessly. "So, you're saying it was a lose-lose situation. That no matter what path I chose, I was screwed. We both were."

Robert smoothed her hair back from her face with a gentle hand. "You speak as though your brother was dead when last you saw him, Beth. Did you not tell me he still breathed when darkness claimed you?"

Sorrow stabbed her as she thought of her last impression of him. Lying so close to her. Blood staining his clothing. Chest rising and falling with short, pained breaths. "Yes. I wanted to go to him, but I couldn't. The pain was…" She shuddered, remembering.

Robert tightened his hold on her and pressed his lips to her temple, lending comfort.

"I managed to reach out and touch his hair." More tears welled. It had been soft and dusty. "He was alive, Robert. I know he was, even though the bullets passed through his vest the way they did mine. But I don't know how long he could've lasted, especially if one of them hit an artery."

"You remember naught after that?" he asked softly.

She struggled to dispel the shadows that shielded those final moments. "Sometimes when I first wake up in the morning, I remember a man looming over me." She frowned. "Not Kingsley or Vergoma. Someone else."

"A third criminal?"

"I don't know. We were only looking for the two, but they could've had help. There could have been others with them." She shook her head. "To be honest, I'm not sure it really happened. The third man leaning over me, I mean. I think maybe my memory is playing tricks on me or I was hallucinating from the pain or blood loss or something."

"Why?"

"Because the man was wearing a long black robe. The kind of robe a monk might wear." And he had smelled of exotic spices. "All he needed was a scythe and he would've been the stereotypical personification of Death."

When Robert didn't offer a response, she leaned back and studied him. His face went blank, which she knew meant something troubled him and he was trying to hide it.

"What is it?" she asked, stomach sinking.

"The man wore a dark robe?"

She nodded. "It had a hood and—as I said—reminded me of something a monk might wear. Although I don't think a monk would have that much hair."

"What do you mean?"

"He had this amazing, long hair that fell all the way down to his waist."

"What color was it?"

"Black."

The most peculiar expression blanketed his features then. One she couldn't decipher.

Did he think it sounded as crazy as she did? A man with hair down to his waist garbed in a monk's robe in the forest outside of Houston, Texas?

Yeah, right.

"I know it sounds weird," she offered hesitantly. "Maybe I shouldn't have mentioned it."

Relaxing, he drew her in and wrapped his arms around her in a tight embrace. "Nay, sweetling. I *want* you to share your troubles with me. Never hesitate to do so."

Relieved, Beth squeezed him back. "Thank you. For listening. I think it helped to talk about it." Though the guilt remained, her spirit did feel a bit lighter.

"Good." Kissing the top of her head, he carefully eased her off his lap and stood. "Have you any weapons you wish to fetch? 'Tis time we were on our way."

Excitement rose as Beth looked up at him. "I can go with you?"

"Aye."

"And I can bring my weapons?"

"Only the smaller ones that can be hidden beneath your skirts."

Woohoo! Throwing her arms around his neck, she pressed a hasty kiss to his lips. "Thank you, Robert! It'll just take me a minute." She would bring her Glock and the .22. And maybe her hunting knife. Could she fit the Ruger beneath her skirts, too?

"I shall go down now and ensure that Marcus has saddled Berserker."

Which reminded Beth of the secret she had been keeping, hoping to surprise him. "I can ride now," she boasted.

His eyebrows rose. "Your own mount?"

"Aye. Adam has been giving me lessons between bouts of cleaning." Much of Fosterly was spic-and-span now.

Robert smiled. "*Adam* has, you say?"

"Aye."

"And did he perchance speak during these lessons?"

Beth laughed. "Not much. Mostly he kept me from falling off the horse while Michael or Stephen or whoever else happened by shouted advice from the sidelines."

Robert chuckled. "Then you shall have your own mount, if you feel confident enough. I will gauge how much you have learned while we ride and take command of your lessons myself."

"Good." Leaning up onto her toes, Beth kissed him and said with a wink, "You've taught me so much already."

He groaned. "Temptress." Turning her around, he gave her bottom a playful swat. "Fetch your weapons before I toss you back in bed and join you there."

Grinning, Beth hurried through the passage.

As soon as Beth disappeared into the secret passage, Robert sank down into the chair behind him. Leaning forward, he braced his elbows on his knees and dropped his face into his hands.

Disbelief gave way to panic, then fury, then dread.

A *gifted one* had been present when Beth had nigh been slain.

He had broached the subject of *gifted ones* once or twice since Beth had revealed whence she came, hoping to ease any fears rumor might inspire and prepare her for her inevitable first encounter with Dillon and Alyssa.

Beth had expressed not fear, but fascination. So *much* fascination that he suspected she would not have believed that there were men and women capable of performing such feats as healing a wound with a touch or moving objects with his or her mind if anyone else had told her. Beth had said she had never heard of such outside of what she called *fiction*, which he believed might be similar to minstrel tales invented to entertain. So he had assumed that no *gifted ones* lived in her time and that whatever miracle had brought her back through time had also healed her wounds.

But the day she had fallen, she had seen a man in black robes with long midnight hair.

That man had been with her ere she had lost consciousness.

And when she had awoken, she had found herself in Robert's time.

Though most of the *gifted ones* Robert knew were women—Alyssa, her mother, her grandmother, her cousin—Robert knew two or three were men. One of them, Dillon referred to as the giant. He stood at least a head taller than Robert and seemed to possess more knowledge and power than all of the others combined. But Robert had never seen his face or hair.

Alyssa's brother, however, was another. And *his* hair was long and black, just as Beth had described.

Alyssa had never divulged what special gifts her brother possessed. But she and her grandmother could both heal with a touch of their hands, so would it not be unreasonable to think Sir Geoffrey could heal as well?

Was it possible his gifts also enabled him to traverse time?

"Please," Robert whispered. There must be some other explanation. *Any* other explanation.

For, if Sir Geoffrey had brought Beth back to Robert's time, he could return her to the future.

And, in so doing, would leave her forever beyond Robert's reach.

Chapter Fifteen

"WELL?" BETH PROMPTED SUDDENLY, A little worried by Robert's pensive expression. They had ridden in silence for some time now.

He glanced over at her. "What?"

Stephen and Marcus rode behind them, with Adam and Michael bringing up the rear.

She motioned to the gentle mare beneath her. "Aren't you going to compliment me on my superior riding skills?"

His lips twitched. "You are indeed a superior rider," he praised with mock solemnity.

Grinning, she blew him a kiss. "Flattery will get you everything."

He quirked a brow. "Although, were you at all concerned with propriety, you would ride turned to one side, rather than riding astride."

Beth bit back a laugh. His jaw had dropped a bit when she had climbed atop the horse and straddled it, her gown rucking up to her knees and leaving the legs she had talked him into shaving for her bare. All she wore beneath were the black panties he loved so much. And she had thought, for a moment, that he would rip his cloak in his haste to remove it, throw it across her lap and cover her.

"I think men just want women to ride sidesaddle because you're afraid we'll show you up," she taunted. She didn't think they called it sidesaddle yet, but they had become surprisingly adept at translating her modern speech, so she suspected they would catch her meaning.

Stephen, of course, took the bait. "Do you imply we fear you will best us?" he asked with some affront.

"Absolutely," she affirmed. "If women were allowed to ride astride, you men would eat our dust."

Stephen snorted. "Aside or astride. If one is skilled, it makes no difference."

"Oh, yeah? Have *you* ever ridden sidesaddle?"

"Do I look like a woman to you?"

"Do you really want me to answer that?" she countered.

"Beth," Robert cautioned as thunderclouds darkened the scruffy knight's features.

Grinning unrepentantly, she tossed him a wink. "I can't help it. He's such an easy mark."

"What is a mark?" Marcus asked.

"A target," Beth clarified.

Robert's lips twitched.

"Who is an easy target?" Stephen barked.

"You are," Michael pointed out dryly.

Stephen grumbled something beneath his breath.

Beth laughed. "Adam wanted to teach me to ride sidesaddle," she told Robert. "But I refused."

"Why does that not surprise me?" he asked with a shake of his head.

"Because you adore my independent spirit?" she quipped.

"Ahhh. You did tell me to keep that in mind, did you not?" he responded with a smile.

Good. She was happy to see his mood lighten.

Quiet descended as they continued their journey.

Birdsong, the occasional hum of insects, and the sounds of small creatures scuttling about out of sight filled the air around them. This place and time was a nature lover's paradise. Trees abounded, so tall their tips seemed to pierce the cottony clouds that drifted above them. Their leaves bore a deep healthy green color.

Closing her eyes, Beth drew in a deep cleansing breath. And the air was fresh and sweet. So much better than the stale, polluted air of Houston and so many other twenty-first-century cities.

An hour or so passed.

Every once in a while, just to keep things interesting, Beth would aggravate Stephen. It was becoming something of a hobby for her and seemed to amuse the others.

"My lady?" Marcus asked her. "Is it true that you were a warrior in your homeland?"

A warrior? "I guess you could say that."

"Your menfolk allowed this?" Stephen groused.

She laughed. "They didn't have much choice."

Robert snorted, his lips curling up in a faint smile. "You had them wrapped around your little finger, did you not?"

Beth grinned. "Absolutely."

Marcus regarded her with some amazement. "Verily, your father did not object?"

Beth reached over to give Robert's arm a squeeze, then fell back to ride beside his squire, displacing Stephen, who joined Adam and Michael behind them.

The sun's warm rays shone down upon them as they left the trees and entered a clearing roughly the size of a football field. Colorful wildflowers bobbed between tall, feathery grasses, infusing the air with a heady perfume. Dense green forest surrounded the meadow like stadium seats. A light cool breeze wove between the trees and set all into gentle, rolling motion.

So beautiful.

"Actually, my father did object," she admitted. "He didn't want me to have any part of bounty hunting. He thought it was too dangerous and wanted to keep me safe. But he died before I was old enough to decide for myself."

Stephen grunted. "'Twas not your decision to make."

Beth's hackles rose. "Hey, where I come from—"

Fwuh-thmp.

Beth jerked her head back as something flew past her nose. Beside her, Marcus's horse made an abrupt restive movement.

She turned to ask Marcus what it meant and felt her stomach sink like a stone. "Marcus!"

His face tight with pain, the squire gritted his teeth and gripped one thigh just above an arrow that was embedded in it.

The other men drew their swords.

Fwuh-thmp.

Beth cried out as a second arrow struck Marcus in his shoulder.

His face blanched. His body began to sway backward.

Beth lunged toward him and gripped his tunic to keep him from falling.

Men erupted from the forest on the opposite side of the clearing, their shouts answered by the warriors at her side.

Panic rose. Beth didn't think she would be able to keep Marcus upright much longer. He might be young, but he still outweighed her by a good sixty or seventy pounds. "Robert!"

"Get to the trees!" Robert urged her.

She tossed a frantic glance over her shoulder.

What appeared to be a limitless number of men poured from the forest, all on foot. Their rough features twisted and contorted as they bellowed battle cries and thrust their swords high.

Michael, Stephen, and Adam raced toward them, the hooves of their horses rumbling and sending clods of dirt flying.

Another arrow flew from the trees beyond the attackers and narrowly missed Beth.

Robert swore foully, his look turning murderous. "*Now*, Beth! Hie yourself back to Fosterly and do not stop until you are safely within its gates!"

Perhaps Beth shouldn't have exaggerated her skills as a horsewoman earlier. For when three men fought their way past Michael, Stephen, and Adam, Robert did the only thing she supposed he could've done to protect her. He slapped the rump of her horse to get her moving, then dug his heels into his own mount and tore off to meet the men halfway.

Regrettably, Beth's balance—as she attempted to aid Marcus—was precarious at best.

As the mare beneath her sprang forward, Beth tumbled out of the saddle.

Marcus went with her and somehow managed to hit the ground first, cushioning her fall as she sprawled atop him, breaking one of the arrow shafts in half.

"Ahhh!"

Beth winced. "I'm sorry! I'm so sorry. Are you okay?" She hastily sought a place to put her hands that wouldn't cause him further harm so she could lever herself off of him.

Fwuh-thitt.

Both of them froze when an arrow impaled the grass barely a foot from their faces.

"My lady, please," Marcus bit out urgently, gritting his teeth as he gripped her arms.

Heart pounding, adrenaline whipping through her, Beth scrambled off of him.

Robert and the others fought the marauders a good thirty or forty yards away. The formerly beautiful clearing was already awash with red, the wildflowers' fragrance befouled by the odors of sweat and death and the metallic scent of blood. Sunlight winked off of flashing swords as bodies writhed in a battle so surreal she could hardly absorb it all.

"My lady, please," Marcus repeated, trying to drag her around behind him as he sat up with a growl of pain. "You must get to the trees, where the arrows cannot find you."

Just as she located Robert, an arrow narrowly missed him.

Terror clutched her heart. *Robert!*

Shrugging off Marcus's hold, Beth parked her butt on the ground by his feet. "Tell me where they're coming from," she ordered, yanking her skirts up to her thighs.

Marcus's eyes flew wide. "My lady!"

The heels of her boots digging into the soft soil, her knees pointing skyward, she began to fumble with the holster she had donned beneath her dress. "Where are the arrows coming from?" she demanded. "I need you to watch and tell me exactly where they exit the trees." *Damn it!* Frustrated, Beth yanked her skirts up to her waist, not caring who saw her black panties. She had to get her 9mm out and take down that damned archer!

Ignoring Marcus's scandalized regard and his constant attempts to drag himself in front of her and serve as her shield, she focused on getting her fingers to stop shaking long enough to liberate her weapon and protect Robert.

Finally!

"My lady—"

"Keep your eyes on the trees!" she snapped.

Yanking the semiautomatic from the holster, she flicked off the safety.

Marcus grabbed her arm and tried to keep her from rising.

Beth would have none of it. Shoving her skirts down, she gained her feet and faced the battle.

Fwuh-thitt. An arrow pierced the grass where she had been sitting.

"Where did it come from? Did you see it?" She wrapped both hands around the grip and raised the Ruger.

The clearing wavered, seemed to change.

Shaking her head, she blinked hard.

For a moment, it looked smaller, the foliage around her drier. Another body—that of her brother—lay before her. Another villain waited in the foliage across from her. Another ambush threatened to take all from her.

"My lady!"

Something tugged at her skirts, nearly toppling her. Scowling, she braced her feet farther apart. "Damn it, Josh, just tell me where the shooter is!"

She spared the boy at her feet a quick glance.

Why was Marcus looking at her so strangely?

"*Where is he?*" she bellowed, out of patience.

He pointed. "There. Above Sir Michael's head. Mayhap ten hands higher."

Aiming accordingly, Beth squinted down the barrel and waited. Another arrow sailed from the trees, a little to the left of where she watched. Making the necessary adjustments, Beth squeezed the trigger.

Pow! Pow! Pow! Pow! Pow!

Marcus flinched and threw his hands up to cover his ears.

Every horse in the clearing bolted.

Birds abandoned the trees in droves, screeching in alarm.

All fighting ceased as men ducked and looked wildly up at a sky that carried no storm clouds capable of producing such thunder.

Wide eyes rolled. Gazes searched the clearing.

As echoes of the gunshots faded, a body crashed through the trees' foliage and landed with a thud on the ground.

The archer had fallen.

Robert spun around to look at Beth.

Instead of being safely on her way back to Fosterly, she stood on the opposite side of the clearing, feet braced apart, clutching one of her odd weapons with both hands at arm's length. One side of her skirt was caught up on her hip, leaving one long, shapely limb exposed.

Marcus lay at her feet, his hands cupped over his ears as he stared up at her with wide eyes and gaping mouth.

A quick look to either side told Robert his men had also guessed 'twas Beth who had felled the archer.

And 'twas Beth who had spawned the terrifying thunder.

Those they fought gradually turned their gazes in her direction as well. Mutters soon swelled, rising on the wind. Several crossed themselves.

Robert took swift advantage of their attackers' distraction and disarmed as many as he could. Michael, Stephen, and Adam joined in. The fighting began anew and soon grew as fierce as it had been before the interruption, though the tide at last began to turn in their favor.

Four men met their end at the tip of Robert's sword, then a fifth. The number of those still combating them thinned. As Robert swung his blade at a sixth opponent, he heard something that sent shards of ice slicing through his veins.

Above the grunts and groans and shouts and sounds of weapons clashing, Beth's voice rang out. "Don't! Stay back!"

Robert looked in her direction.

His opponent's sword penetrated the chain mail covering his left biceps and pierced flesh. But the pain of his wound could not compare with the fear and fury that seized Robert when he saw two men racing toward Beth.

Only one other time had Robert been accused of going into a berserker's rage, killing any and all in his path without pausing to determine whether they were friend or foe. Then, he had been struggling to reach his dying brother's side. Now, as the red haze overtook him, he roared and began to cut a swath to Beth, dispatching any man foolish enough to get in his way.

"I mean it!" Beth yelled in a very un-Beth-like shriek. "Don't make me kill you!"

Marcus struggled to his feet at her side, sword drawn, ready to give his life to protect her.

Robert never slowed his pace. As the last man before him fell, Robert realized he would never reach Beth in time.

The two villains were nigh upon her.

He glanced down, then transferred his sword to his left hand and grabbed the battle-axe his last opponent had dropped. Drawing his right arm back, he prepared to throw it.

Pow!

Flames flashed from the tip of Beth's weapon.

239

One of the two men running toward her jerked to a halt as a hole appeared between his bushy eyebrows and flesh burst from the back of his head. The other man stopped short and gawked as his friend dropped limply to the ground, eyes staring sightlessly up at the sky.

Once again stillness fell over the clearing.

Robert stared, his heart slamming against his ribs.

Just what manner of weapon did Beth wield?

Though everything within him urged him to go to her, Robert instead watched long enough to ensure the second man would not attack her, then resumed the battle.

In short order, he and his men disarmed and restrained the remainder of the marauders. More than one tried to flee, but met with no success.

Marcus restrained the man closest to Beth. That one seemed too afraid to move while her *witch's weapon* was pointed at him.

Once Marcus herded the man over to join the rest, the young squire returned to Beth and sank weakly to the ground at her feet.

Robert didn't think Beth had noticed. She said nothing, just kept staring down at the man she had slain.

The danger now past, Robert strode toward her, his sword still in his left hand, the battle axe in his right.

Just as he was about to call her name, the greenery behind her parted.

A man limped forward, hunched over, the front of his filthy leather armor wet with blood, his blond hair befouled by dirt. His young face twisted with rage as his lips stretched into a sneer that revealed teeth stained crimson. He held one arm, bent at an odd angle, close to his side. The other awkwardly cradled a crossbow, which the man raised under Robert's horrified gaze.

"*Beth!*"

Her eyes widened at his shout, her gaze snapping up to find him.

Robert drew the hand holding the axe back and let it fly. In a move that was stunningly graceful, Beth dropped to the ground and landed neatly on her toes and splayed hands as the axe whistled through the air above her head, spinning end over end until it embedded itself deep in the archer's chest.

The fellow's crossbow fell without releasing a bolt as he collapsed.

Robert ran forward. Beth rolled onto her back and sat up, raising her weapon as he passed her and aiming it at the fallen man.

But the man did not move.

Upon reaching him, Robert studied him closely.

He looked to be no older than Marcus, his features plain and unremarkable.

"Who leads these men?" Robert demanded, watching him struggle for breath.

"I do," the boy said, glaring up at Robert with venom.

This boy led them? "Who are you? Why have you attacked my people?"

"Th-Thief," the boy hissed.

"You are a thief?"

A sound of frustration burst forth as the boy struggled to speak. "Y-You."

Robert stiffened. "I am no thief, boy. I am—"

"Fosterly... sh-should... been mine. H-Hurley... was... m-my father."

Robert frowned. "Lord Hurley had no issue. Had there been someone to inherit, King John would not have given me the land and title. Fosterly would have gone to Lord Hurley's heir."

"B-Bastard born."

This boy was Hurley's bastard? "Did your father acknowledge you?"

Mutinous silence.

"You know you could not inherit."

"That b-bastard witch... that W-Westcott wed will... inherit L-Lord Everard's holdings," the boy snarled.

Fury ignited within Robert as he shifted his sword until the tip pressed against the boy's chin. "'Twas a similar slur that cost your father both his holdings and his life. And, unlike you, Lady Alyssa has been acknowledged by her father and is loved by him as well."

The boy spat a slew of angry curses.

"Who is the man being held at Terrington?" Robert pressed.

"S-Sellsword." The boy coughed, spewing forth blood. "Should have... k-killed your whore... instead of... p-precious squire," he ground out. "W-Wanted you... to suffer."

Then he breathed no more.

Robert stared down at him, finding it hard to believe that this boy had truly been responsible for so much destruction. Finding it *harder* to believe that it was all finally over.

"Is he dead?" Beth asked in a shaky voice behind him.

"Aye."

"Are you sure?"

He met her gaze as she rose. "Aye, Beth. 'Tis over."

She nodded, lowering her weapon until it dangled loosely along her thigh.

Robert made a motion with his hand that sent Michael and Stephen into the forest to confirm that all had been routed while Adam remained with the prisoners.

Sheathing his sword, Robert started toward Beth.

As he approached, she turned away in a slow half circle, her movements stiff and jerky as though she walked in her sleep. Then she stilled and just stood there.

"Beth," he broached softly as he came up behind her.

A breeze ruffled her hair, sending dark strands that had broken free of her braid streaking across her face. She made no move to brush them back as her gaze made a slow foray over the clearing, taking in the trampled wildflowers, the grass painted scarlet with blood and flesh, the weapons that glinted silver and red in the sunlight, the lifeless bodies sprawled wherever they had fallen.

Her face blanched. A muscle in her jaw twitched. Her throat worked with a swallow.

"Beth, love, turn away," he implored gently, reluctant to touch her and soil her with the blood of his enemies.

Again she swallowed. And again. She squeezed her eyes closed and shook her head. A single tear fought its way past her lashes and trailed down one cheek.

"Please, Beth."

Opening her eyes, she blinked several times in quick succession to hold further moisture back. And still she stared.

It reminded him of the moment she had first seen Fosterly, as if her eyes relayed something her mind could not grasp.

For one who had never been exposed to such a battle, it was a gruesome sight. Many a squire and young knight had emptied his stomach when confronted with similar scenes.

Robert cursed himself.

He should never have let her accompany them, should not have put her so at risk.

Reaching up with one quaking hand, she swiped at her damp cheeks.

Robert's heart lurched when he saw the ruby smears she unknowingly left behind. "You are injured?" he demanded. Grabbing her wrist, he swung her around and searched her slender form as fear inundated him. "Where? Where are you wounded, Beth?"

He could not lose her. He *would* not lose her!

When she failed to answer and he did not immediately locate any rends in her clothing that might indicate the blood's origins, he glanced up and found her regarding him with wide eyes. Robert jerked her hand up to draw her attention to the blood that coated it. "Where are you wounded, Beth? Tell me!"

Beth stared at the blood on her hand.

How many times had her fingers been coated with the crimson liquid in recent weeks?

Removing her hand from Robert's hold, she shook her head. "It isn't mine," she whispered, wiping it on her kirtle. "It's Marcus's."

"Are you certain?" he pressed.

Nodding, she moved away to kneel beside his prone squire.

Robert followed and sank onto his haunches across from her.

"I accidentally broke off the arrow in his shoulder when we fell," she explained as Robert tore away Marcus's tunic and went to work on his mail.

"'Tis probably for the best," Robert muttered. "I can feel the tip protruding from his back. With the shaft broken off, we can just push it through."

Sheesh. That was going to hurt like hell. As if Marcus wasn't in enough pain already.

Beth looked to Marcus, who bore Robert's tugging as stoically as possible.

Carefully removing his mailed coif, she stroked the squire's short raven hair back from his face. He was just a kid, really. A teenager.

In her time, boys his age spent their time texting, screwing around on the Internet, playing video games, partying, binge drinking, smoking, getting laid, driving too fast, and doing all kinds of stupid crap to rebel against their parents' so-called oppressive rule. Yet here Marcus studied the art of war, learned how to defend himself and prevail in hand-to-hand combat with all of the seriousness of a man twice his age, and nurtured a strong sense of honor that was becoming more and more rare in her time.

With two arrows already imbedded in his body, he had not hesitated to throw himself in front of Beth to protect her and shield her from their attackers.

"You did well, Marcus," Robert murmured as he cut a substantial patch from Marcus's padded gambeson, finally exposing his wound.

Though Robert's face and voice were calm, Beth recognized his concern.

"You did, Marcus," she praised. Giving his undamaged shoulder a pat, she willed her hands to stop shaking and turned her attention to the arrow in his thigh. "You were very brave." So brave he had almost lost his life trying to protect her.

Marcus sucked in a breath as Robert probed his wound. "Aye, it takes great courage to fall from one's horse."

Robert frowned. "Do not make light of what you did today. You protected my lady when I could not."

Beth scowled as she parted the broken links in Marcus's chainmail around the arrow shaft. *His lady*, she thought, could damned well protect herself. And even if Beth failed, she did not want anyone else to lose his life in an attempt to save her. Not Robert. Not Marcus. And not Josh.

Tears blurred her vision once more. Swearing, she blinked them back.

The trembling of her hands increased.

"Beth?"

Looking up, she found Robert and Marcus both watching her. As one, their troubled gazes dropped to her quaking fingers, then rose to her face.

"I'm fine," she assured them. Of course, the tears over which she apparently had no control chose that moment to spill over her lashes and pour down her cheeks. "I'm fine," she reiterated, trying to sniff them back. "It's just..." Reaction. Delayed reaction to the terror of battle. Of almost losing Robert and Marcus. Of killing a man. And of seeing all of the bodies and body parts littering the field.

But she didn't say that. If she did, they would fall all over themselves trying to comfort her, and then she really *would* go to pieces.

Instead, she motioned to Marcus's leg. "I just can't get his chausses off."

A shadow fell over her. "Ah. A common complaint. Many a maid has wept on my shoulder because she could not remove Marcus's chausses."

Color suffused Marcus's face at Michael's dry remark.

And Beth was surprised to find she could laugh.

Michael squatted beside her. "Mayhap I can be of some assistance, my lady."

She offered him a grateful smile. "Thank you."

As Michael worked, Beth's eyes strayed to Robert and took in the immense amount of blood that coated him. "Robert, were you wounded?"

He sent her a reassuring smile. "Just a scratch, love. You can clean and bind it for me when we return to Fosterly."

She nodded, relieved. "What about you, Michael?"

"I am well, my lady."

"And Adam and Stephen?"

"I have heard no complaints from them, my lady. They are well."

She glanced around, trying not to look too closely at the bodies that littered the clearing. "Where *is* Stephen?" Adam was busy binding the prisoners. But she didn't see Stephen anywhere.

"Once we ensured that no more assassins lurked in the forest, he left to track down our horses." His gaze dropped to the 9mm she had set on the grass beside her. "'Tis quite a weapon you have there, my lady."

She exchanged a look with Robert. "Aye, it is." And would no doubt require an explanation. The question was, how much should she explain?

The ride home seemed to last days rather than hours. Of necessity, they took it slow. But Beth knew every movement must cause Marcus agonizing pain.

One of Beth's classmates in college had had to have an emergency appendectomy. And Beth recalled the woman confiding that every tiny little bump the car had hit on the ride home from the hospital had sent pain rippling through her.

Poor Marcus didn't have the comfort of a cushy car seat in a shock-absorbing vehicle. He rode atop a constantly shifting and moving warhorse,

Michael and Adam on either side of him ready to brace him should he begin to fall.

Beth chewed her lip the whole time, afraid the brave teenager would die before they could get him home. But they made it.

Once at Fosterly, she helped Robert and Michael clean and bandage Marcus's wounds while Adam and Stephen saw the prisoners safely installed in the dungeon. Both Robert and Michael were remarkably proficient at rendering first aid, and Beth marveled at the difference being raised around a gifted healer had made in the two men—both in their actions and their attitudes. Before bandaging the wounds, Robert opted to coat them with healing herbs Alyssa had given him instead of honey or Beth's ointments. Since he had used such in the past with success, Beth offered no objection. But she did encourage him to let her give his squire some ibuprofen for the pain.

"What about you?" she asked Robert. Hadn't he mentioned receiving a scratch? She didn't want some wound he deemed negligible to get infected and end up killing him.

"'Tis paltry," he said with a shrug.

"I want to see it."

Smiling, he looped an arm around her shoulders. "Come. You are weary. You may tend my wound upstairs."

Weary didn't *begin* to cover it. Once the adrenaline had worn off and her hands had stopped shaking, exhaustion had assailed her. Feet dragging, Beth felt as though she had spent the past twenty-four hours working road construction in Houston in triple-digit temperatures.

She leaned into Robert's big body and let him lead her upstairs to his chamber, where a warm bath awaited them. Robert insisted she bathe without him, letting her wash away the day before he *befouled* the water, as he put it, with the blood of battle that coated him.

Beth wouldn't describe the wound on his arm as *paltry*. She didn't think it needed stitches, but it took several butterfly closures to seal it.

A boisterous meal followed in the great hall, one with a great deal of merrymaking as Robert's people celebrated the long-awaited defeat of his enemy with toasts and song and dance.

Beth said little, ate less, and couldn't even manage to muster a smile.

The battle today had driven home yet again just how foreign this time, this way of life, was to her.

And she had killed a man. Again. Had seen the blood spurt from his forehead and life leave his eyes as his knees had buckled and he had crumpled to the ground.

Robert did not comment on her silence. He seemed to understand that she sometimes grew quiet like this when she needed time to think or process events that threatened to overwhelm her.

He really did seem to know her better than anyone else in the world. Perhaps even better than Josh, who had always poked and prodded her into talking about it whenever he thought something troubled her.

Robert just held her hand, his thumb stroking her skin, his fingers giving hers an occasional squeeze to let her know he was there for her.

Damn, she loved him.

Stephen, on the other hand, pretty much made her want to smack him. He either didn't understand or simply didn't care that she had no desire to talk, because he would not let the subject of her weapon go, constantly peppering her with questions.

Beth sighed and looked up at Robert. "We're going to have to tell them, aren't we?"

"Not if you do not wish to, love," he countered.

She found a smile. "If we don't, Stephen will drive us mad, asking about it every five minutes."

"Not if I knock him on his arse."

She laughed. "I'm actually tempted not to tell him just so I can watch you do that."

"'Twould be my pleasure," he told her with a wink.

Stephen muttered something under his breath.

Robert laughed.

Beth shook her head. "Let's just do this and get it over with, then."

She, Robert, Stephen, Michael, and Adam retired to the chamber Marcus had been given for his recuperation, where Beth plunked down her backpack and told them as succinctly as possible that she had traveled back in time from the twenty-first century.

Marcus slid Robert a look.

The three knights all stared at her blankly.

247

Then, leaning toward Adam, Stephen muttered in a loud aside, "I was right. She *is* as mad as the miller's daughter."

Beth laughed. Taking out her cell phone, she knelt in front of the trio with her back to them and held it up to take a selfie.

None were impressed at first, thinking the phone a small mirror of some sort when they saw their reflections. But once she snapped the picture and showed it to them, along with the picture she had taken of Robert and some of the pictures that were already stored on it—including images of herself and Josh that clearly displayed modern buildings and cars and a thousand other things that just didn't exist here—they believed her.

The men's enthusiastic examination of her futuristic possessions and the ensuing barrage of questions regarding the twenty-first century roused her spirits. By the time she and Robert retired to the solar, she felt almost like herself again.

Of course, she also got a nice burst of energy when Robert made passionate love to her. How wonderful it was to shut her mind off and just let her body feel and burn and need. No worries. No regrets. No images of blood and violence bombarding her. Just Robert. His big, muscled body moving over her and stealing her breath, his tender words strengthening his hold on her heart. She really did love him. So much.

The quiet of the keep she had found so unfamiliar in her early days now soothed her and coaxed her toward sleep as she snuggled into Robert's side.

"Beth," he whispered.

"Hm?"

"Do not fall asleep yet, sweetling. There is a question I must put to you first."

She smiled. "You were great. It was wonderful. I loved every minute of it. Just let me snooze for a few minutes, then we can do it again."

A chuckle rumbled through his chest. "The question did not involve my prowess, though 'tis good to know I pleased you."

"Mmm. *Pleasing* me is an understatement."

He nuzzled the hair atop her head. "Beth."

Soooo tired.

He shook her a little. "Beth?"

"Hmm? I'm awake," she murmured. Were her words a little slurred?

"Then open your eyes and look at me," he said, a smile in his voice, "or I shall think you are simply answering me in your sleep again."

Beth tilted her head back, pried her heavy-lidded eyes open, and offered him a sleepy smile. "You are so beautiful."

He pressed a kiss to her forehead. "As are you, my love."

Reaching up, she caressed his stubbled cheek.

Robert turned his head slightly and pressed his lips to her palm. "Are you awake?"

She nodded, fingers fondling his whiskers.

"Beth, I wish to spend every night with you as we have this one."

She bit back a laugh. "I'll bet you do. I do, too."

"And I want you by my side every day," he continued earnestly, "touching and kissing me freely, scandalizing any who care to watch, aggravating me, making me laugh and making me happy in a way I did not think I could ever be again."

Her heart began to pound as he continued, both his tone and expression somber.

"I love you, Beth."

Elation filled her.

"In the short time you have been here," he said before she could respond, "you have become as important to me as the air I breathe." Pressing another kiss to her palm, he pressed her hand against his chest above his heart. "Will you marry me?"

For a moment, warmth and wonder filled her, expanding her chest and making her heart race. Then something like pain ripped through her, shredding the happiness she so wanted to grasp.

A lump rose in her throat. She squeezed her eyes closed.

Robert's heart beat abnormally fast beneath her palm as he awaited her response. She heard him swallow hard, waiting for her to speak.

"Robert," she whispered, her voice and heart breaking, unable to find the words she needed.

Robert wrapped his arms around her and drew her face to his chest. "'Tis all right, love. I have your answer." Though his voice was gentle, sorrow weighted it. His chin came to rest atop her head as he smoothed her hair with one large palm.

How could he comfort her like this when he thought she had just rejected him?

As Beth fought to hold back the tears that threatened, she felt the hand at her back clench into a fist around the covers. Every muscle pressed against her tensed as he fought the pain of the wound she had just inflicted.

Why? she wondered desperately. Why had they not been born in the same time?

His time. Her time. It didn't matter which.

Why had she only found him after she had watched her brother fall?

Why had she been brought here to find love when her uncertain future left her unable to claim it?

Why did she have to hurt Robert when she only wanted to make him happy?

Struggling to find her voice, she leaned back and looked up at him, regret piercing her like needles when she saw his face. "You know I love you," she whispered brokenly.

His shattered cerulean eyes avoided hers.

Her heart clenched. "Robert." Grasping his chin, she forced him to meet her gaze. "I *love* you. Don't *ever* doubt that."

"Yet you do not wish to be my wife."

She shook her head. "I *do* wish to be your wife. But, Robert, we don't even know how long I will be here. For all we know, I might wake up tomorrow back in the twenty-first century."

"All the more reason to take what time we may have together."

"I can't do that. I can't marry you, knowing that I might leave you at any moment. It wouldn't be fair."

"I will not keep you here against your will."

Beth frowned. "What?"

Robert's jaw clenched. "What I meant to say is, I want whatever time we have together to be spent as man and wife. If, after we speak our vows, you should find a way to return to your time and desire to do so, I will not force you to stay with me. I want you to be happy, Beth. I know you miss the comforts of your time and—"

Anger suffused her. "Are you kidding me?" she demanded, her sorrow evaporating. Sitting up, she yanked the covers away from him and tucked them up under her arms to cover her breasts. "You think indoor plumbing and air-conditioning and-and-and freaking rocky road ice cream mean more to me than *you* do? You think *that* is why I didn't say yes?"

Robert sat up slowly, brow furrowing. "I—"

"If it weren't for Josh," she raged, "I wouldn't give a rat's ass if I returned to my time!"

His eyebrows flew up.

Had her language surprised him? Or the temper he had sparked?

Beth didn't know and really didn't care. "Those things," she ranted, her voice rising with each breath, "don't mean squat to me if you aren't there to share them with me!"

"Beth—"

"Which is not to say that I won't try to make changes if I end up staying here, because that garderobe is just *not* working for me, Robert. I mean, we are *seriously* going to have to do something about that."

"Beth—"

"But I'm not so shallow that I'd give you up for a hot shower or chocolate or satellite television or whatever the hell else you think I can't live without. I can't live without *you*, damn it! I'm going to be *miserable* if I go back to my time and have to spend the rest of my life without you!"

"Sweetling—"

"I know I don't fit in here. I keep forgetting to omit modern slang and sometimes can't find medieval equivalents for modern words, so my Middle English probably ends up sounding more like Spanglish to you. And I shake men's hands and curse when I'm pissed off and do a hundred other things wrong every day. But that doesn't mean that I—"

Robert abruptly cupped her face in both hands and pulled her mouth to his.

Caught off-balance, Beth tumbled forward against him as he plundered her lips. Desire rose, swift and strong, commanding her to bury her fingers in his hair and press her breasts to his chest.

Robert softened the kiss and drew back.

Beth stared up at him, her body already tingling.

"Wait." She frowned, her anger not yet spent. "Oh, no you don't. Don't think you can distract me by—"

Again Robert took her lips with his own, seducing and devouring as though he were converting all of the hurt he felt at her refusal into pure lust.

When next he pulled back, her breath came as quickly as his own.

"Okay," she admitted hoarsely. "You win. You made me lose my train of thought."

He kissed her forehead. "Will you listen to me now?"

She nodded. Relinquishing her hold on him (the man was just too tempting), she scooted back to place a little distance between them.

He hesitated a moment. "I loved another in my youth, Beth."

A heavy weight lodged itself in her chest. She had expected him to start enumerating all of the reasons he thought they should marry, not make a confession that sucked all of the air out of her lungs. He had loved another?

"When?" she asked. "How long ago?"

"I was ten and eight." Robert shifted until he sat with his back cushioned by their pillows. "Come here, love, and let me hold you."

She *did* feel a sudden need to cling to him, as though whatever he intended to reveal might tear him away from her.

Beth snuggled up against his side. "Who was she?"

"I was squire to Lord Edmund. She was a handmaiden and a year younger than I."

"Was she pretty?" Though it was totally irrelevant, she couldn't help but ask.

"Aye, she was. In truth, she was somewhat similar to you in appearance, small and dark haired. But she lacked your strength."

"What do you mean? Like physically?" She doubted the women here spent whatever free time they managed to find doing yoga and running marathons.

"Aye. She was plumper and had not honed her muscles to perfection as you have."

"Thank you." Beth didn't think medieval women were as body conscious as women in the future were. At least, the peasant women weren't. Any muscles built here were built through manual labor.

"And, too, she lacked your strength of will," Robert continued. "Eleanor was a timid girl, her feelings easily injured by a mistress cruel enough to take advantage." His voice hardened at the end.

"Why are you telling me this, Robert?"

"I wanted to wed her, Beth. It mattered not to me that I was nobly born and she was not. I wanted her for my wife. Even more so after she bore me a son."

Beth bolted upright. "You have a son? You're a father?" How had she not known that?

He tugged her back into his arms. "Let me finish."

Her imagination exploded with images of a child-sized Robert racing about as she rapidly estimated the boy's age and bit her lip to keep from asking Robert where he was. Didn't they foster children out or send them off to be raised by someone else in medieval times?

"Eleanor was afraid to wed me. The countess knew of the love we shared and took great delight in filling Eleanor's innocent ears with horrific tales of the torture she would endure at the hands of my family, were I to take her home with me."

Beth frowned. "What kind of crap is that?"

Robert shook his head. "Had she not already heard rumors of Dillon's cruelty—"

"I thought you said—"

"He is not."

"Oh."

"Bounteous gossip said otherwise, however, and reached Eleanor's ears ere the countess poisoned them further. It took me until two months after our son Gabriel was born to convince her that all would be well if she returned to Westcott with me."

"I don't get it. Why did the countess want to prevent your marriage? Did she want you for herself or something?" He *was* pretty damned irresistible.

"Nay," he said, his voice like flint. "She simply thrived on the wretchedness of others. The countess was never so happy as when those around her, including her husband, were miserable. Even had the differences in our stations not been an issue, she would have sought ways to prevent Eleanor and me from finding happiness together. And she delighted in spreading foul rumors and speaking poorly of others."

"Oh. One of those." Beth had met people like that in the past. There seemed to be far too many of them in the world. "Robert, *I'm* beneath your station. Why wouldn't it be a problem with me?"

"Because all will believe me when I tell them you are a noblewoman from another land."

Beth considered that. "With no way to disprove it, I suppose they would take your word for it?"

"Aye."

"So what happened with Eleanor? Did you marry her?"

Robert tightened his arms around her and took a deep breath. "Nay. Eleanor and Gabriel both drowned three days after she agreed to return to Westcott with me."

Shock swept through her. "Oh, no. Oh, Robert." Wrapping her arms around him, she hugged him tight. "I'm so sorry, sweetie," she whispered.

His hands fisted in her hair. "I have always regretted not wedding her when we had the chance," he said, voice thick. "I do not wish you to leave me with the same regrets, Beth. Whether you remain here with me in this century or return to your own time, I want you for my wife. I love you."

Nodding, Beth wished in that moment that she would not have to leave. "I'll marry you, Robert," she agreed softly.

His arms tightened around her. "Because you pity me?"

Beth leaned back so she could look him in the eye. "Because you're right. Because I've never loved anyone the way I love you. And, whatever happens, I don't want to have any regrets." Reaching up, she cupped his lean, stubbled jaw in her hand. "Because I love you and want you to be my husband." She pressed a light kiss to his lips. "I want your face to be the first one I see in the morning when I wake up and the last one I see at night before I fall asleep. And I want your voice to be the first and last I hear every day we have together."

Turning his head, he kissed her palm. "I love you, Beth."

"Always."

Chapter Sixteen

EVERY LIVING THING FLED IN terror as the Earl of Westcott and his massive destrier tore through the village toward Fosterly. Women crossed themselves. Children froze in place, watching his approach with round eyes until their mothers scurried forward, wrapped them in protective arms, and led them safely out of sight. Men trembled, ducked their heads, and breathed sighs of relief once he had passed.

Dillon was accustomed to their fear. 'Twas the same everywhere he traveled. Even the damned minstrels sang tales of his ferocity and savagery on the battlefield, exaggerating them to include monstrous acts *off* the field that fascinated and horrified listeners and reduced most to shaking, stuttering lumps in Dillon's presence.

Such had only worsened since he had wed a woman whose supposed sorcery terrified even the king.

Slowing, he scrutinized Fosterly's curtain wall.

The usual number of guards stood atop it. The gate was raised, the drawbridge lowered. He could find naught to indicate that any kind of catastrophe had befallen them, yet his stomach still knotted with tension.

A few nights earlier, Alyssa's sobs had awoken him. Still a prisoner of her nightmare, his wife had not roused until he had shaken her gently, then wrapped his arms around her and held her close to calm her. He had known 'twas grave when she had hesitated to tell him her dream. But he had not expected the worst.

She had dreamed of Robert's death.

And her dreams foretold the future.

Alyssa had tried to reassure him in her usual manner. *Death in dreams more oft than not represents change, much like hallways represent transition.*

And when it does not mean change? he had countered.

She had looked away with furrowed brow, heightening his fears.

The next morning, as they had packed horses and a wagon in the bailey, preparing to leave with two score men, a young messenger from Fosterly had arrived. Dillon's stomach had sunk like a stone. He feared he had inadvertently frightened the boy in his haste to tear the missive from his trembling fingers and read it, expecting news of his brother's death.

Instead, there had been an oddly curt request for their presence penned by Robert himself.

Dillon scowled as he approached the gate.

Fosterly's guards offered no protest as he crossed the drawbridge and rode through the barbican. The men guarding the gate bowed nervous greetings as he passed, too tongue-tied to speak. All wore Fosterly's coat of arms, so at least the keep had not been taken by another.

Or so he thought, until he entered the bailey and saw the bodies strewn across the ground.

Alarm and adrenaline surging through his veins, Dillon drew his sword and prepared to fight.

Naught happened. No one attacked.

Cautiously, he lowered his sword. Guiding his horse forward, he studied the dead.

They lay in various stages of dress. Some in full armor. Some garbed only in tunics, braies, and hose. Others somewhere in between, as if someone had scavenged a piece of armor here and another piece there after they had fallen.

None bore bloodstains. Dillon's sharp gaze could locate no apparent wounds. No weapons either. And, as he looked more closely, apparently no dead.

The men all lived.

Many of them *lay* like the dead, exhausted and gasping for breath. But they lived.

What in hell had happened? Had some illness befallen Fosterly?

Laughter drew his attention to the keep.

Relief poured through him when Dillon spotted Robert, fully clothed and armored, sprawled comfortably on the steps. A substantial number of his warriors, only partially garbed like the others, surrounded him, including Sir Michael.

The rest of the bailey nigh the donjon was crowded with serfs, who strangely had divided themselves into two groups according to gender.

Growing more and more puzzled, Dillon dismounted, barely noticing the quaking man who crept forward to take the reins from him. Dillon scowled as he sheathed his sword and approached the steps.

Some of the men attempted to straighten when they saw him, then gave up and fell backward, still huffing.

Leaning back on his elbows, looking happier and more relaxed than Dillon had seen him in years, Robert finally noticed his brother's arrival.

"Dillon!" Blue eyes sparkling, his smile widening, he leapt up, hopped down the last few steps and drew him into a rough hug. "I did not think you would arrive so soon."

His fears temporarily assuaged, Dillon pounded his younger brother on the back, then kissed both cheeks. Damn, but he looked good. Not at all like he knocked at death's door. "What has transpired here?" He motioned to the men around them.

Robert grinned. "A contest of sorts. The men you see here have all failed in their quest for victory."

Those closest to them either flushed or cursed. One muttered beneath his breath.

Robert laughed and dealt that one a soft kick to the ribs. "She warned you not to underestimate her."

The man groaned and rubbed his side, feigning pain. "I shall never doubt her again, my lord."

Dillon pounced on the word that most piqued his interest. "Her?"

Robert nodded. "Lady Bethany, the woman I intend to wed."

Astonishment rendered Dillon mute.

Robert laughed and slapped him on the back. "Shocked you, did I? I am eager for you to meet her, brother. You will love her as we all do." His brow furrowing suddenly, Robert peered over Dillon's shoulder. "Where is Alyssa? Did she not accompany you?"

Still reeling, Dillon almost missed the anxiety that stole into his brother's voice.

What was this, then? Robert almost sounded as if he hoped Dillon had come alone. "I rode ahead. She and the rest of our party will be along in a few hours."

Something like resignation clouded his brother's features. Then cheering and shouting broke out all around them. And Robert's face lit up as he looked to the west.

Dillon followed his gaze.

A score or more of men appeared beyond the edge of the keep, jogging along the curtain wall. Unevenly spaced. Led by a squire. All but one of the men had doffed his armor. That one tossed aside his heavy gambeson even as Dillon watched. Several nigh the back looked as though they might drop from exhaustion at any moment.

Squinting, he thought he recognized Sir Stephen and Sir Adam just before the group disappeared behind the armory.

Bewildered, Dillon looked around the bailey. No one present engaged in their usual daily labors. Instead, as the runners came back into view, everyone jumped up and down, shrieking and shouting. The men and boys yelled encouragement to the soldiers, calling out names and confirming that two of them were indeed Sir Adam and Sir Stephen. The women and girls praised…

Dillon straightened.

They cheered for Lady Bethany.

Mouth falling open, he realized the squire leading the pack was not a squire at all, but a woman roughly Alyssa's size.

Her slender form was clad in braies and a tunic belted tightly around her narrow waist. Her feet were encased in mannish boots, her long brown hair pulled back in such a way that it resembled a horse's tail that bounced and jounced with every step. Damp curls sprang loose to surround what, even from this distance, appeared to be a pretty, though flushed face.

This was the woman his brother intended to wed?

A shrill, ear-piercing whistle split the air beside him as the group neared the barbican.

Cringing, Dillon gaped at his brother, who grinned widely as he waved to the woman.

Waving back, she smiled and shouted in oddly accented English, "Hi, sweetie! It will not be long now!"

The men behind them all groaned.

Robert laughed and—to Dillon's complete and utter astonishment—blew the woman a kiss.

The crowd's cheering and goading continued until the group disappeared around the eastern corner of the keep.

Two men staggered around the western corner, dropped to their knees, then sprawled backward on the grass, gasping for air.

"Robert," Dillon said.

"Aye?"

"Explain."

Chuckling, Robert clapped him on the back and guided him over to the steps, where Michael and Marcus made room for him.

Dillon nodded to both as he settled himself beside his brother.

"Beth wants to train in swordplay alongside the squires," Robert began.

Dillon grunted. Alyssa would like her then. His wife had ridden into battle at Dillon's side many times and would appreciate any woman who wished to do the same for Robert.

"Faudron and some of the men objected rather strenuously. I was about to intervene when Beth suggested they protested because they feared she would be better than them or *show them up* as she put it."

She thought she could defeat them?

Michael laughed. "I thought Faudron's head would burst."

"Which roused their anger enough," Robert drawled, "that Faudron fell right into her lovely clutches and agreed when she challenged him to an endurance contest of her choice. Beth chose running and invited any man who wished to participate to join them. Most of the knights, men at arms, and squires agreed at Faudron's insistence. I wisely declined." He nodded to the men around them. "Anyone who stops to catch his breath is disqualified."

"And if she is the last one standing?" Dillon asked.

"Faudron must train her."

He frowned. "How many times have they been around?"

Robert shrugged. "I have lost count." When Dillon curled his lip at the exhausted men around them, Robert gave him a hard shove. "I will hear no censure from you, brother. I train my men as vigorously as you do your own."

"Then how is it a woman has bested so many?"

Marcus muttered, "I would say naught disparaging about women in front of Lady Bethany were I you, my lord."

Dillon arched a brow.

Michael grinned. "She is stronger than she appears and has the heart of a true warrior. I can attest to that myself."

Robert smiled as he looked to the west. "In truth, she never ceases to amaze me."

Dillon had never seen his brother so besotted. Was he in love with this Lady Bethany?

Who was she? And how did her presence at Fosterly tie in with Alyssa's troubled dreams? Would she be the catalyst that would bring about Robert's demise?

"Tell me more of this woman," he murmured, looking to the west with the others.

"In good time, brother. I feel no desire to repeat myself and would rather delay the tale until Alyssa has arrived. For now, let us enjoy the entertainment."

Unsettled by the somber undertones in Robert's lightly spoken words, Dillon agreed.

The entertainment lasted another hour. The group of runners slowly dwindled to Lady Bethany, Faudron, Adam and Stephen. When Stephen ceded the battle and staggered over to join them on the steps, Dillon expected a slew of expletives to fly from his lips as soon as he regained his breath. But the crusty knight surprised him, expressing only admiration.

Faudron faltered next, too winded to spew any curses or objections.

Then, at last, Adam tottered, swayed drunkenly, and drew to a halt. Bending over, he shook his head and braced his hands on his knees while he drew in great gasping breaths.

For one brief moment, silence reigned in the bailey. Then the men all groaned and the women burst into loud cheers, jumping up and down and embracing each other.

Still running, Lady Bethany glanced over her shoulder. A huge grin split her damp face when she saw Adam. Throwing her hands up in the air, she shouted, "Woohoo! I am woman! Hear me roar!" and jogged over to the assembly of females.

Every one of them seemed to adore her. The children chattered and tugged on her tunic while their mothers and sisters took her hand or patted her on the shoulder, congratulating her.

"I did it, Alice!" Lady Bethany declared with a grin.

"Well done, my lady!" an unusually tall woman praised with a broad smile, then leaned down to embrace her.

As with Robert, there was none of the usual distance between noble and villein. No aloofness on Lady Bethany's part. Nay, they behaved like one large, happy family.

Robert, Michael, Stephen, and Marcus began to whistle, applaud, and praise Lady Bethany.

Many of the men she had bested did the same.

Dillon rose alongside Robert and watched his brother descend the stairs and stroll forward.

At once, Lady Bethany broke away from the women, skipped toward him, and launched herself into his arms. Bright, tinkling laughter escaped her as Robert spun her around in a tight circle ere he allowed her feet to touch the ground. Ducking his head, Robert spoke something into her ear that Dillon was too far away to hear. Lady Bethany laughed and locked her arms around his neck, leaning her body fully into his.

Dillon glanced around to gauge the response of the other occupants of Fosterly's bailey. 'Twas a highly improper embrace the unwed couple shared so openly. Yet most onlookers either smiled indulgently or paid no attention, as though 'twas a common occurrence.

Stunned, he looked back in time to see Lady Bethany reach up, clasp a fistful of hair atop Robert's head, and playfully rock his head from side to side. Robert grinned and pressed his forehead to hers. Her hand drifted down, stroked his cheek as he rubbed noses with her. Their words grew quieter as he drew her even closer, lifted her onto her toes, then kissed her. Deeply. Thoroughly. One hand drifting down her back and coming dangerously close to her bottom. Pulling her even tighter against him.

Dillon could practically feel the heat from where he stood as the couple's passion flared.

And still those in the bailey paid them no heed.

Dillon looked at Michael, who appeared to be struggling not to laugh at the shock that must be written across his face.

"They tend to forget the rest of us when they are in each other's presence."

Dillon could not remember the last time he had been so confounded.

Descending the steps, he wished Alyssa were there to see it.

Robert looped his arm around Lady Bethany's waist and guided her forward. "Beth, sweetling, this is my brother Dillon, Earl of Westcott."

Strange that he spoke English instead of French.

Dillon waited for the usual cringing, terror-filled reaction his name roused.

Instead, her face brightened as she stared up at him with open curiosity. "You're Dillon? Wow. It's wonderful to meet you." She spoke with an accent he had never encountered before. Still breathing heavily from her run, she thrust out her right hand. "Robert has told me so much about you." Leaning forward, she winked up at him and said as one would to a fellow conspirator, "Only good things, of course."

Dillon would have raised her fingers to his lips, but as soon as he touched her, she clasped his hand firmly in hers and began to pump it up and down.

Discomfited, he looked from their hands to Robert, who shrugged sheepishly, then back to Beth. "'Tis a pleasure to meet you as well, my lady."

Wrinkling her nose, she waved her free hand. "Please, call me Beth."

"As you wish. Might I congratulate you on your victory, Lady Beth?"

She released his hand. "Just Beth. You don't have to be formal with me. And thank you. I hope you will forgive my appearance." Tugging self-consciously on her sweat-dampened tunic, she eyed Robert balefully and nudged him with her hip. "Robert neglected to tell me you were arriving today. Had I known, I would have postponed the race."

Robert held his hands up in surrender. "I knew not he would arrive so swiftly. I thought 'twould take him another two or three days."

"Mm-hmm."

Fascinated, Dillon studied the two. He had never seen his brother behave so with a woman. As though she were both friend and lover.

As though Beth were to Robert everything that Alyssa was to Dillon.

"You must be weary," Dillon commented.

She sent the men around them a wicked smile. "Not as weary as *some* people I know."

When the men groaned, she laughed and leaned into Robert's side. Robert draped his arm around her shoulders and smiled down at her as he toyed with loose tendrils of her hair.

"I can't help it," she admitted gleefully. "They were all so smug when the race began. I have to rub it in a little."

Though some of her words confused him, Dillon caught her meaning and fought a smile. "You *are* the victor. I believe a little boasting is allowed."

She laughed. "Just between you and me, it wasn't a fair contest. I run the Houston marathon every year, so I knew I would win before the race even began."

Houston marathon? What was that? And whence came this Lady Bethany? Why was her speech so peculiar, as if she tossed the words of some foreign language in with the English?

"My lady," Edward called from the top of the stairs.

Beth grinned up at him. "I won, Edward!"

He offered her a proud smile. "I knew you would, my lady."

Grinning, she hugged Robert, who kissed the top of her head.

"I took the liberty of having a bath prepared for you in the solar," Edward informed her.

She started to reply, then cast Dillon an uncertain look. "Would you think me rude if I took advantage of that and left you men to talk or whatever?"

Again it took him a moment to find the meaning in some of her words. "Nay. Mayhap by the time you have bathed and rested, my wife will have arrived."

"Oh." All laughter deserted her. "Sure. I'll meet Lady Alyssa when I come down then." Stepping past him, she climbed the stairs.

Dillon could not help but notice his brother looked equally pensive. Why did Alyssa's impending arrival disturb them both so?

Beth bit her lip as she regarded the kirtles spread across the bed. She really wanted to look her best tonight when she met Alyssa and saw Dillon again.

Cringing, she tried not to remember how rumpled and sweaty and reeky she had been when Robert had introduced her to his brother. Dillon was probably downstairs right now, questioning Robert's sanity and trying to talk some sense into him.

She groaned. At least she wouldn't have to meet them in Alyssa's borrowed clothing. Robert had arranged for several dresses to be made for her that fit her well.

Undecided, Beth continued to survey the array of gowns before her. They were all very pretty, though rather uncomfortable for a woman who was more accustomed to wearing jeans or shorts and clothing made from nice stretchy fabrics. Toying with the belt on Robert's robe, which she had donned after her bath, she narrowed the decision down to either the green or the red one.

"Are you well, my lady?"

Beth turned to Alice, who stood near the door.

Once the two had become friends, Alice had asked if she could serve as Beth's handmaiden.

Beth had thought that might be something along the lines of a personal maid, and had wanted to balk. She just wasn't comfortable with having someone wait on her and perform tasks she was fully capable of performing herself. But she *had* needed someone to help her dress and undress when Robert wasn't around. And Alice had looked so hopeful.

"My lady?" Alice prodded gently, collecting the towels Beth had tossed on a trunk after her bath.

"I'm fine," Beth answered, mustering a smile as she motioned to the bed. "I just can't decide what to wear. Which kirtle do you like the best?"

Alice looked past her at the bed. "I like the green one." She smiled. "But that is only because green is my favorite color. I think the red would look beautiful against your dark hair."

Robert entered the solar.

"Finally!" Beth exclaimed.

Alice bobbed a curtsy, then slipped out into the hallway and closed the door behind her.

Hurrying over to give Robert a quick peck on the cheek, Beth took his hand and pulled him toward the bed. "I want to make sure I look my best tonight, but can't decide what to wear. What do you think?"

His brow crinkled. "Beth, there is no reason for you to be nervous."

"Aye, there is. I want to make a good impression." She grimaced. "Or at least a *better* impression. Was your brother totally offended by my looking like a boy and shaking his hand?"

"Nay, he was intrigued." Amusement sifted into his handsome face. "And no matter your garb, you could *never* look like a boy, sweetling."

Beth rolled her eyes. "I was wearing Marcus's old clothes."

Robert's face darkened. "And do not think the men failed to notice how tight the tunic fit across your breasts or how it and the braies hugged your lovely bottom. Those who ran behind you will receive a grueling punishment on the morrow once I drag their weary carcasses onto the practice field."

"They were *all* running behind me, honey."

His eyes narrowed dangerously. "I know."

Laughing, Beth motioned to the bed. "So, which one?"

"The red is my favorite."

"Red it is. Would you please help me dress?"

Nodding, he set about dressing her as efficiently as Alice would.

Beth couldn't decide whether his being so adept at getting a woman in and out of her clothes was a good thing or a bad thing. Clearly, he had had a lot of practice.

Quiet descended as he laced her up. He offered none of his usual playful leers or teasing touches. Nor did he suggest that they forego dinner and feast on each other instead.

Kneeling in front of her, he straightened a portion of her hem that had folded back.

"Well?" Beth plucked at one long sleeve. "How do I look?"

He stared up at her, his gaze traveling slowly from her dainty slippers up to the hair that fell down her back in long, loose curls.

"I have never seen a more beautiful woman in my life," he whispered, his deep voice hoarse.

Beth cupped his face in one hand, her heart turning over in her breast. There were times when the love she felt for him overwhelmed her with its depth and intensity.

Robert turned his face and nuzzled her palm.

"I love you, Robert."

Still on his knees, he leaned into her and wrapped his arms around her waist.

Beth stroked his hair as he buried his face between her breasts and held her tightly, almost desperately.

Unease sifted through her.

Something was wrong. She had felt it for days now. Between his usual bouts of passion and playfulness, Robert had grown increasingly preoccupied, as though some problem weighed heavily on his mind.

Her mouth went dry. Beth swallowed. "Have you changed your mind?" she asked softly.

"About the red?" he mumbled, his warm breath heating the valley between her breasts.

"Nay. About marrying me."

Leaning back a bit, he frowned up at her. "Why would you ask that?"

She shrugged. "I know I must have embarrassed you earlier and—" She broke off when he loosened his hold long enough to rise and press two fingers to her lips.

"Beth, love, if I could live forever, my only wish would be that I might spend eternity with you by my side as my wife and that you would always love me in return."

Reaching up, she stroked his cheek, rough with stubble no matter how often he shaved. "I do love you, Robert. Enough to know that something is troubling you. What is it? Talk to me. Let me help you."

He closed his eyes. Leaning down, he pressed his forehead to hers. He rested his hands on her waist, his fingers gently caressing her as though he couldn't help himself.

Beth waited for him to speak. Gave him time to gather his thoughts.

His nearness went a long way toward soothing the butterflies in her stomach. His warmth. His strength. His scent.

Drawing in a deep breath, she savored it, that bewitching aroma that was Robert's alone. Unclouded by cologne, it appealed to her senses more than the mightiest of aphrodisiacs.

It still astounded her—how swiftly she had come to know it. To know *him*.

And to love him so completely.

Drawing in a deep breath, Robert raised his head and straightened his shoulders. "There is another reason I asked Dillon and Alyssa to come here, beyond desiring their presence at our wedding."

"Okay." For some reason, she suddenly wanted to flee the conversation. "What might that be?"

A muscle in his jaw jumped. "I asked them to come because I believe Alyssa may be able to help you."

Help her? Help her how? Alyssa was a healer. Beth wasn't sick. What exactly did Robert think Alyssa could help her with?

Her stomach sank as a possible answer hit her.

Alyssa was perfect, right? Hadn't Robert waxed freaking poetic every time he had spoken of her?

Stepping back, she broke his hold and struggled to quell the hurt that rose within her.

It was only logical, right? Beth was from the future and knew very little of the social customs of this time. It shouldn't bother her that, despite his assurances to the contrary, Robert thought she needed some work in order to fit in, that he wanted her to become more like Alyssa.

But it did. It really did.

"So, you asked her to come here and, what, train me?" No amount of effort could keep the resentment from her voice. "You want her to help me be more like a lady? To be more like *her*?"

Robert's mouth fell open. "What?" He looked so aghast that she knew she had guessed incorrectly.

She eyed him uncertainly. "That isn't why she's here?"

He actually started to look a little angry.

Or maybe a lot.

"Beth, have you *never* believed me when I told you I love you?"

She frowned. "Of course I believed you."

"Nay, you did not," he protested with a scowl. "If you believed me, such would not have even occurred to you. You would know that there is naught I wish to change about you. I love you as you are."

Beth held up her hands. "Look, we both know everyone thinks I'm weird."

"I care *naught* what anyone else thinks!" he practically bellowed, startling her into silence. He was getting that red-in-the-face, murderous look that came over him whenever he thought someone maligned Alyssa. "I love you! I love everything about you. Your wisdom. Your wit. Your laughter. Your strength. Your beauty. Your scent. Your touch. There is naught about you that is not perfect and anyone who suggests otherwise will find my sword embedded in his belly!"

Wow.

Just... *wow.*

He actually seemed hurt that she might think he wanted to change her. "I don't get it," she broached hesitantly. "You said you thought Alyssa could help me. If you weren't talking about etiquette lessons, what did you mean?"

"I meant—" He clamped his lips shut. Pacing away from her, he raked his fingers through his hair as he was wont to do when troubled.

"Robert?"

His back to her, he propped his hands on his hips and lowered his head. When next he spoke, his voice was low. Reluctant. As though she forcibly dragged the words from him against his will. "You told me that the day you traveled back in time, a man came to you, garbed all in black."

She nodded slowly. "The monk? Or the guy *dressed* like a monk? Yeah. I mean, aye. But it wasn't real, remember? It was a hallucination."

He turned to face her. "I believe it *was* real, Beth. I believe the man in the dark robe came to you, healed you, and carried you back in time."

What?

She frowned. "Okay. Let's say he *was* real. What does that have to do with Alyssa?"

"I believe Alyssa's brother was the one who brought you to me. The one who brought you back in time." His throat worked. "And if I am right, she can summon him here to Fosterly to take you home again."

Beth stared at him, uncomprehending.

The gears that powered her brain ground to a screeching halt, preventing her from processing whatever Robert was trying to tell her. She didn't *want* to process it. "I don't..." Closing her eyes, she shook her head slightly to clear it. "You think the man I thought I saw after I was shot... you're saying that was Alyssa's brother?"

"I believe so, aye."

Opening her eyes, Beth stared at him.

He kept his expression blank. Only a slight tic in his jaw betrayed his unease.

She must have misunderstood. He couldn't be saying what she thought he was.

Could he? Could she have been such a fool?

Nausea struck, as did a fierce pounding in her head. Her breath shortened. "Alyssa's brother can travel through time?" Her eyes burned as tears blurred her vision. "You knew? All this time, while I've been questioning my sanity and trying to understand what happened to me, trying to figure out how the hell I came here, you *knew* and you said *nothing*?" The pain of his betrayal pierced her breast and made her head swim.

"Beth—"

"Shut up!" Raising a trembling hand to her forehead, she drew her fingers across it. "I can't believe this," she whispered. "I can't believe this. So... what? This was all a game to you?"

"Nay, I—"

"Bringing me here, watching me flounder and struggle to get my bearings, making me fall in love with you—"

"Beth—"

"*Shut up!*"

It didn't make any sense. Robert wasn't cruel. He was *not* a cruel man. She would bet her life on it. She *had* bet her life on it, in a way. How could he have done this to her?

Her head began to swim. "I can't think. I feel dizzy."

Robert swiftly closed the distance between them and, taking her arm, guided her to one of the chairs before the hearth. As Beth sank weakly onto the polished wood, he knelt before her and took her icy hands in his own. "Beth, love, listen to me."

"I trusted you," she whispered.

"And your trust was not misplaced," he vowed earnestly, his warm hands chafing her fingers to warm them. "Please, Beth, let me speak."

Robert had held her while she'd cried. Those first few nights when grief over losing Josh had seemed unbearable, when confusion and fear had overwhelmed her, she had crawled into his bed like a child seeking the comfort of a parent after a gruesome nightmare, and he had voiced not one objection. Despite the discomfort he must have felt when his body had responded to her own cuddled up against his, he had not pressured her for greater intimacy. Nor had he pressured her to explain her tears or grim silence.

He had protected her. He had sheltered her. He had lied about where she had come from so others would accept her, and had done all he could

269

to ease her transition into his world. He had shared his painful past with her, confessed the grief and regret he had felt over the deaths of his lover and their son. He had made her laugh and teased her and tried to please her in a thousand ways.

And he had made love to her with such aching tenderness.

It couldn't have been a lie. It couldn't *all* have been a lie.

"Beth?"

She nodded, giving him permission to speak, needing him to make it right.

"I have told you of Alyssa, of her family and the other *gifted ones*," he began. "How each was born with special talents or abilities the rest of us lack."

"You said she could *heal*." Beth didn't know whether she acknowledged it or leveled an accusation.

He nodded and switched to her other hand. "Alyssa and her grandmother were both born with the ability to heal with their hands. Her mother can scry the future. Her cousin Meghan can move things with her mind and her brother Geoffrey…"

"Can travel through time," she finished for him numbly. She would have withdrawn her hand, but Robert wouldn't let her.

"In truth, Alyssa has never disclosed her brother's gifts. I believe she has avoided doing so because she thinks 'twill make me fear him."

"You said he brought me back in time."

"Sir Geoffrey meets the description of the man you saw after you were wounded. Tall. Dark eyes. Long dark hair. Garbed in the black robes favored by the *gifted ones*. You said such was uncommon in your time."

The robes were. "You don't know for sure it was him?"

"Nay. And I will not until Alyssa confirms it."

She took a moment to absorb that. "Have you suspected this all along?"

Some of the tightness in her chest eased when he shook his head. "I knew not any of the *gifted ones* were capable of such an incredible feat. Not until you mentioned the man in black the morning we rode for Terrington. Ere then, I could find no explanation for what had brought you to me."

"That was three weeks ago, Robert. Why didn't you tell me then?"

"I knew 'twould trouble you, Beth. I knew you would worry and fret every moment of every day until Alyssa arrived and could answer your questions."

No sense in denying it. "So, you were trying to protect me?"

He nodded. "If I am wrong... Had I told you, I would have raised your hopes for naught."

"And if you're right?"

He sighed and pressed his lips to her fingers. "I needed this time with you, Beth."

Her throat tightened as he stared at her with his heart in his eyes.

"If Sir Geoffrey can walk through time and agrees to return you to the future, to take you out of my life..." His Adam's apple bobbed. "I needed this time with you. I needed the memories we have created to help sustain me after you leave, after you return to your home."

Home.

A tear spilled over her lashes and traced a chilly path down one cheek. Her throat grew so thick Beth had to clear it before she could speak. "The thing is, I'm not sure I know where home is anymore, Robert."

She loved him. She would *always* love Robert.

But she loved her brother, too, and had left him bleeding to death in that forest.

Cupping the back of her head in one large palm, Robert pressed a tender kiss to her lips, then wrapped his arms around her and held her close.

Beth fisted her hands in his tunic, pulling him even closer.

They remained thus for a long time.

And though both feared what the future would bring, Robert did not ask her to stay. Not because he didn't love her, Beth knew. But because he would always place her happiness and her desires before his own.

Burying her face in his warm neck, she wept.

Chapter Seventeen

BETH AND ROBERT MADE THEIR way down to the great hall, as somber as a funeral procession.

Beth's anxiety over meeting the wondrously perfect Alyssa had evaporated beneath the onslaught of apprehension spawned by the bombshell Robert had dropped in his solar.

Robert stopped her halfway down the stairs. "Beth, I feel I should warn you…"

She groaned. "Ro-*bert*." She really couldn't take any more bad news today.

His lips twitched. "I only wished to impart that Alyssa's gifts have grown considerably in recent years and—"

"Grown how?"

"She is far more powerful than she used to be. When she touches you now, she can not only heal you and read your emotions, she can also hear your thoughts as clearly as though you have spoken them aloud and glean images from your past."

Crap. That was kind of scary actually. Not in a *She's-a-witch!-Burn-her!* kind of way. But in an *All-your-deepest-darkest-secrets-will-be-revealed* kind of way.

"Dillon and I have each learned to erect a shield of sorts in our mind," Robert said, "so she can only see what we *wish* her to see. Most of the time. But since you cannot, I did not think 'twould be fair for you to meet her without first knowing this."

"Oh." What else could she say to that? "Thank you?"

Nodding, he took her arm and guided her down the remaining steps.

As they entered the great hall, Dillon exited the kitchen with a boy on his hip who looked to be about three or four years old.

As soon as the little boy saw Robert, he squealed in delight, wriggled to get down, then raced toward them, crying out for his uncle Robert.

Beth smiled as Robert picked him up, hugged him, and bussed him on the cheek. Except for the brown eyes, the resemblance was remarkable. Both had jet-black hair. Similar noses. Similar chins, though the boy's was more rounded.

Anyone who didn't know better would probably assume this was Robert's son.

Sadness filtered through her as she thought of the child Robert had lost.

Did he see Gabriel every time he looked at his nephew?

"Beth," Robert said with a grin, "this fierce little warrior is my nephew, Ian." He set the boy down. "Ian, this is Lady Bethany."

Ian performed the cutest little bow.

Utterly charmed, Beth curtsied in response. "Such a strong, handsome warrior. I suspect you shall slay many dragons when you are older."

His eyes lit up. "Dragons?"

Joining them, Dillon smoothed a hand over the boy's hair. "'Twill take a great deal of training ere you can accomplish such a feat. Why not hone your skills by sparring with Sir Stephen?"

His face wreathed in a smile, Ian took off running to the other side of the hall, where Stephen waited with a couple of small wooden swords.

Beth smiled as she watched the two begin a mock battle.

Robert shook his head. "Whatever are you going to do with a daughter, Dillon?" He turned to Beth. "Alyssa is with child again. She carries my niece."

"Oh, my goodness! That's wonderful! Congratulations!" She would've hugged Dillon, but wasn't sure if that would be considered inappropriate and *really* wanted to make a better impression on him.

Dillon nodded, looking both proud and pensive. "In truth, I know not what I shall do with a little girl."

Beth shrugged. "Put a sword in her hands and train her alongside Ian."

Robert grinned.

Dillon eyed her speculatively.

"Hey, every woman needs to know how to defend herself," Beth pointed out. "If she doesn't, what's going to happen to her if she's attacked one day when you're not around?"

Dillon looked ill at the prospect. Turning toward the hearth, he shouted. "Alyssa, I am putting a sword in our daughter's hands as soon as she can hold one, and will hear no objections from you."

"As you will, my lord." The words were spoken not submissively, but with amused indulgence.

Beth followed the soft sounds to the exquisite figure seated before the hearth. "Ah, hell."

Robert's head snapped around. "What?"

"*That's* Alyssa?"

Beside her, Dillon stiffened. "You object?"

"Nay," she said quickly, realizing she had offended him. "It's just..." She gazed upon Dillon's wife, then motioned to her despondently. "Look at her. She's perfect, like Robert said. Perfect hair. Perfect skin. A perfect, pretty face. Perfect posture. She's probably even sewing a perfect seam. How the hell am I supposed to compete with that?"

Robert coughed to cover a laugh.

Beth glared at him, seeing nothing funny about it.

Touching her shoulder, he looked to his brother. "In my attempts to ensure Beth did not fear Alyssa, I might have been a *bit* too enthusiastic in my praise of her. I fear Beth mistook my affection for Alyssa as something more than brotherly and—despite my assurances—remains a bit jealous."

Dillon's eyebrows flew up. "Of Alyssa?"

"Aye."

The older brother's lips twitched.

"Oh, ha, ha, ha. Laugh it up," Beth groused, and the two men shared a grin.

Over by the hearth, Alyssa began putting her sewing away and prepared to rise. She really was perfect. A little smaller than Beth, she bore slender arms and graceful hands. Her long raven locks gleamed in the firelight, providing a lovely contrast to pale, radiant, freckle-free skin. When she rose, her gown revealed a tummy barely rounded, indicating she was still in the early months of pregnancy.

About the only flaw Beth could find was that she looked a little weary.

Robert took Beth's arm and escorted her over to the hearth.

Beth could feel Dillon studying her and fought the urge to squirm like an insect held under a microscope. Robert's older brother possessed

274

an air of intensity that she had to admit was a bit unsettling and doubtless contributed heavily to people's fear of him.

Alyssa smiled when they reached her.

Dillon moved to stand at her side and placed a possessive hand at her back. His countenance softened slightly as he looked down at her and made the introductions.

Beth automatically held out her hand. "Robert told me about the baby. Congratulations."

As Alyssa reached out to touch her, Beth belatedly remembered Robert's warning and jerked her hand back at the last minute. If Alyssa touched her, she would be inundated with images from the future. That probably wouldn't be a good idea until Beth and Robert explained everything.

Hurt flickered in Alyssa's dark brown eyes before a veil descended over her features.

Oh, crap. "I'm sorry." Eyes wide, Beth looked at Robert, who winced, then at Dillon, whose expression darkened as a murderous gleam entered his blue eyes. "I'm so sorry. Really. That was incredibly rude of me," she blurted, talking fast to head off whatever violence Dillon contemplated and to reassure Alyssa. "*Please* do not think I meant any insult by it. I totally did not. I just remembered at the last minute... I mean, I forgot that..." *Get it together*, she ordered herself. "Okay, Robert told me you can read thoughts and... I didn't think... I mean, I thought it wouldn't be wise for you to..." *Sheesh*. She was really bungling this.

She looked up at Robert. "You want to help me out here?"

"Verily, she meant no insult, Alyssa," he insisted. "'Tis only that I told her of your gifts and there are things in her past that she feared would shock you."

Beth stared up at him in dismay. That sounded even worse than her ramblings had! She slapped him on the arm. "Robert! Don't say it like that! You make it sound like I used to be a whore or something!"

"Were you?" Dillon asked insolently.

Beth glared at him. "You know, you are *not* too old to spank."

Robert choked on a laugh.

Alyssa held up one hand to silence whatever retort Dillon planned to voice. "You did not avoid my touch because you fear I am evil?"

Beth frowned. "What? No. Nay. Why would I think you are evil?"

Now Alyssa's brow puckered. "Because of my gifts."

Beth shook her head. "Nay, I do *not* think you're evil. I just come from a place that is very different from this one, and worried that if you saw it in my thoughts…" Well, she wasn't sure what would happen. Robert and Michael and the others had known there was something off about her long before she had told them the truth. Alyssa would just have seen it all cold turkey, no warning.

Beth sighed and glanced up at the man she had come to love so much. "You know what? This isn't going very well. My one shot at making a good first impression on your family has pretty much been blown all to hell, so why don't we just spill the truth and get it over with?"

He tucked a stray strand of hair behind her ear and stroked the nape of her neck. "Forgive me, Beth. Had I thought this through, I could have made this meeting far less awkward." He turned to Dillon and Alyssa. "There is much we have to tell you. And more we must discuss. 'Twould be best if we do so in the privacy of the solar."

Beth offered Alyssa a tentative smile. "Maybe we could start over? I promise—once we tell you everything—you can touch me all you want."

All eyebrows flew up.

Beth groaned. "Wait. That didn't come out right. That sounded sexual, didn't it?"

Stunned silence greeted her.

Shoulders drooping, she looked up at Robert. "I must be more tired than I thought. I keep putting my foot in my mouth."

Chuckling, he drew her up against his side and kissed her hair. "The day has been a long one, love."

"For all of us," Alyssa added, kindly wiping the shock from her expression. "May I congratulate you, Lady Bethany, on your victory over Robert's men? My husband told me of your contest."

"Thank you. And please, call me Beth."

"Then you must call me Alyssa." She smiled. "I wish I could have been here to see Sir Faudron's and Sir Stephen's expressions."

They turned as one to look across the hall at Stephen just as Ian's sword hit Stephen squarely in the groin. Dropping his own sword, the irascible warrior slammed his knees together, cupped himself with both hands, and—whimpering—toppled over onto the floor.

Robert and Dillon both winced.

Beth pursed her lips. "Too bad he wasn't still wearing his armor."

Michael and the other men in the great hall found it wildly amusing, their laughter swelling and echoing off the walls.

Alyssa narrowed her eyes at Dillon. "Do not dare laugh."

"I would not," he said with a grimace. "Ian has done the same to me on numerous occasions."

Robert grunted. "I will not ask if Alyssa healed you with her hands."

Alyssa's cheeks flushed while Dillon donned a naughty grin.

"Perhaps now would be a good time for us to retire to the solar," Beth suggested brightly, hoping to alleviate the other woman's embarrassment.

The others agreed, and—with lighter spirits all around—they exited the great hall.

An hour later, Dillon and Alyssa sat with their heads bent over Beth's cell phone, gazing in astonishment at the photo she had just taken of them, as well as those she had taken of Robert, Marcus and the others.

Thank goodness Beth had packed her solar charger. Without it, her cell phone's battery would have long since died and she wouldn't have had the photos to aid her whenever she tried to convince others she was from the future.

She and Robert had recited her tale as concisely as possible. Through much of it, Dillon had looked angry and suspicious. Alyssa had appeared unsettled. But, as with Michael and the others, Beth's modern goodies—the cell phone and coins in particular—convinced them where words would not.

Alyssa's gifts, however, also afforded them another way.

"Alyssa," Beth said, extending her hand, palm up, "would you like to *see* the future?"

Alyssa glanced at Dillon.

"Do not overtax yourself, sweetling," he murmured.

Beth's gaze dropped to the woman's stomach. "Oh. Will it tire you?" She didn't know how exactly the woman's gift worked.

Smiling, Alyssa shook her head as she handed her husband the cell phone. "Not overly."

"Good." Beth extended her hand again. "Do I just picture what I want you to see?"

"Aye, though I should warn you I may pick up other things along the way," she cautioned. "Things you may not wish me to see. Things you think of often."

Beth bit her lip. That was a bit unsettling. "Then I should probably warn *you* that you are likely to see a lot of Robert naked."

Alyssa's eyes widened as a blush climbed her cheeks.

Dillon released a bark of involuntary laughter.

When Beth glanced at Robert, his eyes twinkled as his lips stretched in a mischievous smile.

"You imagine me naked often, do you?" he murmured, toying with a lock of her hair.

Beth winked. "Are you kidding? You're naked right now."

Laughing, he kissed her cheek.

Beth turned back to Alyssa. "I'm sorry. I couldn't resist. Would you please keep anything personal or embarrassing you might see in my thoughts between you and me?"

"Aye, Beth," she said with a smile. "I would have done so without your request."

"Thank you. Now, why don't I start by showing you my homeland?"

As soon as Alyssa took her hand, Beth closed her eyes and pictured a map of the world laid out before her. "Okay, there's Europe. There's England. And way over here to the west are North and South America."

Alyssa's hand tightened on hers. "I have read ancient scrolls that suggested there was land far to the west, but I never guessed 'twould be so much."

The map in Beth's mind molded itself into a sphere and settled into orbit around the sun with the other planets all in their places.

Alyssa gasped and jerked her hand back.

Beth opened her eyes. "What?"

"You know the Earth circles the sun," Alyssa whispered, then looked at Robert.

Robert raised his hands. "I did not tell her. She already knew."

Beth nodded. "Everyone knows that in my time. The Earth is round and revolves around the sun, along with seven other planets and three dwarf planets."

When Dillon and Alyssa just stared at her, Beth fidgeted uncertainly. "Do you wish to continue?"

Nodding hesitantly, Alyssa again took Beth's hand.

Beth pictured the globe again and let a map of the United States overlay itself atop the North American continent. "This is the country I was born in, the United States. This is Texas." Mentally, she zoomed in on the Lone Star State. "And this is Houston, the city I've lived in all of my life."

"'Tis so large," Alyssa breathed.

"It is," Beth agreed. "I think at last count there were around six million people living in the Houston metropolitan area."

Both Robert and Dillon expressed shock at such a high number.

"'Tis true, Dillon," Alyssa said as Beth showed her the tall buildings and the masses of people. "Look at all of the glass windows!"

Glass windows, Beth had come to understand, were very rare and expensive in this time.

"Oh!" Alyssa exclaimed. "What are those?"

Beth smiled. "Cars. Also called automobiles. You might understand them better as horseless carriages or wagons. Most are powered by a liquid fuel, rather than animals, and can travel three or four times faster than the fastest horse you've ridden."

"Oh, I wish you could see this," Alyssa told the men, her voice high with excitement.

"You know what's even cooler than the cars?" Beth asked with a grin. "Airplanes."

Beth recalled as vividly as possible her last trip to the airport. Walking through the long boarding tunnel, taking her seat, then watching out the window as the plane took off and the land fell away beneath them.

Alyssa abruptly jerked her hand back and broke contact.

Opening her eyes, Beth saw that this time the woman looked pale and shaken.

"You were flying through the air," she whispered.

Robert and Dillon regarded Beth with wide eyes.

"*I* wasn't flying," she corrected. "The plane was. Airplanes are like automobiles, except they can fly through the air and travel at much greater speeds. People frequently use them to cover long distances in the briefest amount of time possible. I'd have to look it up to be sure, but you could probably fly from London to Paris in just a couple of hours."

All three simply stared at her.

Alyssa turned to her husband. "She truly is from the future. 'Tis miraculous, all that she has shown me."

His face unreadable, Dillon brushed the hair back from Alyssa's pale face, then resumed his scrutiny of Beth.

Beginning to feel uncomfortable, Beth turned to Robert, who studied her with astonishment.

"Oh, no you don't," she griped. "Don't *you* start looking at me funny. You already knew all of this."

Robert forced a smile and draped his arm across her shoulders. Encouraging her to lean into him, he kissed her temple, then turned to Alyssa. "Can you tell us if Sir Geoffrey was the man who came to her and carried her through time?"

Beth looked to Alyssa for her response.

"I have never known Geoffrey to accomplish such a feat. He would have told me if he could do so."

Dillon stroked her arm. "When you acquired your new gifts, they unsettled you so much that you would not admit you possessed them and only spoke of them when I forced you to."

Beth would love to hear more of *that* story. Alyssa had acquired more gifts? How? And when?

"Mayhap Geoffrey has done the same," Dillon suggested. "Mayhap he has acquired a new gift and is too unsettled by it to speak of it."

The notion clearly disturbed Alyssa, who extended her hand to Beth. "Show me what happened that day."

Her stomach turning over, Beth clasped the woman's hand once more.

"Robert," Alyssa said, "you will either have to quiet your thoughts or cease touching her."

Beth glanced at Robert.

His eyebrows rose. "You can hear my thoughts?"

Alyssa nodded. "Quite clearly. 'Tis a bit like listening to two people speak at once."

Beth eyed him curiously. "You didn't know it could work that way?"

Frowning, he shook his head.

Alyssa nodded suddenly. "Better. When you are ready, Beth."

Beth replayed the day she had traveled back through time. She tried to leave the gory parts out, but didn't succeed. Whenever she thought of that day, she remembered it all. Hearing gunshots. Racing forward. Finding Josh cornered. Watching three bullets slam into him. Getting shot twice herself. Lying there, choking on her own blood.

Then the man in black kneeling beside her.

"'Tis not Geoffrey," Alyssa murmured just before Beth heard the stranger's words.

I have come for you, Bethany.

She opened her eyes.

Alyssa released her and stared, unseeing, at the hearth. "'Tis not Geoffrey," she repeated softly.

"Was the man a *gifted one*?" Robert asked.

Slowly, she nodded and met his gaze. "I could not glimpse his face clearly, but recognized his voice. 'Twas the giant. When the *gifted ones* came to Westcott to help me birth Ian, he spoke to me."

Beth frowned. "The giant?"

Alyssa nodded. "There are two *gifted ones* we know not. Both are men. One is so tall he dwarfs Dillon."

Beth glanced at Dillon, who stood a few inches above six feet.

"Though he calls himself Seth," Alyssa resumed, "my husband refers to him as the giant."

"I can see why," Beth murmured.

"This Seth is the most powerful of us all," Alyssa continued. "*Far* more powerful than I. And his voice was that of the man who came to you."

"Can you call him to us?" Robert asked her.

"I will try."

"On the morrow, after you have rested," Dillon insisted.

Smiling, she touched his cheek. "As you will."

Dillon met Robert's gaze. "What of the wedding? Now that Bethany has a means of returning to her own time, will it still take place?"

The churning in Beth's stomach graduated to an intense burning, as though someone had poured something highly acidic down her throat.

"Dillon," Alyssa remonstrated, "'tis not our concern."

"'Tis *my* concern," he protested. "I do not wish to see my brother hurt."

"We know not that Seth can return her to her time. We…"

Their voices faded away, drowned out by Beth's heartbeat pounding in her ears. Her time with Robert could very well end soon, if Seth arrived and said he could take her back, said he *would* take her back.

How could she leave? She loved Robert more than she had even known it was possible to love someone. How could she walk away from that? From *him*? How could she walk away from what they shared and return to her own time, knowing she would never see him again? Never know what had happened to him?

Unless you look him up in a history book and find out who he married after you left, a hysterical voice whispered in her head.

Robert cupped her face in his hand and tilted her chin up.

"I don't want to lose you," she whispered, panic rising.

"Nor I you."

She focused on his eyes, afraid to blink, hoping he could somehow quiet the maelstrom of thoughts crashing through her mind. "Do you still want to marry me?" she asked.

Dipping his head, he brushed a kiss across her lips that—though light as air—carried the full weight of his love for her. "I would have you as my wife, Beth, for whatever time we will have together, be it a sennight, a season, or a century."

She blinked back tears. "And I would have you for my husband. I love you, Robert. More than I ever dreamed I *could* love another."

He took her mouth again, this time with a passion that fired an immediate response within her. Wrapping her arms around his neck, Beth let him lift her over onto his lap. His tongue plunged inside to stroke her own as he combed the fingers of one hand through her hair, sending tingles down her spine, then clasped the back of her head to hold her still while he devoured her. He settled his other hand on her waist, then slid it down to her hip. His grip tightened as hunger rose and claimed them both.

A throat cleared.

Robert lifted his head but never looked away from Beth. "Did you bring Father Markham with you?" he asked.

"Aye," Dillon responded.

"Then we shall be wed three days hence."

If anyone said anything after that, Beth neither knew nor cared.

282

Robert's lips once more claimed hers, his tongue doing things that made her want to devour every inch of him, which—come to think of it—was an excellent idea.

Bethany married Robert three days later with Dillon, Alyssa, and what appeared to be every inhabitant of Fosterly as their witnesses.

Father Markham, who had accompanied Dillon and Alyssa on their journey, performed the ceremony. Beth wasn't certain how old he was. She had difficulty estimating age here.

In her time, people in their fifties could easily look, act, and feel as if they were in their thirties. But here fifty was old. Like *nearing the end of your life* old. Beth had met precious few men over the age of sixty-five, and even fewer women. The legal age for marriage was twelve in this era. And birthing one child after another was tantamount to playing Russian roulette. Robert had told her that he would have wed at age twelve himself if the girl to whom his father had betrothed him had not died before the ceremony could be conducted.

Beth attributed Robert's looking so young at age twenty-nine—not to mention attaining a height of six feet—to Alyssa, her healing gift, and the intriguingly advanced knowledge the woman's family possessed and had shared with the Westcott lords. Knowledge passed down through the *gifted ones'* mysterious lineage.

Apparently Westcott was something of a utopia in medieval England, with most of its inhabitants living far longer than their counterparts.

Since Father Markham was Westcott's resident priest, Beth couldn't tell if he was thirty and looked his age or was perhaps younger. He was handsome in a clean-cut, boy-next-door kind of way, and uniquely open-minded, considering both his profession and the time period. Beth liked him instantly. He was very friendly, and not at all put off by her odd speech and mannerisms.

Of course, if rumors held any truth, Father Markham had witnessed a wealth of unusual occurrences since making Alyssa's acquaintance. The residents of Fosterly had, too, during Alyssa and Dillon's frequent visits.

So Beth suspected *weird* had become a kind of norm for them, something that had really worked in her favor. With her modern speech, ideas, and behavior, Beth doubted she would have been so well received anywhere else.

Alyssa produced a beautiful cream-colored kirtle for Beth and helped her don it.

Robert waited for Beth outside the church doors, unbearably handsome in his finest tunic. So handsome that Beth almost tripped walking up the steps, because she couldn't take her eyes off of him.

Fortunately, Dillon escorted her and kept her from falling on her face, his taciturn expression lightening at her no doubt besotted expression.

The ceremony took place outside the church, according to custom.

Wind whipped all present and wrought havoc with Beth's hair. With no extra super hold hairspray on hand, she spent most of the ceremony dragging loose curls out of her eyes and wishing she would've donned one of those wimple head scarf things so many of the married women here wore.

Evidently, the fact that Alyssa didn't wear one was fairly scandalous.

After the ceremony, they adjourned inside for a mass.

Feasting followed. Table upon table laden with huge quantities of food that would likely appall modern doctors and spark lectures on the dangers of high cholesterol and high blood pressure. But it was all *very* tasty and too tempting for Beth to resist. She didn't know if women here were supposed to pick at their food and eat dainty portions. But if they were, then she probably raised eyebrows yet again while she packed away more food than Sir Stephen.

In the bailey, Robert hosted games and contests for the villeins and their children.

In the great hall, lively acrobats and jesters entertained, as did minstrels.

Beth thought the dancing positively surreal. It entailed very little physical contact, aside from holding or touching hands. Nothing at all sensual. A far cry from the dancing she had witnessed at twenty-first-century clubs and parties, in which couples ground on each other to the beat and simulated sex.

And speaking of sex...

Apparently, at the end of the night, there was supposed to be a bedding ceremony of some sort. Beth could never quite figure out what it involved. The whispers she managed to catch seemed to range from Alyssa and some attendants helping Beth change and prepare for Robert to deflower her (a little too late for that one), to Beth's being escorted to the solar by the women, stripped naked, then put on display for Robert and the men who carried him upstairs on their shoulders.

Beth had three words for the latter: Oh, *hell* no.

She didn't know if Robert had nixed such plans ahead of time, or if there hadn't been any to begin with. But when the time came for them to retire, he simply twined his fingers through hers and brought her hand to his lips for a kiss. The tenderness in his blue eyes as they met hers warmed her heart.

"Shall we?" he asked softly beneath the boisterous laughter in the hall.

She nodded.

Smiling, he rose, drew her up from her seat at the high table, then escorted her from the hall.

No one followed, though several of Robert's men called bawdy suggestions after them.

Closing the solar door behind them dampened but did not silence the revelry that took place below.

Someone had prepared a fire in the hearth and left wine for them on the table beside it.

Beth stared up at Robert, her heart pounding wildly in her chest. "I feel nervous," she admitted, "like it's my first time."

He smiled and drew her closer. "It *is*. For both of us." Dipping his head, he pressed a lingering kiss to her lips. "Tonight will be the first time I make love with my wife."

She smiled. "And the first time I make love with my husband." She kissed his chin, then teased his lips with a brief caress. "I love you, husband."

He deepened the kiss. "I love you, wife."

Robert took his time, divesting Beth of her wedding finery. He couldn't resist sliding his rough hands over every bit of soft, pale skin he exposed as he removed each article of clothing. When Beth at last stood before him, wearing only her black *bra* and *panties*, lust pierced him. "You wore them."

She nodded, flashing him a siren's smile. "Now I'll do you."

Every muscle in his body went taut as she placed her small hands on his chest, then slid them down to unbuckle his belt. Every brush of her fingers as she removed his clothes sent fire racing through him. Every caress that followed on bare skin tested his restraint until he shook with the need to bury himself inside her.

Never had he wanted a woman with such a burning need.

As soon as he was bare, he slid his arms around her waist, drew her tempting body up against his, and took her lips in a deep, devouring kiss. "I will never get enough of you," he growled. As soon as he spoke the words, he regretted them.

Instead of expressing his desire, they served as a reminder of how little time they might have together.

Beth's hazel eyes began to glisten with moisture as she looked up at him.

"Don't," he pleaded, easing his hold on her and cupping her face in both hands. "I spoke without thought. Forgive me. I only meant to—"

She curled the fingers of one hand around his wrist and gave it a gentle squeeze. "I know, Robert." Releasing his wrist, she cupped his jaw and stroked the stubble she found there. "Just kiss me and make me forget everything else. No yesterdays. No tomorrows. Just you and me and our wedding night." A teasing glint entered her eyes, banishing some of the sadness there. "And, if you *really* want to distract me and are feeling particularly adventurous, some of the men downstairs had some rather interesting ideas on how we can pass our time up here. Maybe we can give one or two of them a try."

He grinned. "Or three or four." Picking her up, he tossed her backward.

Beth squealed as she flew through the air and landed on his big bed with a bounce.

That was what he wanted to see—her straight white teeth flashing in a happy smile, desire heating her eyes as he knelt on the bed and lowered his body atop hers.

"Mmm. I love to feel your weight on me," she murmured, spreading her thighs to make room for him and wrapping her arms around him. Leaning up, she gave his ear a little nip with her teeth. "The only thing I like better is feeling you inside me." Sliding her hands down his back, she gripped his backside, arched up against him, and ground her core against his arousal.

Robert groaned as he reclaimed her lips. Cupping one breast, he thrust against her as he pinched the rigid tip through the slick black fabric that covered it, eliciting a moan. "How do I get this off of you?" he growled, plucking at the bra.

She laughed. "I thought you liked it."

"Not when it keeps me from tasting you."

Eyes darkening, she thrust her breasts up against his chest and reached behind her back. The fabric loosened.

Robert tucked a finger between her breasts and tugged the bra off, tossing it over his shoulder. Before she could wrap her arms round him again, he reared back and knelt between her thighs.

A few deft pulls, and the black panties joined her bra on the floor.

For a long moment, he just stared at her, his breath coming more quickly with every moment that passed.

She swallowed and spoke in a hushed voice, thick with need. "How can you make me burn with just a look?"

Lightly grasping her ankles, he slid his hands up her calves, over her knees, and along her thighs until his thumbs reached the dark triangle of curls that tempted him so.

She gasped as he toyed with the hidden nub of her arousal. "What are you waiting for?"

He smiled. "Just deciding how I want to take you."

"Fast and hard," she responded instantly, shifting her legs restlessly and arching into his touch. "Take me now. Fast and hard." She moaned. "Then you can do anything you want to me."

The flames burned brighter. "Anything?" he pressed, teasing her with a flick of his fingers.

Again she moaned. "Hell, yes."

Eager to comply, Robert did as she wished and took her fast and hard.

Then, endeavoring to pour a lifetime of passion into the brief time allotted them, he spent hour upon hour making love to her, exploring new ways to bring her pleasure, keeping her so sated and exhausted they did not leave the solar for two days.

How he loved her.

He knew not how he would survive losing her.

Chapter Eighteen

ETH SMILED. WHAT A GLORIOUS day.

A sennight had passed since the wedding. Alyssa and Dillon remained at Fosterly with their adorable son, waiting to see if the enigmatic Seth would respond to her summons.

Beth thought little Ian was currently napping upstairs somewhere, exhausted after another mock sword fight with Sir Stephen. Alyssa had disappeared into the garden with Maude, intent on propagating plants or transplanting them or something along those lines. Shortly thereafter, Robert and Dillon had sequestered themselves in the solar to go over the books.

Beth wasn't sure what exactly *going over the books* entailed, but had decided training with the squires would be much more amusing. And, as luck would have it, it had taken little effort to coax Marcus into being her sparring partner.

Though a blindingly bright sun dominated the sky, for once Beth didn't worry about sunburning. Virtually every inch of her skin was covered.

As in the other days she had trained, she wore a shirt, braies, and tunic like the boys alongside whom she fought. Robert had ordered the armorer to craft special chainmail for her. Until then, she wore a leather hauberk and thickly padded gambeson he had insisted upon when bruises from her initial training sessions had begun to manifest themselves in large numbers and an increasing variety of hues.

On her head she wore a helmet she absolutely detested. It was hot and uncomfortable and reduced visibility. But again, Robert had insisted. He had wanted her to wear mailed mitts, too, but she had talked him down to leather gloves that were more comfortable and provided ample protection from blunted swords.

Sweat trickled down between her breasts as she blocked the powerful swing of Marcus's sword and countered with one of her own. She had made excellent progress, in her opinion, but thought Faudron would die before admitting it. Years of jogging, kickboxing aerobics, and tae kwon do lessons had given her strength, agility, and an excellent sense of balance. Even Dillon had commended her for her growing sword-fighting skills, imparting some instruction of his own.

Beth thought herself a long way from equaling Marcus, however, who had been trained by the best and boasted quite a bit more muscle than she did. Her slighter weight and lesser strength would definitely be a hindrance on the battlefield, but she had found ways to use some of the martial arts moves she'd learned to take her opponents by surprise.

Her breath coming in gasps, Beth called a halt and tugged off her helmet. "Whew! I could use a break."

Marcus smiled and lowered his sword. "You did very well, my lady."

"Oh, please. You're barely out of breath."

He shook his head. "Your skills are advancing far more quickly than mine did. The other squires are envious."

Tucking her helmet under her arm, she waved her free hand. "You're just saying that because you heard me tell Robert that flattery would get him everything."

He laughed. "Were I to admit to such, my lady, Lord Robert would have my head."

"Among other things." Grinning, Beth motioned to the mass of sweating, straining, grunting bodies to her right. "Go find yourself another victim while I rest for a bit."

"As you wish, my lady."

Sliding her sword into the sheath she carried on her back, Beth rounded the corner of the keep and headed for the stairs. Maybe she could convince Robert to take a break and join her for a swim in the lake he had shown her yesterday. The water would be icy cold, but she didn't think her new husband would have any trouble warming her up.

A commotion arose near the gatehouse.

Raising a hand to shield her eyes from the sun, she squinted against the brightness and tried to see what transpired.

A small crowd had formed just outside the barbican. All stared into its darkened interior with a sort of rapt fascination.

She frowned, her steps slowing.

The onlookers suddenly shrank back, parting down the middle to allow a figure to pass.

Beth halted, as captivated as the others.

A knight garbed in midnight armor rode into view atop the largest horse she had ever seen. Its coat was a glossy black, matched by a beautiful mane and long tufts of hair that decorated its legs just above the hooves.

It was huge. As was its rider, she soon saw when he dismounted.

Jeez, the man must be at least six and a half feet tall, towering over every other man in the bailey.

Oddly, he wore no helmet. Perhaps the guards had asked him to remove it and identify himself prior to letting him pass.

The knight's long, thick, wavy hair glinted in the sunlight. As black as his horse's mane, it fell to his waist and was tied back with a strip of leather.

A sick feeling invaded Beth's stomach.

She still hadn't seen his face.

When at last he turned, her knees weakened. Little sparkly things appeared and danced in the air as her vision began to dim.

Straight nose. Dark brows. Dark, almost onyx eyes she could see even at this distance. High cheekbones. Strong jaw. Tanned skin. A countenance handsome as hell.

It was him. The man she had last seen wearing dark robes. The man who had knelt beside her that day in the clearing and carried her back through time.

The man who had come to return her to the twenty-first century and take her away from Robert.

Dropping her helmet, Beth raced for the stairs.

Robert struggled to concentrate on Dillon's voice as the figures before him blurred together. He suppressed a sigh. 'Twas tedious work. He understood now why his brother had grumbled over having to conduct such over the years. Robert would much rather be down in the practice field, sparring with Beth.

Or mayhap coaxing her to slip away with him for a private moment by the lake. His lips turned up in a smile as he imagined peeling away her squire's garb and coaxing moans of pleasure from her whilst the sun bathed her beautiful body. 'Twould be far more exciting than—

The door to the solar slammed open, striking the wall with a thunderous boom.

Robert and Dillon leapt to their feet, their hands going to their sword hilts.

Beth stood in the doorway, her chest rising and falling as though she had run to them as quickly as she could.

Robert barely had time to register the distress on her face before she darted around the table, slammed into his chest, wrapped her arms around him and squeezed the breath out of him. Staggering back a step, he folded his arms around her and watched the doorway, fearing Fosterly was under attack.

Had another enemy risen to take the place of the one he had finally vanquished?

Dillon drew his sword and left the room. A moment later, he returned. "All is well."

Frowning, Robert pressed his lips to his wife's hair. "Beth?" Tremors shook her slender form. "What is amiss?"

Her grip tightened. "I love you."

He cast Dillon a worried look. "And I love you, sweetling. Are you hurt?"

She shook her head quickly.

"One of the squires did not injure you?"

She shook her head.

"Is it Alyssa? Did she reveal a gift that frightened you?"

Again Beth shook her head.

He cast about helplessly. "I know not—"

"I love you," she said again, her voice thick with tears. "I love you. I always will. *Please*, don't ever forget that."

Uneasiness suffused him. "Beth, love, please look at me and tell me what distresses you so."

A deep voice spoke softly from the doorway. "I believe that would be me."

Dillon spun around, raising his sword once more.

Robert tried to push Beth behind him, but could not pry her loose. He could not even draw his sword, because—when he loosened his hold—she shouted, "Don't let go!"

He tightened his arms around her. "Who are you?" he demanded, glaring over her head at the stranger.

The man was so tall he had to duck to enter the room. When he straightened, even Dillon had to look up at him. "You may call me Seth."

Dillon's gaze went from murderous to watchful as he lowered his sword tip. "'Tis the giant."

The dark knight's full lips quirked. "I have been called worse."

Robert addressed Dillon without shifting his gaze from the stranger. "You have never seen the giant's face. Are you certain 'tis him?"

"Aye."

Robert tightened his hold on Beth, felt her squeeze closer, as though she wanted to burrow beneath his skin, and understood now. While Seth would not harm them physically, he would tear them asunder emotionally when he returned Beth to her life in the future.

The panic Robert had read in her face now crystallized in his blood.

The moment he had dreaded had come. With this man's help, Beth would walk out of his life forever. And with her, she would take his heart and all of his hopes for the future.

"I can't do it," she blurted, and his heart stopped. Beth turned her head to look at Seth. "I can't do it. I thought I could, but I can't. I know that makes me a terrible person, a terrible sister, but I can't. I can't leave Robert. I love him too much."

Robert swallowed hard. "Beth," he whispered.

"I know it's selfish to choose my happiness over Josh's, but—"

"Beth," he repeated, stronger. Loosening his hold, he clasped her face in both hands and forced her to look up at him. "You do not have to choose."

Her eyes glistened. "Yes, I do."

"Nay, love, you do not." He pressed his lips to her forehead. "I will go with you."

Dillon made a sound of protest.

Beth's face went blank with shock. "Robert, you can't. Everything you've worked so hard for—everything you've ever wanted—is here. Your *life* is here."

"My life is with you." If he had to give up Fosterly, everyone and everything else he knew and loved, he would do so willingly if 'twould ensure he could spend the rest of his days with Beth and prevent her from suffering over her brother's fate.

A long silence ensued.

Alyssa appeared in the doorway. "Dillon," she said, her face and voice full of concern, "what is amiss? I sensed"—her gaze fell on Seth—"you."

A smile full of affection lit Seth's features as he bowed to Alyssa. "'Tis a pleasure to see you again, my lady."

With a quick glance at Dillon, she hesitantly offered Seth her hand.

His hand was so large it made hers seem like that of a small child as he brought it to his lips.

Alyssa gave him a faint smile. "You are even better at guarding your thoughts than Dillon and Robert have become."

He grinned. "I trust you see naught?"

"I see naught," she confirmed.

He released her hand. "I am delighted to find both you and your daughter well. Her gifts will be nigh as great as your own."

Robert slanted Dillon a glance to catch his reaction, but could not tell if his brother was alarmed at the thought or just surprised.

"If you will forgive me for saying so," Alyssa parried, "you seem greatly concerned with our happiness and well-being. What *are* we to you?"

"You are a *gifted one*," he replied, as if 'twas all the answer she needed.

"Dillon and Robert are not."

"Ah, but Lord Dillon is essential to your happiness."

"And Robert?"

"Has been kind to you."

"What of Beth?" Robert posed.

Seth cocked his head to one side in a way that made Robert wonder if he were trying to decide whether or not he should respond. "She is the key to your own happiness, which I desire as a reward for your kindness to Lady Alyssa."

Alyssa shook her head. "There is more."

Seth's brow furrowed as he turned to her. "Your powers *have* grown. Did you *see* that or merely sense it?"

"Sense it."

He nodded slowly. "I shall have to be more careful. You are correct. There *is* more. Bethany is a *gifted one*."

"What?" Beth blurted. "I can't be. I don't have any gifts or superpowers or whatever."

Robert frowned. "She has demonstrated none of the abilities we have come to understand *gifted ones* may possess."

Seth's shoulders moved in a slight shrug. "The part of her bloodline that comes from *gifted ones* has weakened over time."

"What do you mean?" Beth asked.

"Whenever a *gifted one* weds an ordinary man or woman," Seth explained, "the children born of their union possess gifts that are a little weaker. If those children also wed ordinary spouses, they bear children whose gifts are weaker still. It may not be noticeable during a single life span. But hundreds of years of such can produce great change. Had Beth been born in this time, she would no doubt be able to scry the future and read truth and falsehood with a touch. Instead, those abilities have been dampened enough to seem more to her like..." He seemed to search for the correct word.

"Good instincts," Beth murmured.

Seth nodded. "You knew before you were mortally wounded in that clearing that the men you hunted posed a greater danger than your brother believed. You knew almost as soon as you met him that Robert could be trusted, though your mind tried to instill doubts. And you knew before Robert left for Terrington that he would ride into danger."

"How do you know all of this?" she asked him. "How do you know about *me* and about my brother? How do you know my family's history? How did you even know Robert and I would fall in love? Are you from the future, too?"

His lips curved up in a small smile. "Such questions are best left unanswered."

"Best for whom?" Beth retorted, voicing the same frustration Robert felt.

Seth remained silent.

When Beth scowled and opened her mouth, Robert spoke first to hold off whatever she intended to snap. "Thank you for saving her life and bringing her back to me."

Seth inclined his head. "I regret that I must inform you that what you desire is not possible."

Robert's stomach sank. "I cannot accompany Beth to her time?"

Alyssa took a step forward. "What?" She looked to Dillon, who held his hand out to her and drew her to his side.

"When Beth returns to her time," his brother murmured, "Robert wishes to go with her."

The distress in Alyssa's brown eyes pierced Robert deeply when she turned her gaze on him. "You cannot mean it," she whispered, leaning into Dillon for support. "You would leave us?"

His throat thickened at the thought of never seeing his family again. "I want what you and Dillon have. And I have found it with Beth. If I must travel to her time and live the rest of my days there in order to hold on to it, I will do so."

"You don't have to do that, Robert," Beth insisted again. "I told you. I won't go. I'll stay here and—"

"If I might continue?" Seth interrupted.

All eyes focused on the powerful man.

"As I stated earlier, Robert cannot live out his life in Bethany's time." When Robert opened his mouth to protest, Seth held up one large hand. "Bethany cannot do so either."

Beth's eyes began to burn as she stared up at Seth. She couldn't go back. She couldn't go home. Or to what used to be home.

This was home now. *Robert* was home.

But she would never see Josh again. Would never again nearly suffocate when he engulfed her in a bear hug. Would never tell him good-bye or how much he meant to her.

Grief assailed her. As did guilt, because a tiny part of her was relieved that this decision had been taken out of her hands.

Seth's handsome face rippled like the surface of a pond as tears filled her eyes.

His voice gentled. "Your life in the twenty-first century was meant to end that day, Bethany, either in death or in your retreat to this time."

"If such is true," Robert said, a definite bite to his voice, "why did you not bring her back ere she was injured? Why did you let her suffer?"

Seth took no offense, continuing on in the same soft, deep voice he had used since entering the room. "There were others present. Their fate, too, hung in the balance. Of necessity, I had to allow actions to progress to their natural conclusion."

Had that natural conclusion included Josh's death?

Beth was too afraid to ask.

"What of her brother?" Robert asked for her. "Did Josh survive?"

"He did."

Beth's breath hitched. Tears spilled over her lashes as harsh sobs erupted from her chest.

Josh hadn't died. The brother she loved so much hadn't died alone in that clearing with only the corpses of Kingsley and Vergoma for company. Josh was *alive*.

Robert wrapped his arms around her and held her tight.

"Did you heal him as you did Bethany?" Alyssa asked.

"Partially," Seth divulged. "I could not heal him entirely without raising too many questions, so I numbed his pain, slowed his blood loss, and healed only that which would have impaired him permanently."

He should have made a full recovery then. Had Beth been able to pry her arms from around Robert, she would have thrown them around Seth to thank him for saving her brother's life.

"Does he know Beth lives?" Robert asked.

"Nay. He was unconscious when we left."

She squeezed her eyes shut.

It was her second greatest fear. Josh didn't know she was all right. He probably thought she was either buried in a shallow grave where he would never find her or the captive of some freak sexual predator who had been helping Kingsley and Vergoma.

"Seth," Alyssa inserted into the leaden silence, "there is much I do not understand in all of this, but mayhap one thing most of all. When you brought Bethany to our time, why did you leave her alone, confused and unprotected in the forest with no knowledge of how or why she had come to be there? 'Tis not our nature to be unkind."

"She was never vulnerable," Seth responded. "I placed her directly in Robert's path, knowing mere minutes would pass before he found her."

"But why did you tell none of us this?" Robert demanded.

Beth shared his frustration. So much fear and confusion had gripped her until she had come to terms with the fact that she had traveled back in time.

"I fear ignorance in this instance was necessary," Seth told them. "I risked much to bring her to you. There are others who believe that such interference as this will spark dire repercussions and should be harshly punished."

Beth frowned. "Others like you, you mean?"

"Forgive me, but I can say no more."

Which only made Beth want to *know* more, but she could tell pushing it would be futile.

"Beth cannot go back?" Robert asked, resting his cheek on her hair.

"Nay," Seth said. "Altering her fate in her time would have too many repercussions."

Beth couldn't quite make it all work in her head. "Living in my own time would have repercussions," she said, still trying to silence her sobs, "but living in this one won't?"

He gave her an apologetic *Hey-I-don't-make-the-rules* kind of look. "I am not the architect of your fate, Bethany. I am merely a participant."

Did that mean she had been destined to go back in time all along? she wondered.

Then something in his words struck her. "Wait. You said I can't go back and *live* in my time. Can I go back for a visit? Can I go back long enough to see Josh and let him know I'm okay and... tell him good-bye?"

"'Twould be unwise."

"Why?" she demanded.

"As I said, I risked much to bring you here. Those who fear the consequences of such actions—"

"But I won't be staying. I just want to see for myself that Josh is okay, to let him see that I'm okay, and to say good-bye. That's it. I won't tell everyone who will listen that I've traveled through time." She paused and bit her lip. "I mean, I'll probably tell Marc and Grant. They're our best friends and like family and I don't want them to go on believing I'm dead or being tortured or something. And I don't want Josh to have to lie to them once he knows the truth. But if you know all of that other stuff about my life there, then you know they can be trusted, right?"

He tilted his head to one side, studying her carefully.

"Right?" she repeated when the silence stretched.

"A moment, if you will," he murmured.

Alyssa shifted, her gaze darting back and forth between her and Seth. "Are you reading Beth's mind?"

"Aye," Seth answered.

Beth cringed inwardly. That was creepy. How much could he see? Her thoughts? Her past? *Everything?*

At last, he nodded. "As you wish."

Beth straightened. "What?"

"I will return you to your time for a brief visit."

Elation flooded her.

He held up a finger, staying her before she could speak. "But you must return all of your modern possessions to that time and leave them there."

Damn. That burst her bubble a little. "Even my guns?"

"Even your guns."

Reluctantly, she nodded her agreement. "It's worth it." She would get to see Josh.

So much relief and happiness flooded her that she was tempted to jump up and down like a child viewing presents on Christmas morning. "Can Robert come with me?"

Seth smiled. "Aye, Robert may accompany you."

Woohoo! Now she did jump up and down, jostling Robert and making him laugh since she had not relinquished her hold on him. "I know it's futile to ask , but I have to do it anyway. Can we bring Josh back to this time with us when we return?"

"Nay," Seth informed her gently. "I am sorry, but 'tis not his fate."

That dimmed her spirits. "I'm really beginning to dislike the word *fate,*" she grumbled.

Seth chuckled. "You are not the first, nor will you be the last, to tell me so."

The next morning, Robert, Bethany, Seth, Dillon, Alyssa and Marcus all rode to a secluded glade in the forest outside of Fosterly's walls. While Seth voiced no objection to Marcus joining them, he had refused to allow Michael, Stephen or Adam to do the same.

As usual, he gave them no explanation.

Maybe he just didn't want anyone else to see how he was going to take them through time, Beth speculated as Robert helped her dismount.

Marcus remained uncharacteristically somber.

Alyssa clung to her husband's arm, her pretty face distraught.

Dillon's countenance was more grim than Beth had ever seen it.

They all seemed fearful that something might go wrong and land Beth and Robert in her time permanently. As if they were there to say *Good-bye* instead of *See you when you get back.*

Since butterflies fluttered in her own belly, Beth couldn't blame them. She didn't know how exactly this whole time travel thing worked. And Seth remained infuriatingly closedmouthed about it.

What if something *did* go wrong? All she had been able to drag out of Seth was that he would send them to her time, but could not accompany them himself.

How could he return them to Robert's time if he didn't go with them?

How could he even ensure they ended up in Beth's time—and not the Dark Ages or the Wild West or the friggin' twenty-third century—if he didn't go with them?

Could he even guarantee that they would be together wherever they ended up and not separated by several decades or centuries?

The mere possibility terrified her.

She glanced up at Robert.

If her husband was nervous, he hid it well.

Beth clung to his hand as if it were the only thing keeping her from falling off a cliff's edge. Yet Robert just smiled and stroked the back of her hand with his thumb. Ruffling Marcus's hair, he spoke casually of the weather, the progress he expected Marcus to make in his training while they were gone, and other mundane things as if it were just another day.

Beth rose onto her toes and kissed Robert's cheek, then slipped away from the group. Cloaked by the foliage, she removed her medieval garb and donned the jeans and tank top that weren't bloodstained, topped them off with her bulletproof vest and Bail Enforcement jacket, then added all of her weapons.

Somber faces greeted her return. Embraces ensued. Beth nearly burst into tears when Dillon—such a ferocious, austere man—clasped his brother to him for a long, tight hug, his eyes misty as he murmured something in Robert's ear.

Robert nodded and clapped him on the back.

Once all had said their good-byes, Seth asked the others to leave.

With great reluctance, the group turned away and headed back the way they had come.

Beth looked up at Seth.

"You may have one sennight there," he said. "No more."

A week. Not much time. But she wouldn't make a fuss, particularly since it had taken quite a bit of arguing on her part to get him to allow her more than a day or two.

"Hold tightly to one another," he instructed, "and do not lose your grip."

Beth decided holding Robert's hand wasn't going to be enough and wrapped her arms around him instead.

Still as outwardly composed as before, Robert offered no complaint. His heart pounded rapidly beneath her cheek, however, when she rested her head upon his chest.

"I love you," she whispered, terrified something would go wrong.

"I love you, Beth," he murmured, and pressed a kiss to the top of her head.

It happened so quickly she almost missed it. The scenery around them blurred and elongated as if they were in the *Millennium Falcon* and had just activated the hyperdrive. A strange feeling of weightlessness struck, like that she sometimes experienced in an elevator.

A second later, the world around them stabilized. And then she and Robert stood alone in a clearing vastly different from the one in which they had bid Dillon, Alyssa, and Marcus good-bye.

They now stood in *the* clearing. The one in which she had fallen.

The one in Texas.

Hot, humid air assaulted them, dampening their skin.

Beth leaned back slightly, still holding on to Robert just in case, and examined their surroundings.

Dry, brown foliage. Hard clay soil, cracked by drought. A scorching sun overhead. Parched trees with leaves shriveling and falling from their limbs. Annoying mosquitoes buzzing around. Kingsley's crappy cabin nearby.

"This is it," she said, hearing the wonder she felt reflected in her voice. "This is it, Robert. We're in my time."

Robert loosened his hold on her, sliding one hand down to lace his fingers through hers. Taking a step back, he glanced around. "This is the twenty-first century? This is the clearing in which you were wounded?"

"Yes." She looked around uneasily as memory assaulted her. She heard again the explosive sounds of rifles, shotguns, and handguns firing. Saw blood spurt from Josh's wounds. Felt bullets pierce her flesh.

Her free hand went to the grip of the 9mm in her shoulder holster.

Robert drew his sword and surveyed the clearing carefully. "Do you sense something?"

Beth swallowed hard, trying to quell the irrational fear that built within her. "No. I think it's just what happened here before." Her hands began to shake. "I don't know. I didn't expect it to freak me out like this."

He tugged her closer. "Do you wish to leave this place?"

"Yes. But we'd better not. We need Josh to come pick us up, and he'll find us more easily if we stay here. Let me see if my cell phone will work. I used my solar charger to charge it again yesterday."

Ever alert, Robert kept his sword in hand while she dug the cell phone out of her back pocket and turned it on.

Relief rushed through her, sweeping away her unease. "It's working." And she had a decent signal. Beth dialed their home phone number, her heart slamming against her ribcage.

One ring. Two. Three. Four.

"You have reached the Bennett residence..." An answering machine played Josh's recorded invitation to leave a message at the tone.

Tears filled her eyes.

An annoying beep sounded.

When Beth drew in a breath to speak, it caught on a sob. She hadn't realized what hearing Josh's voice again would do to her. Even in a damned answering machine message. She had thought she would never hear him again. And, to her dismay, she found she couldn't speak as she burst into tears.

Robert's brow furrowed. His eyes clouding with concern, he touched her arm. "Does it not work?"

Helplessly, she thrust the phone toward him.

Robert took the cell phone. "What do I do?"

Beth motioned for him to put the phone to his ear.

"I hold it to my ear?" He would much rather drop it and take her in his arms. He had never seen her so undone.

"Hello?" a voice suddenly spoke in his ear.

"By the saints!" Robert exclaimed, gaping at Beth. "'Tis a voice! I hear a voice!"

That voice proceeded to speak unintelligibly.

Robert looked to Beth. "I cannot understand him." What was it Beth kept calling Robert's language? Middle English?

Attempting to mimic Beth's odd accent, Robert said slowly and deliberately, "Speak Middle English."

A pause ensued. "What?"

"Speak Middle English, please."

Another pause. "Seriously?"

Robert smiled. That had been another of the modern terms he had swiftly learned from Beth. "Aye."

"Who is this?" the man demanded, altering his speech to suit Robert.

"I am Lord Robert, Earl of Fosterly. I seek Josh of Houston, brother of Bethany. Are you he?"

"Yes. Aye, this is Josh." He seemed a little less comfortable with the language than Beth. "Who did you say this was?"

"I am Robert, Earl of Fosterly."

"Robert, where are you calling from?"

"I believe 'tis the clearing in which you and Beth fell." Beth nodded, wiping her streaming eyes. "Aye, 'tis the clearing in which you fell."

"The clearing where she was shot?"

"Aye."

"How did you get that phone?"

"Beth gave it to me."

"Beth *gave* it to you?"

"Aye. 'Tis a most miraculous creation."

"What? When did she give it to you?"

"A moment ago, ere you greeted me."

"Are you saying she's there with you now?"

"Aye."

"Let me speak with her."

"As you will." Robert held the phone out to Beth. "He wishes to speak with you."

Beth took the phone from his and raised it to her ear. "J-Josh?" she managed to choke out in a broken whisper. She listened for a moments, then closed her eyes, her sobs increasing.

Patting her shoulder, Robert took the phone again. "Josh of Houston?"

"Put her back on," Josh gritted.

"She is weeping too hard to speak."

"Why? What have you done to her?"

"Naught you are imagining. In truth I believe 'tis joy that makes her weep so. She has been fair worried about you, Josh of Houston. Knowing you survived and hearing your voice has lifted a great burden from her heart." Robert chuckled when she nodded. "Aye. She is indicating I am correct. 'Tis a fair day all around. I do not always read her so well."

"Look, unless... put her back... phone and... talk to me, I...no way of knowing... Beth or some woman... reward."

Robert frowned as the man's voice faded in an out. He lowered the phone, looked at it, then returned it to his ear. "Josh of Houston?"

No answer came.

He frowned and met his wife's tear-filled gaze. "I cannot hear him, Beth. He no longer speaks to me."

Chapter Nineteen

S TILL TRYING TO CATCH HER breath, Beth grabbed the cell phone from him, put it to her ear, then stared down at it with dismay.

The damned battery had died. What the hell? She had just charged it!

Frustrated with the device and furious with herself over not being able to control her emotions better, she emitted a half-groan half-growl disrupted by a hiccup.

"Beth?" Concern painting his handsome face, Robert sheathed his sword, took her by the shoulders and drew her close. "Easy, love," he murmured. "Take deep breaths and think of naught save my arms around you."

Beth leaned into him and closed her eyes.

Cupping the nape of her neck with one hand, Robert slid the other up and down her back in soothing strokes that loosened the tension she hadn't even realized tightened every muscle. "All will be well," he murmured. "I vow it. All will be well, sweetling. You shall see."

A jagged sigh escaped her as she burrowed her face into his chest.

Robert continued to murmur and make soft shushing sounds until her sobs abated and her breathing quieted.

"That strength you admire so m-much seems to have deserted me," she muttered mournfully. How could she have fallen apart like that? At just the sound of her brother's voice?

When she had been grieving, thinking him dead—sure, she had cried. But this?

Robert kissed the top of her head. "'Tis still there."

Snorting, she glanced around the clearing. "Boy, I really blew it, didn't I? I can't believe I sat there and blubbered while the cell battery died. I have no idea how we're going to get out of here now."

"I can give you a ride," a deep voice offered.

Robert abruptly released her, swiveled and drew his sword all in one motion.

Beth drew her Glock, aimed it, then gaped. "What are *you* doing here?" she asked when she saw the speaker.

Seth stepped from the trees.

A very different Seth.

Instead of knightly garb, he wore black jeans, heavy boots, and a black T-shirt that contrasted nicely with his tanned skin and outlined some very nicely defined muscles. His long, thick hair was pulled back from his face and secured with a strip of leather. A pair of dark shades rested on the bridge of his nose.

Robert sheathed his sword. "I thought you could not accompany us."

"I could not." Reaching up, Seth removed the sunglasses. "I can open the dimensional doorways that allows one to travel through time, but have found that it's best if I refrain from doing so myself."

"Why?" Beth pressed.

Smiling, he said nothing.

She frowned. Well, if Seth hadn't come with them and avoided traveling through time then how was he here? "Wait. Are you saying you've lived over eight hundred years?"

No answer. Just the same handsome smile.

It seemed a confirmation. And a pretty unbelievable one at that.

But Beth had had enough brushes with the unbelievable lately to consider it the truth.

She contemplated him curiously. "Who exactly are you, Seth? Or perhaps the better question would be: *What* exactly are you?"

He strolled forward. "I knew your cell battery would die before you could ask your brother to fetch you, so I thought I would drop by and offer you a ride."

"How did you know the battery would die?" She pounced. "I just charged it yesterday."

He arched a brow. "Shall we go?"

She looked at Robert. "He isn't going to answer me, is he?"

"Nay, he seems disinclined to do so."

"Fine," she muttered, holstering her weapon. "But I gotta tell ya," she groused, "the *mystery* part of this whole tall, dark, handsome, mystery-man thing you've got going can really be annoying sometimes."

Seth's smile widened. "So I have been told."

Shaking her head, Beth looped her backpack and the tent strap over one shoulder and followed him through the dry summer foliage, Robert at her side.

Several steps later, she glanced up and found Robert glowering down at her. "What?"

"You think him handsome?"

"Oh, please." Beth shoved him hard enough to make him stumble slightly. "You know I don't want any man but you."

"Yet you *do* think him handsome."

"Of course he's handsome, Robert. But *you* are the only man who is handsome in a way that makes me want to rip your clothes off and have my way with you twenty-four hours a day, three hundred and sixty-five days a year." She sighed wistfully. "If only there were three-hundred and sixty-six."

His expression lightened with amusement.

Beth smiled up at him, then frowned.

His face was *very* flushed. Perspiration beaded on his forehead and trailed down his temples and cheeks in thin rivulets. He pushed back his mailed coif to let the hot summer breeze comb through his thick hair, which clung damply to his head. But Beth doubted it would help. Summer breezes in Texas were about as cooling as a space heater or a hair dryer.

Concerned, Beth tugged one of her jacket sleeves down over her hand and used it to pat his face dry. "Hey, are you okay?"

Robert nodded. "'Tis hot, is it not?"

Swiping her sleeve across her own face, she sent him a wry smile. "Welcome to Texas."

His look turned skeptical. "Such is common here?"

If his face got any redder, she was going to insist they stop and divest him of his mail and hauberk before they went any farther.

She shrugged. "This kind of heat and humidity is pretty standard for Houston. I may not like it, but I'm used to it."

"I begin to understand why your feet were always so cold at Fosterly."

She laughed. "Only when you weren't there to warm them for me."

306

The trees in front of them parted to reveal a large, sleek black vehicle with windows tinted as dark as the body.

"You drive a van?" Beth asked, somewhat surprised.

"Yes." Pulling the keys from his back pocket, Seth pressed a button that disabled the alarm and unlocked the doors. Beside her, Robert jumped when the van emitted a chirping noise. "Why? What were you expecting?"

"An SUV. Or maybe a sleek sports car."

He shrugged. "This serves my purpose better."

"Mm-hmm. That purpose wouldn't by any chance include sneaking in some afternoon romps in the back with your ladylove, would it?" she teased.

Seth laughed. "Alas, it does not."

Robert sent Beth a somewhat scandalized look, then addressed Seth. "She is quite bold in her speech, is she not?"

"You will find most women of this time speak thusly." Seth turned to Beth. "I realize the gentlemanly thing to do would be to escort you to the front seat. But I suspect Robert's first ride in an automobile will go better for him if you sit beside him in the back."

"Back seat's fine," Beth said.

Robert eyed the van dubiously. "What is it?"

Seth pushed a button on his remote, and the side door rolled back. "Think of it as a horseless wagon."

Beth took Robert's hand and tugged him forward. "Come on. You'll like it. It's fun."

She suspected he would have balked at venturing into the strange conveyance had he not trusted her as much as he did. But he soon settled beside her on a soft bench seat.

"Hey, Seth," she said as he reached for the door.

"Yes?"

"Why did you send the tent back with me? It wasn't with me in the clearing."

He shrugged. "I knew you would be cold." Closing the door, he circled the vehicle and tucked his big body behind the wheel.

When the finely tuned engine hummed to life, Robert started slightly and clutched Beth's hand.

Beth hadn't realized what an unsettling experience this would be for him. Whenever she had imagined taking him on his first ride in a car, she had thought only about how much he would love the high speeds at which they could travel.

That and their ability to regulate the temperature, which Seth did.

Cool air wafted over them when he turned on the AC.

Beth grinned at Robert's amazed expression as he leaned closer to the vents. "Pretty cool, huh?" she asked.

"'Tis *very* cool," he uttered, closing his eyes in bliss.

He *did* enjoy the ride. Eventually. The speed limit on the highway leading into Houston was seventy miles per hour. Having never traveled anywhere near that fast, Robert did seem a tad nervous until the sights distracted him.

Beth found so much around them fascinating when seen anew through his eyes. The wide, smoothly paved road. The other vehicles that came in so many sizes, shapes and colors. The variety of races of people within those vehicles. The red brake lights that lit up on the back bumpers. The brightly colored billboards that Beth had always considered such an eyesore. The huge signs that hung above every store they passed.

What would he think when she took him out after the sun set and let him see how many of those signs began to glow?

The planes and helicopters that flew overhead astounded him. The booming music that assaulted them from neighboring cars annoyed him and made his head pound, although she thought his earlier exposure to the heat could be partially responsible for that. The signal lights enthralled him.

They were idling at a signal light not that far from the forest that had hatched their little road trip, having been diverted from the highway temporarily by road construction, when Robert suddenly leaned toward the darkened window beside him and pointed.

"Beth, look there. Another of your portraits." He frowned. "Or is it a license?"

Leaning across him, she peered at an abandoned gas station that was papered with fliers. Did a picture of *her* reside amidst the assorted ads? "Seth, could we stop here for a minute, please?"

"Of course." As soon as the light turned green, he eased forward, swung into the gas station, and stopped.

Beth hopped out and approached the wall near the boarded-up entrance. Not one, but *several* fliers with her picture adorned it. Most of them were faded, some more tattered than others. A couple had been partially covered by other fliers.

Pulling one down, she took it back to the van and climbed in, sliding the door shut behind her to lock out the heat.

Robert leaned in close as she retook her seat and studied the paper.

A photo took up half the page, showing her from the shoulders up, smiling happily at the viewer. Josh had taken the picture when they had driven to San Antonio back in June. Beside the photo, in neat, dark type was a physical description of her. Height. Weight. Hair color. Eye color. Birth date. The date she had disappeared. The clothing she had been wearing when she had last been seen.

And a phone number. *Their* phone number. Hers and Josh's.

An unbelievably large reward was being offered for any information that led to her recovery. She couldn't imagine where Josh could have come up with so much.

"What is it?" Robert asked. "Is it a license, like the small one you gave me?"

She shook her head. "It's a missing-person flier. People put them up when loved ones disappear in hopes that someone will see it, recognize them, and know where they might be found."

"Does such happen often?"

"People going missing?"

He nodded.

"Unfortunately, yes." She looked at Seth, who had turned slightly in his seat to watch them. "Have you seen these?"

"Aye. He has put up thousands of them since you disappeared, blanketing at least a fifty-mile radius from the clearing in which the two of you fell. He even faxed a copy to other bounty hunters in hopes they would distribute them in other parts of the state."

"Why didn't you tell him I was okay? Why did you just let him think the worst?" What Josh must have suffered...

"Had I approached him and informed him that his sister was alive and well and living in thirteenth-century England, what reason would he have had to believe me?"

"Then you should have sent him back with me!" she declared, anger rising.

"I could not," he said simply.

"Beth, love," Robert said beside her, "please do not mar it."

Looking down, she saw that she had clenched her hand into a fist, crinkling the paper, and relaxed her grip.

Robert took it from her and carefully smoothed it out on his knee, handling it as though it were a priceless work of art.

Seth turned back around, swung the van out into traffic and resumed their journey.

Sighing, Beth leaned against Robert.

"You will see him soon, love," he promised.

Her stomach in knots, Beth hoped so.

Hours later, Beth sprawled in Josh's favorite chair in the living room, wondering where the hell her brother was. The house had been empty when they had arrived.

Thank goodness Seth hadn't just dropped them off, then driven away, because Beth hadn't had her keys with her.

Apparently, among his many other gifts, Seth had pretty impressive telekinetic abilities. One wave of his hand and both locks had unlocked.

Beth had invited him to stay, but Seth had declined.

Click. Click. Click. Click.

The lights turned off, on, off, then on again as Robert toyed with the switch across the room.

Darkness had fallen. Beth's stomach rumbled with hunger, but she didn't eat anything. She couldn't. She was too nervous. Too frustrated. Too impatient to see her brother if he would just bring his ass home already.

Click-click. Click-click. Click. Click.

The flickering lights didn't help, but she could understand Robert's fascination with electricity.

On. Off. On. Off. On-off-on-off. On. Off. On.

Where the hell was Josh? Had he gone to the clearing?

She had tried to call him on his cell and discovered he had left the damned thing at home.

She tried to calculate how long it would take him, in rush-hour traffic, to get to the clearing, search it, then come home.

He should be here by now, if that was what he'd done. Shouldn't he?

Click. Click. Click-click. Click-click.

Off. On. Off-on. Off-on. Off. On. Off. On. Off-on-off-on-off-on-off-on-off-on.

"Robert, honey, you are working my last nerve. *Please* stop messing with the lights." She was so tired and tense she forgot to use Middle English.

"Beth?"

She gasped. *Josh.*

Head whipping around, she looked toward the kitchen.

Her brother stood just inside the living room, his face as white as a sheet, his eyes wide, and his right arm aiming a Glock 9mm at Robert.

Her heart slammed against her ribs. "Josh!" Launching herself from the chair, she raced across the room and slammed into him, hitting him so hard he staggered backward two steps.

He wrapped his free arm around her waist.

Beth looped her arms around his neck and squeezed hard, so damned happy to see him.

"Beth," he said again, as if he couldn't quite believe she was there.

Nodding, she hugged him tighter, tears welling in her eyes and dampening his shoulder.

A throat cleared behind her. "Beth, sweetling," Robert said, "your brother has trained his weapon upon me. Should I be concerned?"

She shook her head. "Nay." Never looking up, she slid one hand down Josh's arm, found the 9mm, took it from him, flipped the safety on, and tossed it onto the sofa.

Josh must have taken that to mean Robert was friend and not foe, because he clamped both arms around her, buried his face in her hair, and wept.

The strength seemed to leave his legs, and the two of them sank to their knees.

Beth didn't know how long they remained there, both crying so hard they couldn't speak, clutching each other desperately, as if each feared the other would disappear if they loosened their hold even the slightest bit.

Then...

Click. The lights went off. *Click.* Then came on again. Off. On. Off. On.

Beth released a watery chuckle. "R-Robert."

311

When Josh reluctantly let her draw away, she sat back on her heels and smiled over her shoulder.

Robert offered her a sheepish grin. "Forgive me. I knew not how much longer you would be and"—he shrugged—"the temptation proved too great to resist."

"W-Well, you lasted longer than Stephen would have," Beth said wryly.

Robert laughed. "Stephen would never have ceased." He started toward them.

Josh rose and helped Beth to her feet.

"Josh," she said, "this is Robert, Earl of F-Fosterly. Robert, this is my b-brother, Josh."

Robert tendered him a friendly smile. "'Tis an honor to meet you."

Eyeing him warily, Josh turned to Beth. "Is this the man who abducted you?"

"No. He's the one who found me. And I don't know what I would've done without him." She smiled up at Robert.

Robert brushed her hair back from her face, his friendly smile turning tender.

"Where did you find her?" Josh challenged. "And why are we speaking Middle English? Why don't—?"

"Josh," Beth quickly interrupted. "It's a really long and truly bizarre story. I'd rather not tell it on an empty stomach." As if on cue, a low growl emanated from her midriff. "Could we call out for pizza or heat something up first? I feel like I haven't eaten in a week."

Robert laughed. "You ate more than I did yestereve."

She grimaced. "I know, but it came right back up again as soon as I left the great hall."

He sobered. "What?"

"I didn't want to tell you because I knew you would worry, but my stomach has been so queasy the last few days that I haven't been able to keep anything down." She hadn't been sleeping well, either, which might explain her new tendency to cry at the drop of a hat. She *had* been pretty stressed of late.

Robert frowned and gently pressed the palm of his hand to her forehead. "Are you ill, Beth?"

"No, I'm fine. It's just nerves. We were waiting for Seth to come. And then, when he did and said he would help us, I was afraid it wouldn't work, or that something would go wrong and we wouldn't make it back here, or that—"

"Make it back from where, Beth?" Josh demanded, his patience visibly fraying. "Where have you been all this time? How did you survive your wounds? The detectives said—"

"The man who took me healed me."

"What man? Was he in league with Kingsley and Vergoma?"

"No."

"Was it Robert?"

"No." She held up a hand, forestalling further questions. "Josh, I know these last two months have been difficult, but if you would just—"

"*Two months*," he practically bellowed. "Two *months?*"

She glanced at Robert uneasily. "I know it's been a little bit more than that, but..."

Disbelief, fury and confusion clouded Josh's features. "Beth, you've been gone for *two years!*" he shouted, abandoning Middle English entirely.

Beth gaped up at him. "What?"

"Two years! I've been looking for you for two years! What happened to you? Did the man who took you...?" He swallowed hard. "Did he hurt you, Beth?"

"No," she assured him, reverting to modern English. "No, he didn't. Actually, he helped me. I never would have survived if he hadn't healed me."

"Well, did he hold you captive or something? Where have you been all this time?"

She glanced uneasily at Robert.

Robert watched them with furrowed brow.

"He didn't hold me captive," she told Josh. "I wasn't a prisoner and wasn't mistreated or anything. But I couldn't contact you or come home. Not until today."

"I don't understand. What the hell does that mean? Were you in witness protection or something?" He motioned to Robert. "And why is he dressed like that? Why does he speak Middle English?"

She bit her lip. "Okay, here's the thing. I'm going to tell you exactly what happened, beginning in the clearing when you passed out and ending with my coming here today, but it's going to sound really unbelievable, and you're going to think that whatever happened to me made me lose it mentally, but it's all true, I'm completely sane, and I want to say right now that I have the pictures to prove it."

Josh stared at her, then looked at Robert, who shrugged, not understanding.

Beth nodded and returned to using Middle English. "Robert, please hand me my cell phone."

Two hours and three pizzas later, Beth sprawled next to Robert on the sofa, so full she could barely breathe. Across from them, Josh leaned forward in his favorite chair, elbows on his knees, and pored over the photos spread across the scuffed-up coffee table between them. He had uploaded them from Beth's cell phone and printed them while they waited for the pizzas to arrive. All colorful pictures taken of Fosterly and its inhabitants.

"Do you believe me now?" Beth asked around a wide yawn. Just as she had known he would, Josh had panicked halfway through her tale, believing she had suffered some kind of mental breakdown. Hence the pictures.

"How can this be?" Josh murmured, spearing a hand through his thick brown locks. "Time travel isn't possible. It just isn't." He shook his head. "Do you know how screwed up the world would be if time travel were possible?"

Robert grunted. "'Tis precisely what Beth told me when she sought to convince me of the truth."

Josh frowned and held up a photo. "Is this William Shatner?"

Beth grinned. "No. His name is Edward. But he looks a lot like him, doesn't he?"

Josh continued to examine the photos. "What about this one? This teenager. Why does he look familiar to me?"

Beth took the picture and studied it. "I don't know. Something about him seemed familiar to me, too, but I could never figure out what. That's Marcus, Robert's squire. I wish you could meet him, Josh. He's the sweetest kid."

"Hmm."

She returned the picture to the array on the coffee table. "Come on, Josh. You *know* me. You know I would never lie to you. I have no *reason* to lie to you about where I've been or why I haven't contacted you. So the only explanations left are that I actually *did* go back in time or that I'm delusional." She settled back against the cushions once more and motioned to the coffee table. "You can't take pictures of delusions. And be honest. Aside from claiming I went back in time, does anything else about me seem off? Anything that would indicate I've suffered some kind of breakdown or have been… I don't know… mentally reconditioned to *believe* I went back in time by some captor?"

He pursed his lips. "You *are* speaking Middle English. Mostly."

She rolled her eyes. "What are the chances I would even remember that language if I'd really lost it?"

Josh sighed and resumed his perusal of the photos.

Robert took Beth's hand and linked his fingers through hers, giving it a squeeze. "Beth?"

She glanced up at him. He looked as sleepy and sated as she felt. "Aye?"

His lips turned up slightly at their corners. "I like pizza."

Laughing, she raised his hand to her lips and kissed his knuckles. "I do, too."

She returned her attention to Josh.

Though his head was still bent over the photos, her brother's piercing brown eyes watched the two of them intently.

Uh-oh.

"Why do I get the feeling you haven't told me everything?" he asked, his voice ominously soft.

Beth lowered Robert's hand to her lap and toyed with it as anxiety rose. "Umm."

"Beth?"

"Do you believe that I was in the thirteenth century?" she asked, procrastinating.

A long pause followed. "Yes."

"You hesitated!"

"Well," he said defensively, "admitting you believe in time travel is a little hard to do. It makes me feel like *I'm* the one who is delusional."

Robert squeezed her hand. "You had a difficult time admitting it yourself, sweetling."

"Thanks so much for reminding me," she grumbled.

"So what haven't you told me?" Josh pressed.

Beth squirmed beneath his gaze, afraid he would blow a gasket when she told him the little part she had left out of her tale.

The little part about getting married.

"The fault lies with me," Robert said. "As you are the head of her family, I should have waited until I could speak with you. But, in truth, I knew not if I would be able to, or that I would accompany Beth here when she left Fosterly."

Josh's face remained impassive. "What are you saying?"

"I fell deeply in love with Bethany and, fearing I would soon lose her to the future, did convince her to wed me a little over a sennight ago."

Josh slumped back in his chair, his expression stunned. "You're *married*?"

Beth leaned forward. "I know. You're thinking I should have waited. Or maybe that I shouldn't have married him at all, because he's a total stranger to you. And it *did* all happen pretty quickly. But I really love him, Josh. And I didn't know if I would ever be able to come back here. And even if I *had* known and *had* waited, we couldn't have gotten married here anyway, because Robert doesn't have a birth certificate or a social security number."

Josh looked from her to Robert to their clasped hands, then back to her. "You're really married?"

"Yes."

"Happily?"

"Very much so."

"You really love him?"

"More than I ever thought I *could* love someone."

"No doubts at all?"

"None whatsoever."

He looked to Robert. "And you love her?"

"Aye. I would give my life for her."

Beth swung on him with a scowl and punched him hard in the shoulder. "Damn it, stop saying that!"

Shrugging, he rubbed his shoulder. "Why? 'Tis the truth."

"Well, I don't *want* you to give your life for me. And I don't want *Marcus* to give his life for me either. Or Michael or Adam or even Stephen, for that matter. I can damn well take care of myself!"

He took her throbbing hand in his own. "I fear, in this instance, what you want or do not want matters little to me, love."

She gaped. "How can you say that?"

He shrugged. "I may have compromised when you wanted to dress and train like a squire. And I did not complain when you were too familiar with my men."

Her brow furrowed. "Familiar how? Like being too friendly with Michael and the guys?"

"But I will not compromise on this," Robert continued as though she hadn't spoken. "If your life is in danger and I must risk my own to protect you, I will not hesitate to do so, Beth."

Before she could open her mouth to rebut, Josh leaned forward and extended his hand to Robert. "Welcome to the family."

Robert hesitated a moment, then shook Josh's hand.

Beth knew men didn't shake hands in Robert's time, but he had seen her do it more than once out of habit.

Josh leaned back in his chair. "So how are you two going to get past the no birth certificate or social security card thing? Robert's going to have a hard time making a go of it here without them."

Her stomach sank.

That was the other little thing she hadn't told him yet.

She glanced at Robert, who squeezed her hand for support. "Actually, the thing is, we can't stay here."

Josh frowned. "What do you mean? Here in Houston? Here in the States? Because, if you're thinking of moving to England, you're going to need passports."

Damn it. When she had asked Seth to let her visit, she hadn't considered how she would tell Josh she couldn't stay. "Josh, the man who took me back in time told me that my life here in the present was supposed to have ended in that clearing, that I would have died if he hadn't intervened. So I can't live here. There would be too many ramifications. He said I have to return to Robert's time."

Josh stared at her. "Are you shitting me?"

"No."

"You think you're going to live out the rest of your life in the Middle Ages?" he asked, voice rising.

"Yes."

"Do you know how short your life will *be* if you do that? That's insane! Their life expectancy wasn't even *half* what ours is. Fifty was *old*. If you go back there, you'll only have maybe thirty years… *if* you're lucky. If you stay here you could have seventy!"

"Josh—"

"And without modern medicine you probably wouldn't even have the thirty. You could die in childbirth or—"

"She will not," Robert interrupted.

Beth looked at him in surprise. Had he actually been following that? Because she and Josh had totally abandoned Middle English somewhere along the way. "I'm sorry, Robert. I didn't mean to switch languages. Did you understand any of that?"

"I understood much of it," he said.

Really? He must have learned more modern English than she had realized.

Robert trained his gaze on Josh. "Beth will not die in childbirth. She will live a long and healthy life if she returns with me to my time."

Josh made a scoffing sound. "According to whom?"

"According to Seth," he replied.

Josh frowned. "The time traveler with all the gifts?"

Robert nodded.

Beth blinked. "Seth really said that?"

"Aye."

"When?"

Robert raised the hand he clasped to his lips for a kiss. "Whilst you and the others supped last night, I drew him aside and tried to convince him to let us live out our lives here in your time."

"Why?" she asked softly. Seth had given them no indication that he might change his mind. And it would've required Robert to leave his own family behind.

"I wanted you to be happy," he said simply. "So much so that I did beg him to let us remain here. But he would not."

"I *am* happy, Robert." She cupped his strong jaw in her free hand. "As long as I'm with you, I'm happy."

He shook his head. "You described such wonders in your world, Beth, that I thought you would have a better life here. I feared living in my time would be a hardship. And, having seen all I have today, I know it *will* be."

"Nay. It won't. Not as long as I have you," she insisted. "And you've only seen the *good* things my time has to offer. There are a *lot* of bad things in my world, too."

He stroked her hand with his thumb. "I believe Seth read my doubts clearly, for he assured me that you and I would have a very long and happy life together at Fosterly."

She sent him a wry smile. "And if anyone would know, he would."

Robert chuckled. "Aye. I believed him."

"I believe him, too." Smiling, she returned her attention to her brother. "It'll be okay, Josh. I know it. I feel it."

"Beth."

"You've always told me to trust my instincts. Well, my instincts are telling me not to fight this."

He must have read her determination, because he ceded the battle. For now. "How long will you be here?"

"A week. Then we have to go back."

And it might take her that long to convince her brother she would be well.

Chapter Twenty

ROBERT SMILED DOWN AT BETH as she took his hand and swung it back and forth.

He had abandoned his armor in favor of *jeans* and a *T-shirt* Josh had generously lent him. On his feet, he wore a pair of Josh's *sneakers*, which Robert decided were the most comfortable shoes he had ever worn. It was like walking on cushions.

Beth was similarly garbed in jeans and a T-shirt, but hers molded themselves to every curve.

Josh had invited their friends Marc and Grant to dinner and expected them to arrive soon.

Beth's pretty face was flushed with excitement. She remained in constant motion, shifting from side to side or bobbing up and down on her toes. As Josh had phrased it, she was *totally bouncing off the walls.*

"I have never seen you thus," Robert murmured, thoroughly entertained. He would not have thought anything could distract him from the miraculous *television* the siblings' living room boasted, or the *gas range* with its stunning blue fire in the kitchen. But Beth enchanted him.

She did a funny little shuffle and dance with her feet that made Josh laugh from his position across the living room. "Do you like it or hate it?"

Robert grinned. "I like it." It made him want to take her in his arms and—

The doorbell rang.

Emitting a squeak of excitement, Beth jumped up and down, then dragged Robert out of the living room and into the hallway that led to the bedrooms and bathroom.

"Do you not wish to stay and greet your friends?" he asked.

She shook her head. "I want to surprise them."

They heard Josh open the door and greet his guests. Two deep male voices joined his. Beth released Robert's hand and covered her lips with her fingers as though she found it almost impossible to hold back the delighted flow of words that threatened to burst free.

She was so adorable that Robert was tempted to drag her into the nearest bedroom and make love to her. But just as he decided her friends would have to wait, she jumped into the doorway to the living room and yelled, "Surprise!"

A charged silence followed.

Curious about these men who were so important to his wife, Robert stepped up behind her.

They were tall, matching his and Josh's height. Both were dressed casually in the jeans and T-shirts that were so common in this time. One of the men had black hair that was almost as long as Beth's. It framed a handsome face graced with dark eyes, a mustache and a beard that covered his chin, but left the rest of his jaw bare.

The other man, however, was the one who drew and held Robert's attention.

His skin was a warm, dark brown. Darker than Robert had ever seen. Was he a Moor, like those Dillon had told him tales of after returning from King Richard's crusade?

The man's head was clean-shaven and shone beneath the overhead lights. His face was handsome, angular, highlighted by brown eyes and a mustache and beard similar to the other man's. But while the first man's short beard was as straight as his hair, the Moor's was wavy and curly.

Both men stared at Beth as though she were a spirit, their faces a study in shock. Then they lunged forward simultaneously.

Beth held up her arms, waggling her fingers and dancing on her toes. The Moor reached her first, sweeping her up into his arms and holding her tight, her feet dangling above the floor. The other man impatiently awaited his turn, his gaze flickering to Robert's and holding.

Setting her down, the Moor stepped back.

Beth leaped into the second man's arms.

Robert ruthlessly tamped down the jealousy that threatened to rise. Loving Beth meant accepting her penchant for openly expressing affection for men she considered her friends, often through physical overtures like this. He knew she meant naught improper, so he resolved not to let it bother him.

When the second man stepped back, the first embraced her again. "Are you all right?"

Though the Moor spoke Beth's modern English, Robert had learned enough to understand his meaning, if not every word.

Beth nodded. "I'm fine."

Loosening his hold, the Moor slid his hands down her arms and grasped her fingers. "We thought—" He broke off, lips tightening, throat working in a swallow. "We thought you were dead or…" He shook his head, unable to continue.

Sniffling, Beth gave his hands a squeeze. "I know. I'm sorry."

"What happened?" the other asked, voice hoarse.

Robert was touched to see that both men battled tears.

"I'll tell you everything. I promise." Beth withdrew one of her hands and reached back to touch Robert's arm, urging him forward. "But first I want you to meet Robert. If it wasn't for him, I wouldn't have found my way back to you."

The Moor instantly held out his hand. "I'm Grant. Nice to meet you, Robert. Thank you for helping Beth."

Robert shook his hand. "In truth, I did very little, Grant."

The Moor cast Beth a look. Robert had tried to speak modern English, but thought his accent had probably distorted it quite a bit.

The other man offered his hand and shook his head. "You brought Beth back to us. Thank you. I'm Marc."

Perhaps his pronunciation hadn't been that bad after all. "Pleasure to meet you, Marc."

Across the room, Josh clapped his hands together. "Okay. Everyone has been introduced. Beth has a long, astonishing tale to tell. I'm sure Grant and Marc are as eager to hear it as I was. My scrumptious Cornish hens are eager to be consumed. So, let's gather around the table and oblige everyone. Beth, don't forget the pictures."

Two days later, Robert found himself standing on the covered front porch of Marc's two-story home. Though he had only been outside long enough to walk here from Bethany's house next door, already damp patches formed on his shirt.

The sun beat down behind him as he turned the knob and pushed.

The door did not open. Perhaps it was barred from the inside. He had not asked Beth the custom for visiting neighbors here. But when he visited castles of friends and acquaintances in his time, he awaited his host in the great hall.

Wiping the dampness from his forehead, he tried the door again, then noticed a strange glowing circle surrounded by a golden ring embedded in the door frame. Curious, he poked it with his finger.

Bing bong.

Glancing up, he looked for the source of the curious chimes, but saw no bells. Pursing his lips, he pressed the circle again. *Bing bong.* It sounded as if the bells might be inside the house. Robert pressed the circle again, experimenting.

Bing bong. Bingbongbingbongbingbong. Bing. Bong. Bing bong. Bingbong bingbong.

The door swung inward. Squinting against the bright light, Marc peered out at him, keeping in the shadows. "My lord?"

Beth had revealed Robert's title the night she had told her friends where she had spent the past two years. Odd, though. For a moment, when Marc had spoken the words, he had sounded almost like an Englishman.

"Ah. Marc. I was just familiarizing myself with your bell here."

"So I heard," he said with a wry smile. "Come in."

Clasping his hands behind his back, Robert stepped inside and stood back while Marc closed the door. Robert was not sure why, but he had felt an instant affinity with this man. Mayhap it was simply because Marc seemed to have the least amount of difficulty understanding Robert's antiquated speech, something that had even surprised Beth. "'Tis wondrous cool in here."

Yawning, Marc nodded. "Air-conditioning is one of the best inventions of this time," he declared, no hint of England tingeing his words now.

Robert must have imagined it. He noticed then that Marc was barefoot. His long black hair was mussed from sleep. His eyelids were heavy over deep brown eyes. Stubble coated the jawline his beard didn't. And the only clothing he wore was a pair of faded blue jeans, which Robert suspected he had donned upon hearing the bells chime.

"Forgive me. I seem to have disturbed your rest."

"No problem. I tend to work late into the night and often don't go to bed until after the sun has risen." Motioning for Robert to accompany him, he shuffled into the adjacent living room, switched on an overhead light, and sank down on the sofa.

Sofas were another grand invention of this time period, Robert decided as he seated himself at the opposite end.

"Beth didn't come with you?" Marc asked, smiling.

"Nay. She had a doctor's appointment. And Josh had some business he needed to take care of."

Marc frowned. "She isn't sick, is she?"

"Nay. She and Josh decided 'twould be best if she had something called a *checkup* before returning to the past."

"I agree. Perhaps you should, too."

Robert stiffened. "Absolutely not."

Marc grinned. "They told you about the rubber-glove exam, didn't they?"

Grimacing, Robert nodded.

"That's what I thought. So, what can I do for you, my lord?"

Robert hesitated. "There is a boon I would ask of you. 'Tis of a delicate nature and I did not feel comfortable approaching Josh with it."

"Well, I'm honored that you chose me. What would you have me do?"

"There is a secret I need your help unearthing."

Marc tilted his head. "A secret?"

"Aye. I saw it on television, and know not where to begin searching for it, only that it belongs to a woman by the name of Victoria."

For a long moment, Marc said nothing. Then his lips twitched. "A secret that belongs to Victoria?"

"Aye."

"I assume you wish to procure some of Victoria's *secrets* for Lady Bethany to take back to your time?"

"Precisely."

A slow grin stretched his lips. "I can definitely help you with that."

"I would be very grateful."

Marc laughed. "I can imagine." Rising, he said, "I believe, my lord, it is time I introduced you to something called the Internet."

Robert eyed him as he stood. "'Tis most curious."

His eyebrows rose. "What? The Internet?"

"Nay. That is the third time you have addressed me as *my lord*."

Marc's look turned guarded. "Is it?"

"Aye." And he had sounded completely natural doing so, unlike Josh and Grant, who had only done it in jest.

"I suppose, considering your title, I deemed it appropriate."

The words rang falsely, though Robert could not say why. "I see no need for such formality, not in this time, and not if we are to become friends."

Slowly Marc's shoulders relaxed. "I believe we already are friends, Robert."

Robert smiled and clapped him on the shoulder. "We are. Now tell me more of this thing called the Internet."

With the help of Marc's computer and a piece of plastic he called a credit card, Robert purchased many *secrets* for Beth that would be delivered the next day. He had been quite dismayed when Marc had told him he could not use the gold coins Robert had brought with him as payment.

"Those coins are centuries old, Robert, and are no longer used in the common market."

"Then they have no value in this time?" Robert had intended to leave whatever coins he did not spend here with Josh as a gift.

Marc snorted. "Those coins are *extremely* valuable. Because of their age and pristine condition, you could probably purchase Victoria's entire store with them. But they must be sold to a rare coin dealer first—or perhaps even a museum—and exchanged for modern moneys."

"Then I will do so and repay you for letting me use your plastic card."

"It isn't necessary, I assure you. In fact, I would much prefer that you repay me in a different manner."

An hour later, Robert and Marc were *sweating buckets*, as Beth would say, and grinning like fools as they hacked at each other with a pair of blunted swords Marc had produced that looked remarkably like the ones Robert used to train his squires.

While Marc had donned shoes, Robert had stripped off his shirt, leaving him in only his blue jeans and *sneakers*. They had shoved all of the living room furniture up against the walls, providing them with a suitably large area in which they could spar. And spar they did. Marc was an excellent swordsman. Robert would not have thought any men of this time would have reason to perfect such skills, but perfect them Marc had.

Apparently, unbeknownst to Beth, he was a member of one of the reenactment groups Beth had thought Robert part of the day they had met.

The two men spoke little as they fought. Occasionally Robert would offer praise or direction, as he did when sparring with his men. But very little direction was needed. More often than not, he laughed out loud with the sheer exhilaration of battling so worthy an opponent.

Bingbong bingbong bingbong bingbongbingbong. Thump thump thump thump thump.

Breathing hard, both men stopped and turned toward the door. Marc took a step forward, lowering his sword tip.

The door burst inward and Beth hurtled past, disappearing down the hallway at top speed. "*Marc!*" she shouted at the top of her lungs. "I've lost Robert! I can't find him!"

"In here," Marc called.

Beth's sneakers squeaked as she skidded to a halt on the wood floor, then backtracked into the living room. "I can't find Robert! I—"

As soon as her eyes lit upon Robert, she let out a huge sigh of relief. "Oh, thank goodness." Wilting against the nearest wall, she pointed an imperious finger at him. "Don't *ever* do that again."

Robert raised his eyebrows. "Visit Marc's home?"

"Aye! I mean, nay. When I got home from the doctor's office, the house was empty and you weren't in the garage or in the backyard or anywhere else that I could see, and there was no note, and I didn't know where you went, and... Do you have any idea how many people live in Houston? Or how long it would take me to go door to door, asking each and every one of them if they had by any chance seen a gorgeous but loony Brit who speaks garbled English?"

Robert frowned. "My English is not garbled."

She turned her frown on Marc. "Hi, Marc."

Marc grinned. "Hi, Beth."

"'Twas not my intention to worry you, love," Robert told her, hoping to calm her temper.

"Well, you did. I haven't been that scared since I was shot." Straightening suddenly, she noticed for the first time the new furniture arrangement and the swords in their hands. "What are you two doing?"

"Sparring," Marc answered cheerfully.

Her eyebrows nearly met her hairline. "You know how to wield a sword?"

"Aye," Robert said. "And, after sparring with him, I must admit Marc is my equal."

"No way!" she exclaimed incredulously.

"I wouldn't go so far as to say *that*," Marc mumbled. And damned if he didn't flush at the compliment.

"I would," Robert insisted. "You are a worthy opponent who would give even my brother a challenge."

"Wow," Beth said. "That is high praise indeed, Marc."

Incredibly, Marc blushed an even darker crimson.

"Wait," she said, straightening. "You're speaking Middle English."

Marc nodded. "I'm a member of a reenactment group."

Her mouth fell open. "You are?"

"Aye."

"Wow. It must be one of those really fanatical ones if you learned to speak Middle English."

Robert grinned at Marc. "She thought I was a member of such when she first met me."

Marc laughed.

"Hey, Robert?" Beth remarked casually.

"Aye?"

"Have I told you how hot you look in jeans?"

He had learned that *hot* in her time did not always refer to temperature. "You have."

She looked at Marc. "You look hot, too, by the way."

Marc darted Robert a nervous glance.

He smiled wryly. "Beth has already assured me that I am the only man who is hot in a way that makes her want to tear my clothes off and have her way with me."

"Something I would love to do right now," Beth said, grinning mischievously, "but I have news." Skipping forward, she clapped her hands rapidly in the manner of a child who has been promised a sweet and was fairly bursting with excitement. "Guess what! Guess what! Guess what!"

Thoroughly charmed, Robert grinned back. "What?"

"I'm pregnant!" Then, squealing, she jumped up and threw herself into his arms.

The sword Robert held clattered to the floor as he caught her. Shock rippled through him. "What?"

She laughed. "I'm pregnant! You're going to be a daddy!"

Joy swept through him as her words sank in. Squeezing her closer, he spun her around in a circle. A babe! Beth was carrying his babe. *Their* babe. Their son or daughter.

Setting her on her feet, he covered her face with kisses, then hugged her close again.

A happy smile wreathed her face when he released her.

"Congratulations," Marc said, smiling as he pulled her into a hug, then offered his hand to Robert.

Robert shook it and thanked him, his heart full.

"I don't know why I was so surprised when Doctor Cohen told me," Beth said, taking Robert's hand and swinging it back and forth between them. "I mean, it wasn't like we were using birth control or anything. But you could have knocked me over with a polo mallet! No wonder I've been crying so much lately. I thought it was just stress."

Marc laughed.

Robert shook his head.

"You *are* pleased, aren't you?" she asked him.

"More than I can say." Spinning her into his arms, her back to his front, Robert rested both hands on her tummy.

She smiled up at him over her shoulder and placed her hands atop his. "I love you."

"I love you, too, sweetling."

"Now give me your sword," she went on in the same dulcet tones. "I want to see just how good Marc is."

Beth took Robert's sword.

"You can wield a sword, Beth?" Marc asked.

She laughed. "Hell, yes, I can. Let's do this."

Robert backed away, smiling.

Marc went easy on her at first. But once he saw she knew what she was doing, he relaxed into it and soon fought her as Robert would, even offering some instruction.

The longer they sparred, the more familiar it began to feel to Beth.

So much so that she paused. "Robert, honey, would you please get me a glass of ice water? Or maybe some Perrier on ice?"

Marc lowered his sword. "I'll get it."

She held up a hand and shook her head. "Let Robert do it. He'll enjoying playing with the ice dispenser and he likes the bubbles in the Perrier."

Robert's face lit with curiosity. "Ice dispenser?"

Beth nodded. "Press the button on the outside of the refrigerator door and little chunks of ice will come out."

Robert headed for the kitchen.

Marc told him where to find the glasses, then looked at Beth as Robert disappeared from view. "Are you sure I shouldn't show him?" he asked in modern English.

She shook her head. "He'll be fine."

He nodded.

Beth studied him, instincts yammering in her ears.

"What?" he asked.

"You're him, aren't you?" she asked.

A clatter came from the kitchen.

"By the saints!" Robert cried.

Marc laughed. "What?"

"You're him, aren't you?" she repeated. "You're Marcus."

Marc lost his smile. His look turned cautious. "Who?"

"Robert's squire. Marcus, heir of Dunnenford."

"The boy in the pictures from the Middle Ages?"

She nodded. "That's why he kept feeling so familiar to me. He's you, only younger."

"Beth—"

"I've never seen you without the long hair, mustache and beard. And his more youthful face threw me. But he's you, Marc. You're him." She motioned to him with her free hand. "You move the same way. You tilt your head the same way. And, now that I've heard you speak Middle English, you even phrase your words the same way. You're him. You're Marcus."

In the kitchen, more ice clattered, accompanied by exclamations of awe.

Marc lowered his eyes and poked the floor with his blunted sword tip. "That man Edward in the pictures looks just like William Shatner. That doesn't mean—"

"Marc, don't." She stepped closer to him, lowering her voice. "Please, don't deny it. I know you're him. I feel it. Seth said I'm a *gifted one*, that my intuition isn't just ordinary intuition. And I believe him. I know I'm right." A moment passed. "Tell me I'm right."

Slowly, he nodded. "I am Marcus, heir of Dunnenford." This time, when he spoke, his voice carried a British accent.

She smiled, excitement filling her at his admission. "That is so cool! How can this be? Did Seth bring you forward in time?"

He shook his head. "I can't tell you."

"Why?"

His lips curled up in a smile that contained a hint of bitterness. "Seth does not wish me to alter my fate."

She grimaced. "That whole dancing around fate thing is really annoying."

"Yes, it is."

"I mean, why is it okay for him to bring *you* to this time to live, but not okay for me and Robert to stay here?"

Again, he glanced down at the floor.

Seth *had* brought him forward in time, right?

Not necessarily. Back in the clearing, hadn't she drawn the unbelievable conclusion that Seth had not come forward in time from the thirteenth century, but had instead simply lived long enough to see them again in this one?

Had Marcus done the same?

"How long have you known Seth?" she asked, hoping for a clue.

"Forever, it sometimes seems," he murmured, then said no more.

The crack and fizzing sounds of a Perrier bottle opening carried to their ears.

"Are you going to tell Robert?" she asked softly.

He shook his head. "I only want him to know me as I used to be, not as what I've become."

She frowned. What did *that* mean?

Beth didn't know and opted not to push him. "Well, I'm glad you told me." Wrapping her arms around him, she hugged him hard. "Seth said I can't take anything from this time back with me." Withdrawing, she smiled up at him. "But now I'll have *you* there."

Sadness tinged his smile. "The boy I was then won't know you from this time."

"It doesn't matter," she insisted. "It'll still be you."

Amusement lightened his sober expression. "Sending the tent back with you was my idea, by the way."

She laughed. "It was?"

He nodded. "I remembered Robert frequently mentioning your icy fingers and toes and hoped it would keep you warm that first night."

"Thank you," she said wryly, then frowned. "Wait. So you knew—when you told me to bring the backpack—what was going to happen that day?"

"Yes. But Seth would not let me warn you."

Trippy. "Well, if you *had* warned me, things would've turned out differently and I never would've met Robert. So I'm glad you didn't."

Robert returned, carrying a glass full of ice and bubbling Perrier.

"Thank you." Beth took a sip. "How much ice did you spill on the floor?"

Robert gave her a sheepish grin. "A lot. But I picked it up and put it in the sink."

All laughed.

The evening before they were to return to the past, Robert went to bed early, leaving brother and sister alone. The two siblings stayed awake all night, talking, reminiscing, and trying to cram decades of teasing into the few hours they had left together.

When the sun painted the sky with the first flush of dawn, they rose without speaking, donned their jogging shoes and went for their final run together.

It was hard. Harder even than the Houston Marathon. Her throat kept tightening up. Her breathing was choppier than usual. Tears posed a constant threat.

The impending departure weighed heavily upon them both. Their spirits lifted only slightly upon returning home when they found Robert, decked out in his medieval garb, baking yet another pizza.

Then it was time to leave.

Somber silence accompanied the drive. Beth and Robert, clad once more in his chain mail, rode with Josh in his SUV. Marc and Grant followed in Marc's Prius, which had windows tinted as dark as those on Seth's van.

Seth awaited them in the clearing, clad in jeans and a black T-shirt, eyes hidden behind dark glasses, leaning casually against a tree. He raised one eyebrow at the backpack Robert carried—a backpack full of *secrets* Robert wouldn't disclose—but offered no protest. Nor did he examine the contents, so he must approve of whatever was in there.

A sense of unreality invaded Beth, accompanied by near panic.

This couldn't be it. It couldn't be time for them to say good-bye. She wasn't ready.

Then Grant wrapped his strong arms around her in a hug. "Be happy," he whispered hoarsely.

She clutched him tightly. "You, too," she forced past the lump in her throat.

He nodded, eyes glimmering.

Marc approached her next, hugging her so hard she could barely breathe. "I'll miss you."

Tears spilled over her lashes. For a moment, she couldn't speak. "I'll miss you, too. I'll have to tease you mercilessly in Robert's time to make up for it."

He loosed a hoarse chuckle before he drew back, eyes damp.

Grant shook Robert's hand. "Take care of her."

Robert smiled. "I will."

Marc took Robert's hand, then surprised Beth by pulling him into a rough hug. "It has been an honor, my lord."

"Robert," her husband corrected with a smile.

Marc nodded. "It has been an honor, Robert."

"For me as well."

Beth embraced both friends again and told them she loved them. "Watch over Josh for me."

"We will," they promised.

She turned to her brother. Rising onto her toes, she wrapped her arms around his neck and held on tight.

Josh buried his face in her hair and clung just as desperately.

"I love you," she murmured brokenly.

"I love you, too."

Many long moments passed before he reluctantly pulled away. "Cause lots of chaos when you get back to the Middle Ages," he ordered, tucking a few curls behind her ear.

She forced a wobbly smile. "You can bet on it. Maybe I'll do like they did in the *Back to the Future* trilogy and arrange for Western Union to deliver a bunch of letters right after we leave."

He returned her smile with a sad one of his own. "Western Union didn't exist then."

"I know. But I'll think of something," she vowed with false confidence.

Josh gave Robert a big hug. "I couldn't have chosen a better husband for her."

"Nor I a better brother-in-law," Robert replied. "I want you to know that I have never loved anyone more than I do Bethany. And I shall strive every day of my life to make her happy."

"I don't doubt that you'll succeed." Josh started to back away from them, then stopped and pulled Beth into another fierce hug.

Tears flowed freely down Beth's cheeks.

Not yet. Please, not yet.

She bit back a sob as he loosened his hold. She could barely see him through the moisture filling her eyes as he dipped his head and kissed her forehead.

"Tell my nieces and nephews about me," he said, his voice thick. "Tell them I love them even though I'm not there to give them piggyback rides."

She nodded helplessly. "Tell mine about me."

Nodding, he backed away to the outer fringes of the clearing.

Robert wrapped an arm around Beth's shoulders.

Marc and Grant moved to stand behind Josh in the shade.

Dimly, Beth was aware of Seth's approach. But her eyes clung to her brother's.

Then Josh's face and the clearing blurred. That peculiar feeling of weightlessness swept over her, lingering several seconds.

And the world swam back into focus.

Once more, she and Robert stood on Fosterly land in the clearing from which they had departed a week ago.

Seth stood nearby, now sporting medieval garb.

A party on horseback was just disappearing into the trees on the far side. One member turned to look back over his shoulder.

It was Marcus. The faithful squire's mournful expression brightened as soon as he spotted them and realized that Beth's clothing had changed and her weapons were gone.

Apparently Seth had returned them mere minutes after they had left.

At Marcus's joyful cry, Dillon and Alyssa spun their horses around and, spying the couple, urged them swiftly forward.

Her thoughts on her brother, Beth buried her face in her husband's chest and wept.

A horse skidded to a halt. Its rider dismounted.

"My lord," Marcus broached hesitantly, "did Lady Bethany not find her brother?"

Robert smoothed his hands across her back and rested his cheek against her hair. "She found him, Marcus," he answered softly.

Epilogue

"JOSH?" BETH GLANCED AROUND THE great hall, but did not see her quarry. "Josh!"

A handsome nine-year-old boy with brown hair and hazel eyes, who was the spitting image of his namesake, exited the kitchen, still chewing whatever treat Cook had slipped him. "Aye, Mother?"

"Honey, go up and see what's keeping your father. He should have been down here by now. And do not *dare* wipe your hands on your tunic."

Grinning, he gave her a smart salute and left on his quest.

Shaking her head, Beth turned to Monsieur Tiveau. "Forgive me. 'Twill only be a few more minutes."

He smiled affably and adjusted the large blank canvas that rested on the easel beside him. "I am here at your pleasure, my lady. You should not apologize."

"Of course I should. We are always late, and you are always patient."

He was an immensely talented artist. It had taken her the entire first year of her marriage to find him after Robert had let it be known they were searching for someone of his abilities.

Pierre Tiveau had been only a year older than Marcus when he had arrived at Fosterly. Beth had almost decided on a much older man to serve her purposes when she gave young Tiveau some parchment and told him to spend the day sketching the people of Fosterly. The results had been so detailed, so like a photograph, capturing every thought and emotion reflected in his subjects' faces, that she had hired him on the spot.

He had lived at Fosterly ever since, an artist in residence, and had been given his own chamber here in the castle. Most days he sketched the family going about their various pursuits. Robert training his men. Beth sparring with Robert or Marcus or even Dillon when he visited. Beth dancing with

Robert or her sons. Robert, Marcus, or Michael roughhousing with the boys. Beth snuggling with Robert in his great chair before the hearth.

Tiveau captured it all in beautiful detail, amassing piles and piles of sketches. Every year he painted a formal family portrait as well. And every year or two, Seth dropped by for a visit and Beth coaxed him into working his magic on the artwork and the letters she wrote to her brother, doing whatever he could do to preserve it all for Josh to uncover in the twenty-first century down in the hidden oubliette, which was now free of spikes and skeletons.

How Josh would know it was there and where to look for it she hadn't quite worked out yet. But she would. And through this, Josh would know she had lived a very happy life.

Beth turned her attention to the two boys seated near the buttery. "Michael, Alex, give those to Maude and come over here. You can have them back as soon as Monsieur Tiveau is finished with us."

Both children stilled, glanced over at her, then obediently handed Maude their practice swords.

Beth smiled with pride and a great deal of love as she watched her youngest sons approach. They looked so like their father, with jet-black hair and bright blue eyes. They even possessed his forbearance, standing still and offering no complaint while Beth brushed off their tunics and smoothed their hair.

"Maude, will you please have Alice bring Vanessa down?"

"No need," a deep voice rumbled softly.

Beth turned and watched Marcus approach, her sleeping infant daughter cradled gently in his arms. Her smile widened. "Must you charm *all* of the females of Fosterly?"

"All but one," he teased, his dark eyes sparkling.

Beth laughed. "Don't kid yourself. You charm me all the time."

Maturity had molded Marcus's boyish good looks into the strong, handsome countenance of her beloved friend Marc. She was so glad he had stayed on at Fosterly after attaining knighthood. It was like having a little piece of home with her. And he provided yet another excellent role model for her children, all of whom he cherished.

Especially Vanessa.

The Fosterly men *adored* Vanessa, her father most of all.

Her older brothers and Marcus, Michael, Stephen, and Adam fawned over Vanessa and thought her the most clever little girl in the world. And while most infants were left in the care of wet-nurses and maids, Vanessa was forever being stolen away by her brothers, paraded about by her proud papa, or tucked into the crook of a warrior's arm and told tales of battle and warfare a little girl just shouldn't hear.

As Marcus deposited her daughter in her arms, Beth heard a commotion erupt in the stairwell that led to the solar and chambers above.

Rolling her eyes, she called out, "Don't muss your hair!"

Vanessa jerked awake with a grunt of surprise.

Robert and Josh stepped into view. Josh's head was wedged under his father's arm, his laughter filling the hall as he struggled to escape. Robert met Beth's gaze, smiled sheepishly and released him, then helped his son right his hair and tunic.

Meanwhile, Vanessa's little face puckered up as she prepared to have a good long cry over her sleep being so rudely interrupted. Contrite, Beth rocked her and tried to soothe her as the first wails erupted. Marcus lent his aid as well, cooing and making funny faces that made Beth laugh but had no effect on her daughter.

Robert joined them and gave Beth a light kiss. "Did I not tell you? She bears your temperament as well as your beauty, sweetling."

Marcus laughed.

"Oh, ha-ha," she responded, not at all upset. The fuzzy hair atop Vanessa's head was the same brown as Bethany's, her eyes an expressive hazel. Robert had made no secret of his delight in having a daughter who resembled her mother so closely, confessing only last night that he had been hoping for such ever since Beth had agreed to marry him.

Taking their daughter and settling her in his arms, Robert bent his head and rubbed his face against her tummy, making growling sounds that instantly transformed her wails into giggles.

Robert had changed very little in the years they had been together. His body was just as firm and muscular as it had been the day she had met him. His hair was still black as night, something about which Beth complained often because her own was already lightly peppered with gray. While her face remained smooth and unwrinkled, his now sported laugh lines at the outer corners of his eyes. Laugh lines for which he deemed her responsible.

He was so handsome, still able to steal her breath with just a look. Beth didn't know why everyone believed married couples never had sex. She and Robert made love all the time, their relationship full of never-ending passion and laughter.

Robert kissed Vanessa's forehead, then handed her back to Beth and herded the boys over to the hearth, where a padded bench had been placed.

Beth sat, smiling when Robert bent and carefully adjusted her skirts for her, stealing another kiss in the process. When all was to their liking, he sat beside her and lifted Alex onto his knee. Young Michael and Josh stood close on either side, according to Monsieur Tiveau's directions.

Robert wrapped his free arm around her waist.

Josh rested a hand on her shoulder.

Beth glanced at her husband, at their children gathered around them, thought of the life she had left behind in the future, and knew no regrets.

As if hearing her thoughts, Robert leaned down and whispered in her ear, "Have I made you happy, Beth?"

Lifting her lips to his, she met his gaze and smiled. "The happiest."

"I love you. You are my world."

She kissed him again. "And you are mine."

Bonus Scene

In every manuscript I write, there is always at least one scene I cut either to reduce the word count or because I ultimately decide that—although I enjoy the scene—it doesn't advance the plot. The following is just such a scene, but I thought both readers of The Gifted Ones series and those who enjoy my Immortal Guardians series would be interested in it. It takes place shortly after Robert and Bethany arrive in her time to visit Josh.

IN THE QUIET OF THE master bedroom on the second floor of Marc's modest two-story home, a rhythmic thumping and muted laughter filtered in from outside, breaking the silence. Drawing back the curtains of the window that overlooked his front yard, Marc carefully avoided the scorching afternoon sunlight and remained in the cool shadows while he watched the activity below.

His lips twitched when the basketball Robert hurled toward the goal careened off the backboard without so much as brushing the rim.

Robert was appallingly bad at the sport and clearly grew frustrated. To a man who could throw an axe or a dagger with astounding precision, sending a rubber ball through a net must appear a simple task. But Marc suspected Robert's inability to master it was only partly responsible for the frown that drew down his brows.

While fall temperatures cooled northern states, temperatures in Houston still hovered in the mid-nineties. The heat index or *feels-like* temp was probably a good ten degrees above that.

Perspiration trailed down the sides of Robert's flushed face and saturated his T-shirt. His arms and the thickly muscled legs left bare by the shorts Josh had loaned him were damp as well. The Earl of Fosterly was definitely having a difficult time adjusting to the new climate, and had to pause frequently to guzzle the cold water Beth kept in the shade of the front porch.

While Josh loped off after the ball, Beth smiled up at Robert and offered him advice and encouragement.

What an unlikely couple they were. Born and raised eight centuries apart, they had nevertheless found enough similarities between them to fall deeply in love.

In deference to Robert's medieval mind frame, Beth had foregone wearing shorts herself (Robert balked at her revealing so much tempting bare flesh to others) and instead wore jeans and a T-shirt. Even these, Marc knew, had met with some disapproval. And he could understand why.

The jeans were a pale, pale blue and hugged her slender legs and firm, shapely ass like a second skin. They rode low on her hips, the waistband falling beneath her belly button, and allowed teasing glimpses of muscled abs and the soft white skin of her narrow waist every time her T-shirt drifted up. Several damp patches darkened her red shirt, making it cling to her full breasts and small frame in alluring ways.

Her dark brown hair was pulled back into a ponytail that jounced and danced with every movement. Damp curls had sprung loose, and clung to her temples and the back of her neck. Her pretty face glistening, she caught the ball Josh tossed her, flashed Robert a grin, and effortlessly sent the ball sailing through the net.

Marc's hand curled into a fist around the loose curtain fabric.

She was so damned beautiful. Her laughter so musical.

And he had missed her so much the two years she had been gone. How could he withstand losing her again when she returned to Robert's time?

"You can't," a voice said behind him, where seconds before no one had stood.

Marc stiffened. "Can't what?" he asked, abandoning his faux American accent and letting his native English accent color his words.

"Do what you are thinking," Seth informed him somberly.

For many long moments, Marc said nothing. He simply continued to stare at the play below.

Robert attempted another free throw and missed the backboard entirely. Sailing over the top of it, the ball hit the roof so hard it rebounded and flew clear across the street. Robert swore foully and began to stomp down the driveway after it. But he only made it a few steps before a smiling Beth leapt onto his back. Laughing, he stumbled forward, then tucked his arms beneath her knees and carried her with him, piggyback style, grinning at her over his shoulder when she pecked him on the cheek.

"Would it be so bad?" Marc whispered finally, loathing the despair and vulnerability the question revealed.

Seth sighed. An unhappy sound. "You know you cannot tell her who you are."

"I would not have to," Marc pointed out. He had thought it all through very carefully, how he could approach her. What he could say that would produce the desired results without exposing all. "I could—"

"Bethany is an exceptionally bright and perceptive woman, as you know. She may even yet figure out who you are. But you cannot tell her *what* you are or what *made* you what you are."

"Then *you* go to her." Desperation driving him, Marc glanced over his shoulder and located Seth lounging in the darkness just inside the doorway. "You were the one who took her back in time. She knows you possess knowledge the rest of us do not. She would listen to you. *You* go to her. Then she would not have to know who I am. She would not have to know what I have become. You could—"

"Marcus—"

"*Let me finish!*" Silence descended in the aftermath of his shout. Marcus closed his eyes and mentally swore.

One did not yell at Seth.

No one yelled at Seth.

The immortal's power was incalculable. His true age, in what millennium he had been born, *where* he was born, remained a mystery. All anyone knew with any certainty was that he had lived long enough to have witnessed biblical events, and it was extremely unwise to cross him.

Yet Seth's face, when Marcus dared to look again, remained impassive.

"Very well," Seth stated softly. "Continue."

Marcus strove to moderate his voice, present a calm argument. "As I said, you would not have to tell her who I am. She knows you are gifted, that you can do things and *know* things that others don't. All you would have to do is go to her and tell her you have had a vision or a dream and that she should do all in her power to keep Marcus from journeying to London in September of the year 1213 or a terrible fate shall befall him."

"If memory serves, she *did* attempt to prevent you from going to London—"

"Because she loved me like a brother and *missed* me whenever I was away," Marcus gritted. "If she had thought some harm would befall me, she would have fought tooth and nail to keep me at Fosterly. She would have chained me to the damned walls of the dungeon if necessary. Lord Robert would have, too. If you tell her now, they *will* do so."

"And then?"

Marcus returned his attention to the scene next door. "And then all of this will be wiped away," he said tonelessly. "None of it will have happened. I would not be immortal and..." He shook his head. "All would be as it should be."

"You cannot change your fate, Marcus."

"*Why* can I not? You altered Beth's fate. She would have died that day had you not plucked her from the present and delivered her to the past. And there is no telling what would have become of Lord Robert without her."

A series of whoops and shouts erupted below as Robert scored his first basket.

Marcus had not anticipated what seeing Lord Robert again would do to him. The memories it would stir. The longing to recapture the deep, abiding friendship and camaraderie they had shared in his youth. Robert had been the only real family Marcus had had, though they bore no blood relation. When, upon her return to the present, Beth had innocently *introduced* the two of them, Marcus had damn near broken down and wept.

"You misunderstand," Seth spoke. "Bethany was always meant to live out her life with Lord Robert in the past. Just as you were always meant to live out your life as you have. I did not in any way alter her fate. Nor can I alter yours."

"Fate," Marcus snarled. "How I detest the word. If everything that happens is *fated*, how can there be free will?"

Seth sighed as if the complaint were not a new one. "The day before I brought Bethany and Lord Robert forward to this time, I watched Lord Dillon engage his toddler son in a foot race."

Sadness flickered through Marcus. He had not thought of Lord Dillon or Lady Alyssa in years.

"Lord Dillon clearly had the advantage. And yet I knew before the race even began that he was going to let his son win." Seth paused. "Did my knowing ahead of time that Lord Dillon would throw the race in any way prevent him from making the decision to do so of his own free will?"

Marcus's fist tightened around the curtains. "No."

"So it is with fate. You were fated to travel to London in the fall of 1213—"

"And be transformed against my will."

"Yes. Some things cannot be changed, Marcus, even when it appears we have the power to do so." Great sorrow weighted Seth's voice.

But not nearly as much as that which suffused Marcus. He shook his head, wanting to shout a denial.

It had been foolish to hope. Pointless.

His eyes fixed on Beth, followed her every move. His ears strained to hear every laugh, every teasing comment she made.

"I am weary of this life, Seth," he whispered despondently. "So incredibly weary that I must struggle to find a reason to rise each evening."

"Did you rest at all today?" Seth asked in the most gentle voice Marcus had ever heard emerge from him.

"No. I don't want to. Not while they are here. Not while *she* is here. I don't want to miss a moment of it." He swallowed hard against the lump that rose in his throat. "I will only have her for a few more days, Seth. What will I do when she is gone?"

Below, Beth squealed when Robert growled and swept her up in his arms, then dangled her upside down in response to her taunts and teases.

"Eight hundred years," Marcus continued softly. "I have lived for over eight hundred years, and the only happiness I have ever experienced was during the years I lived at Fosterly as Robert's squire, then his knight, and this last decade I have spent living near Beth."

"Your life span is that of a babe's compared to mine."

Marcus continued as though Seth had not spoken. "There were decades... entire centuries really... when the only thing that kept me going was the knowledge that I would see her again one day. That if I could just hold out another century—then another and another and another—I would be rewarded with her presence once more. I could see her smile. Hear her laugh. Feel one of her sharp jesting punches to my shoulder. Have her hugs. Her friendship. Her affection."

"You could have had more than that, had you wished it," Seth commented cautiously.

Marcus nodded. "That has been the sweetest torture of all, I think, knowing that she could have been mine."

Beth, Josh, and Grant began playing a game of twenty-one while Robert took a few minutes to cool down in the shade.

"When I was Robert's squire, she told me that she had once been smitten with her next-door neighbor. I did not realize until we met again all of these centuries later that she spoke of me, here in this time. That she…"

"That she could have loved you?"

Just hearing it spoken aloud was painful. "Not like she loves Robert. Not like he loves her. She could have been *content* with me. But they belong together. They were made for each other. Even you have admitted that. And I love them both too much to ever betray them by acting on my feelings."

Robert brought Beth some water and was rewarded with a kiss.

"How I adore her," Marcus murmured. "She is my light, Seth. My candle in the darkness of this existence. When she and Robert return to the thirteenth century, that light will forever be extinguished. I will never see her again, will have nothing to look forward to, nothing to keep me going. What will I do?"

When next Seth spoke, he sounded infinitely weary. "You will do what we all do, Marcus. You will survive. And perhaps, in time, you will receive another, sweeter reward."

Beth jumped up and down and cheered when the ball she had just thrown swirled around the rim twice, teetered, then finally fell through the goal.

Marcus shook his head. "There can be none sweeter."

If you would like to know more about Marcus and whether or not he will find love and happily-ever-after for himself, you can read his story in Night Reigns, *Immortal Guardians Book 2.*

Thank you for reading **Rendezvous with Yesterday**. I hope you enjoyed Robert and Bethany's story. It's one I've wanted to tell for quite some time now. If you've read my *Immortal Guardians* books, you received snippets of this tale when I revealed Marcus's history. I hope seeing it unfold in full—as well as getting a glimpse of Marcus and Seth's lives in the Middle Ages— proved entertaining. If you haven't read my *Immortal Guardians* books, you might be interested in knowing that there is some crossover between that series and *The Gifted Ones* series. Seth, Marcus, and Roland are all major players in my *Immortal Guardians* books. So, if you are interested in seeing more of them, I hope you'll give that series a try.

If you liked this book, please consider rating or reviewing it at an online retailer of your choice. I appreciate your support so much and am always thrilled when I see that one of my books made a reader happy. Ratings and reviews are also an excellent way to recommend an author's books, create word of mouth, and help other readers find new favorites.

Thank you again!

Dianne Duvall
www.DianneDuvall.com

About the Author

Dianne Duvall is the *New York Times* and *USA Today* Bestselling Author of the **Immortal Guardians** and **The Gifted Ones** series. Reviewers have called Dianne's books "fast-paced and humorous" (*Publishers Weekly*), "utterly addictive" (*RT Book Reviews*), "extraordinary" (Long and Short Reviews), and "wonderfully imaginative" (The Romance Reviews). Her books have twice been nominated for RT Reviewers' Choice Awards and are routinely deemed Top Picks by *RT Book Reviews*, The Romance Reviews, and/or Night Owl Reviews.

Dianne loves all things creative. When she isn't writing, Dianne is active in the independent film industry and has even appeared on-screen, crawling out of a moonlit grave and wielding a machete like some of the vampires she so loves to create in her books.

For the latest news on upcoming releases, contests, and more, please visit www.DianneDuvall.com. You can also connect with Dianne online:

Website — www.DianneDuvall.com
Blog — dianneduvall.blogspot.com
Facebook — www.facebook.com/DianneDuvallAuthor
Twitter — twitter.com/DianneDuvall
YouTube — www.youtube.com/channel/
UCVcJ9xnm_i2ZKV7jM8dqAgA?feature=mhee
Pinterest — www.pinterest.com/dianneduvall
Goodreads — www.goodreads.com/Dianne_Duvall
Google Plus — plus.google.com/106122556514705041683

57744436R00214

Made in the USA
Lexington, KY
23 November 2016